Gem of the Crown

Aquaria Oceana Series: Book Two

J.A. Johnson

For my beautiful girl and my wonderful husband.

Trigger Warning: reference to and talk of rape.
Domestic violence, physical and emotional abuse.

PART ONE

1

The dark gray sky had been a constant for months. The chilling wind blew through her hair as she stood on a cliff, watching the ships sailing into port. Hoping for his ship to come back, even if for just a day. She wanted him back. Wanted to know he was safe. The sound of steel driving into the soil pierced her ears. Grabbing her dagger from her hip, she turned to see who was behind her.

His auburn hair and dark hateful eyes threw her back. That was the last merman she expected to see. And even worse, he was digging a deep hole. Large enough to fit a body.

"Macsen." She growled. Her dagger clutched tightly in her hand.

"About time you notice I was here. Lost in your desperate search for your human?"

"What are you doing here?"

"I came for you."

"To kill me and bury my body?" She snapped.

"Never. This is for me."

"Cause you know I'll kill you if you touch me again?"

"No. Not by your hand. I could never let you suffer having that on your conscious."

"Your death wouldn't be something I'd regret."

"As cold as ever I see."

"Why are you here?"

"I came to give you a warning. Something I overheard Delanson saying."

"Visiting Shelby again?"

He went back to digging, eyes focused on the dirt. "You know I have no choice. I would be with you if allowed. You know that."

"I've never wanted to be with you. Now would you please get on with why you're here?"

"I don't know what it means, but I know it has to do with you. Something I wasn't supposed to hear. They're already hunting me down. I'd rather not go through another torture session with Delanson. He can't do what you do to me. But his version of torture is weeks long. I won't go through that again. Especially if it puts you at risk. I'd rather die than put your life in jeopardy."

"So what's your plan after you tell me this? Bury yourself alive?"

"No." He pulled a crystal out of his pocket. Pressed it to his temple. He shut his eyes as the crystal began to glow. His eyes opened when it stopped glowing. "Take this." He extended the crystal to her. "It's every memory I have. Keep it. Destroy it. Give it to your father or Nikoli. I don't care what you do with it. Just don't let Silas see it. Don't let Delanson or Fjord see it."

"Hmph. So you don't trust him either."

"Not with anything to do with you."

"So your going to kill yourself?"

"Obviously."

"How?"

"You really want to know?"

"I need to know."

"I'll slit my throat."

"No. That won't work."

"Of course it will. It'll kill me."

"No I mean… it won't keep them from getting your memories. My family can retrieve memories from the deceased for up the three years after death… unless…"

"Unless what?"

"Your head has to either be cut off… which is why we could never get my mothers memories... or any other major damage to your brain. It has to be where your memories are stored... otherwise my brothers can retrieve them when they find your body."

"Show me where and I'll put a dagger there."

She looked down at the crystal in her hand. He really did care about her wellbeing more than his own life. She actually meant more to him than just a position of power. In his own twisted way, he loved her. She let out a sigh.

"I'll take care of it for you. I'll have to bury your body anyways. So tell me this warning and we'll finish this once and for all."

"Follow the blood to find your true king. Until you two are reunited, crimson is the only shade you'll see. On that day, many will finally be free, but that is just the beginning of your war. You can't run from this, it will always find you. The bodies that fall because of your hand, are those who will oppose our one true queen."

"What's that supposed to mean?"

"That's something you'll have to figure out." He looked at the hole and jumped in it. "Think this is good enough?"

"It should be fine."

"Good."

He sat in the hole, removing his cuff. His tail came back almost instantly. An innocent childlike smile formed on his face as she climbed into the hole to finish him off. The hate in his eyes had finally vanished. This wasn't the Macsen she had known and hated. His soul was at peace.

She sat in front of him. Straddling his tail. His smile reaching his eyes. She placed the crystal next to his hip in the torn fragments of what used to be trousers. A firm grip on her dagger. Her heart pounded hard in her chest. She looked him in the eye. This was going to be her first kill. She never expected it to be someone she knew.

"Are you ready?"

"I have one last request. One last kiss. Let me die with one moment of bliss."

"Just one."

He grabbed the back of her head, assaulting her lips with his. There it was, the same old Macsen. Same aggressive sea scum she's always known. She pulled away.

"Thank you. Go ahead a drive that dagger into my skull."

"No. I'm going with the other option. I can't risk missing."

She stood up grabbing the shovel off the ground. She pushed him down with her foot. Making sure his head was down.

"Thank you, for giving your life for me."

"Aquaria. Nothing would give me greater joy than giving my life for you. I lo-"

She drove the shovel hard into his throat. Refusing to let him say that to her again. It didn't cut his head off. But it had sliced through enough to reach everything except the spine. The light faded from his eyes. Blood spluttering out of his throat. Watching the blood soak the soil. She drove the blade of the shovel into his throat a few more times. Blood splattering her clothes and the dirt. By the fourth time. She finally succeeded. His head was off. She reached down into the bloody mud. Grabbing the crystal as the blood dripped from her fingers. She climbed out of the hole. Her nails digging into the grass. Leaving a crimson trail behind her. Hands trembling as she grabbed a shell and lighter out of her pocket. She pulled a piece of paper out of the shell and lit it on fire. Putting it back in the shell and throwing it into the grave.

A blue ring of fire appeared in the hole as a tall muscular man walked through it. The blood on the paper let him know how urgent his presence was.

"Why in the underworld am I standing on a dead body?!" He shouted to her.

She looked down in the hole. Face covered in blood.

"What happened?"

"He asked me to. I need help making his body unrecoverable."

"How unrecoverable?"

"My brothers can't find him."

"Why?"

"Delanson is searching for him. He wants his memories."

"Well you severed the head."

"Yeah. But I don't want the possibility of them ever finding him. If they find his headless body, they'll know there is a memory crystal out there, and my location."

He grabbed the shell and climbed out of the hole. He handed the shell back to her. Taking a black handkerchief from his pocket, handing it to her.

"You're going to do it. I'll teach you how."

"Alright."

"Why didn't you get Styx to help you?"

"She doesn't know… she wouldn't understand anyways."

"Trust me. She would. She had me do this exact same thing for her."

"I'll talk to her about it later. Now what do we need to do."

"Place one hand on the ground. Close your eyes and feel the earth. Feel the actual earth not just what's below your hand. Search for the center."

She closed her eyes. Searching for the deepest part of the earth. The center of everything. Her eyes opened, glowing gold. He knew this meant she found it.

"Good. Now pull the body to where you are."

The body began sinking into the bloody soil. Disappearing into the deepest part of the earth. She blinked her eyes and was back. She looked into the grave. The body was gone. Even his torn trousers, blood and shovel were gone. all that remained in the grave was his cuff. She climbed down into the grave grabbing the cuff. She climbed back out. Shoving the bloody cuff and crystal into her coat pocket.

"Thank you. Father wouldn't understand. He would've kept him alive for more intel."

"Your father doesn't understand that sometimes, it's best to just end a life." He wrapped his arm around her shoulder. "Want to explain the crystal?"

"It's his memories. That's all I know. He told me to give it to my father."

"Are you going to?"

"Eventually. I don't see a point right now."

"I'm surprised this saddens you."

"It doesn't."

"Then explain your hair."

"Oh. That's something different. I'm just really missing Kelley right now." She looked over her shoulder at the water, letting out a deep sigh. "I was watching the ships coming in when Macsen got here.

I was hoping his ship would come to port today. Once again. I was wrong."

"Well my dear, I will unfortunately be of no help for you with those matters. I deal in the matters of death."

"Which is exactly why I asked for your help with this situation."

"I'll walk you back. It feels like it's been ages since I've seen Styx."

"You saw her last month." She laughed as they began walking back.

"I'm still not a fan of her being in hiding. She has no need for it. We're the only ones who even remember her existence."

"That's true. But she enjoys a peaceful home life."

"Styx was always a little different than the rest of us."

"You know she hates you calling her that."

"Why do you think I do it?"

His sly grin and wiggling of his eyebrows filled her with a laugh no one had heard from her since before Kelley left. He knew all the best ways to cheer her up.

2

Peggy froze when she saw them walk into the house. The handkerchief may have gotten the blood off her face and hands but her clothes and hair were still covered. Her glare went right to Hades. She stormed over to him, pulling the two of them up the stairs into Gemma's room. Locking the door behind her.

"What in the underworld did you make her do?" A deep growl rolled off her lips.

"I didn't do anything. She called me here for cleanup. A similar cleanup to a few you had me do for you."

"We agreed to never speak of that again."

"What does it matter? It was hundreds of years ago."

"You know you're not supposed to talk about that when you're here! What if Lucy hears? Or even worse, if Patrick hears?"

Gemma walked over to her wardrobe to change out of the blood soaked clothes while they argued. She wanted Macsen's blood off her. She pulled the crystal and cuff out of her coat pocket, placing them in a drawer on her desk. She waved her hand over the drawer. Placing a magical seal on it. Protecting it from prying eyes. Last thing she needed was someone getting ahold of it. When she finished undressing they were still arguing. She wrapped herself in her robe. Gathered clean clothes to take to a bath. She headed for the door but was stopped by Peggy.

"Where do you think your going? We still need to discuss this?"

"Well, seeing as how you two have been bickering for the past twenty minutes. I figured I would go wash the blood out of my hair before Patrick gets home. Unless you think he would have no problem seeing me covered in blood again."

Peggy let out a sigh. "Make it quick. We need to discuss what happened."

"My uncle can fill you in."

"No. I want to hear it from you."

"What's it even matter? I took care of it. It's all done and over now. Nothing more to say."

"Who was it?"

"It was my kind. No laws broken. It was his request."

"Who."

"Macsen. The merman that showed up to the solstice party three solstices ago."

"Why?"

"He was giving me a message. Then was planning to kill himself. I did it myself to be sure his memories would never be found. Now if you don't mind. I prefer to remove this degenerate's blood from my hair."

She stormed out of the room, locking herself in the bathroom.

The water quickly turned crimson as the blood was washed from her skin. She ducked under the surface. Freeing her hair from the vile blood that had taken over. She opened her eyes underwater. It was dark. She couldn't remember the last time she had been in that bloody of water. She brought her face to the surface. To keep from seeing the darkness.

Darkness. She went there again. To that dark place she had been warned to never go to. She felt no remorse for killing him. She felt relief. Freedom. And worst of all... joy. That part worried her. She enjoyed killing him. That darkness called her regularly. Especially since Kelley left. When he was around, her darkness laid dormant. But now that he wasn't around her, it pushed to come out.

"I need him." She muttered to herself.

She drained the tub and waited for her tail to dry. As soon as her legs were back, she threw her clothes on and returned to her room. Peggy and Hades were still bickering, but it was about something else. Something they didn't want her to know about. She sat at her desk. Pulled out a piece of paper and began writing Kelley a letter. This one was small, but urgent.

Kelley,

I've gone to a dark place. Darker than I remember ever going. The darkness has been trying to consume me. I need you. I need you to be my light. Please guide me from the dark. I need you home. Please come home. Tell your captain it's urgent. I don't know how much longer I can hold back the darkness. I'm begging you. Come home.

Love

Your Gem

She placed the letter in an envelope, stood up and walked over to Hades, handing him the letter.

"This needs to get to Kelley immediately. I need him to read it right away. Can you please deliver it to him for me?"

"I'm not a mail service."

"I know. And I wouldn't be asking if I didn't think this is an emergency."

"What's the emergency?"

"Read me and you'll know."

He looked into her eyes. Digging deep into her soul. His eyes widened. He made a quick flame, disappearing into the fire.

"What was in the letter?" Peggy asked.

"I just need him right now."

A hand flew to her mouth. "The darkness has gotten to you, hasn't it?"

"Yes. I enjoyed killing him. I wanted to dismember him. I wanted it to be slow and painful. But I was on a time limit. So I couldn't."

"What can sending Kelley a letter do?"

"I'm hoping that my uncle will bring him back... even if it's just for a day. I need him desperately right now. I've never felt so good about doing something so bad before. I felt at peace about it. I don't want to enjoy killing someone so much."

"You don't really think Hades would bring him back do you?"

"If anyone can… it would be him. He read my soul and saw what I felt. He knows that My soul regularly rides a fine line of light and dark. I prefer the light… but the dark feels so good. Kelley is the only thing that can get me out of the place that my head is going. When he's around… I don't feel a desire to even consider the darkness."

"What do you think your father would do if he finds out that Kelley did sneak back?"

"It doesn't matter. I need him. And if he knew why… he would agree to it. He doesn't want me to turn out like two of my brothers. That much I know for sure."

A blue ring of Fire appeared right where he had left from. Kelley was pushed through the ring as Hades walked in behind him. Kelley seemed disoriented. A little off balance and confused. Then his eyes locked on her. He scooped her up in his arms. Holding her tight. Her head resting on his chest. Leaving a kiss on the top of her head. She felt light again. Not heavy, sinking deeper into the darkness.

"How long do we have?"

Gods she missed that voice.

"We can get away with 24 hours. After that… the crew might become suspicious when they leave port."

"Can you leave us for a few minutes. I need to help her get her head in the right place."

Peggy and Hades left. Gemma magically sealed the door. Keeping everyone out of her room. Her grip on his shirt tightened. She couldn't bare the thought of him leaving again. A single thought ran through her head… time to run.

He sighed. "You know we can't."

"Can't What?"

"We can't run away. Trust me… I've tried. A few times. I always get dragged back to the ship."

"At the lagoon… they can't-"

"Yes they can. Your uncle can find us anywhere."

"I'm sure he would-"

"No he won't."

She dropped back down onto the bed. "I don't want you to go. I've got this horrible feeling that something bad is going to happen."

"Is that why you sent for me?"

"No… I felt that as soon as we touched."

"Then why did you send for me? What happened?"

"Did you read the letter?"

"Yes. Now what happened?"

"I killed Macsen."

His fist balled. "Macsen?"

That was a new growl from him. It was as dark as she felt. Filled with an untapped vengeance ready to explode.

"Y-yes… he gave me his memories, then told me he was killing himself. So I did it for him."

"Where's the body?" Lightning was now crawling up his arms.

"Hades helped me bury it. No one will ever find it."

He sat beside her, pulling her in close. "It was a rush, wasn't it?"

"Yeah. I feel like I'm a horrible monster for even feeling that way. But after everything I've gone through with him. Him giving up his life to protect me… it felt like I did the right thing. And it felt so good."

"I know that feeling. But here's the thing. You have to decide deep down what's better. That high you get from taking someone's life? That darkness that was rushing through you, filling you with a temporary joy. It all goes away. And it goes away fast. Each time you kill someone, the high lasts for less time. And when you look back… do you want all that blood on your hands? Is that what you want to remember?"

"Of course not. I don't want to be that way… but that feeling-"

"Will disappear quickly. Then you'll hit a deep low. One that can change you. That's when deep down you decide. Do you go dark?" He opened his fist to reveal a star made of his sparks. "Or do you stay in the light?" He pushed the star up as it floated near the ceiling. A new trick he learned while being away. He didn't know how long it would last, but knew it would help her while he was gone.

"I can't find the light when your not here."

"You need to. You need to find a way. We still have over a year until I can come back."

"How do you stay out of the dark? I know you ride that fine line like I do."

"I think of you. I think of what you would think if you saw me turn dark. I know killing people won't stop for me. But mine is for survival. If I don't have to, I won't. But if it's keeping me alive to get back to you. Then I'll kill anyone that tries to come after me. Because even when you're not with me, you're the light in my darkness."

"I don't know if I can."

He lifted her chin. His eyes always made her melt into a puddle. "You can. Trust me. You can." His lips stole hers. Sending a fire through her. Gods she missed his lips. He knew all the right ways to mend her. Never forgetting a single inch of her.

3

Peggy had called the docks, asking them to keep Patrick out late and to take him to Callie's pub. She followed that call with a call to Callie asking her to keep him there until the next afternoon. She couldn't let him know what was going on. And especially couldn't let him see Hades. He believed he was dead, after he posed as her father for multiple years. She brought him a cup of a special tea that he loved. One that only Gods could drink. She sat across from him. Watching his every move.

"Are you just going to stare at me?"

"Maybe."

"Why are you acting so weird this time?"

"Because you brought her home covered in blood."

"I was just clean up. You remember how that is. All I did was teach her what you should've been teaching her."

"Sorry. I'm just on edge lately."

"Care to explain?"

"I'd rather not."

"Styx. Nothing you've ever said has ever shocked me."

"I'm just having some regrets."

"Like giving up your powers? Passing them to Kelley?"

"Of course not. He needs them. I'm now wishing I had given him my immortality too. I should've... but stupidly I didn't."

"Why didn't you?"

She shrugged. That was a hard one for her to answer. But she knew if he got a read on her, he would know. Thankfully she still knew how to block even him.

"I didn't think he would need it."

"And now you think he does."

She gave him a small nod. "I worry about them both. They can't handle being apart."

"She needs some part of him that she can always have."

"That's not an easy task."

"Well... there's one way..."

"That didn't work out so well for them last time. He still doesn't know. She's afraid to tell him."

"Hmm... maybe have him get her a pet... like a cat. Something she can take back and forth with her. I would normally recommend a dog... but she needs something less maintenance right now."

"That's something you'll have to talk to him about."

He scratched his chin. "I wonder if it could survive here."

"What?"

"A soul vixen."

Her eyes widened. She hadn't seen one in centuries. The only place they can be found is in the underworld. They were crafty little things that could appear to vanish. They looked like a normal cat to humans. But the gods knew better. To "vanish" they would make it seem like their fur exploded for a moment and were gone, when really they just went invisible. But the best part of them, you could attach a soul or part of a soul to it.

"It would be the perfect thing for her."

"Do you still have that book I gave Kelley about our kind of animals?"

"I believe it's in his room."

She ran to Kelley's room to grab the book. She ran back downstairs handing him the book. He flipped through the pages until he found it.

"Hmm... well... it can work... it will be difficult though. We'll definitely have to keep your husband out of the house for the night. Lucy should be fine... but it might give away who I really am... in turn give away who you really are. You might want to talk to him about who you really are. He's known what you are since before he left but nothing about you specifically."

"That would be a fantastic question to answer."

They turned to find Kelley standing behind them. Gemma glued to his arm. Refusing to release him.

"Come have a seat. It'll take a while to explain. But first, Hades has an idea for something to help Gemma while you're away."

They looked at one another a small glimmer of hope filled them both. They sat on the sofa next to Hades. Ready to hear whatever idea he could possibly have.

"Kelley, have you read this book that I gave you?"

"Maybe 10 years ago I haven't touched it since. Didn't see much of a point in memorizing animals I'll never see."

"Do you remember what a soul vixen is?"

Gemma's eyes widened. She had forgotten about those. She had wanted one for years when she was younger, but they can't survive underwater.

"Can they survive here?" She asked eagerly.

"Yes... the process to imprint a soul will be a little difficult is all."

"Why?"

"Because he's still alive. I've been trying to find one that can live underwater so your father can have one, but it never works."

"I don't really remember those. Can you explain what it is?"

"You can imprint a soul into it. Leaving a piece of you with it so you'll always be with the person that owns it."

"So why is it difficult to imprint a living soul."

"They're normally done with the deceased. And they can only be taken care of by our kind... and for a living soul... they have to be our kind."

"What do you mean by our kind?"

Hades sighed. "The gods."

"But I'm not a-"

"Yes you are." The three said in unison.

He looked over at Peggy. "Ma?"

"Tell him a yes or no, then I'll explain while he gets it."

"Will it kill me?"

"No. It's just saving a small part of you."

"Then go get one."

Hades made a circular motion with his hand, then walked through the ring of fire.

"Alright ma, what's going on. Who are you?"

"I used to be a goddess. I gave up my immortality. And passed my magic down to you. It's why you have the ability to resist all siren abilities, and wield a trident. You're a god. Like how Gemma is a goddess. However you're not immortal."

Kelley shot up from his seat. "Why didn't you tell me before? It could've helped me understand all of this. You could've told me."

"Your father doesn't know."

"Oh…" He dropped back onto the sofa.

"I didn't and still don't want to know what he would do to the three of us if he found out. You know how much he hates the gods. It's why Hades and Sephy only show up when he's not here."

"Which goddess are you?"

"One you've never heard of. Hades and Poseidon took me out of the books years ago to protect me."

"Why?"

"Because she's the reason Zeus is gone." Gemma interjected. She knew how hard talking about it was for Peggy. "She removed him. My father and uncle needed to protect her from the possible wrath of the other remaining gods. You have both his powers and your mothers. It's why you create lightning."

"So I'm a mortal god? Is that even possible? Don't both of my parents have to be gods?"

"Not necessarily. Gemma is a goddess and only her father is a god. If one parent is a god or goddess and the other parent has some kind of magical abilities. Then it can still be possible."

"But Da doesn't-"

"He's from a long line of moon chasers. Making it possible."

"And Lu?"

"She's human. She didn't inherit many magical abilities aside from talking to animals and being a moon chaser. She has the hair of a goddess, but that's it. All my powers were given to you."

"Why?"

"When I had you, I didn't know if I would be able to have another child after you. So I gave it all to you. Zeus' powers were hiding within me and I didn't know they were there."

"Then how do you know I have his powers."

"The lightning that you produce. That crawls up your arms when your angry or stressed. I never had that. Only One god ever had that."

"So who am I?"

"What do you mean?"

"Am I myself? Am I Zeus? Am I someone or something else?"

"You're not Zeus. You're not some other god. You are yourself. You've been this way your whole life. It's just something that I kept secret from you. I was trying to protect you... mostly from your father."

He crossed his arms. "Hmph. A lot of good that did."

"It would've been worse if he knew. You might not have made it past your birth... I might not have made it past your birth... you know how-"

"Yeah Ma. I know. But you should've let me know earlier. Like when Gem moved in with us. We could've been working together on our magic the whole time. Taught me how to control this shit. Instead I'm just a mess that explodes magic when I get bloody pissed."

"I couldn't risk it. I couldn't risk him finding out and doing something to get rid of the three of us. I know he has it in him to get rid of gods and goddesses. He's done it before and gets joy out of it."

"What? How?" Gemma asked.

"Your father tasked him with removing a few that were trying to create a coup and overthrow him. They were more minor gods, but he reveled in their deaths. I knew from then on that I could never let him know."

"Was I born yet when you found out about that?" He clenched his fist. This was something he should've known before leaving at the very least.

"No, I was pregnant with you and had already drank the elixir that passed my powers to you." Her hands trembled thinking of what Patrick would do to the three of them. "It was my only way to protect you and Lucy. You can defend yourself now but Lucy wouldn't stand a chance."

He let out a breath, unclenching his fist. "Is there anything else that you know that I don't? Anything that might get me killed or help keep me alive while on this bloody ship?"

Her eyes flitted to Gemma, then back to him. She couldn't tell him, that was for Gemma to tell him. "Don't ever sing around anyone. You're like Gemma siren strength wise. I spent years helping you not put people in trances by just talking or touching them."

"Nothing else?"

"Nothing that will make a difference. When you come home for good, I'll fill you in on my life story."

He gave her a small nod before looking at Gemma. She was sweating. He had felt her tense up and hand get clammy when he asked his mother if there was anything else she was hiding. He also didn't miss his mother's eyes dart to Gemma. Gemma was hiding something. He knew better than to ask her though. If she hadn't told him, it meant it was something she was having a hard time even thinking about let alone talking about. He would just have to wait until she was ready.

4

The ring of fire appeared in the fireplace. Hades walked in holding a black, blue and purple ball of fluff. It was smaller than she thought it would be. He squatted down in front of the two of them holding out the little ball of fluff. He looked over at Peggy giving her a nod. She got up, locked the doors and closed the curtains. She remained in the kitchen. Digging through the cabinets. He grabbed Kelley's hands placing the ball in one hand and the other on top of it.

"It took me a while to find one that has never had a soul attached to it. I didn't want it to have any relapses of past souls. This little one has never been active."

"What do I have to do?"

"Styx is getting you the elixir mixed up right now. She used to help Sephy and I with these."

"What will happen to me? Will it kill me?"

"No… but you will feel weak and drained for a few hours. You'll need to rest for most of today. I don't mean you have to sleep, but you'll have to avoid using any magic. Which includes blocking everyone from getting a read on your soul."

"Alright." He looked at Gemma, her eyes were glued to the ball of fluff. She was entranced by it. Peggy nudged him, handing him a cup of what looked like tea, but was glowing and smelt like jasmine and honey.

"Just take one sip."

"What is it?"

"It's an elixir of the soul. It'll pull a small piece of you into the creature. But only take one sip. The more you drink, the more of you that will transfer to it."

"So you're the goddess Styx?"

"Yes. But I'm still your mother. So you better not start calling me Styx. You understand?"

He gave her a small nod. He took a decent size sip. He wanted to be sure it has more than a tiny piece of him. He knew she needed more than that. His arms and hands became incased in lightning. The lightning was absorbed by the ball of fluff. When the sparks vanished, the fluff began to shift in his hands. He opened his hands to allow it to get out. Hades closed Kelley's hands around the fluff.

"It's not done yet."

He wrapped Gemma's hands around Kelley's. Having her hands hold his closed. She could feel it moving in his hands. Then it stopped. Kelley felt a sharp sting in his hand followed by a burn racing through his veins. His eyes turned white as he let out a scream. She knew that kind of scream. It was a siren scream. It went on for a couple of minutes. When he stopped screaming his eyes returned. The creature began moving in his hands again. Kelley's heavy breaths and pale face worried her. She wanted to make sure he was alright, but she knew better than to let go before she was told to. Hades took her hands off Kelley's.

"Kelley, when you open your hands, bring it to your face, look it deep in the eyes. Once you see the spark in its eyes, bring it to Aquaria's face. She must be the first living thing it sees after you. Once their eyes connect it will acknowledge who she is. It will be loyal and obedient to only you two. No one else. It will give her the feeling that you're still here with her while you're gone. Do you both understand."

They gave him a small nod. Kelley brought his hands to his face and opened them. The little ball of fluff stretched. It looked like a mix between a kitten and a baby fox. It's dark black fur with shimmering hues of cobalt and magenta. As he looked at it closer, he saw what looked like sparks jumping through its fur. It looked like an entire galaxy was hiding in its fur. It's big bright crystal blue eyes were entrancing. Their eyes met and he lost himself in there. Every memory he had of him and Gemma flashed through his mind. As the years of memories ended, a spark flickered in its eyes. He quickly shoved it in Gemma's face, letting their eyes connect. Her face softened as it moved towards her. It rubbed up against her, letting out a soft hum.

"What's that sound?" She asked as it climbed onto her shoulder.

"It's like the purr of a cat."

"Won't people ask questions about it?"

"No, to human eyes it looks like a black cat. It even sounds like a cat to humans. Don't let that thing out of your sight for a week. If you do, it will become depressed and try one of two things: get back to the underworld or to find Kelley. After a week, it will be fine on its own. You'll even be able to leave it for a couple days."

"What does it eat?"

"That's the tricky part. And another reason why Styx being here is a good thing. It normally feeds on souls. So Styx will help you train it to eat the right souls."

"How? We can't even see them."

"Actually… I can." Gemma's voice went meek as her face turned a soft pink. The vixen rubbed against her cheek, calming her down as fast as Kelley did.

"What?"

"Yeah… I've always seen souls. It's something that I usually ignore… but today…"

"You saw his soul leave his body today."

"That's why I agreed to retrieve you and brought her the Vixen. I'm one of the only ones who knows she can see them. I felt it when I read her soul." Hades explained.

"So how do we get him souls?" Gemma asked.

"First of all, it's a her. The males can't come into the mortal world."

"So this girl vixen is part Kelley?"

"Yes."

"Ha ha. Kelley. Look. We have a girl version of you!" She teased.

"Gem. It's not that funny."

"You say that now! Wait till Lucy finds out."

"Don't you dare tell her."

"Oh I'm telling her."

Hades cleared his throat. "Can I continue with what I was saying?"

"Yes… Sorry." She lowered her head looking back at the vixen.

"It doesn't have to be human souls. Rodents and birds will be fine. But the bigger the body, the bigger the soul. The bigger the soul, the less often it needs to feed. A mouse will last two days. A rabbit a week. A Fox a month. A human… 6 months."

"How do we get her the souls?"

"She'll disappear when she senses a soul escaping a body. She'll go get it herself."

"But this first week?"

"I'm sure there are mice in the barn and plenty of birds outside."

"Will she always be this small?"

"No. By the end of the week she should be about the size of a normal adult house cat."

"So what does she do for Gem?"

"Gives her comfort… the way that your presence gives her comfort."

"Can it protect her?"

"No… they're actually quite skittish around confrontation. She can turn invisible to human eyes and will usually do that if she's scared. She is nothing more than an emotional companion for Aquaria. Something to keep her from the darkness."

"I have a feeling Patrick will never see her." She muttered to herself. She forgot that everyone in that room could hear as well as she could.

"Gem. What aren't you telling me?"

"It's nothing. He just hates our kind."

"If there's anything else going on-"

"I promise, I'll tell you. You're the one person I would tell."

"Wow. You wouldn't even tell Gerard?"

"If your not here I will. But otherwise no."

"Not even Astrid?" Hades asked.

"I'm not allowed to have contact with her, or anyone else. So I have no way of telling her, now do I?"

"No need to snap at me. I'm always here for you when you need me."

"Yes, but just like everyone else. Your hiding that one big secret from me. I deserve to know."

"Gem. It's alright. He's here helping us, right? Let's just drop it for now and see if there's anything else you need to know about this thing."

"It can't die. Even if Kelley died, it would still keep living. It would get depressed for a few weeks, but instead of Kelley's soul going to the underworld, it would return to the vixen. I wouldn't even know if he died because his soul would go straight to the vixen."

"Is there anything else she needs to know?"

"I don't believe so. But Styx can help. She helped me take care of some for about a century or so. She can help you learn about it. They're quite self sufficient. She'll just need your attention."

"Do I just call her Kelley or can I call her something else?"

"Call her something else. It would get confusing if you call her Kelley. She would get confused anytime he's around because she's part of him."

"Does eating other souls imprint them on her?"

"No. That's a different process. Her eating of souls isn't like eating and isn't like imprinting. She just absorbs the energy that comes from the soul. And no. She can't steal souls of the living. They have to be deceased. Any other questions?"

They shook their heads. It jumped down from her shoulder landing in her lap. Curling up to go to sleep. She began petting the little ball of fluff as it began to hum.

"Good. I'll be back in the morning to get Kelley and take him back. Get her head in the right place. Last thing any of us need is for her to turn out like her brothers. She enjoyed killing Macsen a little too much for my comfort."

"Thank you Uncle Hades."

"You know I'm always here to help you my dear. Don't tell your father about this. And especially don't tell him about that." He pointed to the vixen in her lap as its ear twitched in its sleep. "He's still upset that I can't get one that will survive underwater with Theia's soul."

The ring of fire appeared in the fireplace. He stepped into it, closing it behind him. Gemma looked over at Kelley. He was still off and looking exhausted. She helped him to his feet and took him upstairs. They curled up in her bed together. The little Vixen curled up between them. Snuggling into them, feeling the warmth of both of their bodies.

5

They woke up to the sound of the front door slamming shut, and feet rushing up the stairs. They knew it was Lucy. Patrick didn't sound like that that when he climbed the stairs. They didn't know if they should even tell Lucy about Kelley being back for the night. Last thing they needed was to deal with was explaining all of this to her. But they didn't really have much of an option as the door flew open. Lucy's hair was in shambles as she panted trying to catch her breath. They looked at her.

"Gemma! Are you okay?" She paused for a moment as they watched her face go from terror to confusion. "Kelley? What are you doing here? How are you here? Does Ma' know you're here? What about Da? Oh I have to go tell Gerard! He'll be so thrilled your home! How long are you here for?"

"Lu." He grumbled. "I'm just here for the night."

"Wait... but your ship wasn't in port... how did you get here? Are you the reason there's blood all over the front door? Why Ma's scrubbing blood from the tub?"

"No... actually that was me." Gemma said. "Along with Kelley being here is because of me... well actually my uncle. He kidnapped Kelley for a day for me."

"So he's only here for the day?"

"Yes. Now can you let me get back to sleep. I'm exhausted. I need to sleep."

The Vixen peeked up from between them. She rubbed against Gemma's cheek. Letting out a soft hum of a purr.

"Oh. My... what is that thing?"

"We'll explain later. Just let me rest. We'll talk at dinner."

"But Kelley. You're only here fo-"

"Not now Lucille! Let me rest. We'll be down in an hour."

"Fine. But you better bring that thing down with you." She stormed towards the door. "Don't you dare try to tell me its just a cat! Cat's don't have fur like that." She slammed the door behind her muttering to herself.

Gemma rested her head on his bare chest. Listening to the steady beat of his heart. She had been listening to it since they climbed in bed. Ensuring he was recovering. But most of all, just to hear it once more. The sound that put her to sleep faster than anything else. The vixen squeezed herself between them. Forcing their skin against hers.

"Are we sure she doesn't have your soul? She's being quite demanding." He laughed.

"She's acting just like you do when you want my attention. Nuzzling your face into my hair. Ensuring our skin is touching at all times. She's being as possessive as you are."

"Well..." he picked her up and got a better look at her. "Do you have any idea what you're going to call her?"

"I was thinking Lux."

"Lux?"

"It means light. And since she's going to be like a little light to keep me out of the darkness. I thought it was appropriate."

"Hmm. Well. You're the one that's going to be living with her. As long as you like the name."

"I do." She stroked its soft fur, causing its hum to intensify. "Do you think it will help?"

"I think that if your uncle specifically got this for you to keep you from the darkness, that he believes it will work. And this way, you'll always have me with you in a way."

"I hope she helps. It also might be helpful that she can disappear."

"Yeah… people might think its weird if a cat is following you around everywhere. And I think your right on Da' not knowing she is what she is."

"I'll just tell him you sent me a cat. To keep me company. He doesn't need to know any more than that."

"He'll probably wonder why I would send a cat."

She shrugged. "Not something I need to explain. If he wants to know that he'll have to ask you."

She went back to listening to his heart. Memorizing the sound and the feeling against her cheek. There it was again. That chill shooting up her spine. She was starting to think it was her nerves getting to her. But then she noticed Lux. She began shaking. Curling herself closer to Kelley. Pawing at his chest. Rubbing her head against his hand. She felt it too. Something was going on. Either he was hiding something from her… or he didn't know it was coming either.

She didn't let go of him. She stayed by his side as much as possible. Lux trotting along side the two of them. Not letting either of them out of her sight. Even when Lucy was holding her while they explained everything to her, Lux's eyes remained on them.

"I don't get it. You said only gods can see what she really looks like. How come I can? I'm not special like you two."

"That's a fantastic question." He turned his head towards the kitchen raising his voice for Peggy to hear. "Maybe Ma could answer that for you."

She glared at him, ignoring the comment. Gemma knew how hard she worked to keep her identity a secret. She had kept it a secret for two years now. Not to mention her own identity. It was something that they understood, that no one else in the family could.

"Where's Da? Isn't he coming home for dinner?"

"No. He's staying at the pub tonight. We didn't want to have to explain to him how Kelley got here… he's not a fan of my uncle."

"To be fair, not many people are."

"True. But he's actually quite wonderful. Most don't realize he's much more understanding than my father."

"I don't get why everyone hates him. I get along great with him. Always have. Ask Ma. She knows how nice he's always been to me and Lu."

Gemma elbowed him in the side. "Leave it alone. She doesn't want her to know. So leave her alone." She muttered softly.

"It's not fair to us. We should know this. It's part of who we are."

"Leave it alone. It's for her protection."

"What are you two arguing about? I thought you two would be sickeningly lovey dovey the whole night."

"It's nothing. Don't worry about it." Gemma quickly responded as Kelley got up to go into the kitchen. Lux's eyes followed him. She jumped off Lucy's lap curling up next to Gemma's shoulder. "Where's Gerard? I thought he was going to join us for dinner."

"He is. He should be here anytime now. He must've been stopped on his way here or something. Is everything alright with Kelley?"

"I don't know. I mean, I doubt it. It's obvious that it's been a rough year and a half... but I don't know. I think he's just a bit shaken by everything that's happened today."

"I wish he could stay longer."

"Me too. A day isn't long enough with him."

"What's he saying to ma? I know you can hear them."

"Don't worry about it. They'll tell you when they're ready."

Lucy jumped up as the door opened. Running into Gerard's arms. As soon as she finally released him, he gave Kelley a hug. Lucy dragged him to the living room. She wanted to test what they said about Lux looking like a cat to humans.

"Um Lucy... when did you get a cat? You didn't have it yesterday... or say anything about it when we had lunch."

"She's mine... well mine and Kelley's." Gemma smiled as lux hopped into her lap again as Kelley moved back to the sofa.

"Why'd you get her a cat?"

"I didn't. Her uncle brought it to us after he brought me here."

"Wait... that's how you got here? The god of the underworld?"

"Yeah. And it's not a cat. It's a Soul Vixen. He attached part of my soul to it for Gemma. Something to help her while I'm gone. Mainly to keep her from going completely dark. Like she almost did today."

"Oh gods. What'd she do this time?"

"Killed someone."

"He deserved it. After everything he's done, I was merciful in making it end quickly." Gemma snapped "Besides, he asked me to."

Gerard scrubbed his face. "I don't want to know. So back to the cat."

"Her name is Lux. She'll be with me at all times now."

"It's not a cat." Lucy jumped in. "Just look at its fur. It's got blue and pink and it sparkles... kinda like the sparks that come out of Kelley's hands."

"Lucy... it's just a black cat."

"No it's not! I mean, look at its face! It looks like a fox and a cat had a baby."

"It's looks like a black kitten. Are you sure your feeling alright?"

"I'm fine! Ugh! Fine! You two win! He can't see what it really is. Now why can I?"

"Ask Ma."

Lucy ran into the kitchen, begging Peggy for answers. Peggy brushed off the questions as she handed Lucy food to put on the table.

"So... is Lucy right? Does Lux not look like a cat?"

"Not really. I mean a little, but you can tell she's not a cat. And if she gets scared she'll disappear." Gemma stroked Lux's fur, as she hummed softly.

"Like run away?"

"No, like poof! Invisible!"

"Really?"

"Supposedly. We haven't seen her do it yet, but my uncle says it's what they do."

"Can she protect you?"

"No... she's emotional support. I'm constantly between being a good person and going completely dark like a couple of my brothers. Kelley somehow manages to keep me out of the dark just by being with me. I don't know how to explain it... but it's how it is between us. And lux having a piece of his soul means she will help me stay out of that darkness."

"How dark are we talking? Like you in a bad mood or..."

"I thoroughly enjoyed killing Macsen. I wanted to slowly

dismember him. I wanted to watch him suffer. When I got back here, I took a bath to wash off his blood. That's when I realized that I needed Kelley. That I was going down that dark path I try so hard to avoid. I gave my uncle a letter to bring to Kelley and let him read my soul. He knew in that moment that Kelley was the only thing to get me back from going darker."

"So Lux will help with that?"

"Supposedly."

"Why is Lucy so upset about me thinking it looks like a cat?"

"Because humans are the only ones that can't see what she really is... and well... she can see what she is. So she's trying to figure out why."

"Why can she?"

"It's complicated and not our story to tell. That belongs to someone else, when they're ready."

"Really? Huh. I guess my suspicions about Peggy have been right then."

"What?! You knew?" They exclaimed.

"I always thought there was something she was hiding. I would occasionally hear her speaking clear and fluent Greek. If you caught her off guard her Irish accent would be gone. But I think the Solstice is what really got me. I saw Poseidon take her to another room to talk privately. I knew something was off. He knew her on a very personal level."

"I didn't know about that." Kelley voice was weakening, he needed to rest more. The one hour wasn't nearly long enough.

"Oh I did. She told me about it a few weeks after the club banquet. I think she's enjoying having someone to talk to about it all, and knows I won't tell anyone her secret." Gemma's smile faltered as she looked at Kelley. He was getting paler by the minute.

"So why can't Lucy know?"

"Da. Why else?" Kelley rolled his eyes, thinking Gerard of all people should know that. "He hates the gods. Who knows what he would do if he found out he married one and produced one and another with god blood. It's something that we know for a fact that he would lose his mind."

"Yet another reason we have to keep this a secret. If he asks you about Lux, make sure you stick with her just being a cat." Gemma looked back at Gerard for a moment.

"Don't worry. Your secret's safe with me. Lucy is the one you need to worry about."

"I'm going to talk to Peggy about this. Lucy won't drop it, and if Gerard already figured it out on his own, then I don't see any point in her not knowing."

"Gem-"

"Hold Lux for me. I'll be back in a moment."

She pulled Peggy aside and began whispering to her.

"What's she saying."

"Something in Greek. I still can't believe you figured it all out. I only know because they told me this afternoon."

"It's probably because I'm not her kid. You two probably wouldn't notice the things I noticed because you were raised by her."

"I guess you're right." He scratched Lux under her chin. Her hum getting louder by the second. She nuzzled into his hand. Begging for more attention.

"Are you sure it's not Gemma's soul imprinted? She's acting just like her."

Kelley let out a light chuckle. "I said the same thing, then she reminded me that I'm just as bad as she is when I'm wanting her affection."

"Think it'll help?"

"I bloody hope so. I don't want her to go down that dark path." He peeked over his shoulder looking at her trying to convince Peggy into telling Lucy. "She only lets two people read her soul, Hades and me. I've seen how fine of a line she's on between her light and going dark. And that darkness... I've felt it... it's freeing. It feels damn good, and is horribly addicting. But it doesn't last long and you crave it nonstop."

"And how've you been holding up?"

"The thought of her is the only thing keeping me from fully embracing all that darkness that I crave. But I know the cost of that darkness."

"And what's that?"

"I'll lose her."

6

No matter what he tried, he couldn't sleep. He held her tight in his arms, not ready for dawn to come. The little vixen curled up on the pillow above her head was as wide awake as he was. He looked at the little creature.

"So this is how it's gonna be, huh? You only sleeping when I'm asleep? She won't like that."

She blinked up at him, before turning her focus back to Gemma.

"I know." He sighed. "But what else am I supposed to do? You're part of me... you know how I feel and what's going on. I don't want to leave. I want to run away. I've tried. But they always find me. I ran away to the lagoon once and was dragged right back to that blasted ship! I just wanted to spend a couple of days with her, but no. I'm under strict orders to stay away until he says I can return."

"Until who says that?" She mumbled.

"Your father."

"He doesn't make it easy for me to not hate him." She rested her head on his chest. "Can't sleep?"

"No. I don't want to waste a second I have with you on sleeping. I'll sleep on the ship."

"I wish I could say I couldn't sleep... but what I did took a lot out of me."

"Killing Macsen?"

"No... my uncle taught me how to control the earth enough to pull the body and blood deep into the earths core. No one will ever find it. But that kind of magic will drain you."

"Sorry I wasn't there to help you."

"It's alright... it was something I was meant to do alone... and I was lucky enough to get you back for the day."

"I'm sorry I have to leave tomorrow."

"Me too, but I got you here now. It's better than nothing... and when I needed you most, you were right here for me."

"I'll do everything in my power to be here for you when you need me. And if I can't, now you have Lux."

"Whom you seem to have been having a conversation with."

"Yeah" he scratched the back of his head letting out a soft chuckle. "It's like I can hear her talking in my head when I look at her."

"Well... she has part of your soul, so that might explain that."

"How much do you know about these things?"

"Not much. But I'll read about her. Try to understand her more. I'm sure your mom will be a huge help with her."

"Yeah... ma... what all do you know about her?"

"A lot actually. The river Styx that takes you to the underworld was named after her. My aunt and uncle are her best friends, have been for centuries. When it's just the two of us, we sit and talk about everything. She helps me with understanding my role in life. How to come to terms with the fact that I'm a goddess not just a mermaid or a princess. She helps me understand how to control some of my magic. While she didn't have most of the powers I have, she does understand how to control them. She's been helping me the most while you've been gone."

"Why did she tell you who she was?"

"Ha! She didn't. I figured it out on my own. I've known since my birthday when she pulled me away from everyone after they all dropped to their knees."

"And it didn't bother you that she's been lying?"

"Darling, everyone lies to me about almost everything. Even you have a secret you can't tell me. So I'm used to it. It's become a game to me to find out what people are keeping from me."

"Sorry I have to keep some of this from you right now. I would tell you everything if I didn't know for a fact your father would erase your memory again. I don't know how he does it, but somehow he always finds out."

"How many times have you tried to run away?"

"Maybe 20 times. Nothing ever worked. He would somehow always find out. Even the men on my ship wouldn't know, but he somehow would. It's been exhausting."

"I'm sorry he's doing that to you. I desperately wish that we could run away together. That there was a way."

"But there isn't. Trust me, I've tried. At least now you'll always have a piece of me. Lux will always be here for you."

"I know. And I hope she helps me. But it won't be the same."

Before morning arrived, he had finally drifted off to sleep. She slipped out of his embrace, making her way to her desk. She had been contemplating how to tell him what happened. Every time she tried to tell him, she would throw the paper away. After that feeling she had been getting since he arrived, she knew this time, she had to tell him.

She wrote down everything she could think of. Her tears falling on the page, smudging the ink. She didn't care. Her tears hadn't ruined the important parts. Once she sealed the letter, she curled back up in his arms drifting off to sleep herself.

Hours passed before they were woken up by someone shaking them. She swung her arm at the one shaking her awake. Her wrist was caught in a soft, delicate hand.

"It's just me dear. Unfortunately Kelley needs to get up. Your uncle is downstairs waiting to take him back."

Peggy's soft voice was much more soothing than that of her uncle. Reminding her of her mother when she would attempt to wake her. Keeping her from going into her usual morning rage.

They climbed out of bed and headed downstairs. Lux trotting along behind them. They sat at the table to eat so Kelley wouldn't go back starving. Hades never minded delays when food was involved, especially Peggy's cooking. Peggy had even packed food for Kelley to take with him and for Hades to bring Persephone.

The table was quiet. Just the sounds of silverware hitting the plates. She snuck away upstairs to grab the letter. As she reached the bottom of the stairs, Kelley was saying goodbye to everyone, again. She walked up to Hades and pulled him into another room.

"I need one more favor from you."

"And what would that be?"

"Give this to Kelley as soon as you close the portal." She held out the letter. The tear stains seeped through the envelope. "I know what your going to say. 'I'm not a mail service.' And I know that. However, your the only one I trust to give it to him."

"Why me?"

"Because you won't read it. You respect my privacy when it comes to a letter."

"What's in the letter? Plans to run away together? Because I won't support that."

She sighed "No, not this time. I know that won't work. It's just something personal that Kelley needs to know, but I don't want my father to know."

He looked at the tear stained letter. He had a feeling he knew what it was about. "It's better if you tell him in person."

"It won't make a difference. Neither of us can do anything to fix it. It's easier for me to tell him this way."

"Are you sure? I remember when Seph went through it and-"

"It's been months since it happened. He needs to know, but I can't relive it again. So can you please give it to him."

He sighed, staring at it. He gave her a small nod. "Under one condition. Next time you see him in person, you two talk about it. Got it?"

"Alright. Thank you."

He took the letter from her as he left the room. She followed him out wiping away the tear that betrayed her stoic expression. Her heart ached at the thought of what she had put in that letter. She wished she could tell him in person, but she knew she would breakdown worse than she will when he leaves.

She was pulled out of her thoughts when she felt his soothing arms wrap around her. His touch healed her heart. A feeling she wasn't ready to lose.

"Are you going to be okay?" His eyes searching hers.

"No. But we don't have any other choice right now. I have Lux, maybe she'll help."

"Try to keep yourself busy. It'll make the time go by faster. And go to the lagoon as much as possible. I'll try to sneak over there if we go to that port again."

She gave him a small nod. Trying to hold her tears back, as they threatened to betray her again. She could never cry in front of her uncle if anyone else was around. That was only allowed when it was just the two of them, or if Persephone was there. Lux rubbed her head against Gemma's leg. It soothed her enough to hold the tears back.

"I'll be back. I promise." He leaned in close to her ear. He knew that even if he whispered his mother and hades would hear him. But he wanted their focus on his voice, not his hand as he slipped a note in the pocket of her skirt. "I love you more than anything. I promise I'll marry you as soon as I get back. Please stay out of the darkness and wait for me."

"I will. I promise. I love you so much. Please don't fall for anyone else while you're gone. I will kill any woman who lays a finger on you."

He kissed her forehead. "I would expect nothing less."

He held her tight. Her face buried in his chest. He didn't look back up until Hades cleared his throat, gesturing to the open portal.

"I love you more than anything."

"I love you too."

He kissed her lips once more before stepping through the portal. Hades looked back at her, giving her a small nod. Pulling the letter out and handing it to Kelley as the portal shut. She collapsed to the ground. Her tears flowing freely. Peggy helped her to the sofa. She curled up, unable to stop the tears.

"It will go by fast my dear."

Peggy left her to give her space, forcing Gerard and Lucy out of the room. She pulled out the note he slipped into her pocket.

"Don't trust what they say about me. Not even death will keep me from getting back to you."

7

It was a windy day, a storm was coming in. She could hear the thunder behind her, racing to beat the rain, that would ultimately cause her to change. She was on horseback, riding faster than usual. Trying to get back in time. She left Lucy in town, she couldn't wait for her. Her hair blowing wildly in the wind, not stopping for anything. The only thing on her mind was getting back in time.

Repeating to herself, "Come on, go faster! I can't be late! I can't miss him again." She finally got back to the house and saw she was already too late. She felt her heart begin to sink in her chest. She would have to wait another full week for a chance.

"Gemma dear. Nik left a letter for you." Peggy handed Gemma the letter. She still had a somewhat disappointed look on her face. "Don't worry, I made sure that he took the letter you wrote."

"Thank you, Peggy!" She said while giving her a big hug.

She ran to Kelley's room and closed the door behind Lux, who had become her little shadow. She sat on his bed to read the letter, it made her feel as if he was with her, when she would read his letters in his room. She was ecstatic about getting letters from him. He wasn't supposed to be sending her letters, but Captain Jones and Nik allowed them to exchange letters once a week. That was the fastest that Nik could exchange the letters, especially since Kelley was always somewhere different.

My Gem,

I miss you more than anything in the whole world. We haven't stopped very much, there are not many islands where we are currently. I wish I could tell you everything right now, however I can't. I promise I will tell you everything when I return. Captain Jones has been having me help his first mate chart our courses. Apparently, I have a knack for this kind of thing. We had a new man join our crew this week, he wasn't afraid of anyone, that is until he heard my last name. Da' must have really left a name for himself while he was a pirate, everyone is petrified when they hear that name. I can't wait to have you back in my arms, I want nothing more than to just be with you. We have already made it a year and a half, we can make it through this. I will come back for you, even if you are already married, I will come back and save you. You are the light in my dark. Nothing will ever change that. I love you and miss you more than anything.

All my love, Kelley

She curled up with the letter on his bed, Lux snuggling into her neck, with a soft humming. It killed her being away from him, but she was happy just to be able to get his letters every week. It was the only thing she ever looked forward to anymore. After she laid there for a while she got up and put the letter back in her room. Lucy finally came back home over an hour later. Gerard came back with her to have dinner with everyone. Gemma was already wishing it had been a week, so she could get her next letter to him. After dinner, she went right back upstairs and went to bed clutching the letter in her hands.

The next week Gemma waited patiently for Nik to arrive, she didn't want to risk missing him again, so she stayed at the house all day. Most of the day she just sat at the window in her room, watching for him. As she headed downstairs for lunch, halfway down the stairs she felt a sharp pain in her stomach. She grabbed onto the rail. Trying to hold herself up. But failing miserably. She stumbled to the bottom step. The pain getting worse with each step. She gripped tight to her stomach. Letting out a scream as she fell to the floor. All she saw was double vision. She couldn't move. She couldn't speak. Everything was muffled. Then it all went black.

When she could finally see again she was in her bed with Peggy sitting beside her. Lux curled up next to her sound asleep.

"Oh thank the heavens you're alright."

"Peggy? How-how did I get here?" She rubbed her eyes trying to focus again. "What happened?"

"That's what I'd like to know. You stumbled down the stairs then began screaming and collapsed. You were screaming for ten minutes. Clutching your stomach. You passed out when you finally stopped screaming. So what in the underworld happened?"

"I-I don't... know... it was weird. I was fine. I was just a little hungry so I was coming downstairs for lunch... then... I don't know. I started to feel a pain in my stomach. It just kept getting worse. I remember falling to the ground but nothing after that." Lux woke up and began rubbing her face against Gemma's hand.

"Does you stomach still hurt?"

"No. It's completely fine. Like nothing ever happened."

"Hmm. I don't really know what to tell you. Maybe we should talk to Nik about this. It might be a mermaid problem of some kind. We know it's not what happened before."

"No... it's definitely not that. It doesn't feel the same as that... this... it felt like I was stabbed. The pain I felt in my leg from Liam but in my stomach. And it was so much worse. I've never felt a pain like that before. It burned at the same time. I felt weak. Do you know what color my hair turned?"

"When it happened?"

She nodded.

"It was turning black."

"Black? Are you sure? Maybe a dark blue?"

"No my dear. It was clearly black. Lucy was in a horrible panic. She thought you were dying."

"Why would she think that?"

"Your eyes rolled back. Your heart nearly stopped. Your breathing was so weak. We've been trying to get a hold of Nik. We know he's coming today, but he's taking so much longer than usual."

"I-I don't know what to say. I don't know what happened. But now I feel perfectly fine, like it never happened."

"Hopefully Nik will be here soon. Try to take it easy today. I'll even bring you your dinner if you would like."

"I should be fine. Thank you though. If I'm not feeling right when I try to stand. Then I'll stay in bed. But I honestly feel normal."

"Alright. Well, try to rest. I'll come check on you in a little bit."

Peggy left the room closing the door to give her some peace. Gemma curled back up in bed. Lux curling into her chest as they both drifted off to sleep.

8

The next evening Nik finally showed up. Every time he was around she had a smile on her face. The only time anyone ever saw her smile since Kelley left. But this time something was different about his visit. it was much later than usual, it was already dark. Dark enough that she didn't notice that he wasn't alone. She quickly searched her desk for the letter she wrote and ran downstairs to greet him. She ran right to him and gave him a hug, she was so excited to get the letter. This time he didn't let go of her hug, he held her tight.

"Alright Nik! No need hug me so tight, it's not like you don't see me every week." She laughed.

"Gemma, I need to talk to you about something."

"If it's about yesterday. It's nothing. I'm fine. Sure it was weird but I'm completely fine. See?" She spread her arms with a smile on her face.

"What happened yesterday?"

"I'm not sure. I felt a sharp pain in my stomach and collapsed. Peggy said I was screaming and that my eyes rolled back. My heart nearly stopped and I stopped breathing for about a minute."

"What?"

"The weirdest part is she said my hair was turning black. Which is impossible. The only time I've ever seen anyone's do that was father's hair when my mother died. And I mean look at it now. It's definitely not black."

"I'll talk with Peggy about this later. But that's not what I need to talk to you about."

"Did Kelley not send a letter this time? It's okay if he didn't, I understand if he couldn't get one to me this week. You can still bring him my letter though." The smile didn't leave her face as she tried to hand him the letter.

"He sent a letter, but… Come have a seat."

"Nik you're worrying me. Where's everyone else?" She noticed that everyone was gone, dinner abandoned hastily, in the middle of preparation. The smell of lamb stew simmering on the stove, filled the room. "They were here right before I came downstairs."

"Aquaria stop talking!" He snapped, he dropped his head and shoulders, letting out a breath. "I need to tell you something, you have to listen to what I'm going to tell you. Okay?"

"Alright…." She froze hearing him say her name on land. She had never heard Nik speak to her with that tone. He had lost his temper at her before, especially the times she ended up in the cells. Though, it was never like this. Lux finally made it downstairs. Jumping onto her lap. She stroked the little vixen, but it wouldn't hum.

"Something happened."

Gemma gripped the chair as her chest tightened. Lux rubbed herself hard against her arm. Begging her to focus her attention on her.

"Kelley's ship was attacked yesterday. The fight got rough, there were many who were gravely injured and unfortunately didn't survive."

"Nik, stop. You're starting to scare me." Her highlights began to fade into a darker blue.

"Aquaria…" he grabbed her hands, placing the letter in one hand. "This is the last letter you will get from Kelley." With every word he spoke, the darker the blue got. Her hands trembled holding the letter. He took a deep breath, "Kelley did not survive the fight."

"No…. No, I don't believe you." The blue turned black. Just like her father's.

"He died, yesterday afternoon."

"I... I don't believe you. He's an amazing fighter! He can beat anyone." She shouted.

"There were apparently multiple pirates that attacked him at once."

"No! This is just some trick to get me to not love him! So I'll go along with that gods-forsaken arraignment and not run away with him when he gets back "

"Why would I make up his death? If I was going to keep you from loving him, I would have made something up about him being with someone else. I wouldn't lie to you about his death."

"But... he was fine yesterday. You said it yourself that he gave you this letter and…. He was fine!"

Poseidon opened the front door and came into the room, Gemma saw through the door Patrick was holding Peggy and Lucy in his arms. They were both crying.

"No…" Her hands flew to her mouth. As tears soaked her cheeks. "No! It can't be true."

"My Pearl, come here." Poseidon said.

She couldn't move, she sat there crying so hard that she couldn't breathe. She had never felt this kind of pain before. The tightness and pressure on her chest were becoming unbearable. She wanted to rip out her heart to make the pain go away. She gripped her chest, digging her nails into her skin, begging the pain to stop. Her breathing was nearly nonexistent, complete uncontrollable crying. Lux was trembling in her lap. Her usual soothing hum was missing. Her eyes darting between Nik and Poseidon. Giving them a cat-like glare that if she were human, it would be the same glare Kelley gave.

Poseidon walked over to Gemma and stood in front of her. "My pearl, I'm so sorry. I know how it feels to lose the one you love." He placed his hand on her shoulder. Lux jumped from her lap. Darting upstairs to Kelley's room.

She threw his hand from her shoulder, stood up quickly and ran upstairs. She went right to Kelley's room, slamming the door, before curling up on his bed. She clung to the letter that Nik had just given her. Her heart felt like someone took a sledgehammer to it, shattering her heart into a million pieces. Nothing could fix the pain she was feeling.

Poseidon came into the room, finding his daughter completely devastated. He didn't know what to do, he just sat next to her and pulled her in, holding her tight as she cried. He pulled a crystal out of his pocket and tapped it with his trident.

"Aquaria, hold this to your head and think of every memory you have of the two of you. This way you will be able to see them anytime you want. You know how these things work." He placed the crystal in her hand, closing her fingers around it. He kissed her head and got up to leave. "I love you my pearl. I'm sorry for this loss."

Gemma continued to cry, she couldn't even think about speaking to her father right now. None of this would have happened if he hadn't sent her away. Poseidon went back downstairs to get Nik so they could leave. Gemma could hear Nik and Patrick shouting, she couldn't understand what they were saying, all she could hear was shouting. Peggy came into Kelley's room, she sat on the bed with her and held her tight. They cried together, the two of them were the most broken hearted over his death. Lucy and Patrick were devastated as well, but nothing like what Gemma and Peggy were going through. Neither one of them left his room for the rest of the night. Lucy had to call Gerard to have him be with her, she couldn't be alone. Gerard's parents came with him. Shannon finished making dinner for everyone, knowing that no one in the house would be up to the challenge that day. It was a hard night for all of them, Gerard and his parents stayed the night. Gerard and Lucy fell asleep on the couch together, her eyes were red and puffy from crying. Gemma and Peggy fell asleep in Kelley's room. Kelley had a spare bed in his room for when Gerard would stay the night. Peggy slept on the spare bed, while Gemma slept in Kelley's, they both cried themselves to sleep.

In the morning, Shannon had made everyone breakfast, she brought it up to Gemma and Peggy. She couldn't imagine what they were going through, and just wanted to help them in any way possible. Gemma didn't wake up when she came in. She looked at Gemma and saw her eyes were still red and puffy, which told her that she had not been asleep long. When Gemma finally woke up it was around lunch time. Gerard and his parents left, taking Lucy with them. She didn't want to be home right now, it was too hard for her to be there. Gemma didn't leave Kelley's room, she hardly even left his bed. She couldn't eat, think, or do anything besides cry. She still hadn't opened the last letter, clutching it even tighter in her hand knowing she would never get another one again. She then remembered what her father had given her, she pulled it out and pressed it against her head. Thinking of every memory that they had together. It began to glow, when she stopped she put the crystal in a glass of water. The crystal shot out a beam of light, all of her memories of him played out in front of her. She watched them silently crying to herself, knowing this was the only way she would ever see him again. She heard someone coming, she quickly grabbed the crystal and put it in her pocket. The door opened, it was Peggy, checking on her. She saw the tears in Gemma's eyes and held her tight. Seeing Gemma so heartbroken, made it even harder on her. She lost her son, and had to watch the girl he loved, fall apart because of it.

9

It had been a week since they got the news, it was now the day of Kelley's memorial. They had received word that his body was recovered, but would take at least a month before they could get it back to them. By the time it would get there, it would already be completely sealed in a box of salt. Gemma sat on her bed, completely in black, her hair still hadn't changed back. Lucy knocked on the door, to see if she was ready to go. She saw Gemma staring at the ring on her finger, not ready to move.

"Gemma, it's time to go, everyone's waiting."

A tear rolled down her cheek, she felt as if half of her was gone forever. She got up and followed Lucy to the carriage. Gemma sat with Peggy at the service, Peggy held her hand tight, trying to help one another get through this. Gerard held Lucy tight, giving her comfort when she needed it. Patrick stood off to the side, not speaking to anyone, just glaring at Gemma. She had noticed Gerard wasn't crying. He didn't even look sad. He was pissed. The anger rolling off him was hard for anyone to miss, especially Gemma. She had never felt anger from him so strong before.

After all of the blessings, they returned home. Everyone who was at the memorial went with them, giving their condolences. Patrick sat in a corner of the kitchen drinking rum, the entire time the guests were there. Gemma learned quickly that things were done very differently there after the memorial. They didn't believe in mourning, they believed in celebrating the life of the person who died, with lots of food, stories and of course plenty of whiskey. She couldn't act like everyone else, she was unable to really talk at all, so she sat quietly by herself.

All of the Brothers of the Club she and Kelley were part of, personally gave her their condolences. They were all close with both Kelley and Gemma. The club was special to them, no one ever questioned the two of them, and supported them whenever they needed it most. Henry came and sat with Gemma for a little bit, he knew how close she was with Kelley, before they made everything public. He told her if she ever needed anything to just come find him. Many of the boys that Kelley had gone to school with also attended.

"Gemma, I'm so sorry. If you ever need anything, please let me know." Finn said. Gemma just nodded.

She didn't really say anything to anyone the whole day. She had tears most of the time, but very few words, just an occasional nod. Gemma became tired of everyone telling her how sorry they were, so she went upstairs to be alone. She curled up on Kelley's bed, tears running down her cheeks, but didn't make a sound. She wanted to go to her room to get Lux. But Peggy told her Lux shouldn't leave her room until all the guests were gone. But she needed Lux. That was all she had left of him.

Later that night after everyone had left, Peggy tried to get Gemma to come down for some dinner. Gemma told her she wasn't hungry, and just wanted to be alone. When Peggy returned downstairs without Gemma, Patrick became furious. He had been drinking all day, every day since Kelley's death. He stormed upstairs to Kelley's room and started to yell at her. Peggy quickly ran back upstairs, to try to calm him down.

"Get out of his room!" Patrick shouted.

"What?" Gemma said sounding a bit confused.

"GET OUT! You don't belong here! Now get out!"

Gemma couldn't speak, she was too shocked and confused as to why he was acting this way. She stood up and walked to her room silently, she didn't want to upset him further. She could tell he was drunk and being irrational.

"Patrick what's going on up here?" Peggy asked

"She has no right to be in here. She has no reason to be upset like this. She's a child, who was just playing with his heart!"

"Patrick! Leave the poor girl alone. She's hurting, just like we all are!"

"She knows nothing of the pain we feel!"

"She knows more than the pain we feel. We may have lost our son, but she has lost much more than that. She has lost her love, the one person that made her happy."

"She knows nothing of love. She's just a child."

"She is much more than just a child. She has been through more in her young life than we ever had at her age." Peggy shouted.

Patrick stormed into Gemma's room "All of this is because of you. He would still be here if you had never come here." He shouted

"How is this my fault?" Gemma asked, starting to get irritated.

"He would never have been sent to the ships if it wasn't for you."

"I had nothing to do with him leaving. I was the one trying to keep him from leaving. YOU SENT HIM AWAY!" Gemma shouted back at him.

Patrick was fuming by this point. His blood was boiling. "You are the worst thing to have ever happened to him. Your kind are the worst thing to ever happen to this family." He shouted

"Patrick you don't know what your saying!" Peggy shouted.

Gerard had stayed for dinner, after hearing all of the shouting he came rushing upstairs with Lucy.

"You know I speak the truth. If she had never showed up he would still be here."

"NO! This has nothing to do with her, and everything to do with that contract with her father. And you know very well that she has nothing to do with any of this!"

Gerard pulled Patrick out of Gemma's room. Gemma was crying on her bed, Lucy came and sat with her trying to calm her down.

"Let go of me boy!" Patrick demanded

"Damnit Patrick! You're drunk and don't know what you're talking about." Gerard shouted

"I know exactly what I'm saying!"

"No you don't! Go outside and cool down, before you do something you regret."

Patrick stormed down stairs and went outside, slamming the door behind him.

"Gemma, are you alright?" Gerard asked

Gemma continued to cry.

"Gerard, can you take the girls to your house for the night? This isn't the place for them tonight. Make sure you find Lux. She won't survive without Gemma."

"Yes, of course. Lucy, can you gather some things for you and Gemma for tonight?"

Lucy nodded and quickly gathered a couple of bags for them. Gemma put the letters from Kelley, the key's and necklace for the lagoon, and her memory crystal in the bag. She wanted to be sure those things always stayed with her. She put Lux in a small satchel, keeping it open for her to breath. They quickly snuck out the back door, Gemma hopped on her horse, while Lucy and Gerard, shared Gerard's horse. The three of them rode off into the night. Unfortunately, it was still raining, they had to pull off to the side, Gemma had changed back into a mermaid.

"Gerard, you need to ride with her. I can ride on my own, Gemma can't ride as a mermaid." Lucy said.

Gerard climbed onto Gemma's horse and helped her. When they got to his house they rushed in, he carried her upstairs into one of the guest rooms.

"Gerard, what's going on?" Shannon said as he rushed past her. "What happened to Gemma?"

"Shannon, I'm so sorry to do this to you, could we stay here for the night?" Lucy asked

"Of course my dear. What happened? What's going on? Why is Gerard carrying Gemma? Did she get hurt?"

"Things are not going well at home right now, especially for Gemma. We just really needed a place to stay tonight."

"Is she alright?"

"She'll be fine."

Lucy ran upstairs to the guest room. Gemma was still in mermaid form, curled up on the bed, she stopped crying, but wasn't speaking.

Lux crawled out of the satchel, curling up close to her heart. Feeling it beat against her fur. Lucy sat next to Gemma, she brushed Gemma's hair out of her face. She looked up at Gerard, they both had the same look of hopelessness on their faces. Then Shannon came into the room.

"Is everything alright?"

Gerard quickly ran to the door and pulled her out. "Everything will be fine mum, she just needs to be alone right now."

"Gerard, is she a mermaid?" Shannon exclaimed.

"What? No! of course not."

"I swear I just saw a tail on her."

"No mum, you're just tired, we all are. We should all just get some sleep."

"Don't you lie to me son. I saw a tail." She pushed Gerard out of the way, and saw Gemma on the bed. She had dried off enough that her tail was gone.

"I told you mum, you're just tired. Now go get some rest."

"Alright, I'm sorry I thought you were lying to me. I must be more tired than I thought. Goodnight everyone." She gave Gerard a kiss on his head and Lucy a big hug, then went to bed.

"That was close." He whispered to Lucy. "Thankfully she changed back before mum came back in."

"We should get to bed as well, I'll help Gemma change into something dry, then I'll come say goodnight to you."

"I'll leave you to it. Gemma, I'm sorry for everything today. I hope you sleep well." He kissed Lucy and headed for the door.

"Thank you Gerard. For everything." She muttered.

Lucy took Gemma's wet clothes so she could hang them to dry, then left Gemma to go to bed. She went to Gerard's room and curled up with him.

"I don't know what to do." Lucy said

"What do you mean?"

"I'm afraid to take her home. Da' hasn't stopped drinking since we found out. He apparently has it out for Gemma now."

"She shouldn't go back for a little while, it's not good for anyone. My parents would let her stay as long as she needs, but it's not safe. They'll figure out what she is eventually."

"Where can she go?"

"We can take her to the lagoon, it's the safest place for her. Patrick won't be able to get there."

"That sounds like a good plan, but… what about you? I won't see you while we are there."

"I will take you both there, and come back on the weekend, to see if you both are ready to come home."

"How will you get back in?"

"I'll ask Gemma if I can hold onto her necklace or key, this way I can come and go as I please."

"I hope this works. This past week has been really hard. I don't know what I would have done without you."

"Don't worry my love, everything will be alright eventually." He kissed her and went to sleep.

"I love you" She whispered as she fell asleep in his arms.

10

The next morning Lucy and Gerard quickly packed their car with supplies while Gemma slept. Gerard filled his father in on what happened and asked if they could borrow the car. He agreed that It was probably safest to get her away from Patrick until he cooled down. Lucy called Peggy to inform her of the plan, and to not tell Patrick until later that night. Peggy agreed that it was the best plan, after everything that had happened. She said she would join Gerard over the weekend, and bring them anything that they might need. As soon as Gemma got up, Lucy had her get dressed quickly and get into the car. They weren't sure if Patrick would try to come find them, so they wanted to get out of there fast. The girls thanked Shannon for allowing them to stay the night, then they left quickly. Lux was invisible the entire time they were at Gerard's house. She finally made herself visible when they were leaving and jumped back into the satchel. Curled up in Gemma's lap the entire drive. Not separating from her for even a moment.

When they finally got to the lagoon, Gemma felt relived, like she had reached a sanctuary from all of her problems. They all took their things to their rooms, Gemma made sure to give her aquamarine necklace to Gerard so he could return after he left. Gemma went straight to the lagoon. She dove into the water. The one place she could actually be alone. Lucy and Gerard filled Marsali in on what had happened. Making sure Lux was in the house before he left. He grabbed himself a sandwich for the drive home. He didn't want to leave Lucy like this, but he had to get his parents car home and had work the rest of the week.

Lucy and Gemma didn't talk much that first week there. Not that Lucy didn't want to talk to her, Gemma just didn't want to talk to anyone. She spent most of her time in the water, she thought if she practiced her magic it might take her mind off of everything. It didn't seem to work, it actually made things harder. When she wasn't in the water she was hiding in her room, usually talking to Lux.

That Thursday night she went into the kitchen to help Lucy with dinner.

"I just can't get it." Gemma said, slamming her fist on the table.

"What can't you get?

"My magic to work… even the stuff I could do before, I can't do it anymore."

"Well, then take a break from it. Just relax a little, I know it's hard, but it might be what you need to help you. Maybe read a little."

Gemma sighed, "Maybe you're right. I just wish I had something to really take my mind off of everything."

"Gerard and Ma will be back tomorrow. I'm sure Gerard will fight you if that would help."

"That would actually help a lot. Thanks Lucy." Gemma gave her a hug and a slight smirk.

"Have you read the letter yet?" Lucy asked nervously

"No. I just can't seem to even open it."

"Why not?"

"If I do, I won't ever get a chance to open something from him again. This is the last thing I have from him. I don't want to lose that."

"You will have to open it eventually."

"I know, I'm just not ready. I know it will say things like how much he loves me, and that we will be together when he returns. Promising to save me from who I'm supposed to marry."

"I'm sorry."

"For what?"

"Asking, and that he can't keep his promise."

"You're just curious, it's my fault. I haven't been talking to you about everything."

"You shouldn't have to. But if you ever need someone to talk to, you know I'm here for you."

"Thanks Lucy. You truly are the best friend I could ever ask for."

"How's Lux? I haven't seen her much."

"She's been off... I don't know if it's because it's a new place for her and she's trying to sort through Kelley's memories to make sure she knows where she's at... or if she's still trying to sort through having Kelley's entire soul in her."

"Is she at least helping you?"

"Yes... when I'm around her she is. Talking to her is like talking to myself... but at the same time, like I'm writing a letter to Kelley. It's hard to explain."

"Well... as long as she's helping you, that's what matters right?"

"Yeah... I just miss him. It's not the same."

"I know. I miss him too."

"I'm gonna go to bed. I'll see you when I get up."

When Gerard and Peggy arrived in the morning, Gemma was sitting on the patio reading a book quietly to herself. Lucy told Gerard about her idea to have him practice fighting with Gemma, he agreed that it might help her a bit. Peggy brought them some food and extra clothes, when they left they only grabbed two day's worth of clothes, so this was something they really needed.

"How long do you think you girls will be staying here?" Peggy asked

"I'm not sure. I finally got her to talk a little last night. She spent most of the week down at the lagoon, alone. She really isn't doing well."

"I didn't expect her to take it well, she has had a lot of loss in her young life. First her mother, then shipped away from home, and now Kelley. This will take her some time, she just needs to find a way to put all of this in the back of her mind. She will never fully get over all of this, but eventually she will be able to put it behind her."

"I really hope so, I'm worried about her."

"We all are."

"How's Da'?"

"I don't really know, he spends all day drinking at the pub, sometimes he comes home, sometimes he doesn't. When he comes home he goes to bed without saying a word. This morning before I left, I tried to grab a couple of things from Kelley's room, hoping it would make Gemma feel better. But he put a lock on the door. I guess he didn't want me to bring her anything."

"Why is he doing this? It's not her fault. Why would he blame her? She tried to run away with him so he wouldn't have to go."

"I guess he just needs someone to blame, someone other than himself. And Gemma is just the casualty in this whole mess."

"Well he needs to stop whatever this is. Its ruining our entire family. I know Gemma's not our blood, but she is the closest thing I have to a sister, I can't lose her too."

Peggy grasped Lucy's shoulders, her eyes focused on hers. "Don't worry darling, things will get better eventually. I promise it will get better.".

11

Lucy watched as Gerard went to talk to Gemma. He took the book from her hand, and handed her a sword. She looked up at him, as they left to go fight. She had become quite rusty, she hadn't fought anyone since Kelley left. She didn't have a desire to fight anymore without him there. Gerard made it easy for her to relax, she knew she could beat him, which made her feel good. She fought with anger for what had happened, and how Patrick was treating her. She was more aggressive than usual, but Gerard didn't get upset. He knew she wasn't trying to be this way towards him, she was just trying to get all of her anger out. She scratched him a little bit while fighting, not on purpose, but when she saw what she had done she instantly dropped her sword and began to cry.

"Gemma, its okay. It's just a few scratches, it's nothing too bad."

"I'm so sorry! Lucy's going to kill me." She sat on the ground and cried some more.

"Well it could give you a chance to see if your healing magic is working again."

"I haven't been able to get any of my magic to work. I can't even get my hair to turn back. I'm stuck with these black strands of hair."

"Well if you look on the bright side, you don't have to worry about people seeing your hair change color. You could go out in public with your hair like that. Tell them you dyed the strands black. Come on just give it a try on my arm." He sat down next to her.

"Alright, I'll try, but I can't promise anything."

She wiped away her tears. pressed her hand firmly on his wound, thinking to herself please heal, please heal! Gerard looked at her hand and smiled, her hand had a glowing blue light coming from under it. She was finally getting her powers back. When she opened her eyes, and lifted her hand she smiled.

"It worked!" she exclaimed

"I thought it would." He laughed.

"But how?"

"You have had a lot of pent up anger because of all of this. You tend to let your emotions get the best of you. It can be a good thing at times, but also it can also hinder your judgement. Sometimes you just have to let your emotions out in the right way, and for you it's usually fighting."

"It does always seem to make me feel better."

"Whenever you decide to come back, we can go to the Club. Any of them would practice with you. They understand that sometimes we need this. Most of the men there use fighting to get through all of their emotions as well. Many of them have a hard time getting over past battles they had."

"Thank you. I would like that." She gave him a slight smile. "Can I ask you something?"

"Anything."

"Why is it so easy for me to talk to you? I used to be able to tell Lucy anything, and now… Well now I'm afraid to tell her anything."

"Probably because I'm an outsider like you. We're not part of the family, so for us it's harder to say things to any of them. You can tell her anything though, she loves you like a sister. She's worried about you, especially since you won't talk to her."

"I just don't know what to say to her. I just feel like every conversation we have is going to end up with one of us upset."

"It will get easier with time. I mean you're talking with me just fine."

"Yeah, but it's like you said, you're not the family. And they're the ones I can't talk to. I honestly don't know if I will ever talk to Patrick again."

"I don't think anyone can blame you for that. He had no right to say those things to you."

"Thank you for getting him out of my room, and taking me away. I don't know what I would have done that night."

"Come on you know I would do anything to help you." He said nudging her shoulder. She gave him a small giggle. "Look at that, a smile for once. See things will get better. It'll just take time. Just remember we are all here for you anytime you need us. We all love you very much."

"Thanks Gerard. You always know what to say to make me feel better." She gave him slight smirk.

"What are friends for. And seeing as how Kelley was my best friend, I only feel it's right that I look out for you, for him."

"I'm sure that's what he would want. Thank you."

"How's Lux? I don't see her around anywhere."

"She's a bit off... I don't know what's going on with her."

"Have you talked to Peggy about it?"

"No... but I should. I tried asking my uncle, and he said she might be adjusting."

"Did he see Kelley's soul in the underworld?"

"No. It went right to Lux. So he didn't even know what happened until I asked him. When he gave her to me he told me that if anything happened to Kelley that his soul would be immediately absorbed into Lux. It would never go to the underworld. So he's technically still here with us... but as Lux... and she's been in a mood."

"What'd ya mean?"

"She's always taking off... I mean I'm sure she's hunting for mice souls or something... but she's been giving me more space than I want right now."

"Well... maybe it's cause you're in the water so much. Has Lucy seen her much?"

"No... that's the weird part. She's been avoiding Lucy... like Kelley would when he was hiding something from her. She's acting just like he does when he hides stuff from us. And I think that's the part that worries me."

"You should talk to Peggy about it. I'm sure she'll know something. Didn't you say she used to help your aunt and uncle take care of these for years in the underworld?"

"Yeah. I just hope she knows what's going on and that she gets back to herself soon." She looked out at the water crashing down into the lagoon. "I really miss him."

"Me too."

Gemma sat outside for a while longer, looking out at the lagoon. She eventually went inside with everyone for dinner. Everyone was talking, trying to be happy again. Gemma didn't say much but would interject in the conversation occasionally. She went to her room and put her memory crystal in a cup of water. Lux jumped on the bed, curling up in her lap. She sat and watched all of their memories play out in front of her, holding onto every second of happiness that they had. Then Lucy came into her room.

"What's this?" She asked.

"My father gave it to me last time I saw him. It's called a memory crystal. I put all of mine and Kelley's memories on it, so I can never forget. I gave Kelley one for his birthday, so he could always have me with him." Gemma said quietly not taking her eyes off the memories.

"How many times have you watched this?"

"Only twice. It is actually making me feel a little better."

"Do you mind if I watch with you?"

"Go ahead, some stuff you might not want to see though." She joked.

"Whatever Gerard did to help you today, I'm glad."

"What do you mean?"

"You laughed a little and are actually smiling."

"He helped me get out a lot of anger, and other emotions. Then we talked for a little bit. I was able to heal a cut I accidentally gave him. He really made me feel a little more like myself."

"You know you can talk to me about anything."

"I know, it's just harder."

"How is it harder?"

"You're his sister. Gerard and I... we're not part of the family, so it's hard for us to talk to any of you about how we feel. You loved him in a different way, you've been there his whole life. Gerard and I, we're not part of the whole family dynamic. So for us to hurt from him being gone, is hard to talk to you about."

"Gemma, I know how much you love him. I know there is nothing in the world that would ever change that. Yes, your love for him was different, but look at this." She pointed to the images from the memory crystal. "This kind of love, that's impossible to get over. I've never met anyone else who loved someone as much as you two loved each other. This was a pure love that you two had. There was no hesitation of your feelings from the moment you met. You both knew in an instant that you were meant to be together. That's something that will take a long time to get over. If you ever get over it. Just know I will always be here for you. Da' is completely wrong, you were the best thing to ever happen to him. He had never been happier than when he was with you."

"Thank you Lucy, I'm glad we can talk about this."

"Anytime." Lucy said smiling, then she stopped and paused for a moment. "Umm when did this happen?"

Gemma quickly covered Lucy's eyes. "You're not supposed to see this." She laughed somewhat embarrassed.

"Obviously!" Lucy laughed, "Is there any way to skip past this part?"

"No, sorry. I haven't learned how to do that yet. Just have to go through the whole thing."

"I can't watch this." She said covering her face with pillow.

Gemma laughed and took the crystal out of water to stop the images. "I'll watch this a little later, when I'm alone."

"I won't come in and bother you when you're watching this again." Lucy laughed

"You can watch the beginning stuff... it just gets a little racy during his birthday. Sorry you had to see that."

"It's okay. But what was going on right before that?"

"What do you mean?"

"You two were fighting about something, then it flashed quickly to a gazebo and you two were kissing."

"Oh... that... over his birthday we got into a huge fight. I don't really want to talk about it, it wasn't a very good moment for us. We fixed everything when he found me at the gazebo."

"Where is the gazebo? I haven't seen it here before."

"If you go through the orchard then towards the cliff where the water fall is, it's up there. There is a swing that goes over the cliff."

"Do you mind if I take Gerard there tomorrow?"

"Go ahead. He would love it. Can you let him fight with me first? I want to get as much fight time as I can before he has to leave."

"That's fine, he enjoys it too. He misses having Kelley to spar with."

"Me too."

Lucy got up and went back to bed, she wanting to give Gemma time to herself.

12

The next day while Lucy and Gerard went to the gazebo and swing, Gemma went to the cave behind the waterfall. She took her trident with her and gathered some extra crystals. She saw how much Lucy liked being able to see her brother, so she wanted to give some to all of them. So they could see their memories whenever they wanted. When she returned to the house, she saw Peggy in the kitchen, she looked like she was in the middle of baking a pie, but stopped part way.

"Peggy?"

Peggy looked up, and quickly wiped her eyes. "Oh Gemma, I didn't see you there. Did you need something?"

"Actually, I have something for you."

"For me? But what for?"

"Well, my father had given me something that day, and last night Lucy helped me realize that it might be helpful for all of you to have one too." Gemma pulled a crystal out of the basket she was carrying.

"Where did you get this?"

"It's a memory crystal, it stores your memories of whatever you are thinking about. So I thought we could store your memories of Kelley on here, and then whenever you missed him, you could see him."

"I know what it is dear. But where did you get them? They're rare these days."

"The cave behind the waterfall. The walls are filled with them."

"That's incredible! I haven't seen these in centuries. Your father's worked hard to keep them all to himself."

She gave her a shrug. She had no idea what her fathers plans were and why he would leave the crystals in her care. But the look of Peggy's face was relief, not rage. A tear rolled down her cheek as she pressed the crystal to her head. When she was done, Gemma put it in a cup of water. A light burst from it projecting images of Kelley, starting from when he was just a baby. Gemma stood there and watched. Peggy wrapped Gemma in her arms, tears rolling down her face.

"This is the best gift anyone has ever given me. Thank you." She kissed the top of Gemma's head.

"Your welcome. Thank you for letting me watch with you."

"My dear, you can watch this anytime you want. You deserve to know him when he was younger."

"Thank you." Gemma said with a tear in her eye. They continued to watch all the memories Peggy had of Kelley. Then memories of Gemma with Kelley showed up, Gemma looked at Peggy.

"You put the memories of me with him on here?"

"Of course my dear, you were a big part of his life. And he loved you with his whole heart."

Gemma continued to watch and noticed that Peggy had known about them the entire time. She was finally seeing how others saw them together. She could see the way her hair turned pink every time Kelley touched her, and the way they looked at one another. How closely he held her when they danced in the living room. The way they talked to one another, even when they thought they were alone, Peggy managed to catch small glimpses of them. She saw how they danced at the festival, and how everyone stopped and watched them. Everyone could see how much they loved one another, just by the looks on their faces. When he stayed by her side all night after she was attacked, Peggy saw him holding her hand tight. Kelley asleep in her bed with her on her birthday. Peggy didn't miss anything at all, she always knew what was going on, but kept it from Patrick.

Gemma started to tear up, "Oh this is one of my favorite memories of you two." Peggy said making sure Gemma was watching.

Gemma was watching and saw her and Kelley fighting. "This was our fight, why is this one of your favorite memories?"

"Because of the look on his face when you won." Peggy said smiling.

Gemma watched and saw as soon as Gemma won he had pulled her into a kiss, after he had the biggest smile on his face, he couldn't take his eyes off her. He had a look pride, joy, and love all at once. It was such a busy moment for her, she didn't even notice how he was looking at her. She started to tear up some more, she hugged Peggy again and told her she needed to go. Peggy stopped her.

"Gemma, you need to see the rest. The last memories I have of him, are of you two together. I had only ever seen him this happy and confident in himself when he was with you. He would have never stood up to anyone before you."

Gemma continued to watch, they reached the moment that Kelley left, Kelley said goodbye to everyone, then it was just the two of them. Peggy couldn't hear what they were saying, but she saw everything. Gemma realized then that Peggy saw him slide the ring on her left hand, promising himself to her. She watched herself say goodbye to him and break down in tears. Gemma began to cry, wishing she could just stop him from leaving them.

"It doesn't matter what Patrick thinks, you were the best thing to ever happen to him. He doesn't see it now, he is hurting too much, but he will. It will take a while, but he will realize that you were the best thing to ever happen to Kelley and this family."

Gemma hugged her once more, then ran out of the room, and back to her room to cry. There was no point in going into his room there, he only slept in his bed a couple of times, they spent all their time in her room. It was their escape. The only place they could be in love together. No one could truly stop them, the tunnels made it possible to be together.

Later that night Gemma gave Lucy and Gerard each a crystal, she told them what to do to save the memories and then to replay them anytime they wanted. She gave an extra one to Peggy to give to Patrick when she returned home. She placed it in the center of the table.

"When he has a clear mind again, then and only then will I give this to him."

13

Lying on a rock in the lagoon, her tail gently swishing in the water. She was trying to work on controlling water, and currents. Just something to take her mind off Kelley, and the fact that she would never see him again. The excruciating pain she felt in her heart, that kept her feeling as if nothing mattered anymore. She would pull a little water into the air with her hand, and start bending it into different shapes. She made a few fish out of the water, having them swim around her in the air. She made them jump and play, swimming happily. Then she noticed that one of the fish wasn't happy like the others. It was slowly swimming alone, going off in the other direction. She tried to get it to come back, but it would just swim in a small circle, then continue to swim off on its own. She put the water fish back in the lagoon, but that one fish wouldn't go back. She didn't understand why she wasn't able to control something that she created. It started swimming towards the waterfall.

"Wait! Come back!" She shouted at it.

It swam back towards her a little, then back to the waterfall. She went into the water and started to swim after it. It swam into the waterfall, she stopped and stared at the waterfall. The fish swam out of the waterfall, then back in it. Telling her follow it. She dove down and swam through the tunnel to the cave. The little fish was swimming around, circling the crystals, making them light up. It swam over to her, circling her trident, then back to lighting up the crystals. It continued several times until the tips of the trident began to glow. She watched trying to figure out what the fish was trying to get her to do. Then it hit her, she pointed her trident at the crystals that were glowing.

A bright white light exploded from her trident hitting only the crystals that were glowing. The fish swam back to her and stayed next to her shoulder. The crystals shot out images of her and Kelley. They were not like from her memory crystal, they were different. They were as if someone was watching them. It was only memories from in the cave. The crystals stored every memory of the two of them. Most were of the two of them just being alone together, but there were a few others. Her 16th birthday, where Kelley was holding her, and crying. She had never seen what he had gone through that day.

She looked at the fish with tears in her eyes and shouted. "Why? Why would you do this to me? I created you just to get stronger with my magic. Why would you torture me like this?"

The fish swam up to two more crystals lighting them up like the others. Kelley was sitting by the side of the pool, holding her, both of them looking terrified. She then saw Lucy and Gerard run in. Something was trying to pull her underwater, as the rest of them tried to get her out of the water. Lucy was in the water with her as they were both pulled under the water. Kelley was instantly trying to go after them, but Gerard tried to stop him. Kelley didn't listen and dove in to try to get them. Gerard followed him, but they were both quickly brought back up to the surface by Nik.

"Damn it Kelley! You're going to get yourself killed." Nik shouted.

"I have to save them!" Kelley shouted.

"They're fine. You know we have to keep you alive. If you die everything will be ruined, you can't be so reckless." Nik said quietly.

"What are you talking about? The only thing that matters is Gem, and something took her and Lucy. Let me go, I have to get them back."

"They're both fine. They're with Poseidon. I was sent to come get you two. Go to the stairs, I will get you both through to him. You have to stop this recklessness, we need you alive."

"What does that even mean? I'm of no importance to anyone but

Gem."

"You still haven't read that letter from Poseidon?"

"Of course not. Lucy has that."

Gerard sighed as he chimed in, "You need to get that letter back from Lucy. You need to know what it says. She doesn't think you're ready… but you need to know."

"Read the letter, everything will make sense. Don't tell Aquaria what's in that letter though."

She didn't remember any of that, but all it did was make her want to have Lucy tell her what was in those letters. The memory faded, not even a second later another memory showed up. This was yet another one she didn't remember. It was two little kids. A boy who looked just like Kelley in the memories that Peggy showed her. He was carrying her into the cave through the waterfall, in her mermaid form. He placed her in the water and sat next to the pool with his feet in the water. She was crying and Kelley was upset as well. She couldn't help but smile at how cute he was when he was little.

"What were they talking about?" He asked

"I don't know, but if we heard it and we're not allowed to know, he will wipe this from our memory. Possibly even us ever meeting."

"But why? Why wouldn't he want us to remember meeting?"

"I don't know, it has something to do with what he was talking about. I just don't understand. All I know is they said we are meant to be together."

"Then why won't they let us?"

"I don't know" She began to cry again. "They're not going to let us see one another for a long time. Who knows when we will see each other again."

"Here take this." he took off his necklace.

"What is it?"

"Ma gave it to me a long time ago. It's supposed to ward off harm, but I want you to have it. Something to always have that belongs to me. Maybe it will help you remember me."

"Thank you! I will keep it forever, and the flower crowns you gave me." She said as he put the necklace on her. "I have an idea of something for you, but I don't have it with me, I'll have to get it from my father."

"He probably won't let you give it to me, whatever it is."

"I won't give him a choice!" She said confidently, "This is too important."

"I promise, I will find you one day." He said smiling at her, "We can come back here."

"Sounds perfect!" She smiled back at him.

Gemma instantly recognized the necklace, it was one she had for years, and wore it everywhere. She always felt safe when she wore it, and wondered why she felt it was so important to her. She had forgotten it when she left, and was angry at Nik for not letting her go back to get it. She tried to figure out what flower crowns she was talking about in the memory, then it came to her. She had a pair of flower crowns that hung from the sides of the mirror of her vanity. They were enchanted so they would never fall apart, and Nik always refused to let her get rid of them. She had no idea where they came from, but when she would have a bad day, she would wear one and just look at herself in the mirror. Feeling better almost instantly after placing it on her head. She thought harder about the crowns and recognized the flowers, they were the exact same ones that Kelley gave her for her birthday.

She felt angry, and even more heartbroken than before. She so desperately wanted to know what they were talking about, and why her father had taken that memory from them. she began to fill with rage again. Smoke began to rise from her head, there were little red glowing specks in the black streaks, like embers from a fire. She set her trident on the side of the pool, knowing that she couldn't calm herself down, and at any instant a red bolt would be shot from it. She could feel her hands beginning to shake from the anger that filled her. She just wanted to scream and cry all at once, just get it all out of her for once. She couldn't hold it back any longer. She had been holding it in for nearly a month, and couldn't do it anymore. She started to scream in anger, causing the whole cave to start to shake, as well as most of the lagoon. Then a red burst exploded from her. Sending a shockwave through the lagoon temporarily giving the water of the lagoon and waterfall, a red glow. There was a loud boom, sounding like a cannon being fired, when the burst exploded from her. When she finally stopped screaming, she fell to the seabed of the cave. She began to cry, even harder than before. She was so hurt that she couldn't do anything else but cry.

The little fish came back to her, but was now a bubble. "Why would you torture me like this? Why would you make my grief so much worse?" She cried. It remained motionless, just staring at her. "Just leave me alone." She mumbled as she swam off.

She swam to shore and pulled herself out of the water. She realized that she left her trident in the cave. She sat on the shore and tried to calm herself down enough to call her trident to her.

"Revenio" She shouted, and nothing happened. "Revenio" She shouted again, this time reaching her hand towards the waterfall. Still nothing happened. "Revenio damn it! You stupid thing! Come back so I can go inside." She screamed.

The trident flew back to her and landed in her hand. Then she noticed something else come with it, the little fish. "I thought I told you to leave me alone. Go back to the water where you belong." She said, trying to use her powers to make it go away. But it didn't, it stayed by her side.

She used the trident to get her legs back and started storming up the hill. The fish continued to follow her. She would turn towards it and shout at it to leave her alone. But it wouldn't, it just kept following her. She made it back to the house and found Lucy in the kitchen getting ready to work on dinner.

"Are you alright? The water in the lagoon turned red and the whole place was shaking for a bit." Lucy said.

"I'll be fine." She mumbled. "Just having a bad day."

"Anything I can do to help?"

"Yeah, help me get this stupid thing to stop following me." She grumbled while pointing at the fish.

"What is it?" Lucy asked, while curiously looking at it.

"You know I can make water morph into different shapes and kind of bring it to life. Usually it will do what I tell it to, and if touched it will fall apart. But this one won't. I can't get it to do what I want, I can't get it to just turn back into water, even when in water it just turns into bubbles. It won't stop following me, and to make matters worse, it showed me all these memories of Kelley and I, even some I don't remember. Some I had no knowledge of. Like you and I getting sucked underwater from the cave and taken away. And Kelley and Gerard trying to go after us, but Nik stopping them and yelling at

Kelley. Then a memory of Kelley and I when we were little kids. We were talking about some argument we got into with my father and how we were supposed to be together. It just makes no sense. None of this. And this little fish is just making things worse right now. Like I don't have enough pain right now, this thing is just forcing me to feel even more pain."

"Alright. Well have you tried asking it what it wants?"

"Not what it wants, but why it was doing this to me. And all it did was show me memories that I don't even remember." Gemma shouted. "I just need to be alone. Can you try to keep this thing with you for now, until I figure out how to get rid of it?"

"I can try. I don't know if it will stay with me if it keeps following you."

Gemma walked into the library and placed her trident against the wall. She started searching the books trying to find anything to get the fish to leave her alone.

14

Lucy managed to keep the fish away from Gemma by treating it like a pet. She noticed that the fish seemed sad, just like Gemma. So she decided to try to keep it occupied and give it her full attention. She decided that she needed to ask what it wanted, why it still there. The fish started to swim away, so Lucy followed it. She followed it up the stairs to Kelley's old room. It waited outside the door for Lucy to open it. Once she opened the door the fish quickly swam inside and started swimming around as if it was looking for something. Lucy followed it in to see what it was looking for, but it was just swimming around aimlessly. She began to turn to walk out when the fish rushed over to her and started swimming around her frantically. She turned back around and sat in a chair in the room, and let out a deep sigh.

"I don't understand you." She sighed. "You're just swimming around aimlessly. Show me what you want me to see."

The fish then swam over to a the book case and swam under it. It swam back out to Lucy then back under the book case again. It did this about five more times before Lucy finally reached under the bookcase. She felt a small piece of paper, she pulled it out and looked at it closely. It was a letter to Kelley in Gemma's hand writing. She sat down in the chair and began to read the letter, she got halfway through the letter and knew why she never sent it. Another reason why Kelley's death was so hard on her, and why she was so sick for a few months after Kelley had left.

"She was pregnant?" Lucy asked the fish. "But… why would she keep this from me?"

The fish swam over to the letter and circled it, trying to get her to finish reading it. "Alright, I'll finish reading."

She continued reading and noticed right after she wrote that she had lost it, the letter stopped. None of the normal I love you, I miss you, come back to me. That were normally in her letters, it just stopped. She knew that meant that she never even told him, he had no idea that they were going to have a baby but lost it.

"She must be so lost… I mean… I know she was only 18, but she would have loved that baby more than anything. It would have been a piece of Kelley with her always. Is this why you won't leave? Because she lost so much of him?" The fish swam over to her shoulder and stayed close to her. "You're not going anywhere for a while are you?" The fish just stayed at her shoulder. "What are you?"

The fish quickly swam out of the room and down to the study. Gemma had already left but there were books sitting all over the room. The fish swam to the top of the bookshelf and remained still in front of a book. Lucy pushed the ladder over to where the fish was, climbed up and grabbed the book. She climbed down and sat on the sofa to read it.

"What page?" Lucy asked, "Swim in the shape of the numbers."

The fish started to swim making the numbers 9 and 3. Lucy quickly flipped to page 93 to read what it said.

"Loss of a soulmate." She read, then looked up at the fish who swam to her shoulder again.

"Merpeople who are strong enough to create living creatures out of water, can unintentionally give it a purpose. When a merperson is grieving over the loss of their soulmate, they can give the creature the mission to help them through their grief. They will not know they did this, it will seem like the creature is trying to torture and torment them. The creature cannot leave until the merperson has figured out how to live without their other half. Not even Poseidon himself can send the creature away, only when the creature feels its mission is complete will it leave.

We're going to be here for a long time, aren't we?" Lucy asked this fish. "Well we better get used to you. Just give her a little time tonight, you really made things worse for her today."

The fish slowly started to swim away, as if it was upset again. "Come on little fish, you can just stay with me tonight. Gerard should be back tomorrow, he should help her feel better."

She walked up the stairs and to her room, the fish slowly following behind her. occasionally it would act like it was going to go try to find Gemma, but then Lucy would call the fish to follow her. It acted like a lost puppy how much it followed her.

15

Gemma had gotten frustrated with not finding anything in the books and decided to go down to the cellar, somewhere she could be completely alone. She wanted the pain to go away, she was willing to do anything at this moment to make it stop. She looked around at all the barrels and bottles. She grabbed a bottle just hoping this could take even a little bit of the pain away. She started to drink the whiskey, knowing it was stronger than the wine. She started drinking, tears running down her face. She finished an entire bottle, but she felt nothing. No buzz, no numbing of the pain. She felt exactly the same. She knew she had a high tolerance, the only time she had ever been able to get a little bit of a buzz was before she was 18. She grabbed another bottle and chugged it. Still nothing. She chugged two more, doing nothing but causing her to have to vomit. She thought to wait a few minutes to let it sink in. But nothing. She tried to test her aim with her dagger, and it was still perfect.

"You've got to be fucking kidding me." She paused for a moment as her rage began to fill her up. "I can't even get fucking drunk? I can't drink this pain away or blackout or anything?!" She screamed, causing the entire palace to shake. "That's it, I need to talk with him… now!"

She got up off the floor and stormed up the stairs. She called her trident as she entered the foyer, stormed out the door to the lagoon from the kitchen. She stomped the entire walk down the hill to the water. Cursing under her breath as she made her way into the water. Throwing her clothes on the ground before diving off the dock. She swam to the stairs leading to where she met up with Nik on her eighteenth birthday.

She opened the door at the end of the stairs and swam through, hunting for either Nik or Poseidon. One of them would give her a damn answer. She was not leaving until they did.

She went directly to the study, Poseidon was usually there or the war room, and she didn't feel safe going to the war room. She listened outside the door, she heard quiet murmuring from inside. She cracked the door open to make sure it was only those she trusted in there. Then she heard her voice, she couldn't believe it. She threw the door open and swam in. Poseidon and Nik had conflicting expressions of shock and anger on their faces. Then the mermaid turned around and squealed in excitement as she swam to her. Nik swam to the door closing it and locking it.

"I've missed you so much little A! I can't believe you're here!" She held her in a tight hug then pulled herself back. "Wait… how are you here? You're not supposed to be here… you're supposed to be on land for another two years."

"It's good to see you too Astrid, but I need to talk to father."

"This could not wait until you saw Nikoli again?" Poseidon growled. "You are not supposed to be at the palace, it is too dangerous for you here."

"I can handle myself just fine to get here from my palace. Now explain to me why I can't get drunk?"

Nik and Poseidon gave each other a puzzled look, then went back to her. Poseidon started laughing, a startling response to her demand.

"Nikoli, get her some lightning shots. The kind that work on me, apparently my daughter discovered that its impossible for her to get inebriated."

"Seriously? That's terrible!" Astrid exclaimed. "I get drunk just about everyday."

"That's part of your job my child. Both of you sit down while we wait for Nikoli to return."

The girls swam to the seats in front of his desk. Astrid couldn't stop smiling, she had missed her so much. If it hadn't been for her, Poseidon wouldn't have adopted her and her twin.

"Alright, now why else are you here?" Poseidon asked.

"I created a water creature... it was a simple angel fish... but now it won't go away... it's torturing me. Showing me memories of me and Kelley... some that I don't remember." She growled at the last remark. Looking him dead in the eye.

His eyes widened when she mentioned the ones she didn't remember. "The fish is an easy solution. It is made from your grief. You have to let it help you. It is trying to help you find a way to get back to your fully functional self. Your magic has been spotty lately, has it not?"

"Yes... how did you-"

"The same thing happened to me when your mother died. It is why I could not see you before you left. I was trying to work through my grief. You have to follow it, do what it wants you to... it is the only way."

"Umm... Who's Kelley? And what happened?" Astrid asked

"My boyfriend, the love of my life... who was killed a month ago because someone sent him to spend three years on a pirate ship." She growled.

Nik swam back in with a jar of black and glowing purple gel. He grabbed a few shot glasses and set them out on the desk while pouring each of them a shot.

"Ooo... I've never seen this color lightning shots before." Astrid was eying the shots. She knew all the different colors of lightning shots, but not this one.

"This is a blend that is the only thing that works for them. For a normal merperson, it would be the equivalent of three jars in one shot." Nik replied as he handed the girls each a shot. "These two... well... they might get a very small buzz off of about five shots. An entire jar is needed to get them a good buzz."

Gemma took the shot back without hesitation. She slid the glass back to Nik and had him pour her another. She kept downing and refilling her glass. Desperate for anything to numb the pain.

"Aquaria, you might want to slow-"

Astrid stopped when Poseidon held his hand up. She knew it was him telling her to leave it alone when Aquaria shot a glare at her. Aquaria finished what was remaining in the jar before she spoke again. There was still very little noticeable difference.

"Nik, I'm going to need as many jars as it will take to get me drunk enough to blackout."

"That's not possible." Nik replied.

"Why? We don't have enough?" She snapped, rolling her eyes at him.

"No, it's because you physically can never get drunk. When you gained your full powers… your ability to get drunk was destroyed. This is the most it will ever do to you, but only this kind of lightning shot, and the rum that is at your palace can do it. Nothing else."

"This is bull sharks! Why me? I've seen my siblings drunk at every event, why doesn't it work for me?"

"Because you are immortal," Poseidon sighed.

"What?" She shouted loud enough to cause the room to quake.

"You are immortal like myself. None of your siblings are, just you. We do not know why, we just know you are."

"Because you should have died when your mother did." Nik added.

"Little A, didn't you always wonder why Pops was so protective over you? Never let you do anything?"

"Pops?" She gave Astrid a confused expression. She had never referred to Poseidon as pops in front of him. He looked like he didn't mind though, a small smirk grew across his face when she said it.

"You know I call him that. Anyways, haven't you ever wondered that? Why you're so much stronger than your siblings?"

"Of course I have. You know that. It's been frustrating as hell growing up like that."

"Well it's because you're a full-blown goddess, just like pops is a god. You're different from your siblings, because you need to be."

"Father, is this true?"

Poseidon rubbed his temples and blew out a breath. "Yes, all of it is true. Astrid only knows because Asteria figured it out and told her before she left."

"Who left?"

"Both of us. I work as a spy now & Asteria and Atlas swam away."

"Well neither of those are a big surprise." Aquaria looked down at her empty glass, desperately wanting to cry. She held it in the best she could. "Father… can I speak with Astrid alone? I need some time with my sister."

"We will be right outside."

Nik and Poseidon swam out of the room, as soon as the door shut she broke down.

16

Astrid swam over to her, wrapping her arm around her as she cried. She let her get it all out. Even though they were not blood, they had always had a close bond. They knew they could always count on the other to help them through anything they were going through.

"Do you want to talk about it?"

"I hate my life so much. Every time I find something that makes me happy, it's ripped away from me. I hurt all the time, I can't make it go away. And that stupid fish I made, it's making everything worse. I wish so desperately that I could go back in time and stop him or save him."

"You know you can't. And even if you could… it wouldn't change the outcome. If he was destined to die at that time, death will come hunting him down. You know this."

"I know… it just hurts. I love him so much, my heart feels shattered. My body aches for his touch, his embrace. I crave him at all times, but then that reminder that I will never see him again floods my system. It feels like everything in my body stops working except the ability to cry." She took a breath of the salty water, letting it fill her lungs. "I'm lost without him."

"He must have been quite something. Did you to ever?"

Aquaria nodded, "even more reason for my desperate desire for him. No one will ever make me feel the way he did. I felt complete when I was with him. I'm pretty sure everyone could hear us… and I might have set off a few bursts and earthquakes." Her flush cheeks caused Astrid to grin from ear to ear.

"That's when you know you've found the right man. I have to say, sex on land is so much better than in our natural form."

"Really?"

"Trust me. It's not as sensual here. It's natural instinct in our form, but when you're on land… oh the things you can do. Mermen can learn a thing or two from these humans."

"Like what?"

"Well, they care more about pleasure. Not just their pleasure, but your pleasure. It gets them off when you're in pure ecstasy. Mermen don't come near our breasts because they see them on a regular basis, it's nothing special to them. They don't kiss their way down your body, caressing every curve, soaking in the touch of your skin." Astrid's cheeks went flush. "There's this one pirate, his touch makes me tremble. The heat of his breath on my neck sends chills up my spine. He… fuck… let's just say he has a gift for what he does to me."

"Gods, that sounds like how Kelley is to me… well was." She looked down at her hands holding the empty glass. "Do you think I will ever move past this?"

"I don't know… I've never felt a love like that… I know you're bound to find someone who can make you feel good, but it will take some time… as you know… death isn't something you can just get over." She grabbed Aquaria's hands while letting out a sigh. "We've both been through the loss of those we love. Through death and through other circumstances…" She trailed off, looking down.

The two of them had been through so much. Astrid's parents had died when she was young. The orphanage kicked her and her identical twin out, because their siren abilities were too strong for them to handle. When Aquaria found them, they were living in an abandoned house, using their siren abilities to get people to buy them food. She convinced her mother to talk to her father about taking them in. He ended up adopting them, making them legal members of the royal family. Unfortunately, Astrid's twin, Tove went missing. Vanishing in the middle of the night. A couple months later Theia died, and Aquaria went into a coma. They both understood loss, and their desperate need for one another when dealing with a loss.

"Still no word?"

Astrid shook her head.

"I wish you could come back with me... even if just for the night. Lucy tries to help... but its hard, she doesn't fully understand... and Kelley's her brother..."

"Say no more, let me ask Pops. He owes me... I've been keeping that whole you're a goddess thing a secret from you for so long."

"What?!"

"Oh yeah, I've known since before that accident." She gave her a mischievous smirk and whispered.

Astrid swam out of the room, Aquaria could hear the sounds of their whispering and murmuring through the door. She hated when they kept things from her, it infuriated her, but this time Astrid was using her amazing blackmail skills to get something to help her. Astrid swam back in with a huge smile on her face.

"I get to stay with you for the weekend... He said he might erase it from my memory, but he said he thinks this will help you. Possibly having me there will help with that troublesome little fish."

She swam to Astrid giving her the biggest hug she could imagine. "I can't believe he said yes!"

"He will be grilling me on what we talk about... he said if there is something that comes up that you're not supposed to know yet, that he will erase that portion of our time together. He wants to be sure that everything goes the way his plan is set for you."

Aquaria rolled her eyes, "Story of my damn life. I'll accept whatever terms he has this time. I need this desperately."

"Great! Grab your trident and lets go! Nikoli is going to escort us to your palace."

"Well... you should know, its on land."

Holds up wrist, showing her the gold seahorse bangle with glowing crystals. "Got it covered. Now lets go."

As they swam down the hall to the secret tunnel to the Lagoon, they all remained silent. No one was supposed to hear them, no one was supposed to know she was there. She gave Nik a hug, then the swam through the door to the lagoon. Astrid's eyes widened when they made it to the surface. The beautiful tropical flowers all around them, the breathtaking waterfall that she desperately wanted to jump off. Then she saw the palace. It was lit up with the lights from inside, giving everything a golden glow. She couldn't swim fast enough to the shore to get out and explore.

"Little A, this is all yours? This is incredible!"

Aquaria had stopped and was looking at the flowers glowing in the moonlight. Astrid swam right to her.

"You alright, Little A?" She wrapped her arm around her shoulder.

"Yeah... I... umm... forgot that those flowers glow in the moonlight is all."

Astrid looked at the flowers blowing in the trees along the shore. They were glowing a bright pink, that seemed to leave a sweet melody as the wind hit the petals. She grabbed Aquaria's hand and pulled her to shore. As soon as her legs came back, she stormed over to the flowers in the trees, picking a few. She sat in the sand next to Aquaria, putting the flowers in her hand.

"He gave you these, didn't he?"

Aquaria nodded as she wiped a tear away.

"Get up and pick one of those damn flowers. You need help getting through this pain, I'm here to help. Now get up and pick a damn flower, or so help me I will drag your royal ass over there and force you to."

"You can't do that!"

"Wanna bet? Now get up and pick that flower!"

"What good will that do me?"

"You need to learn how to be around everything that reminds you of him. How to do things you used to do with him, but now without him. This one small task will be hard, and hurt like hell at first, but you need this little push. Now do it."

She stood up, bushing the sand off her naked body. She walked over to the flowers, watching them glow in the moonlight. Her hand trembled as she reached up. She pulled her hand back grasping at her chest. The ache from the memory of Kelley pulling them from the tree and placing them in her hair. It killed her.

"Little A, grab that flower, do exactly what he did with it."

Tears rolled down her cheeks as she reached up again. She slammed her eyes shut, pulling her arm back down, only to be caught by Astrid's hand. Astrid pulled her arm back up to the flowers. She held it there until Aquaria grasped the flower, pulling it from its stem. She pulled her hand back, holding it close to her chest. She dropped to her knees crying, grasping the flower at her chest. Astrid sat on the ground next to her, letting her cry it all out. She wrapped her in her arms, holding her tight. Astrid continued to hold her, even when she fell into her.

"Just let it all out. I've got you." She rubbed her back, as her skin was soaked with tears. "When your able to, do what he used to do with the flower... Can you say what it was?"

"He would put it in my hair, then kiss me... Tell me he loved me, that we would find a way to spend the rest of our lives together."

Astrid let out a sigh as she held her tighter. "I know its hard, but I need you to put that flower in your hair... You need you to put that in your hair."

"You don't understand... I lost more than just the love of my life... I-"

"How about we go inside your beautiful Palace that pops had built for you. We'll get something hot to drink... maybe grab some cookies or something. Sit on your bed and talk there. How does that sound?"

Aquaria nodded. Astrid helped her stand and they began walking back to the house. She grabbed her clothes from the dock, tossing them on herself. She knew she would need to get some of Lucy's clothes for Astrid for a couple of days. Astrid was right around the same size as Lucy.

17

Aquaria and Astrid were sitting on Aquaria's bed, backs against the headboard, holding their mugs of tea, with a plate of delicious cookies between them. Lux was curled up on her lap sound asleep. Aquaria wasn't eating, speaking or doing anything other than staring blankly at the doors to the balcony. Watching the wind blowing the sheer curtains.

"You're going to tell me eventually. So just say it, then you can get past all of this. I promise I won't tell Pops whatever is eating you up inside. I know its more than just his death. There is something else going on with you, I can feel it."

She let out a sigh, closing her eyes as she leaned her head against the headboard.

"I knew the moment I saw his eyes, that I wanted to spend the rest of my life with him. That kind of feeling doesn't come more than once in your life. Now knowing I'm immortal and can't die... I will forever feel the crushing pain of losing him."

"Alright, but that wasn't what I was talking about. What were you going to say on the beach?"

She blew out a breath and wiped a tear away. "Only Kelley's mother and uncle Hades know about this... I haven't told Lucy, and she's my best friend… I told him in a letter I forced uncle Hades to give him when he took him away from me." She began crying harder again. "Gods why is it so hard to say?"

"Because it hurts, but you know this will help you. I'm not even saying to get past it, move on, or anything like that. I mean it will help you live your life again. It will help you from crying at the mention of his name or seeing something that reminds you of him. Just say it quickly."

"Gods I hate this… all of it."

"Just say it."

"I was pregnant."

She looked at her, not saying a word. But it was all over her face. She felt for her.

"We were going to have a baby… I lost it, five months into it. I lost him… I lost our child… I lost our happiness… our chance… If we had just kept going… if we didn't stop… Gods I wish we hadn't stopped. Cause he would be here right now, we would have our son or daughter in the next room… and we would be happy. I would be curled up in his arms… or tangled up in these sheets. But we would have been together." She wiped the tears from her eyes, clutching tighter to her cup. "Even if he had died… If I hadn't lost our child… I would've still had part of him with me. Some beautiful piece of him, born from two who love each other more than anything in the world. But even that was taken from me."

"I had a feeling that's what it was."

"How?"

"I've seen the look on women's faces when they've lost a child. Not just by miscarriage, but by death after birth as well. Its something that will remain with you forever. I've helped a few women with that pain. You know how we can remove someone's pain and suffering… well I do that for them… unfortunately, I can't for you. So I am going to help you through this as much as I can the next couple of days."

"Isn't this going to cut into your work?"

She let out a sigh. "I should be fine. I just hope Jamison doesn't come by while I'm here… That would be a tragedy. That man… gods he can have me anytime he wants. I don't have to mess with his head even. He just gives me whatever information I want, as long as we fool around. He was the one I was telling you about. I swear there must be a requirement on that ship to be ridiculously handsome."

"What do you mean?"

"Its one of the most powerful, dangerous and vicious ships out there, but everyone I know from that ship is gorgeous. And they all know how to properly take care of a woman. Their captain, shit, all I did was kiss him once, and what he did with his tongue was like sex in my mouth. I can only imagine what he is like in bed."

"I'm surprised you didn't get him in bed. Wouldn't a captain of a ship be a little old for your taste?"

"No, I mean, he's probably in like his 40's but it's part of my job."

"So why haven't you gotten him into bed?"

"A couple of reasons, first: I've only met him once and his ship was about to leave. He was getting the rest of his crew. Secondly: He's a Captain. Pop's says I'm not allowed to mess with the minds of Captains. If I do. It's breaking some rule of the accord. But I'll say if he's the captain you're going to marry... you're in good hands in the bedroom."

"Not something I'm overly enthused to think about right now. I just want Kelley back... I don't even care who I marry... It's not Kelley."

"I understand that... but there isn't anything you can do to change that he's gone. Eventually your going to have to move on. I'm not saying now, or even with your husband... but eventually, one day, you'll have to move on. Maybe you'll find him in another one of his lives. You can't die, so you'll find him again... eventually."

"Astrid... Can we please stop this for the night? I can't anymore tonight."

"Are you going to cry yourself to sleep?"

"Actually... I don't think I'll be able to... I'm pretty sure I'm out of tears right now." She set her glass down on the bedside table and snuggled deep into the fluffy pink blanket. "I'm so tired... everything hurts so bad, but I'm too tired to cry anymore today. My body is drained."

"That's normal after what you've been through. Just rest. We'll talk more tomorrow. I can't wait to meet your friend Lucy."

Aquaria let out a yawn, grabbing Astrid's hand. "Thank you for being here with me. I needed you."

Astrid put the cookies and her cup on the other bedside table, curling up with her. She brushed the hair out of Aquaria's face, trailing her fingers down the side of her delicate features. She began to hum a tune that Theia would sing to them when they had a rough day. Something that helped sooth them into a deep sleep, melting all their worries away, even if for just a moment. She stroked her hair as Aquaria drifted off to sleep.

"Don't worry, I'll protect you. I'll find out who he is. I'll make sure he is a good man, one that will give you the love you deserve and deserves your love. I won't let you go through this pain again."

Aquaria gave her a small smile before she drifted off.

18

"Good morning, my favorite princess of the sea."

Aquaria groaned as the pillow was snatched from her head. "You're one too. Let me sleep." She threw the pillow back over her head trying to get back to sleep.

"Not really, not like you. Anyways… its time to get up. Time for breakfast."

"What is wrong with you? Its early. You know I don't do mornings" She grumbled under her pillow.

"Come on! I want some breakfast. I would go get it myself, but I don't want to scare your friend Lucy. Still haven't met her yet." Astrid was jumping on the bed, trying to drag Aquaria out of bed.

She pulled the pillow off her head and smiled at her sister. "Somedays I hate you."

"Ha! Like I would ever believe that! You love me. I'm your favorite sibling." She dropped hard on the bed laughing at her.

"Well it's hard for you not to be, you're not blood and you're not trying to kill me. So you instantly win the favorite sibling spot." She gave her a sly grin, then rolled her eyes. "Fine, I'll get up. Gods, Lucy is going to be shocked to see me up this early."

"I thought all humans woke up early."

"Oh, they do, but you know as well as I do that I'm not human. Lucy knows that too, which is why she lets me sleep however long I want. She doesn't want me throwing shit at her head again."

"Yeah… I know that feeling. Remember that one time you chucked that massive crystal at my head? Still got the scar from that!" Astrid teased.

"That's your own fault. You already knew better by that point." She climbed out of bed, tossed some clothes on, and tossed Astrid a robe. "Wear this downstairs. I'll ask Lucy if you can borrow some of her clothes for a couple of days. You're closer in size, so you should be fine."

Astrid shrugged as she put the robe on. "You know I adapt easily."

They started to walk out of the room when Aquaria stopped her. "Umm, I almost forgot. Everyone on land calls me Gemma… No one is supposed to know my name, Lucy and her fiancé do, but they tend to forget because they have only ever heard Kelley call me that on rare occasions… basically when I wouldn't listen to him."

"Like when Pops calls you Tritonia?" She teased.

"Exactly," she let out a small laugh, which made Astrid smile. "Also, Gerard, Lucy's fiancé, will be here this weekend… knowing him he's already here or will be here any minute. I'm begging you, do not flirt with him. Lucy will lose her damn mind. And that includes inappropriate comments. Gerard can dish them back, but Lucy will be pissed off, and we will all have to suffer for the rest of the weekend. So please, don't make any advances on him."

"Don't worry, I won't. Besides, it will be nice to get a few days off from constantly using my abilities, and flirting. It loses its luster after doing it every day for a year."

They began walking down the hall and to the stairs.

"I'm sure it does… I hardly use that ability at all… only when I'm alone, just so I don't lose my control over it."

"You don't really need it though, its not like your working for Pops, trying to get information from everyone."

"True, I guess-" She stopped when she saw the front door open and Gerard walk in with a smile on his face. Lucy ran from the kitchen and tackled him to the ground in kisses. She smiled watching them. She knew they had no idea she was up yet. "Well Gerard is here."

"He's... wow... yeah... this is gonna be hard."

Aquaria laughed at her. "See why I begged you to not flirt with him?"

"Yeah... He's gorgeous. Gods, look at that smile. You could melt glass with that."

Aquaria laughed at Astrid's response. She knew her reaction was going to be like that. Gerard and Lucy heard her laughing and looked up at the stairs from the floor. They got back up, when they noticed someone with her. Lucy was sound asleep when they had gotten back, so she wasn't able to tell her.

"Shit, what time is it? Am I really that late? I thought I still had a couple of hours alone with you." Gerard whispered while trying to look for the clock. The girls started walking down the stairs when they saw them get up.

"You're here the same time you always get here... I think she just woke up early or something." Lucy whispered back

"Who is that with her?" Gerard gripped his dagger on his belt.

"I have no idea."

Aquaria gave them each a hug when she made it to them. Hugging Gerard extra tight, pulling his hand away from the dagger. "You won't need that."

He was confused at first, but he knew to trust her.

"This is my sister Astrid. She's going to be staying with us for the weekend. She's helping me through some things. Astrid, this is Gerard and Lucy. They're my closest friends here."

"Your sister? I thought your sister was eighty or something." Lucy was giving Astrid a suspicious eye.

"Its great to finally meet you. Gemma's told me so much about you." Gerard said with a smile.

"My father adopted Astrid when she was thirteen. She doesn't like to talk about how it happened... so just leave it be. She was one of my closest friends before father adopted her. So please, be nice."

Lucy sighed, "Sorry, we're just a little overprotective of her. Her past couple of years here have been... well... interesting to say the least. Its nice to meet you though."

"Thanks, and I can believe it. She always seems to cause all sorts of trouble. Gods the amount of times we got thrown-"

Aquaria quickly covered her mouth, stopping her from revealing her past indiscretions to them.

"They don't need to know that, because its in the past and I'm not like that anymore."

"Really? That's surprising. I thought that by how she said its been interesting that you got yourself into trouble again."

"Different kind of trouble."

"Oh, we're so talking about this later."

"No, we're good."

"Trust us, you don't want to know what she's been through the past couple of years." Gerard said, he then extended his hand to her. "I'm Gerard, its nice to meet you."

"Nice to meet you as well. And I actually need to know what's gone on with her the past couple of years. I'm here to help her get rid of that damn fish she made... which where is it? I haven't seen it the entire time I've been here."

"Oh... I have it distracted." Lucy said with a smile.

"What how?" Aquaria said

"Yeah Pops said you can't distract those things, or keep them from their creator." Astrid replied.

"Well obviously I can. It's in the kitchen, I have it helping myself and Marsali with breakfast... I should probably get back to it. That thing gets so upset when I leave it for too long. It took so much work to keep it from your room last night and this morning."

"Wait... who's Pops?" Gerard asked

"Our father... Poseidon." Astrid rolled her eyes, she couldn't understand how he didn't get that right away.

"She calls him Pops? Do you call him that too?" Gerard gaped at her.

"Hades no! He would kill me if I ever called him that. She's the only one allowed to call him that. And I mean the only one! I can only ever call him father."

"I'm pretty sure he would send you to some kind of intense remedial studies again if you called him that."

"Ugh... I don't even want to think about that again. It was torture. Two whole weeks with Silas breathing down my neck about respect for authority."

"Silas is a fucking eel! I keep telling Pops not to trust him, but he doesn't listen. I need more proof, still working on it. I'll talk to Angus when I see him next… maybe he can help me with that."

"Right… I'm going to get back to breakfast. Astrid, is there anything in particular you like for breakfast?" Lucy began walking into the kitchen, as everyone followed her.

"I usually eat eggs and bacon with some toast."

"I don't have bacon, but I have sausage."

"That works." Astrid had a smile on her face, she was excited for breakfast, and to find out what had been going on while Aquaria had been away.

"I'm surprised you eat human food… Gemma struggled with it for a week when she first moved here."

"Oh… I live on land. I rarely eat food from the sea anymore. Just when visiting Pops."

"Why do you live on land?" Gerard inquired. His eyes studied her, but in a curious way.

"It's for work. Pops set me up with a great position."

"Doing what?"

"She's a siren. And one of the most powerful ones out there. How long is your post supposed to be?"

"However long I want. I own the place I work at. Pops bought it for me. He also has a cottage for me on the palace grounds for when I come home to visit and for good."

"I'm glad he's keeping his promise to mom and taking care of you."

"You know pops loves me. He would never screw me over."

"True. He says all the time he's surprised your not actually a blood relation."

Gemma had sent Astrid to grab some of Lucy's clothes, Lucy wasn't too fond of a gorgeous siren just in a robe around Gerard. They were all sitting at the table eating while Astrid began her interrogation of the past couple of years.

"Little A, are you sure I've never met them?" She whispered.

"Positive. Why?"

"I don't know. Something about him is familiar. Like… I feel like I know him. How he speaks, his voice, his facial expressions, it's all so familiar."

"If you've ever met him before, I don't know about it. I don't think Delly ever took you to Ireland for training."

"No, never to Ireland."

"Then you couldn't have met him. I don't think he's ever left."

"Gerard, have you ever left Ireland?"

"A few times, why?"

"You just seem familiar, like I've met you before."

"Oh thank the gods. I thought I'd lost it. I've thought that since the second I saw you."

"You have?" Lucy asked.

"Yeah. There is something oddly familiar about her. I swear I've met her before."

"Ever been to France?"

"A couple of times, it was a long time ago, I think I was around 6 or 7."

"Hmmm… that would have been before. Anywhere around the time you were 16 or 17?"

"I went to England for a week, but that's about it. That was a weird couple of years for me."

"How so?"

"I have some gaps in my memory. Kelley and I didn't talk for like 6 months. A lot happened then."

"Tell me about these gaps."

"Why would you want to know about gaps in his memory." Gemma asked

Astrid looked Gemma deep in the eyes and growled "our father."

Her eyes widened. "Gerard, tell her."

"Not much to really say about it, I just don't remember certain times."

"When did they happen?"

"Well… the longest one… it's like a full week I can't remember… maybe longer. It was while Kelley was in a coma, about three weeks or so before Gemma got here."

Astrid looked at Gemma then back at Gerard. She let out a deep sigh. "I have a week missing from that time as well. I have a feeling we've met, but that memory has been wiped."

"Is that the week you were visiting the ship they had Kelley on?" Lucy asked.

"What are you talking about? I was never on a ship while Kelley was in his coma."

"Yes you were, ask your parents. I was staying with you during that time, I think I would remember you disappearing for a week to be on a pirate ship."

Everyone froze, eyes wide as what she said sunk in.

"What was the name of the ship?" Aquaria asked.

"I believe it's the same ship Kelley was sent to. I'm not really sure. I wasn't allowed to go see him while he was there. Ma and da were only allowed there when they brought him there and brought him home. Gerard was the only one I knew that was allowed there."

"Bloody hell. What happened on that ship?" Gerard mumbled.

"Apparently you were seen as around town a few times with some girl, you were caught kissing her in the alley by the cafe."

"What?!" Gerard jumped from his seat. "What are you talking about? You're the only girl I've ever kissed."

"It was going around town like crazy for a week. Apparently she was really pretty and had several boys flirting with her. They said you were fiercely protective of her."

Gerard dropped to his knees, grasping her hands. "Lu you can't believe those rumors. It didn't happen, it couldn't have, I would remember."

She gave him a soft smile. "It doesn't bother me even if they are true. We weren't together yet. I'm just letting you know what happened in that time. I was hoping it would jog your memory of that week."

Astrid's head was in her hands. A small grumble escaped her lips. Before she lifted her head up. Looking directly at Gerard. Her deep blue eyes glowing. "Aquaria, call uncle Hades immediately."

"What, why?"

"Because the memory is trying to come back but it's burning in my mind. He has a spell on that memory. I don't know how much longer I can hold it back before the spell consumes my mind."

Aquaria grabbed a scrap of paper and a pen, writing emergency on the paper, before lighting it on fire with the candle. Seconds later a ring of fire appeared in the dining room. Hades rushed out, worry strewn across his face.

"What's the emergency?" He looked around the room and saw Astrid's eyes glowing.

"Help me uncle hades! This memory is burning my mind." She let out a scream. Lucy and Gerard covered their ears to protect themselves from her siren scream.

"Lucy, take Gerard out of the house, now!" Hades commanded. He watched them run out of the room as fast as they could. He went over to Astrid placing his hands on either side of her head. "What memory is it?"

She let out a small scream. "When she was in a coma. Please help me. Please just make it stop."

He closed his eyes as a blue light beamed from the palms of his hands, going into her head. The glowing stopped but his hands remained still. The glowing reappeared, but coming from her head into his hands. Once the glowing light was fully in his hands he pulled them away from her head. He sat in the chair next to her, turning her towards him. He looked into her eyes ensuring the glow was gone.

"How do you feel now?"

"Much better, thank you."

"Aquaria, could you tell the others they can come back in? I'll keep an eye on Astrid."

Aquaria left the room, he waited until he heard the kitchen door close. He looked back at Astrid. "Do you still have that memory?"

"Yes. Are you going to remove it again?"

"No. That spell Poseidon made me put on all of you was dangerous. At the time it was our only option. Do you have the full week back?"

"No, just small pieces. It's really only the memories of Gerard."

"Interesting. Why only him."

"Probably because that was all Lucy knew about. She told us about the rumors going around their town."

"No one can know what happened during that time."

"I know. I won't say a word."

"I'll be leaving as soon as Aquaria gets back. Please help her through all of this. And do us all a favor, pretend like your memory has been wiped of that memory. We can't have her thinking she can weasel it out of you."

She gave him a nod. Her eyes darted to the doorway, hearing voices and footsteps. She turned back to Hades just as he was walking through a portal. She composed herself, putting a blank stare on her face. She knew how people looked after a memory wipe. Gerard and Lucy walked in, sitting back down and cautiously began eating. Aquaria stopped in her tracks as her eyes landed on Astrid. She ran to her side, grasping her shoulders.

"Where is uncle Hades?" She was frantic, she had something she needed to ask him.

"Uncle Hades? How should I know, I haven't seen him in months." Astrid was a little too good at pretending to have her memory wiped.

"What are you talking about?! He was just here with you."

"No he wasn't. I've been sitting here alone waiting for you."

"Not again." She groaned, dropping her head. "He wiped your memory."

"Why would you think that my memory has been wiped?"

"Because our father likes to hide things from us. This is what he does. He thinks us being ignorant is better than us being knowledgeable about our own lives. And uncle Hades just goes along with his plans." Gemma growled.

"Little A, You know he only does it for our own safety-"

"NO ITS NOT!"

The room quaked as she spoke. Lucy and Gerard held onto their glasses, ensuring that their drinks didn't spill. Astrid glared at her, ensuring her eyes didn't leave Gemma's. She needed someone to challenge her and remind her not to let her emotions get the best of her. The only other person who could ever do that was Kelley.

"You know I'm right."

"Don't." She snarled.

"Don't try to deny it Little A! We both know-"

"Stop defending him! Stop defending his actions!"

"Not this time. I know when it comes to this situation, he's right."

"He's the reason Kelley's dead!" She shouted.

The room went quiet once the quaking stopped. She saw Lucy and Gerard out of the corner of her eye. She shouldn't have shouted that around them. She shouldn't have ever even said it, even if it was the truth. She pushed Astrid out of her way and ran to her room, slamming the door behind her.

19

Lucy sighed as she stood up. "I'll go talk to her."

"No. Sit and finish your breakfast. She needs to be alone. I'll talk with her when the storm passes."

"I know you're her sister and all. But you haven't been here for her the past two years. You don't know what she's gone through." Lucy stood up and began walking to the door.

"And you haven't sat by her side in the castle cells over 60 times. Stayed by her side while she was in a coma for three months. Been beat halfway to death with her in arena training, and swam through one of her hurricanes, staying by her side until she calmed down." She stood up and walked to Lucy. "I might not be her blood. But I sure as hades know her well enough to know when to give her time to cool down. Her hair won't change back from black because she lost her soulmate. She might not know that, but I do. I know exactly what our father's plans are. I know as much as Nikoli does. So trust me on this. There's a reason for everything I'm doing, and aside from Kelley, I'm the only one who can help her. I was sent here for a reason."

"Luce, listen to her. She knows more about Gem and all of this than we do."

"But-"

"Let her do what she came here to do."

"I'm not asking. I'm royally ordering you to back down and leave it alone."

"You don't understand the pain she's going through! I do. It was my brother. You could never understand that pain."

"I know better than you think. You at least know he's dead." Astrid walked off, heading upstairs to check on Gemma.

"What's that supposed to mean?" Lucy snapped.

"You really don't listen to Gemma, do you?" Gerard sighed.

"What do you mean?"

"I mean, she's told us Astrid's story like ten times."

"She has?"

Gerard shook his head. "Astrid and her identical twin Tove, were adopted by Poseidon. Gemma found them begging for food because the orphanage rejected them for being too strong of sirens. Their parents were killed and they had been living on the streets for a year. Her twin sister vanished in the middle of the night, about five months before Gemma got here. They still haven't found her. So she understands losing family, but she's lost a lot more than you have. Let her take care of her sister."

"But-"

"Leave it be. She's here to help her. There's obviously a reason Poseidon sent her here. Something we don't know."

"I don't get it though. She's supposed to be in hiding. Why send her sister here when they haven't even been allowed to have any contact for two years? How do we know Poseidon actually sent her?"

"Because Gemma said he did. I trust her. Don't you?"

"Yes, but-"

"Just leave it be. Let's go find something to do today... Gemma being up early interrupted our original plans."

"I don't trust her."

"You just said you trusted her."

"No! Not Gemma. I mean her sister. I don't trust her. I think she's up to something."

"Why? Because you don't know her?"

"Obviously, But also... I don't know. Something just isn't adding up. Why now? Why not right when they told us? Why wait a month?"

"That's a question for Gemma." He picked up his plate and left the room. Leaving Lucy alone to think everything through.

When Astrid made it into her room, she didn't see her anywhere. Until she noticed a light glowing behind the bookcase. She walked over to it and slipped in through the cracked door. Gemma was sitting on the ground, glaring at a mural, tears rolling down her cheeks. She sat next to her, wrapping her arm around her shoulders.

"Let it all out. I'm not going anywhere."

"Yes you are, you leave on Sunday."

"I'll stay as long as you need me."

"Father won't allow it."

"Pops can piss off. I'm staying with you until that fish is gone. You need me here. So I'm not going anywhere."

She gave her a little smirk as she wiped her tears away.

"Mom would have said everything I said."

"I know." she sighed. "Sometimes it's just hard to remember that. Especially after everything that's happened. God's my brothers would never believe it. They think everything in my life is perfect. They would never believe what has actually happened to me."

"Care to elaborate?"

She shrugged, then lifted up the side of her blouse, exposing the long scar along her side.

"Who did this to you? And why in fathers name didn't you heal yourself or get father to?"

"Kelley saved me from what the boy was trying to do to me. Gerard carried me out of there. It's how he found out what I am."

"You didn't answer my question."

"I didn't have my healing powers yet."

"And why didn't father heal you?"

"He doesn't know. Nik found out after I had healed. I kept it from both of them. I didn't want Kelley's family to get punished for not protecting me well enough, when there wasn't anything they could have done to prevent it."

"I wish I could say he wouldn't, but you and I both know he

would. So I get it. I wish we had been allowed to have contact the past two years. You know I would have been there in a heartbeat."

Gemma laughed, "Yeah and killed whoever did this to me."

"What happened to him?"

"He's dead."

"By your hand?"

"Mine and Kelley's."

"But... what else happened to you? What are you so afraid of father finding out about?"

She lightly shrugged her shoulders while staring at the tiles of the mural.

"Your hiding something."

"Macsen paid me a visit."

"Yeah, I heard all about that."

"No... another time after that... after Kelley was sent away."

"Alright... what did that eel want this time?"

"He gave me a warning... one I've been trying to decipher, but I can't."

"What did he say."

"Follow the blood to find your true king. Until you two are reunited, crimson is the only shade you'll see. On that day, many will finally be free, but that is just the beginning of your war. You can't run from this, it will always find you. The bodies that fall because of your hand, are those who will oppose our one true queen."

Astrid stood up and turned to the the door and began walking out.

"Astrid, wait. What's it mean?"

Astrid turned quick on her heel and looked her dead in the eye. Color had drained from her face as she became as pale as a deceased sea biscuit.

"I need to speak with father immediately... you should too. He needs to know this."

"Why? What does it mean?"

"You're in more danger than we thought. Now where were you when you saw him? Where did he go after that?"

"I was just outside of clew. Sitting on a hill by the bay. Just staring at the water. Looking for the ship Kelley was on."

"Where did he go?"

"No where... I killed him after he told me that. He said he would rather take his own life than let Delanson find out what he knew. He said he loved me, and was sorry I had to witness it, but it was for my safety."

"Did anyone else know he was there?"

"Only three people... but you can't tell father who knows."

"Why?"

"Because it was uncle Hades. He helped me bury the body deep into the core of the earth. Then Peggy found out... which she's actually the Goddess Styx."

"Peggy?"

"Kelley and Lucy's mother. But he brought Kelley to me that day... I went dark."

"How dark?"

"Delanson dark. He got me Lux. She is actually a soul vixen... with Kelley's soul. But he doesn't want father to know that he got one for me. He's been trying to get one to survive underwater with mom's soul. But hasn't been successful and father would be pissed at him for getting me one and not one for him."

"Yeah pops would be livid about Lux... but he needs to know about Macsen."

"Astrid, what's going on?"

"If what he said is true... he knows who your fiancé is and others might too."

"What does he have to do with any of this?"

Astrid ran out of the room fast. She took off down the stairs and ran to the lagoon, leaving a trail of clothes along the hill. Gemma was running behind her. Shouting at her to stop and answer her. But she didn't listen. Astrid dove into the water, straight for the tunnel. As soon as she reached the door, Gemma darted in front of her, blocking the door. She had forgotten how fast Gemma was in the water, it was nearly impossible to catch her.

"What's going on?"

"Aquaria, you need to move right now. I need to tell father about this."

"Why?! Why does he need to know?"

"Come with me to find out. I don't have time to explain it all. So move!"

20

Gemma moved to the side and followed her back to the study in the palace. She made Gemma stay there as she fetched Poseidon. Within minutes Astrid, Poseidon and Nik were in the room. Nik and Poseidon checked her over as Astrid locked down the room. A special protocol for only members of the royal family. Nik was usually part of those lockdowns as well.

"Father, what's going on?" Her voice shook. She had never been this worried about her own safety in the palace.

"What happened to Macsen's body?"

"I buried him… on a cliff in clew."

"Did you save his memories on a crystal?"

"Yes, but-"

"What did you do with the crystal?"

"It's in my room at the O'Reilly's, in my desk drawer."

"Nikoli, go retrieve it now."

Nik swam out of the room, Astrid locking the door behind him.

"Did he do anything to you?"

"Nothing out of the ordinary for him."

"Meaning?"

"He kissed her and probably groped her like he always did."

Astrid snapped. "We need to fix this now."

"Fix what?"

"What he said to you was part of your prophecy. He was just a pawn for someone else."

"So? What does someone knowing some prophecy about me do them any good?"

"If we're lucky, they don't understand it correctly. Astrid. You know who we were talking about yesterday?"

"Yes..."

"That's him. Go warn him now. You're going the only one I trust to know this besides Nikoli. Go now and come right back. Do you understand?"

"Yeah, but where is he?"

"Guest quarters. The room across from Nikoli's."

"He's here?!"

"Yes. Go immediately."

"Where do you want him to go?"

"He will know. Now go!"

Astrid swam out of the room. Poseidon waited by the door, refusing to speak until she was back. Every time she tried to ask him something, he would hold his hand up. Not releasing a single word. Astrid and Nik returned at the same time, the door being locked behind them. Poseidon used his trident to magically lock the door and seal the room. No matter how hard someone tried, they wouldn't be able to hear a word that they said.

"Does someone want to explain what's going on here?"

"No!" All three shouted in unison.

"Then I'm leaving. I'm safer at my palace."

"Tritonia!" The room quaked as his loud thunderous voice bellowed through the room. "Sit down. You are staying here until we say it's safe."

A note slipped under the door. She quickly grabbed it before Poseidon could. She read the short note before he snatched it from her fingers. She knew that handwriting.

"Let me out now."

"No."

"I said let me out! I know that handwriting. I need to know who delivered it! Now let me out of here."

"It's not safe."

"The letter asked if I was okay. Now let me prove to whoever this is that I'm fine."

"No!"

"Fine. Renovo." Poseidon's trident flew into her hand. Astrid gaped. No one could ever take that trident from him. She unlocked the door, opening it to find nothing more than an empty hallway. She slammed the door and turned back to them. "Who sent that?!"

"Someone who reports to your fiancé."

"You're lying! Where is he?"

"Hopefully reporting to your fiancé."

She held the trident at his throat. "I might not be able to kill you. But it will still hurt. Where is Kelley?"

"He's dead. You know-"

"You think I don't know his handwriting? That's his hand writing! Now where is he? Tell me before I wreck havoc on the palace searching for him."

"Tritonia!"

She used the trident to throw all three of them into a corner of the room. Holding them in place until they gave her the answers she wanted.

"I want proof that he's dead."

"You went to-" Nik barely squeezed out.

"That doesn't count Nikoli! No one saw the body! We just placed a memorial headstone for him. Now prove to me he died."

"Top right desk drawer. The black crystal. Watch it." Poseidon growled.

"What is it?"

"It's the memory of one of the crew members who saw him die."

"How come none of us knew about this?"

"Because it's too painful to watch. I had to leave the room when I saw it." Nik hung his head low. She knew how close he was to Kelley.

She froze. If Nik said it was too painful for him… she might never recover. "Who left that note?"

"Someone who works on your fiancé's ship. He's one of my spies who relays messages between us."

She released them. Gripping the trident tighter. "What Macsen said to me… what does it mean?"

"It means your fiancé is being hunted by your broth-"

"No… the part about the true king? Being reunited?"

"That's probably just a message that your brothers believe one of them is the rightful king."

"And the reunited? Because according to that message, crimson is the only color I'll see until then."

"Delanson wants to use your strength to overpower me. Meaning he will be killing many till he gets what he wants."

"Or he dies." Astrid murmured.

Nik gave her a sly smirk. He knew they were both thinking the same thing.

"And the line, our one true queen?"

"He was in love with you. He always called you his queen." Astrid scoffed.

"Then why the security? Why the panic?"

"The other part. The You can't run from this, it will always find you. The bodies that fall because of your hand. Those are direct lines from the prophecy about you. The fact that he knew those exact lines means that someone told him. Someone got ahold of the prophecy."

"Who all knows it?"

"The three of us, your mother, your uncle and your fiancé. That's it. And the six of us are the last ones who would ever tell your bro-"

"How can you be so sure to trust my fiancé? How do you know he isn't working for him?"

"He's not." They snapped.

Rage bubbled inside her. She was about ready to explode. "I'm going home." She swam back to the door throwing the trident on the ground. Stopping as she reached for the handle. "Don't worry. His body will never be found. Uncle hades helped me bury him deep enough that no one could ever find him. I also severed his head so no one else can get his memories." She swam out of the room. Leaving the door wide open.

"Astrid, go back with her. We'll take care of this."

She gave him a nod and took off after her. She turned to look back at the study, watching a dark haired merman swim in. Closing the door behind him. The glow of the protective shield sparkled around the door.

"He's still here." She mumbled to herself as she continued down the hall.

21

Gemma sat on the beach waiting for her legs to come back. The little fish was back to following her everywhere. Thankfully Lux hated the thing and kept trying to bat it away. She watched Astrid come back to shore. She sat beside her. She knew Astrid wouldn't tell her anything. She was forbidden.

"Who did father send you to talk to?"

"Another spy. The one who works for your fiancé. I still haven't seen him... I've only spoken to him through a door or coded messages."

"Thank you for not mentioning Lux."

"It wouldn't do anyone any good if he knew. It would probably make things worse. Are you okay?"

"No. I'm pissed. I hate that I'm not allowed to know anything about my own life yet everyone else seems to know. Even Lucy and Gerard know stuff I'm apparently not allowed to know. I'm sick of this. Sick of all the secrecy. Sick of my life not being my own."

"Well... you're royal by blood. Your life will never be what you want it to be. But I know how hard all of this is for you. I hate keeping these secrets from you. You know that... but some of these, I have no choice."

"When this is all over. No more secrets between us. Understand?"

"I understand. And if I could tell you everything right now, I would. But Pops..."

"I know." She let out a sigh as she pulled her freshly formed legs to her chest. "But as soon as I'm married and his ridiculous plan has played through. You and I are going to meet up and chat about everything. I want to know everything you've been hiding from me. Deal?"

"Deal. But you have to tell me everything you're keeping from me."

"I will. It's just hard. Those are the things that I have a hard time talking about... or even thinking about. The things I push so deep in my mind that I wish father would pull them from my memory. But he won't. Last time I asked him to remove that kind of memory, he refused. Saying that those are the memories that I learn the most from." She looked up at the sky, letting out a deep breath. Her chest tightening with the mere thought of any of those memories. But an agreement with her father was unbreakable. She had to tell her sister everything... no matter how hard it would hurt. "Let's go back to the house. I just want to sit in my room for a bit. I need a break from his realm."

"Can I ask you something?"

"What?"

"Do you have any photos of you two together?"

"Just one. I'll show it to you when we get to my room."

As soon as they walked through the kitchen, Lucy began bombarding them with her snooping questions. Gerard pulled her away. He knew Gemma wasn't up for one of Lucy's relentless interrogation sessions. Gemma handed Astrid the photo once they got to her room. Her hands shook. Color drained from her face. She gripped her chest. She had only seen Astrid do this one other time, when Tove vanished. The photo fell from her trembling fingers.

"What's got you so freaked out?"

"I've seen him before. About three months ago... he's from Jameson's ship."

"Are you sure?"

"Hard to forget a person whose soul can't be read. That touching their skin causes my mind to go completely blank. Forgetting my own name even."

"Yeah… that's him alright. Siren abilities don't work on him."

"How?!"

"Father says he's an anomaly. But I know the truth. He has god blood. His mother is the goddess Styx. She didn't teach him how to do any magic except how to block a soul read."

"But his sister… I could read her soul and remove pain by the slightest grazing against the skin."

"She received hardly any magic. Just her hair, control of animals and her moonchaser genes."

"I remember every second of that encounter. I felt him walk into the pub. That same intense magical feeling I get when you or pops are near. But I didn't know it came from him. He was looking for someone… I think he was the one they sent to get Jameson."

"How were you able to get him to let you touch his chest?"

"He sat down at the bar and handed the bartender a note. I sat next to him because something was drawing me to him. I quickly placed my hand on his chest before he could reject it. But then it all went blank. I pulled my hand away and he gave me the worst glare I've ever seen. It was like he could read my soul by looking into my eyes like uncle Hades does. The weirdest part was what he said though."

"Which is what?"

"Good try. But not even the gods can read me without my permission. He got up and left. Jameson chased after him. That's how I knew they're from the same ship. I couldn't work the rest of the day. I had to come home and talk to pops. He assured me he knew who I was talking about and not to worry. But…"

"What?"

"Something about those eyes. I swear he was reading my soul too."

"He may have and didn't realize it. His mother didn't teach him how to control his magic… but I taught him how to read a soul."

"How? Why?"

"He finally allowed me to read his soul and when I did, it felt so good. Gods it felt as good as sex. I actually moaned from it."

"Seriously?!"

"Yeah. It felt like his soul was made for me. I wanted him to feel that too. So I taught him how. And then… well… let's just say it ended in the hottest sex we've ever had."

"Well I can believe that. Your souls were completely open to the other. Holding absolutely nothing back. So it makes sense."

"I was surprised he let me read his soul. Uncle Hades has tried for years and wasn't able to."

"That should tell you how much he trusted you. To be the one person he opened up to."

"It does. But now it just hurts."

"Why has Hades been trying to read his soul for years?"

"Uncle Hades is Kelley's godfather. He would spend at least one day a month with him. He trusted and cared for uncle Hades more than his own father."

Astrid sat in a chair across from the fireplace. She stared at the photo. Studying every detail. The swords at their feet. The arena like setting. They were in a fight.

"Where was this photo taken?"

"In the ring. They hold an annual sword fighting competition. I was the first girl to ever compete… and I won the whole thing."

"That's not surprising. I bet Pops would've been so proud to see you fight like that. I know he was always proud of me in the arena, but I know it would be nothing compared to what he had hoped for you."

"He was. He saw that fight. I've never seen him proud of me before. It felt nice… like he actually cared."

"You know he cares."

"It rarely feels like it. I only seem to matter to him when it's something to do with this master plan. I'm just a pawn to him."

"No Aquaria. You are the plan. You're not a pawn. YOU are the whole plan. Everything is for you and about you. You think Nik and I would let him put you through all this if it wasn't the right thing for you? Everything is for your protection. Father sent me to a town that pirates who frequent Delanson and Fjords waters. I'm there to get intel to protect you."

"Do you know how little I care about any of that? I don't give a damn about some stupid prophecy. I want no part of it. I only want to live my life how I want to. If I could renounce my title I would, but I can't because I'm the only true heir to the throne. Not like it even matters because father is immortal."

She walked over to Gemma, wrapping her arms around her. Holding in a tight hug.

"I promise to help you escape 24 hours after your wedding. If you want to escape I will be there."

She gave her a small nod as she hugged her back. She had missed her sister so much. She was thankful to have her helping her through this.

After being with them for over a month, Astrid had to leave. She had worked hard at helping her sister with her grief. The hardest part besides leaving, was controlling her anger. The slight mention of anything related to their father would cause her to lose her temper. But she was able to accomplish her task of getting rid of the annoying little fish made of water. It was purposely torturing Gemma. Making Lucy spend all her time trying to distract it, while Lux would chase after it and bat at it.

They stood in the sand at the edge of the water. Astrid stripped down into nothing but a bra and small magical gold skirt.

"It'll be hard, but you're strong."

Gemma scoffed. "Have you forgotten, I'm the weakest in our family."

"Trust me, you're the strongest. You've gone through more hardships than the rest of your siblings, and you're still standing tall. And no I won't claim them… Bash and Delly sure, but not the rest of them."

"You forget that you've gone through worse than me."

"You may think that, but I always had someone I could rely on. You, Tove & Angus. You've had to go through everything alone. Sure you had Nikoli, but that's not the same. When mom died, I wasn't allowed to see you and pops was trying to get rid of his fish. When

Tove vanished, you had to be my rock as I fell apart. You couldn't grieve for my sake. You were sent away from everyone and everything you know, and not allowed to communicate with anyone except Nikoli. And this time… you only had Kelley's family and friend. You didn't have your support by your side. You've always had to be strong and hold it all in because of your title. But when you're here, don't. This is a place where you can let it all out and not have to be strong."

The sun was almost to the horizon. Dinner with their father was always when the sun reached the horizon. Gemma wrapped her arms tightly around her sister's neck. Holding onto her as if she was the last bit of oxygen. Astrid hugged her back. She really didn't want to leave. But she had already been away from her work for over a month and she didn't even want to think of how her pub looked. She always worked hard to keep it looking nice. She never knew when Poseidon would pop in for a report.

"I really have to go. Last thing either of us want is to make pops angry."

"Promise you'll try to keep in touch?"

"I'll do my best, but pops is going to probably erase this from my memory so I can't tell anyone where you are. If you can manage to get a letter to me I'll make sure to write back. I love you."

She squeezed her tighter. "I love you too."

Astrid let go and walked into the water. Disappearing under the surface.

PART TWO

22

Gemma and Lucy stayed at the Lagoon for a full two months before returning. They thought about returning earlier, but Peggy and Gerard agreed that it was not in Gemma's best interest to return. Patrick was in a constant drunken rage. Blaming Gemma for Kelley's death.

It was only a week until Lucy's 18th birthday, she was excited, it meant that this was her last year of school. Which meant that she could start planning her wedding. Gemma had gained full control of many of her powers. There was still one power that she refused to practice anywhere but the cave behind the waterfall. The one thing that mermaids were known for, she had to do alone. She knew how powerful her singing could be and refused to put anyone under that kind of spell, especially Gerard. She wanted to make sure he belonged to Lucy.

The girls went into town one day before Lucy's birthday. Gemma wanted Lucy to have a wonderful gift, she was so good to Gemma and gave up so much to help her through everything. She knew she had to do something amazing for her. Nothing could live up to the gift from Gerard last year, but she wanted to do something special for her. Lucy went to the market to spend time with Gerard, and go to lunch with him. Gemma went to a few different shops to find a gift for Lucy, she couldn't seem to find anything just right. Then she found her the perfect dress. It was one that Lucy had been looking at before they left. While going through the shops she ran into Finn.

"Gemma?" He said

Gemma turned around and saw Finn. "Oh, hello Finley, how are you today?"

"I feel like no one has seen you in months."

"Well they haven't, besides Lucy, Peggy and Gerard. Lucy and I went away for a while."

"Where did you go?"

"My father has a house, about three hours south of here. We thought it was best for me to stay away, with everything that happened."

"Yeah, the whole town heard. Are you okay? Callie has thrown Patrick out of the pub several times while you were gone."

"I'll be fine, things just got a little uncomfortable at their house. I needed to get away from there. Lucy didn't want me to be alone, so Gerard took us to the house. He visited every weekend, Peggy visited a lot too, it was just hard to you know, come back."

"How long are you back for?"

"I don't know, maybe a while. It all depends on how things go with Patrick."

"Well I hope you stay. You know the festival is this weekend. Are you going to fight this year?"

"I don't know, I haven't practiced much, but I also worry that people might think Kelley let me win, if I don't compete and win again."

"Well I hope you at least come to the festival, I would love to have a dance with you."

"Well if I go, I will save you a dance."

"Really?"

Gemma slightly laughed, "Really. It might be nice to dance again."

"Great! I will look for you." He said, right as a young girl called his name, "Oh I have to go. I will see you there."

"Maybe…" She shouted back, he didn't seem to take the maybe for an answer.

* * *

She decided that she should stop by the Club and Pub while in town. Her first stop was the Club, she wanted to speak with Henry, she hadn't seen him in months and wanted to know how everything was going with the festival and fights this year.

"Gemma! It's great to see you again. We were all wondering when you would be back. You missed the ball this year, we had an award to present to you there." Henry said.

"Hi Henry. I didn't really feel up for the ball this year, Lucy and I went away for a little while. I needed to recover a bit from what happened."

"Oh we all know why, Gerard keeps us well informed and told us you were at a house your father owns. How are you doing? Planning to fight this year? We have a fight for the girls now, but you are more than welcome to be in either of the fights."

"I don't know if I'll be fighting this year, I haven't practiced much since… well you know."

"I understand. Well, we still have an award to present you with."

"What for?"

"Come to the meeting tonight and we'll give it to you there. Here I have something to show you, come with me."

Henry took Gemma down a hall full of portraits of all the members, she saw the picture of Gerard, but he looked a lot younger, then she saw Kelley. She stopped for a moment, just to see his handsome face. When they got to the end of the hall she saw it, in a gold frame, with a plaque under it that said "First Woman of the Club". It was a portrait of her. She had never seen a portrait of just herself before, she didn't know how to react.

"You deserved a special place. We had a feeling you would not want to fight this year, after what happened. We were thinking that if you wanted you could join us at the judges table this year."

"What?" Gemma was shocked by his request, "But I've only ever competed once. Why would I be a good judge."

"We had a meeting last week, you were the only one not to attend, which is fine, don't worry. And everyone voted that you would be the perfect choice. Now that we have female fighters, we need someone who understands how they move. You are the only one we could think of."

"So everyone wants me to judge?"

"Yes. The Club loves you. We all missed having you around."

"Ummm… I guess I can. I don't quite feel qualified though."

"Don't worry we will be there with you, and if you want I can send you home with the rule book, if that would make you feel better."

"Actually it might make me feel better."

"Fantastic! I will tell the others later tonight. Will you be attending the meeting?"

"I guess I can, I will ask Gerard if he could escort me home. He should be fine with it."

"Great! We will see you at six."

She made her way to Callie's pub across the street and remembered that she wanted to talk to Callie before she went back to the house. She walked in and didn't see Callie anywhere, she asked the bartender where she was. He told her she stepped out for a little while and would be back soon. The bartender was new, she had never seen anyone in there besides Callie. She then went to the Market where Gerard worked to ask him if he would mind escorting her home. However, he wasn't there, he was on his lunch break with Lucy, which meant they could be anywhere. She started to feel a bit upset, when she saw Nik go into the pub. She quickly rushed over there, she didn't want to be alone.

"Nik!" She said as soon as she got into the pub

"Gemma? What are you doing here? I didn't know you were back yet."

"We got back yesterday. What are you doing here?"

"Well its poker night tonight."

"But that's not until 7, why are you here so early?"

"I'm always here this early for Poker night. I stop in for a drink, catch up with everyone and deliver the package that your father sends. Which Peggy has put in your room for you."

"Oh, thank you."

"Something's wrong. Here, have a seat, lets chat." He pulled out a chair at a table in the corner. He waved to the bartender to bring them three drinks.

"I was trying to find Callie, I wanted to ask her something. I couldn't find her, so I tried to find Gerard and Lucy, and once again couldn't find them. I'm just trying to keep my mind off of it, but it is hard when I'm alone."

"Well Callie should be here any minute, she always has a drink with me when I arrive. What did you need to talk to her about?"

"Henry asked me to be a judge in the fights this year, because I don't feel like I'm up to fighting this year. I haven't practiced much in the last couple of months and I'm not fighting as well. I just don't know if I feel like I'm ready to judge the fights."

"Judging the fights is much easier than fighting. As long as you know the rules, you will be fine. That's nothing to worry about."

"I wanted to ask Callie if she would help me fight better. I don't have Kelley to help me anymore, Gerard is a good fighter, but even when I'm rusty, I still beat him easily. Callie is such a good fighter I want to learn how to fight like her."

"Well, all you have to do is ask." Callie said walking up to the table with all three drinks.

Gemma looked at her drink, they had given her rum. "You would really teach me?"

"Well you showed a lot of promise last year, I can see you are a dedicated fighter."

"I used to be, these last few months were hard, and I only had a sparring partner once a week."

"Well you can come here three times a week and I will help you, but I can only offer two hours a day."

"Really? Thank you so much."

"Of course. Now drink up girl, these men will steal that from you. Anyways, Kelley had asked me to help you practice before he left. I told him only if you asked."

Gemma started to drink her rum, it was strong. She never had rum before, only the wine and whiskey her father kept in the cellar at her palace. Callie and Nik laughed at her reaction to the rum.

"It takes some getting used to." Nik laughed.

"Obviously." She said

"Now you should get going, we will begin practicing tomorrow." Callie said.

"Thank you." She said as she got up, she gave Nik a hug and left.

"I'm surprised you agreed." Nik said after Gemma was out of earshot.

"Well, she needs to stay sharp. If it was anyone else I would say no, but from what I saw last year, she won't need much teaching, just someone to practice with her."

Gemma was walking back towards the market hoping that Lucy and Gerard were back. When she got there she found Gerard was working again, but she couldn't find Lucy.

"Gerard?"

"Hi Gemma. Lucy just left, she should be close by."

"Alright, but I was actually looking for you."

"Oh really? What for?"

"I talked to Henry and he wants me to come to the meeting tonight. But I would need someone to take me home after. Would you take me home after the meeting?"

"Of course. We can have Lucy stay at my house while we are at the meeting."

"Great. Thank you. I will see you at 6 then?"

"Actually, meet at my house at 5, we can all eat dinner before we go."

"Alright. See you then." Gemma left with a smile on her face.

That evening at the meeting Gemma finally felt at home. Everyone talked to her as an equal, not as a child, or a fragile princess, but as their equal. They all joked around, no one was afraid of offending anyone. It was like a breath of fresh air. During the meeting they talked about the festival, and how they would select who fights who in the first rounds. Then they brought up the fights for the girls, how they would be set up, when they would fight. Then Gerard stood up.

"I think our newest member will be a lot of help in this discussion.

She is the only woman to have ever fought in a ring before anyways, she could give us a clearer idea of what would work best for them."

"Well Gemma, what do you think we should do?" Henry asked

"Honestly, the hardest part, was the crowds. I didn't have much support from the crowd, and it made me nervous. It made me actually consider backing down. Maybe if we have the girls fight only one day, it would make things run smoothly."

"Which day would you suggest?"

"Either early on Saturday before the boys fights or Sunday before the finals. There are not many girls that signed up, so it won't take too long for their fights. Either way if the fights are before the boys, the stands won't be completely full yet, so it won't be as daunting."

"Why can't we just have them at the same time just in the practice ring?" One man asked.

"If you have them in the practice ring, it will make them feel as if they are seen as not worth watching. Which will make them not want to fight again, and then losing the girls fights all together." she answered.

"There are a total of 8 girls who have signed up, so that would give us a total of 7 fights. So let's give them an estimated total time of 45 minutes. That should be more than enough time, we will have them fight on Saturday. The winner of the girls can then be added to the first round with the boys if she would like." Henry said.

"Why only 45 minutes?" Gemma asked

"Well on average, the fights last about 5 minutes each, so 45 minutes should be more than enough time for 7 fights."

"I swear my fights were longer than that." Gemma mumbled to herself.

Henry saw the confused look on her face, he whispered to her. "Gemma, you and Kelley had the longest fight in the history of the club. No one had ever lasted that long in the ring."

Gemma smiled when he said that.

They finished all the business of the meeting and then spent some time mingling.

"Gemma, come with me for a moment." Henry said, Gemma signaled to Gerard that she would be back soon. He took her into another room, it was full of plaques and medals.

"Gemma I wanted to show you something. You never got full tour of the building, but this is our trophy room. Remember how I told you there was an award that we were never able to present to you?"

"Yes, I thought it was my portrait."

"Oh no, everyone gets one of those. You and Kelley won an award together. For the record length of a fight." He pointed to a golden plaque with hers and Kelley's names together, she had a small tear run down her cheek. "We have this for you as well. We had a photographer at the fights, and he took this one of you two. We thought you should have it."

Gemma took the picture from his hand, it was of the moment that she had defeated Kelley and he kissed her.

"How did they get this? It was so quick."

"I don't know, but we all agreed that you needed to have it."

"Thank you, this really means a lot. It's funny the only two pictures I have of us, are from the same moment."

"What do you mean?"

"The newspaper reporter had taken a similar picture, but it was from when I was announced the winner. That's it. Just these two." She looked down at the photo, a slight upward turn of her lips. "Thank you. You have no idea what this means to me."

Gemma went back to the other room to grab Gerard, when they got back to his place Lucy was fast asleep in his bed. They decided that it was best for Gemma to stay in the guest room for the night, and just go back in the morning

23

The festival had arrived, Gemma was ready to judge this year. She stayed with Henry the whole time, this was the first year that Gerard couldn't fight, he was 21 and age limit for the fights was 20. Gerard and Lucy wanted to watch the girls fight so they sat next to the judges. Gemma watched the fights closely, most of the girls were barely fighting at all. Barely blocking, jumping away from every swing. Gemma just sighed.

"This is not how I thought these fights would go." She said to Henry.

"Maybe they need someone to show them how it's done."

"What do you mean?"

"One of the girls just dropped out, we have a match open for you. You're already dressed for a fight, you might enjoy it."

"I know I will enjoy it, but I won't be as good as last year."

"That doesn't matter, go have some fun. If we don't have someone fill the spot, the other girl will automatically move to the next round. Go on, we can handle to rest of the judging."

"I didn't bring my sword with me."

"Here Gemma, take mine. You know I never leave the house without it. Like you with your daggers." Gerard said handing her his sword. "You've used this one before, you know how it handles."

"Thanks, Gerard. Alright Henry, when am I up?"

"You're up next. Get down there."

Gemma gave them a soft smirk and made her way to the ring. The crowd started to cheer. As soon as people saw her they began chanting her name, enticing more people to fill the stands. She went into the ring, there was a young girl in the ring. She looked to be about 15, and looked terrified. Gemma walked up to her and shook her hand.

"Are you scared?" She asked, the girl just nodded.

"Don't worry, it will be fine. It takes a lot of practice, just don't be afraid of getting hurt."

The girl just nodded again, she still looked terrified. They dropped the flag and the fight began. Gemma went slow for the girl, trying to coach her through the fight. Gemma was able to help boost the girl's confidence. Then after a few minutes, the girl got scared and dropped her sword and backed away. Gemma won the round, and left the ring. After she went to speak to the girl that she fought.

"What's your name?" Gemma asked sweetly.

"Molly" She said shyly.

"How long have you been practicing?"

"A couple of months."

"Who has been teaching you?"

"My older brother, he's coming over here now."

"Thank you Gemma for being gentle on Molly. I know it was probably hard for you to hold back." Finn laughed

"Finn this is your little sister? You should have told me, I could have trained her a lot better than you did."

"Well I'm not much of a fighter, I don't partake in the fights ever. Not really my thing."

"Well Molly, if you ever want to know how to fight, just ask. I will teach you how to really fight."

"Really?" Molly exclaimed

"Sure. We can start out at once a week." She said smiling at Molly.

"That would be lovely. Thank you, Gemma!" Molly said grinning from ear to ear. She then ran over to her parents to tell them.

"You know you didn't have to do that." Finn said

"What do you mean?"

"You don't have to teach her how to fight, she only wanted to learn because she saw how good you were last year."

"Well, that is a good enough reason for me to want to teach her. Just because you're not interested, doesn't mean that she isn't." She said giving him a slight smirk, "You're just afraid she will beat you if she starts training with me."

"I know she will beat me if she trains with you. You're too good."

"And maybe she will be one day as well. Give her a chance, why should she have to be exactly like every other girl. Let her be unique."

"You are very different from all the other girls. You know that?"

"I get told that a lot. Well it looks like I'm up again."

"Can we talk more after your fight?"

"I don't see why not." Gemma shouted back as she walked into the ring.

She wasn't as easy on the rest of the girls, they were all a lot closer to Gemma's age. She won the girls tournament with ease, and prepared for the boys to begin. She told Henry she wanted to continue on into the boy's tournament. She knew that was where she would really find out how rusty she was. She had practiced a couple of times with Callie that week, it was her first week of training with her. She was no match for Callie, and Callie refused to go easy on her at all. Gemma was the last one to go in for the boy's tournament, so she had a while to wait.

"You really know how to make an impression don't you?" Finn said walking up to her.

"Well I can't very well just let them win. They wouldn't survive one round with the boys, how they were fighting. Their brothers are going too easy on them."

"They're girls. What do you expect us to do, fight them like we fight the boys?"

"That's exactly how you should teach them. What's the point in them learning how to defend themselves if they can't fight anyone off?"

"Well that's what their fathers and brothers are for."

"And when they are not around to protect them? Who will be there to keep them safe?"

"I guess I never thought of it like that."

"Do you remember why I started fighting?"

"To spend more time with Kelley?"

"Yes, but also because I was attacked by Liam. I knew from then on that I couldn't always count on other people to protect me. I needed to know how to protect myself." She purposely left out the part about who she was going to marry.

"I've never really thought about my sister being alone somewhere. She's only 15, and doesn't go anywhere without one of us with her."

"You know that will be changing soon. I was only two years older than her when I was attacked."

"I didn't know that. I'm sorry."

"You have no need to be sorry, I just want you to understand why this is so important to me. I hope you realize that it should be important to you as well. Teach her how to really fight, not for fun, but to keep her safe." She touched his arm, using her siren abilities to reassure him that she wasn't trying to be mean. His cheeks flushed, he wasn't expecting that.

"It looks like you're up. You should get in there before they think you forfeited."

"Trust me, Henry knows I would never forfeit." She laughed as she walked into the ring.

"Who's Henry?" He shouted to her.

"A good friend of mine." She smiled back at him.

She went back into the ring, she was up against the boy that Kelley fought in the semi-finals. The boy looked scared, he knew exactly who she was. She went to shake his hand and he was shaking.

"You look familiar, did I fight you last year?" She asked

"No, I fought Kelley right before you did."

"Why do you look so scared?"

"He said you show no mercy, and after watching you fight him, I know he was right."

Gemma just laughed. "Well he's not wrong."

The flag dropped and the fight began. She didn't hold back. She was back to her normal self. She finished the round fast, he didn't stand a chance. The crowd cheered for her every time she walked into the ring. All the girls wanted to talk to her, find out how she got so good. She told them all that she just practiced a lot, and always told her trainers not to hold back or go easy on her. Everyone was in awe of her, she was something no one had ever seen before. She was thrilled, but her hair never changed color, it stayed black. No matter how happy she was about anything, she was still completely heartbroken over Kelley's death. She won every match that day, not one opponent stood a chance against her.

24

That night Gemma joined Lucy and Gerard at the dance. She wore a simple, knee length black dress, she pulled her hair into a low side ponytail. She wore the hair comb that Poseidon gave her when she won. Always wearing the necklace and ring Kelley gave her, along with her ring from the club. Gerard walked in with both girls on his arms, it was Lucy's idea. She didn't want Gemma to be bombarded walking in again, she had been through enough lately. Lucy and Gerard danced most of the night, occasionally stopping to spend time with Gemma.

Gemma talked with Henry and some of the brothers of the club. She was the crown jewel of the club, they all loved her. Anytime someone would ask her to dance, the members would wait for a signal from her, stating that she didn't want to dance with them. They would all quickly pull out their daggers and warn the boy to leave. She felt safe with all of them, it was as if Gerard and Kelley were surrounding her. She knew none of them would let anything bad happen to her. Then Finn got the courage to ask her to dance, she accepted and headed to the dance floor with him.

"I was worried that they wouldn't let me dance with you." He said

"I let them know it was okay for you to ask." She said with a little smile.

"Thank you... I think."

Gemma lightly laughed, "They're protective, but they also know that I can take care of myself."

"Should I be worried about my safety?"

"As long as you're respectful and don't try to hurt me, you'll be fine."

"I'll do my best. You know you slightly scare me."

"I've gotten that a lot today." She laughed

"Well I hope that we can be friends. Who knows maybe when you are teaching Molly how to fight, you can give me a few pointers."

"I would like that... you know the friends part." She smiled

"And the pointers?"

"We will see, maybe after your sister can beat you."

The song ended and he walked her back to the club members, knowing that she felt best with them. After chatting with them for a little longer Gerard grabbed Gemma and pulled her on the dance floor. "Come on Gem! It's time for you to have a little fun." All of the other Brothers just chuckled. They knew Gerard and Gemma were close like siblings.

"You should try enjoying yourself tonight." He said

"I am enjoying myself. Who says I'm not?"

"Lucy, she saw your face. An occasional smile and slight chuckle won't fool her."

"Well I'm not trying to fool anyone. I'm just trying to be as happy as I possibly can. She's going to have to realize I will never be like I was before."

"She knows. She just worries about you. You've rejected everyone she has sent to dance with you."

"I didn't want to dance with them. She knows that I don't like when people do that."

"She thinks that dancing will make you feel better."

"Fighting makes me feel better. Dancing actually makes me miss Kelley a lot."

"You danced with Finn though."

"He had asked me earlier this week. We talked a lot today, it was really nice to just talk someone who doesn't really know me."

"What do you mean?"

"Mean I can talk to you and Lucy about everything, but at the same time, it's nice to talk to someone who doesn't know everything about me. He doesn't know who I really am, he doesn't know what my future entails. And most importantly, he doesn't know how deeply in love I am with Kelley, and the fact that I'm still so completely broken hearted. So much so that I feel as if half of me is gone. Talking with Finn, made me feel like I don't have explain my heartbreak." She explained in a somewhat somber tone.

"I never realized you felt like that. You don't have to talk to me about this type of thing all the time. You can talk to me about anything. But if talking to Finn makes things easier for you, then I'm glad. Just don't rush into anything."

"It's nothing like that, I like him as a friend, nothing more."

"Well just so you know, he likes you as more."

"I figured. He's too afraid to make an actual move, for now at least."

"I just want you to be careful. Like you said he doesn't know who you REALLY are."

"Don't worry I will be. I'm going to teach his little sister how to fight. I think just teaching her to fight will help me get through this. The more I fight the better I feel."

"Well if you ever need any help, I will be there."

"Thanks. And can you do me a favor?"

"Anything."

"Don't call me Gem, only Kelley ever called me Gem. When you pulled me on the dance floor, and called me Gem, for a moment, I thought you were Kelley."

"I'm so sorry. I won't do it again. I promise."

"Thank you."

Just then Lucy came up to them. "Mind if I cut in?"

"He's all yours." Gemma said smiling at her, "Thanks for the dance and the talk."

"Anytime Gemma."

"Did you ask her why she won't dance with anyone I send over to her?" Lucy asked once Gemma was out of earshot.

"Yes, and she said you need to stop. She hates it."

"But dancing will make her feel better, more like her again."

"No, it doesn't. Fighting does, why do you think Henry and I set it up for her to fight today?"

"Wait I thought someone backed out."

"No, Henry and I have been planning this before you two came back. The only time we have seen her be herself since Kelley died, is when she has a sword in her hand. So we told her she was going to be a judge, and knew that if someone dropped out last minute, that she would jump in. Once she was in, she would keep going. She was as happy as she could be, she will never be where she was before."

Lucy sighed, "I just want her to be happy."

"I know, and so does she. Just let her come to us when she needs help on this, okay?"

"Alright. But if she was happy today why is her hair still black?"

"I don't think it will ever change back."

"Why?"

"She said that she feels as if half of her is gone. And honestly, I don't think that feeling will ever go away."

"Unfortunately it won't, she loved him too much."

"That's why I said I don't think it will change back."

"You two talk about this stuff a lot, don't you?"

"She feels like there are things that are easier for her to talk to me about. Even before we were together, it was always easy for her to talk to me. How do you think she helped get us together?"

"I never knew she got us together."

"I was afraid to ask you to dance, I always thought you just considered me a friend. She told me to dance with you, and she danced with Liam to be sure that I got that chance."

"I always liked you as more, I just never thought I would have a chance with you. You were such a big shot, every girl wanted you. Plus, you were my brother's best friend, I thought you saw me as just his little sister."

"Well, I have always loved you. Nothing can change that." He said when he kissed her.

"I love you too. I can't wait to be married and start our own family. When can we start planning?"

"You know your parents said after your birthday we can plan, but we can't get married until you're 18. So after next week you can start planning for a wedding the next year. I want to be working at the bank and have a house before we're married."

"It's so long, but completely worth it." She said grinning from ear to ear.

They continued to dance, Gemma looked over at them and smiled, she was glad they were so happy. The dance ended and Gerard went home with the girls, Patrick and Peggy didn't attend the festival at all this time. Peggy had Gerard sleep on the couch, Patrick still wouldn't unlock the door to Kelley's room. Not even for Gerard to have a place to sleep.

25

When they arrived at the festival the next day, Gemma was ready for a fight. She looked in the stands and saw it was already completely filled. She went to Henry to sign in, and speak with him for a moment.

"I'm a little nervous today." She said

"Why is that?" Henry asked

"I've never had so many people watching me fight before. What if I don't win?" She asked

"Then you don't win, they know that fights are unpredictable. Everyone here is hoping to see a fight like last time. They will be sadly disappointed." Henry replied

"Why is that?" She asked

"Well You and Kelley, were a perfect match. He was the only one who could keep up with your speed and actually rival you. So far, you have completely annihilated everyone that you have come across this year." Henry answered.

"Well I still have two more fights, maybe one of them will be able to keep up."

"Not likely, you and Kelley have a different style of fighting from everyone else. That is what made you both so good. Everyone else fights like Gerard, classically trained. You two fight for survival, and on top of the survival, you fight gracefully. His moves were rough, yours are swift, as if you planned every move ahead of time." He explained.

"I never really thought we fought so different from everyone else."

"Well you do, and I just hope to never get into a real fight with you. I won't last two minutes."

"Thanks Henry." She laughed.

Gemma waited by the entrance to the ring, ready for her fight. She looked up in the stands, Lucy and Gerard were sitting by the town leaders again. She smiled at them, happy she had someone there to watch her. She looked around some more, she saw Callie on the sides, Nik was with her. She wanted to go see Nik, but decided to wait until after the fights. She took a deep breath and walked into the ring. The crowd was chanting her name, they were louder than usual, somewhat distracting. She had to tune it out, knowing that her sole focus should be on her opponent. She went to shake his hand, but he refused. She got into her ready stance, twisting her wrist, making her sword look as if she were spinning it. The flag dropped and the fight began. He was better than everyone she fought yesterday, but he was still not a challenge for her. She easily blocked every hit that came near her. She cut his arm, causing him to drop his sword. She picked it up, he tried to get it back but it only caused him to get his hands cut. He tried to take a swing at her, she quickly ducked and hit his nose with the butt of her sword. His nose was bleeding so he backed off and went to the medical tent for his minor injuries.

She waited outside the ring watching the next match, trying to study her opponent. They both fought like everyone else, no instinct, just classic fighting. It was time for her to go into the ring again. It was the final fight. She took a deep breath and walked in. Her heart was pounding, which drowned out the sound of everyone cheering. She shook her opponents hand, and looked him up and down. He was tall, but not very muscular, just skinny. She knew that meant he would be fast and that he could quickly dodge things. Meaning to her that she had to be tricky, not just fast. She took one more deep breath, then the flag dropped. She advanced first, just so she could see what she was up against. He blocked decently, but she managed to cut him a few times. He finally began to fight back, but not in passionate way, trying not look bad. She decided she was ready to end the fight, he couldn't challenge her skills. She quickly hit the butt of his sword, causing it to go flying in the air. He became so focused on trying to catch it that he didn't realize Gemma had a sword to his throat. She was not going to take her eyes off him, even for a second. His sword hit the ground behind Gemma, then he looked down and saw it. There was no way out, she had defeated him without him realizing it. He backed away admitting defeat. The judges came down to announce the winner. Nik entered when Lucy and Gerard went into the ring. They all gave her hugs and told her how proud they were of her. She smiled, but it wasn't like last time when she won. It wasn't a worthy victory for her, she felt like it was too easy. Nik whispered in her ear that he needed to speak with her privately in a moment. After the celebrating died down, Gemma had Gerard and Lucy come with her to go speak with Nik. Nik was standing outside of a tent, Gemma knew that meant one thing, Poseidon was there. She told Gerard and Lucy they could go, she would meet back up with them in a few moments. She walked in and gave Poseidon a hug, tears beginning to well up in her eyes.

"My Pearl, you were wonderful today. Why are you crying?" Poseidon said

"I'm just glad to see you is all. I had hoped you were watching when I saw Nik out there."

"I would have come yesterday too, but I did not know you were fighting."

Gemma laughed, "Neither did I until I walked into the ring."

"You mean you did not sign up?"

"No. I was supposed to judge this year, one of the girls dropped out so I took her place."

"Well I am glad you did, however your opponents this year were nowhere near your skill level. Were you holding back?" He asked.

Gemma sighed, "It was really hard to, but yes. Especially with the last fight, I felt bored. There was no challenge today."

"Well you just need to find someone who challenges you again."

"I'm training with someone three times a week now. She really challenges me."

"And who is this?"

"Callie, she owns the pub in town."

"Nik has told me about her, she would be a good match for you to fight." He smiled at Gemma, she tried to smile back, but he could tell it was fake. "What is wrong? You know I can tell when something is wrong."

"I don't know, I just can't seem to be happy anymore. I don't know what to do."

"Is this about Kelley?" He asked

Gemma nodded.

"Aquaria, this might be something that you can not get over. You just have to find a way to be somewhat satisfied. It will help."

"I can't even feel happy about my victories today. They just feel empty now."

"I can not help you with that. You need to find something that will give you a little joy in life. Thrive off of that little bit of joy. That is what I had to do."

"What worked for you?" She asked with a small tear rolling down her cheek.

"Keeping an eye on you. You are the most unique of all my children. You will change the world one day. I love you my little Pearl." He said.

Gemma tried to smile for him but it was no use he could still see how forced it was.

"I must go, it is almost time for you to go to the dance. Here, this is for you." He handed her a small wooden box. Pulled her in for one more hug, kissed her head then left out the back.

Gemma found Lucy and Gerard, they went to Gerard's house to get ready for the dance. They had already told Peggy that they would just stay there for the night. Gemma wore another black dress, this one had more fancy details to it, but still very simple and black.

"Gemma you know you can wear a color other than black." Lucy said.

"I don't want to. This is what I feel is right for me to wear right now." Gemma replied

"Alright."

Gemma had Lucy put her hair up, making sure that she used the hair comb that her father gave her last year. Then Gemma looked at the box he had just given her. She wanted to open it, but at the same time, she wasn't sure if now was the right time.

"Just open it." Lucy said

"What?"

"The box you have been staring at it the whole time I was doing your hair. Just open it. It's just a gift, probably something for you to wear tonight." Lucy said.

Gemma sighed and opened the box. Lucy was right, it was something to wear tonight. It was a golden armband with shells and a very small trident, not noticeable to the untrained eye. She put it on, it made her look a little more formal than before, but also made her feel like she was going to an event back under the sea.

"That's very pretty." Lucy said

"Thanks, I used to wear it to every event back home. I guess he figured I would want it back." Gemma replied.

"Your father really likes gold doesn't he?" Lucy asked.

Gemma laughed, "More than anything. Everything he gives me is made of gold."

"You know that's not a bad thing right?" Lucy laughed.

"I know. Do me a favor tonight. Don't send anyone to come dance with me. I'm fine with Gerard dancing with me occasionally, but I don't want a parade of boys asking me to dance." Gemma said.

"I won't, Gerard already told me how much it upset you. I'm sorry. I was just trying to help." Lucy replied.

"I know you were. I just wanted to make sure you didn't do it again." Gemma said

"I won't." Lucy said with a smile.

Once they were ready they went down stairs to get ready to leave. Gerard walked both girls into the dance. Once it seemed like no one else was going to be arriving, Henry presented Gemma with her award. Everyone cheered, she had a small smile on her face. After she received her award she went to spend time with the brothers of the club. They made her feel at home. Every single one agreed that there was no true competition for her this year. They told her stories of their pasts. A few of them had survived run-ins with pirates, while others spent a very short time aboard a pirate ship. All of them said, that she fights the way some of the best pirate's fight. She was meant to fight opponents like that, these boys were just children who would not last two minutes in a real fight. They made her feel good about herself. She had felt so terrible all day, just for the fact of how easy the fights were. She was wanting a real fight, something to challenge her.

Finn came up to her and asked her for a dance, she danced with him for a few songs. They talked the whole time. He would occasionally make her laugh a little bit. She had a real smile on her face, for the first time in months. He never once brought up Kelley, or her past, he only talked to her about things he noticed while watching the fights. It made her feel good to have someone to talk to. He never pulled her close, or tried to make a move. He just treated her as a friend, which is exactly what she needed right now. She couldn't handle anything else.

"So Molly wanted me to ask you when you can start training her." Finn said.

Gemma laughed, "Well she seems eager to start."

"After watching you fight today she is very excited to learn how to fight like you." Finn laughed.

"Well I have training three days a week. So I can train her on Tuesdays after she is done with school. Where did you train her?" She asked.

"In our barn, why?" He responded.

"Then we will meet there. Patrick won't like me training anyone at his house, so your place would be best."

"Alright, we can just walk back to my house after school."

"I will meet you outside of school. I don't go to school with all of you. Peggy teaches me at home. She says I don't really even need to have my lessons anymore, or at least not as often." She replied

"Oh, okay. Will you be allowed to ride over here by yourself?" He asked.

"It will be fine. I will make sure of it." She said with a smile.

"Thank you, for doing this for her. I have never been that good at fighting, so when she asked me, I tried to teach her the best I could.

After what you said yesterday, I want her to really know what she is doing."

"I will teach her to fight well. I want her to be safe." Gemma smiled at him, then left the dance floor. It was getting late, and she was ready to leave. She found Gerard and Lucy, they were both ready to leave as well. The dances were not as fun for Gemma without Kelley there. The three of them left and went back to Gerard's place for the night.

26

In the morning Gemma and Gerard left early, Lucy took her time and went to school at the normal time. Gerard had to get to work, and Gemma had to get to the pub before it opened. When she arrived at the pub she saw Callie moving some of the tables and chairs out of the way. She knocked on the door and Callie let her in.

"You're early today." Callie said

"We stayed at Gerard's house last night, it made more sense."

"Very well, you can help me get ready."

Gemma helped Callie set up the room for them to fight. Once they started to fight Gemma began feeling better. Callie really was the best teacher she could have asked for. She understood how Gemma should move her body, how to fight someone who is a lot bigger than her. She never went easy on Gemma. She wanted to be sure that Gemma was prepared for anything. Unfortunately, some things you can't prepare for, like your reflexes. She explained to Gemma that wearing her fighting gloves were the best thing she could do for her hands. If anyone cut her hand, no matter what her reflexes will drop the sword. They practiced for three hours, she helped Gemma become more swift than she already was. She gave her encouragement to not be afraid of anyone that challenges her. After they finished training Gemma helped her put everything back in place. It was much faster with the two of them, than just Callie.

"Gemma, I have a proposition for you."

"What is it?"

"How would you feel about working at the Pub with me on the days that we train? I could use the extra help and it will help you get experience standing up to the drunken scum that comes through that door."

"That sounds great. But would I have to stay till closing?"

"Of course not, you could leave at the same time that Gerard gets off work if that would make you feel better."

"That would make me feel better about the time I would get home. Please don't tell Patrick, if he finds out he will make sure I never get to even train with you."

"Don't worry I will take care of Patrick."

"Thanks Callie."

"Here come in back with me, I'll get you something more suited for work, and then teach you what to do when working."

She showed Gemma where everything was, and told her everything that she needed to know for working there. She warned her that the men that frequented 'there would try to be inappropriate with her. So she must keep her daggers on her at all times. She also warned her that if they try to get rough that she is more than welcome to use her dagger to get them to leave her alone. The laws of the town do not apply to Callie and her employees within the walls of the pub.

Gemma enjoyed working at the pub, it wasn't the best job in the world, but she loved doing something different with her time. She got to know all the men in town, and even the ones who would just be in town for the night. The ones who were just there for the night, were usually rougher than the locals. She had to throw a few daggers a day, and threaten a few for trying to be fresh with her. Practicing while working made her no longer afraid of being around this sort. She would get up early every morning that she had training and ride

Kelley's horse into town, train for a few hours, then work the rest of the day. Gerard always came and picked her up from work, he felt she would be safer if he picked her up.

On Tuesday's she would meet Finn and Molly at the school house, they would go back to Finn's barn and Gemma would teach Molly everything she knew. She could see that Molly really enjoyed learning to fight, she was a quick learner too. Molly followed every step that Gemma told her, she picked up everything easily. Finn would come watch from time to time, but for the most part, it was just Gemma teaching Molly. She had Molly fight Finn one day, and knew that Molly had gotten a lot better, she wasn't afraid to fight anymore either.

"I don't know how you did it!" Finn said

"Did what?"

"Get her to fight so well, so fast. She's really good now."

"Well that was kind of the point. I want her to be a good fighter. Not just for the ring, but for her own safety."

"Thank you for taking your time to teach her. I really appreciate it. I can't fight as good as either of you." Finn said with a smile.

"I enjoy teaching her, she's a quick learner. I just hope she is enjoying it as much as I do."

"She loves it. All she talks about at dinner is her fighting lessons. My mum hates it, but my Da' thinks it's great that one of us wants to fight." He lightly chuckled.

"Well my father loves that I fight too, Patrick on the other hand hates that I fight, and constantly argues with me about it." She said as she rolled her eyes. "Luckily what my father says goes, no one can argue what he says."

"What does your mum think?" Finn asked.

"Ummm... She died right before I came here." She said quietly. "It's part of the reason I was sent to live with the O'Reilly's. I know she would have loved it though. She used to fight back home."

"I'm sorry, I didn't know." Finn felt embarrassed for saying anything, he watched Gemma's face and remembered he shouldn't ask about her family.

"It's alright, not many people know about my past, I try to keep it that way." She said quietly.

"I won't ask again."

"Thank you." She paused for a moment, looked outside, it was getting dark. "I should get going, Peggy will be upset if I'm late for dinner again. She doesn't like it when I ride home alone in the dark."

"I could take you home if you like." Finn suggested.

"No, it's alright. I might call her and just stay at Gerard's tonight, I have to be back in town early in the morning anyways."

"Why do you have to be back so early?" He asked.

"I have training, then work right after that."

"I didn't know you worked in town. Where do you work at?" He asked.

"I work at the pub, Callie trains me, then I work the rest of the day." She replied.

"I can't picture you working at the pub." He laughed.

"I actually really enjoy it."

"Aren't you afraid of men that go in there?"

"I was at first, but I've gotten used to it. I can stand up for myself, and I'm not afraid to prove it to them."

"You are very different from the girls from here." He said taking a step closer to her.

Gemma laughed, "Well that's a good thing, especially since I'm not from around here. Shows you that people all around the world are different."

"I've never thought of it like that. I have never been away from here before."

"Well one day, you should get away. See somewhere besides this place, it would be good for you." She said with a smile.

"I might do that one day." He took another step closer to her, her smile made his heart race. He so badly wanted to make a move on her, but knew she was not ready for that yet.

"I really should go." Gemma gathered her things and put them in the bag that was on the back of her horse.

"Have you ever thought of a car?" He asked.

"What?"

"A car, it would be a lot easier for taking things to and from places. It might actually feel a little safer going places at night."

"I couldn't imagine getting one for myself." She replied, feeling a bit embarrassed.

"We have one, I could take you for a ride in it sometime. Maybe next Tuesday, I could just pick you up from your house and then drive you home." He suggested.

"That might be nice, but you won't want to do that if Patrick is home. He wouldn't approve."

"Well I will talk to you about it later this week, see if you want me to pick you up."

"Alright, we will talk later."

Gemma climbed on the horse and took off to Gerard's house. They told her she could stay the night, so she called and let Peggy know that she would not be coming home. Peggy told her that it was no problem, to just come home tomorrow night after work and bring Gerard with her. Gemma agreed, she ate dinner with Gerard's family, then went to bed. His family was always extremely accommodating to her. They didn't know everything about her, but they knew that she was a close friend of their son, so they trusted her.

27

Gerard and Gemma left at the same time the next morning. She showed up to train with Callie, but Callie had just left a note on the door for her.

Gemma,

Come on in, something came up late last night. Open up at regular time, I will try to be back in time for you to get off of work. If I am not, kick everyone out and lock up.

Callie

Gemma just shrugged and went and practiced on her own. She looked at the time and it was another hour until opening. She put everything back in its place and then changed. She still had a decent amount of time until opening so she went to the Market to talk to Gerard for a moment.

"Gemma, what are you doing here? Shouldn't you be getting ready to start work?" Gerard asked.

"I am, I just needed to ask you if you could do me a favor." She said.

"Sure what is it?" He asked.

"I don't know if Callie will be back at all today, so I won't be able to get lunch today. Do you think you could bring me something on your break?" She handed him a couple pieces of copper for her lunch.

"Of course, but it won't be for a few more hours."

"I know, I just don't know if I will be able to get out to get anything."

"Don't worry I'll bring you something."

"Thanks! I will see you a little later."

Gemma went back to the pub and opened it up. A few of the regulars came in right away. They were the ones that were always nice to her, not the ones who would cause problems. Then right around lunch time a big group of men came in, they were from one of the merchant ships that just came into port. They were rowdy and constantly trying to be inappropriate towards her. She just brushed it off for the most part, trying to ignore all of them. She was cleaning up one of the tables when Gerard came in. She brought him a drink so they could have lunch together. Some of the men were yelling obscene things at her in front of Gerard. He clenched his fist, getting ready to start a fight with them.

"Don't." She said simply.

"Gemma you shouldn't take them talking to you that way!"

"I can handle myself, besides if all they're doing is talking it's nothing. It's when they try to grab at me, that's when I pull out my dagger and kick them out." She said as she continued to eat.

"Kelley would have hated you working here. I can get you a job at the market if you really want to work. You don't have to work in a place like this."

"It doesn't bother me. I enjoy working with Callie. It's not always like this, just when the degenerate scum come into port. Friday is usually our bad day, that's when we usually get one of the pirate ships into port. Besides, if Kelley was here I wouldn't be working here. But he isn't and this is something that makes me feel better."

"I don't feel good about you working here."

"It's not up to you though. This is for me." She was starting to get irritated.

"Alright, but I still don't like it."

"You don't have to like it, just be here for me when I need you. Anyways, I was thinking about going to the Lagoon this weekend, would you and Lucy want to come with me?"

"Sure, but what about Patrick and Peggy?" He asked.

"Peggy can come if she wants, but I'm going whether they want me to or not. I need to go back there for a couple of days."

"Alright, we will go. I'll leave work a little early Friday, we can leave as soon as Lucy is done with class."

"Sounds great." A small fight began to break out. Gemma sighed, "I have to get back to work. Come get me when you get off today, okay?"

"Alright, do you want some help before I leave though?"

"No I got this." She said with a little smile.

Gemma got up and pulled a dagger from her boot and threw it at the men fighting. It glided through the air, right into the middle of the fight. Landing into one of the men's fist that was just about to throw a punch. The man groaned in agony. Everyone froze and saw Gemma coming at them with her sword and another dagger.

"You're all cut off! Get out before I start to slice each of you, limb from limb." She shouted in a voice that Gerard had never heard come out of her before. It was commanding and regal. Definitely something she inherited from her father. The men quickly left money on the table and left.

"I guess you can take care of yourself here." He laughed.

"I told you, I can handle it." She smiled

"Well if you need anything, you know where to find me."

"I know. Thank you for lunch. I'll see you this evening."

That evening when Gerard and Gemma rode back to the O'Reilly's house they got there just in time for dinner. Before going in Gemma had to remind Gerard not to say anything about where she worked. Patrick still didn't know, and they were all trying to keep it that way. At dinner Gemma told Peggy that she wanted to go to the Lagoon this weekend. Patrick told her she couldn't go alone, and that Peggy had things to do this weekend. Gerard interjected that he would go with them so they wouldn't be alone. Gerard knew how much Gemma desperately needed to go to the lagoon this weekend. She needed to escape from all of this.

After dinner Patrick left for the pub, like he did every night. He didn't return home until morning still drunk, and shouting through the house. Gemma quickly put a chair in front of her door and hid under her desk. She knew she could fight him, and beat him, but she didn't want to risk Peggy and Lucy being upset with her for killing him. Patrick was pounding on her door, screaming at her through the door. She could hear Peggy yelling at him to leave her alone, and to just go to bed. He didn't listen, he kicked, and pushed on the door until he was able to get it open. She started to shake while under her desk, clinging tight to one of her daggers. He pulled her out from under her desk by her hair. Once she was out from under the desk he let go of her hair squeezing her arm tight. Screaming at her about how everything was her fault. She tried to pull herself away from him, but his grip on her arm was too tight. She remembered what Callie had told her about reflexes, so she cut his hand with her dagger. He instantly let go of her, she started to run, but he caught her. He balled his hand into a fist and hit her right in the eye. She fell to the ground, and didn't move. He didn't knock her out, but she knew if she pretended that he did, he would walk away. He kicked her and yelled at her for not getting up and fighting, but she didn't move. Gerard came running in, Patrick tried to fight Gerard as well. Gerard gave Patrick a bloody nose and shouted at him.

"Get out and sober up! Or so help me I'll find Poseidon myself and tell him what you did!" Gerard shouted.

Patrick just glared at him, "You wouldn't dare."

"Try me." Gerard was now clutching a dagger, ready to fight back if necessary. Patrick stormed out of the house and took off on a horse.

"Gemma are you okay?" Gerard asked

Gemma sat up and looked at him, she had tears in her eyes.

"Gemma, we have to tell your father, he needs to know what's going on. This is two days in a row that you have been beaten by Patrick. Your father needs to know what's happening to you." He looked at her face, her eye was already starting to swell, and Patrick's hand print gripping her arm. He tried to touch her face to see how bad her eye really was.

She groaned as his fingers lightly grazed her swollen eye.

"Sorry, come on, let's get you down stairs and put something on that."

"I'll be fine, don't worry about me." She placed her hand over her eye. A blue light glowed beneath her hand, when she moved her hand from her eye, it looked as if nothing had happened.

"Just because you can heal yourself, doesn't mean you should put up with this." He snapped as he helped her up.

"If we tell my father, he will punish him, and might punish Lucy and Peggy as well. I can't let anything happen to the two of them. They always try to protect me. Anyways, what are you doing here so early?"

"I was leaving the house for work, when I saw Patrick leaving the pub. He was stumbling all over the place and yelling at everyone. So I ran to the stables to get my horse, and rushed over here to try to help you. You have to know Poseidon won't punish Peggy and Lucy for this. If you just tell Nik what is going on, he will make sure nothing happens to them. You know he would be sure of that."

"Well I'm fine, but thank you. I should go check on Peggy, she probably has a few bruises that she would like for me to make disappear for her. You need to check on Lucy, she is probably hiding in her room right now."

"I will go check on her, but I'm serious you need to at least tell Nik. Maybe he can find somewhere else for you to stay besides here. You're not safe here anymore. Or just come stay at my house."

"I will be fine, now go check on Lucy."

Gerard went to make sure Lucy was alright, she was hiding in her wardrobe crying. He wrapped her in his arms and held her until she calmed down. He packed bags for both girls, with enough clothes for them to stay at his house, and at the lagoon. When he made it down stairs, Gemma had just finished healing Peggy. Peggy was crying and upset, she felt terrible for what Gemma was going through, but didn't know what to do besides send her somewhere else that would be safe.

"Gemma, pack some extra clothes. We are going to keep some of your clothes at my house, so whenever you stay with us you will already have clothes there. Lucy please do the same. I want you both to be safe." Gerard said in a firm voice.

Both girls ran upstairs and packed some more clothes, Gemma

packed almost all of her clothes, she grabbed everything that reminded her of Kelley, and a decent amount of her weapons. She hid a few daggers around the room, so she had something for when she was there.

28

Gemma had a rough rest of the day at the pub, so Callie told her to go home early. She began walking down the street to stop at the market where Gerard worked. She needed to ask him if she could stay at his parent's house until he got off work. There were so many pirates in town that day, she hadn't seen this many pirates in town in one day in a long time. There were apparently 5 pirate ships that came in that day. Something about a meeting with the captains and the town leaders. She knew that meant her father probably sent Nik in his place. She kept her head down and continued to walk down the street. Some would make crude comments at her, others would bump into her and yell at her for being in the way.

She was almost to the market when she was grabbed from behind and pulled into an alley. She quickly grabbed her dagger and stabbed the man in his left shoulder. She tried to run but he grabbed her again and threw her against the wall. She kicked him, and tried to slice his throat with her dagger, but he grabbed on to her wrist and twisted it until he heard the snap of her wrist breaking. She screamed but didn't stop trying to get free. Everything she tried he would just hurt her more. She tried to see his face but he kept it covered. He held her throat tight as he tried to stop her breathing enough for her to stop struggling. She begged him to stop but he wouldn't. She tried to use her other hand to fight her way out, but he just turned her around pressing her face hard against the wall, twisting her other arm behind her back. He took the dagger that she had tried to use to defend herself, and slowly pressing it into her ribs. As she screamed she accidentally let out one of her bursts, this time it was blue. The man didn't notice that the burst exploded from her. The rain was starting to really come down, but the alley was covered so she wasn't going to change from the rain. He slapped her for screaming and pushed her head into the wall even harder.

"Shut up! Your brother didn't tell me it would be this hard to kill you." He snarled.

After a few more moments of her screaming for help, someone finally showed up. He pulled the man off of her and punched him in the face. He pulled out a sword and tried to fight the man. The man saw her rescuers face and quickly ran in the opposite direction. Gemma had dropped to the ground and held her side. When her rescuer came to save her, the other man pushed the dagger in deep. He looked over at her saw all the blood covering her. She looked up at him, he was soaking wet from the rain, water dripping from his light brown hair. They didn't say anything to one another. She just looked into his dark blue eyes, and knew he wasn't going to hurt her. He picked her up in his arms, and carried her to Callie's pub. She curled up in his arms, feeling terrified but relieved that someone was there to save her. The rain had stopped thankfully so she didn't have to worry about turning. She was becoming weak from all the blood she was losing. Having a hard time staying awake, she was nearly unconscious. She knew needed to get somewhere alone to heal herself. When they got to Callie's he took her towards the back room so she could rest in there while he got Callie.

"Thank you for saving me." She said as she gently kissed his cheek. Then ran into the room locking the door. He lightly touched his cheek, it tingled from the magic within her kiss. She began healing herself quickly. She didn't know how much time she had left with all the blood she was losing. Once she healed her side she began healing her wrist and everything else. She made sure to keep some bandages on her wounds so no one would ask questions. She wrapped her wrist up, to appear as if it was still injured. Then there was a knock on the door.

"Gemma let me in." Callie said

"Hold on." She said, she finished wrapping her wrist then opened the door.

Callie froze, eyes wide, horrified at the sight of her injuries. Gemma didn't get a chance to heal her face yet. She had a busted lip, and her faced was scratched and bruising from being pushed against the rough stone wall multiple times. Her eye had begun to swell. She healed most of the cut on her neck, leaving just enough to show a cut of some kind.

"Gemma what happened?"

"I was attacked again." She said flatly. "This man beat me, stabbed me, hurt my wrist. I tried to escape but I couldn't get away."

"Well thankfully Jamison brought you here. He is out searching for the man now." Callie said, "Would you like me to call Peggy or Patrick to come get you?"

"No!" She said in a frantic shaky voice. "Can you just call the market or the bank instead? Have Gerard or William come get me? I don't want to know what Patrick would do to me if he finds out."

"Why would Patrick do anything to you for being attacked?" Callie cocked an eyebrow at her.

"Don't worry about it. You wouldn't understand. No one would." She said looking at her wrist.

"Gemma what's going on? You haven't been this upset in a long time. Is something going on with Patrick?" Callie asked in the most caring voice she could.

"Really, I'll be fine. You have no need to worry about it. Just call Gerard or William. They will come get me, and take me back to their house."

"I will call them. But you know you can tell me anything that is going on. I will help you in any way that I can."

"I know. Thank you. I need you to teach me how to fight off someone that would attack me like that. I need to be able to escape from that."

"We will work on that next week. We won't let this happen to you again. Do you understand?"

"Thanks Callie. And can you thank the man who saved me?"

"You mean Jamison?" Callie asked

"If that is who brought me in here then yes. He is the one who saved me."

"Alright I will thank him as soon as he comes back in here. I've never seen him act like this before. You must have left quite an impression on him."

"I didn't do anything to try to leave an impression on him."

"Well something about you made him want to go after whoever did this to you."

Gemma sat there thinking about what had happened and realized that she released a blue burst. All she could think is that he might have been affected by it and that is why he was acting differently. She knew she had to see him, just to get him out of the trance. Callie came back into the room and gave her some clean clothes and a hat so she could use it to cover her face if she needed. She told Gemma that Gerard would be there in a few minutes to take her home. Gemma began to change her clothes as soon as Callie left the room.

Gerard came into the room and quickly got her out of there. She saw Jamison, he was sitting with a drink close to the room she was in. Making sure that he was facing it to be able to see her when she left. She walked up to him, gave him a hug, and discretely waved her hand as if gently pulling something from him. She saw a faint blue sparkle come from him as she pulled it from him. Confirming that he was under the spell of her blue burst. She let go of him and thanked him again then left with Gerard. Gerard rushed her back to his house and took her upstairs to the bathroom, so she could heal herself fully before he took her home. He left her alone for a few minutes to change. She looked at herself in the mirror and saw all the damage the man had done to her. She quickly washed off as much of the blood off of her as she could. Crying and frantically trying to remove any feeling of him. She healed her face and looked fine, even though she felt anything but fine. She finished getting dressed and just sat on the floor and cried. Gerard knocked on the door when he heard her crying.

"Gemma? Can I come in so we can talk?" He said. She got up and opened the door and let him in. She broke down and cried into his chest. He hugged her and let her just cry it out.

"Gemma, what happened?"

"I don't want to talk about it. Please." She cried

"Alright we don't have to talk about it. Just tell me one thing, was this Patrick that did this?"

"No, not this time." She cried.

She continued to cry for a while, then Shannon came upstairs after hearing Gemma crying.

"Gemma? Why are you crying dear?" She asked

"She doesn't want to talk about it mum. She won't even tell me."

"Come here my dear." Shannon said wrapping her arms around her. "Let's get you a warm drink. You can curl up on the sofa while I make it for you."

Gemma nodded and followed her back downstairs. She curled up on the sofa, Gerard brought her a blanket and she wrapped herself up in it. Shannon brought her a warm drink. Gemma looked down at it, it wasn't tea, it was something else. It smelled wonderful.

"What is it?" She asked as her voice cracked from crying and screaming so much that day.

"It's called hot chocolate. Whenever any of us have a really bad day, I make it to make your day a tiny bit better." Shannon said with a smile

"It's really good, and always makes me feel better." Gerard said smiling at her.

"Thank you." She said as she took a sip. "It's delicious."

"Well I hope it makes you feel even the tiniest bit better." Shannon said. She gave Gemma a hug then went back into the kitchen to make a cup for herself and Gerard.

"Gemma, you can tell me what happened whenever you feel ready, alright?" He said

"Alright. I don't know if I will ever feel ready to tell anyone about what happened today." She said as a tear rolled down her cheek. "I really need Kelley right now." She said as she wiped the tear away.

"I know. I'm sorry that I can't get him for you. I would try to get Lux but she always thinks it's a game when I try to catch her."

"Don't worry about it. Even he wouldn't be able to fix this, but I would at least feel better knowing that he is here. And she does that because she has his soul. So she thinks she's playing with her best friend."

"I know."

"Would you two like some cookies as well?" Shannon asked as she handed Gerard his cup of cocoa.

"Thanks mum."

"Thank you Shannon."

"Gemma, you are more than welcome to stay here tonight or any night you want. I know things have been hard over there. You never have to ask, just come over." She said handing Gemma a key.

"What's this?" She asked

"It's a key to the house. You can now get in anytime you need. We won't ask questions. Just know you are always safe here." Shannon said. "We love you and want to keep you safe."

Gemma wiped another tear from her eye. "Thank you. This means a lot to me." She gave Shannon another hug.

"Well you are the closest thing to a daughter I will get, besides Lucy. But I don't have to worry about you running off to be alone with him." She teased.

Gemma giggled as Gerard started to blush. "Mum. Stop it, Lucy and I are engaged. It doesn't matter anymore."

"Oh sweetie, I'm just teasing you. You know how much we love Lucy and can't wait for her to be part of this family."

The three of them continued to sit in the living room chatting, trying to make Gemma feel better. Also knowing not to try to question her about what had happened. The last thing they wanted was to upset her again. They knew something horrible must have happened with how much she was crying. This wasn't like when he would save her from Patrick, this was something much worse. He wanted to ask her but knew she wouldn't tell him right now, if ever.

29

It had been a rough week at the pub, everyday there were more and more fights breaking out. Gemma was beginning to get exhausted from dealing with it everyday, she just wanted to make them all stop and act civilized. One afternoon Nik showed up early for poker night. Callie took him and another man, that came in with the crew, into the back room, then suddenly all the liquor was instantly locked up. Chaos broke out, she tried throwing daggers, but they didn't pay any attention. She tried getting between some of them and fighting them off, but there were too many of them for her alone. A few of them grabbed her and she tried to get away, but that just made them more rough with her. She stabbed a few with her dagger, just to get them to leave her alone. This was a particularly rowdy crew, and the usual tactics were not going to work on them. She knew she had only one option left, she had to sing. Singing is what sirens were known for, dragging men to their deaths by the mere sound of their voice. She hated the possibility of revealing her identity, but she was out of options. She took a deep breath and climbed on top of the bar. Then she began to sing a song she had been taught from a very young age. The one that could stop all humans in their tracks and do her bidding.

"You've been out to sea for far too long,
and now it's time you hear my song.
The land has missed you tearfully,
now you're stuck here fearfully.
Follow me into the depths below,
I'll take you where the mermaids go.
You'll try your best to hold your breath,
but soon you'll find you need some rest.
So follow me into the deep blue sea,
I'll show you where you're meant to be.
Don't try to fight it,
you're already in too deep,
you can't escape you're here for me to keep."

All of the men had stopped, completely stuck in a trance. Her voice sounded like the heavens were singing to them. None of them had heard anything like it before. Once they all were stuck in a trance, she began to walk around while singing. Convincing them to sit down quietly. Then suddenly she was grabbed and dragged into the corner of the room. She turned around, it was Nik.

"What in the underworld do you think you are doing?" He shouted.

"I needed to stop the fighting. It was the worst fight I've ever seen in here. I was doing everything I could to stop it, but nothing was working."

"Do you realize how reckless you are being?" He growled at her. "People could figure out who you are, you are exposing yourself."

"It'll be fine. They won't even remember anything. I don't see why this was such a big deal."

"If anyone else had seen you, they would have known. Putting you in danger!"

"What else was I supposed to do? I tried to stop the fighting, I was fighting them off and they wouldn't stop."

"Did any of them hurt you?"

Gemma looked at her arm, and saw that she was bleeding. She pressed her hand on her arm firmly to heal it. "I'll be fine."

"You working here is reckless and dangerous, you are constantly exposing yourself by working here. Someone will find out who you are. How do you think Kelley would have felt about you working here?"

"Why does everyone keep saying that to me? It doesn't matter how Kelley would have felt. He's gone! I have to live my life the best I can without him!"

"Gemma, its more than just you working here. It's the running off on your own, staying out late every night, the not coming home at night. You are out of control!"

"Out of control?" Gemma gave a dark chuckle as she leaned back in the chair, crossing her arms firmly against her chest. "You call that out of control? I promise you haven't seen reckless yet. When I do decide to lose control, the entire ocean will feel it."

"You have to stop this now! No one has any idea where you are. How is Patrick supposed to protect you if he doesn't know where you are?"

"Tsk. Like he actually protects me." She rolled her eyes. She would have better protection from the scum in the pub than Patrick. "I let Peggy know where I'm at, at all times. Gerard walks me to and from the pub every day. When I don't go home, I'm at Gerard's house and Peggy knows I'm there. I run off on my own because I can't sit and wait all day for people to take me places. I'll be 20 next week, I think I should start being allowed to be in control of my life a little."

"Why is Patrick not informed of any of this? He didn't even know you were working here."

"Patrick doesn't even know what day it is! He's been drunk since that day and wouldn't even be able to tell you that it's been months since then. Peggy and I communicate everything to one another. So if there are any problems, talk to her. She knows everything going on at all times. I'm not out of control, for the first time in my life I'm in complete control of myself! I know what I'm doing at all times, and I own up to all of my decisions. Don't ever say that I'm out of control again!"

Gemma was angry, but her hair didn't change from black. Then a small red energy burst exploded from her, all the pirates in the room became angry again. This time instead of fighting each other they all got up and started walking towards them.

"Gemma, calm down. You just sent out an energy burst." He whispered.

Gemma looked around and saw the angry pirates approaching them, all glaring at Nik. Gemma relaxed, then waved her arm in a swift motion. As if waving them away. There was a red sparkle that floated up from all of them to the ceiling. They all snapped out of it and went back to what they were doing before.

"This is what I'm talking about. You lost control and look what happened."

"And I took care of it with ease. I'm in control, stop questioning it."

"Are you even listening to what I'm saying?"

Gemma took a deep breath, trying to control her emotions. "I understand you, but are you listening to what I'm saying? I have been taking care of myself just fine. No one can help me with any of this. This is something I have to learn to do on my own. And you telling me that I'm out of control is making things more difficult for me. Can you just trust that I know what I'm doing?"

"What about this boy's house you go to every week? He picks you up and drives you home very late. You think that is controlling yourself? What if he finds out who you are? What happens if it rains?"

"I'm just teaching his little sister how to fight, he didn't feel it was safe for me to ride a horse home so late at night by myself. I told him I was fine, but he insisted, and so did his father. Gerard knows when I'm there, and lives just down the street from Finn. When it rains he comes right over to get me."

Gemma had never seen him so upset with her before. She didn't understand why he was acting like this towards her this time.

"Damn it Nik! I'm almost 20, the same age Kelley was when he was shipped off. If I was home I would've been treated as an adult two years ago! I'd be on my own like Astrid is, who is also working in a pub doing exactly what I just did. You've known that I work here for months. What's so different about today? Who was that with you and Callie earlier? You were fine until he came in."

"He works for your fiancé. And what you did, what he saw, is reckless. If he takes this back to the captain, he could tell your father. And you know how he feels about you using your powers around humans while in hiding."

Gemma stood in shock. "My fiancé is here… at port… right now?"

"Yes, his whole crew was who you just put under a trance... twice now."

Gemma ran out of the Pub. Nik chased after her and grabbed her arm and pulled her back before she reached the street.

"Don't even think about it!" He growled.

"Think about what?" She snapped.

"You know what. You can't go find out who it is. You cannot go to that ship."

"You want to bet?" She said pulling her arm away from him.

30

She took off down the street, colliding with a sturdy figure as she looked over her shoulder. Strong arms caught her before she hit the ground, Nik ran over to her, picked her up, and tossed her over his shoulder.

"Gemma? What are you doing?" Finn asked

Gemma looked over Nik's shoulder. "Finn? What are you doing here?"

"I was coming to see if you were alright. I knew a pirate ship came in today, and wanted to make sure you were okay. Why is this man carrying you?"

"Nikoli put me down." She ordered.

"Are you going to go where you were trying to go before?"

"No, I will not." Gemma sighed.

"Fine. I'm staying here to make sure you don't run off again."

"Gemma what's going on? Who is this guy?" Finn asked

"This is Nik, he's... let's just call him my uncle. He's just trying to stop me from doing something reckless, as he would put it." She rolled her eyes.

Finn pulled Gemma to the side a bit, and spoke quietly, "Are you okay? Do you need me to help you get away?"

"I'm fine, really. He's just looking out for me."

"Are you sure?"

Gemma looked over at Nik, he still had a scowl on his face. "Yeah, I'm sure. It's nothing to worry about. I should get back to work. I will see you later."

Finn glared at Nik, not trusting him. "I'll come with you."

"Thanks, but I'll be fine."

"I don't trust this guy, please let me walk you back to Callie." He whispered to her.

"Trust me, he's not the problem, I am. He was just looking out for me. Nik, is a good guy. He really is just looking out for my best interest."

"Are you sure you don't want me to walk you back?"

"I'm sure. Nik and I need to talk about some stuff in private. I will see you on Tuesday."

"Okay, but if you need anything, I'm here for you."

"Thanks Finn."

Gemma and Nik walked back to the pub. Finn didn't take his eyes off Gemma for a second. They walked back into the pub, and sat at a table in the corner of the room. Some of the crew had already left the pub, while others were finishing their drinks.

"Gemma don't try to find out anything about your future husband. Don't you trust me at all?"

"Of course I trust you Nik. You are one of the few that I completely trust, you know this."

"Then trust me when I tell you not to do something. I'm just looking out for you. We can't risk people finding out who you are. You will be in danger if they do."

"Why am I in so much danger? What's going on?"

"Things back home are not going well. Some things have happened, all you need to know is that being at the O'Reilly's and the lagoon are the safest places for you to be. As long as you don't blow your cover."

"What happened?"

"There have been whispers of a possible war starting."

"But isn't that why I'm here? Because this marriage will stop a war?"

"Yes, but this is one we didn't see coming, this is different. I want to tell you more, but right now…. I can't." Nik looked around the room, then back at Gemma, "It's not safe. There are very few places that are safe to talk about this."

"I don't understand."

"It's better that you don't know, the less you know the safer you are."

"Nik, is my father in danger too?"

"He's immortal, he will be fine. You are the one everyone is worried about."

"Why is everyone so worried about me? I can take care of myself. I obviously know how to protect myself. And oh that's right, I'm also immortal."

"It's your identity we are worried about. We just want to keep you safe. We care about you, stop pushing away all of those that care about you. I have been your personal guard since the day you were born. Your mother personally picked me to protect you, and I will continue to do so until the day I die. If you keep acting like this, you are just going to be making my job harder."

Gemma sat back in her chair, she folded her arms, she was irritated with him. She knew he was right, but she was still irritated. "Why did my mother choose you to protect me? What was her reasoning? I'm not trying to be rude, you know I love you, you're like my family. But how did she choose you?"

"I gained their trust. Ranked up fast. Have a special ability not even your father has. That's how. Please be careful. And don't sing. You and I both know that you can put someone in a trance just by speaking. Sometimes just by touch. You know better than to sing that song around humans in a crowded place."

"I won't sing that song again, unless it's an emergency."

"You're lucky that they don't remember anything."

"No one ever remembers anything after one of my trances."

"You could have completely blown your cover. Then we would have had to move all of you away from here."

"Is that such a bad thing? Why can't I just live at the lagoon?"

Nik sat there wide eyed, he didn't say anything.

"So there is no reason why I can't just live there?"

"We can't just uproot the O'Reilly's, and you are supposed to be staying with them, for protection."

"I've been protecting myself since Kelley left. Patrick and I haven't had a conversation that didn't end in a fight since then. It's been six months since he died, and I've been protecting myself that whole time."

"You can't be there by yourself for a year."

"What about if during the weekends, Lucy comes and stays with me? Like I said Patrick and I don't speak. It's as if we are in completely different houses anyways. Can I please go there, so I can be somewhat happy?"

"How about this, I will talk to your father, and maybe we can figure something out where you spend a week there and then a week here. This way you can still get your training here that you enjoy so much, and you can spend some time with Peggy, Lucy and Gerard."

"Thank you Nik!" She said giving him a hug.

"I said I would talk to him about it, that doesn't mean he will agree. I will let you know next week. Alright?"

"Alright!" She was smiling, happy that she might have a chance to spend more time there.

"Anyways, shouldn't you be here helping Lucy plan her wedding?" He asked

"She isn't letting anyone help her. She said once she has figured out the grand idea in her head, then she will let Peggy and I help her execute it. But until then, she won't let anyone know what she is even thinking."

"Well, go get back to work. I'll talk to your father tomorrow. I will let you know what he says next week. If he is okay with it, you also have to talk to Callie about it. She might not be too happy about you only working every other week. Don't stay late tonight, it's poker night, that means Patrick will be here soon."

"I understand. Thank you!" Gemma got up, gave him another hug then went back to work.

31

She sat knees pressed against her chest, rocking herself on her blood soaked bed. Unsure if she truly wanted him to wake up or not. Sure, if he didn't wake up, she wouldn't have to endure this torture any longer, but he was Kelley and Lucy's father. The bastard who was supposed to protect her until her wedding. And now? He's lying face down in a pool of his own blood. There was a possibility that he would live if she didn't heal him. It was slim, but still possible. She didn't know what to do now. After what he just did to her, he didn't deserve to live. *Sharks.* Kelley would have killed him without a moment of hesitation if he saw. Then why is she so damn worried about him not dying? Why doesn't she just let him die?

She looked down at her torn, bloody nightgown. Her hands trembled as she thought about what to do. She wished more than anything that Kelley was there. He would at least understand and not hate her for what she did to save herself. She had to do it. She had no other choice by this point. She was still having issues with her magic. Ever since Kelley's death she couldn't get it to work when she was scared. By the time she had gotten the knife out of his hand, the blade was at her throat, and he had almost climaxed.

"Curses. I have to save your degenerative life. You should be happy I don't tell my father what you just did to me."

She slowly and carefully crawled off her bed. Placed her hand on the deep wound on his neck and watched the glow under her hand. Of course, now her magic was working when trying to save the life of this degenerate piece of sea scum. Where was her magic while she was trying to save herself? As soon as the glow was gone, he began to wake. It wasn't fully healed, but he would live. She grabbed a thick book that was sitting on her bedside table. Bashing him in the right temple, knocking him out again. She dropped the book on his head, running out of her room. Leaving a trail of bloody footprints. She ran downstairs and outside to the stables. She grabbed Kelley's horse and took off to Gerard's. Screw leaving a note for anyone, or even grabbing her jacket. This was life or death now. And she wasn't going to risk her life for the likes of Patrick.

She put Kelley's horse in their stables and ran to the front door. Pounding as hard and as fast as she could, trying to keep the tears at bay. She couldn't risk crying outside and turning. William answered the door. She had never seen such a horrified look on anyone's face before. What did she expect his reaction to be though? Here she was at 2 am standing in a blood soaked, torn to pieces nightgown, which by this point, she might as well have worn nothing at all. Gerard came running to the door, but his expression was pure rage. He was ready to take off and finish what she started. They pulled her inside quickly. Wrapping a warm blanket around her.

"Is he alive?"

"Gerard. What kind of a question is that?"

He ignored his father's question. He held her shoulders and looked deep in her eyes. He needed to know if Patrick was alive or dead. She began to cry, unable to speak. He headed for the door to finish what she started, but was stopped by her cold bloody hand grabbing his wrist.

"She would never forgive us."

He looked back at her tear-filled eyes. He knew she was right. Lucy would never forgive either of them if they killed Patrick, no matter what the reason.

"If anyone is going to kill him, it will be me. I could never live with myself if I was the reason for Lucy to not love you. Just leave it be."

"Gemma. I need you to tell me what happened. Exactly."

Sharks. William was in his town leader distinguished persona. He had never done that before. She looked at him but dropped her head in her hands as she cried harder. He walked to their telephone and started making some calls. Sharks. She knew he was calling the other town leaders to his house immediately.

"Gemma, what happened?" Gerard whispered.

"Something Kelley would have killed him for." She looked at her nightgown. It was obvious what happened. She wrapped the blanket around her tighter. She wanted to wash everything off her. The feeling of his hands on her skin. Clenched tightly around her throat. She felt sick thinking of the rest. "I can't tell them. If Morgan tells my father... I can't. She would never forgive me."

"Patrick doesn't deserve to live after what he just did. You should have let him die."

"You know why I couldn't."

"Did he... finish?"

"No."

"Are you sure?"

"Positive. I stabbed him in the neck before he had a chance to."

William finally came back to them. She had never seen him so upset before. They waited silently for the others to arrive. William didn't say anything about them coming, but they knew. Shannon was thankfully asleep. She would be screaming in terror at the sight before her. William stepped out of the room to make Gemma some tea. Gerard wrapped his arms around her, hugging her as she cried into his shoulder.

"Is Lucy..."

"She was still asleep. Everyone was asleep."

"You can't stay there. You need to stay here with us. At least for a few days."

"Can we not tell my father?"

"No. He needs to know."

"But what if he blames Peggy and Lucy too? What if they get punished as well?"

"He would never blame them for this. You need to tell him."

"What if you're wrong? What if he does? Could you live with yourself knowing that us telling him is the reason she's tortured the rest of her life? Cause I know I can't live with that."

There was a knock on the door. She jumped. Her heart wouldn't slow down. Gerard began looking at her closer. There were cuts under all the blood she was covered in. He did a number on her this time. Enough that the town leaders would insist on the doctor seeing her. He whispered in her ear to heal some of the cuts, especially the deep ones, before they noticed. She quickly began healing herself as the town leaders entered the room.

She had never been one on one with Morgan and Rackem, but she knew by the looks on their faces, that they had the same thought as Gerard.

"Someone get Nikoli here now." Morgan said. "He'll lose his shit if he finds out this happened to his niece and we didn't tell him."

William ran to his phone and called Callie to contact Nik immediately, telling him it was an emergency.

"Niece? Nik isn't my uncle? And how did you know his name was Nikoli?" They didn't hear her, or they chose not to listen, or quite possibly… she only spoke in her head. She wasn't sure at this point.

"Her father will kill us all if he finds out we didn't keep her safe from this. I would rather not deal with his wrath again." Rackem replied.

"My father?"

"He will lose his mind if he finds out. Dealing with Nikoli is one thing, but her father… the whole town will be feeling those repercussions." Henry said.

William walked back into the room. "He'll be here shortly. An emergency message was sent to Atlantis. He should be here in about 10 minutes."

They were standing talking quickly to one another about what to do. Completely ignoring everything she was saying, which pissed her off. She didn't know that the words weren't actually coming out of her mouth. She stood up and turned towards them. The ground began to quake beneath their feet. She dropped the blanket so they could see exactly what they were dealing with.

"I swear on Poseidon that if you don't tell me what in the underworld is going on, I will make you all personally regret it."

"Gerard, you should leave. There are things about her you don't understand." William said.

"He knows who and what I really am. He's known the whole time. Now how do all of you know?"

"Your highness, this is not a situation we can take lightly. Do you understand what your father will do to the town when he finds out?" Morgan said.

"Then he won't find out. Send Nikoli home. Tell him it was a false alarm."

"You don't understand everything. Your father will find out, and if we don't at least inform Nikoli, the entire town, including Gerard and Lucy, will be punished. We have to protect everyone and get Patrick away from you."

"How did you know it was Patrick?"

"Because I told them." William said. "It's our job to be informed of everything in this town. I figured it out quickly on my own. You're not safe in that house."

There was an urgent knocking at the door. Gerard rushed to the door, expecting to find Nik. But when he opened the door, he went sheet white. There stood Lucy, black eye and busted lip, holding a bleeding Peggy who was clutching her side. He pulled them inside, taking Peggy to the sofa. Gemma rushed to Peggy's side, as the town leaders stood horrified at the increasingly horrific scene unfolding in front of them.

"Lucy, what happened?" Gerard asked as he wrapped her in his arms before looking her over for more damage.

Gemma looked over Peggy's wound, making sure there wasn't any other wounds worse than that. She quickly began healing Peggy, who at this point was barely conscious.

"We both woke up to the front door slamming shut. We went directly to Gemma's room to see if she was alright. But we found Da in there waking up in a pool of blood. But he wasn't bleeding, so we knew it had to be her blood. Da tried to get past us, and we fought back, trying to give her time to escape. He hit me a few times. But when he got to Ma, that's when he brought out his knife. He started yelling at her saying she's a bitch for choosing Gemma over him. Ma fought him off but he cut her a few times in the process. Then he stabbed her in the stomach. I found a heavy book and hit him over the head repeatedly until I was sure he was unconscious. Then I helped Ma get here. I didn't know where else she would go." She began sobbing into his chest. He was furious.

Gemma had finished healing the large wound on her stomach, and was moving to all the other wounds.

Peggy gave her a weak smile. "Thank you dear. I would be dead if it wasn't for you."

"You shouldn't have gotten involved. You knew he would come after you two. You need to protect yourself and Lucy, I can take care of myself."

Peggy looked her up and down. Her heartbreaking as she took in the sight. "I'm sorry for what he did. If I had known I would've stopped him."

"I know. I tried to scream but he was choking me so hard I couldn't get any noise out." She checked for anymore wounds, not seeing any she stood up and walked over to Lucy. "Are you hurt anywhere besides your face?"

"No, he just went for my face."

Gemma began healing her black eye then her lip. Once she was finished she looked over her shoulder at Peggy. "Gerard, how many guest rooms do you have?"

"A few. Lucy take your mom to the guest room next to my room, she needs to rest, I'll bring her some water in a few minutes." He kissed the top of her head as she left to help Peggy to the guest room. She wasn't looking good, but then again none of them were.

There was a pounding at the door. William went to the door to answer it. But she stopped him.

"You don't want my wrath on top of my father's. If he finds out. This whole town will be leveled."

"We have no other choice right now."

William opened the door and Nik stormed in. He stopped when he saw her. He clenched his fist, a rage filled within his eyes that she had never seen before. *Sharks*.

32

"Who did this?" Nik growled through his teeth. She had never heard him like this, and for once was scared of him. "Who the bloody hell did this?"

"Patrick." Morgan replied.

His eyes widened, he quickly ran to William's phone and called Callie. He lowered his voice so only she could hear him. He was so caught up, he forgot her hearing was impeccable, and she could hear every word he said.

"It happened, he was right. I know. He's going to make our lives miserable for a while. Yeah. I'm more than well aware. Well who's going to tell him? Me? Why do I have to tell him? Have David tell him."

Henry overheard the mention of his brother and knew who he was talking about. He ran to Nik and grabbed the phone out of his hand. "Do NOT tell David. I'll deal with this. All of it. But whatever you do, don't tell David."

"Why not? Sam and him are close. Hearing it from him might be easier."

"No it won't. David and Patrick were best mates their whole lives. It will break David to tell Sam. Trust me on this. You have to tell him… or someone else who is close to Sam." Henry and Nik peered into the other room. Then back at each other. "There's your best option."

"Not happening." Nik snapped

"Why not? He wouldn't trust it from anyone else anyways."

Nik scrubbed his hands down his face, groaning in defeat. "Damnit. He's going to kill us. Alright. He can be the one to break it to him… I'll figure out how to get them together. Now what am I supposed to do about my Niece? I can't let her continue to live there. You realize that Sam is going to lose his mind when we tell him."

"Anyone would lose their mind seeing this. I don't know how you are staying so calm right now."

"Because unlike you… I've seen what she's capable of. I know what happens when she releases her wrath. It makes Poseidon look like child's play. She just doesn't remember any of it… ever. If I don't remain calm and do as she wishes, we are all in for worse than anything Poseidon would dish out."

"Fine. Then what do we do?"

"We get her out of that house. We protect her like we're supposed to do. I'm taking her away for a few days. Her birthday is this weekend… it will give us time to figure it out."

"And Sam?"

"I'm not ready to deal with that hurricane. When he finds out what Patrick did to his future wife… he's going storm over here himself and kill him."

"Hades is going to love this."

"If Hades finds out what happened to his favorite niece… you can kiss clew goodbye. She's the only relative that Hades likes. His wife has spoiled her, her entire life. None of you truly know or understand who she is."

Gemma stormed over to Nik, grabbed him by the collar of his shirt and pulled him down to her level. "You have a lot to explain. Now start talking."

"Damnit Aquaria. Sit down. We'll discuss this in a moment. Right now we have to deal with how we keep this situation from your father before he levels the damn town."

She raised her brows, "You're not telling him?"

"Hades no! Do you think I've lost my mind? This stays between all of us. Your father and uncle are to remain in the dark about this, for now. Is this the first time? And I mean any physical harm."

She began rubbing her wrist, still covered in blood. "This is the first time this, has happened, but-"

Gerard stepped in, knowing she wouldn't tell him. "He's been beating the shit out of her since we were told about Kelley. Lucy and I have been begging her for months to tell you, but she wouldn't. She's afraid Poseidon will punish Lucy and Peggy for what Patrick has done. She can't go back there. I don't even want Lucy there after what happened tonight."

"Morgan, Rackem. I need you two to go to the O'Reilly's house. Pack up Aquaria's stuff. Then drag Patrick to the cells for the night. After he's locked up, return here so we can discuss things further."

"Try to get Lux. She's a little black cat. When calling for her say you're taking her to Gemma and she'll come right to you." Gerard said

"If she isn't invisible." She mumbled.

"Invisible?" Nik glared at her. "What is Lux really?"

She ignored him.

"She's something called a soul vixen, with Kelley's soul attached to it." Gerard said.

"I won't tell your father, but is there anything they should know about finding her?"

"She wasn't in my room when it happened. So I don't know where she is. She likes to hunt for rodent souls at night." She said.

"Check the stables if you don't find her in the house." Gerard instructed.

They bowed to Gemma and left quickly. William escorted everyone else to his office. She had never been in there before, but to hers and Gerard's surprise, Nik had.

"That's a new addition." Nik gave William a smile holding up the picture of Gerard and Lucy together on his desk.

"Well, she'll be my daughter soon enough. Thought she deserved a place on the desk as well. Her royal highness might be getting a spot soon too. She's here enough that we've started to think of her as family." He smiled at Gemma.

She didn't know what to think at that moment. They all knew exactly who she was. They had known the whole time, meaning when they didn't send Liam away for punishment. It was because they didn't want her father to find out what happened. Not because of any law or special kind of punishment. It was to keep Poseidon from leveling the town. Gerard came back into the room with a shirt for her to wear. She took off the tattered night gown, throwing it to the floor. The rest of the room had turned away when she changed. Nik told her to sit down and get to healing herself while they talked. Gerard stood behind her. He placed his hand on her shoulder. Ensuring she felt some sort of comfort, she was the closest he would ever have to a sibling, and he would protect her with his life.

"Alright Nikoli. Start talking. Why do they keep calling me your niece? How and why do they know exactly who I am?"

"Where to begin..." He let out a sigh and looked back at her. "Theia is... was my sister. My only sibling. We kept my familiar relationship a secret to keep the rest of the guards from believing that I got my position because of who I am to your mother. Although she had a little to do with it, it wasn't the reason. I moved up fast before your parents met. She just requested me as her personal guard then moved me to be yours when you were born."

"Wait... so your saying, all these damn years you've been my uncle and never once had the decency to tell me?! What else are you hiding from me?"

"More than you could imagine. But I can't tell you until you're married. It's for your protection that you don't know until then. You'll be safe after your wedding. Don't ask me how I know this, I just do."

"Fine... We'll discuss this later. Now how do they know?" She gestured to Henry and William.

"They're the town leaders. You really expected your father to send you somewhere and not have protection for you? You know you're different from your siblings and that they want you dead. They're your extra protection here. And it seems like all of us failed in that department tonight."

"None of you failed. I'm good at keeping that to myself. But I refuse to go back there."

"We know. We're figuring it out."

"She can stay here." William said. "She already has a key and basically lives here anyways. Either way you're both staying here tonight."

"Is that alright with you?" Nik asked.

"Yes. But I need out of here for a few days."

"I'm taking you, Gerard, Lucy and Peggy to your palace tomorrow morning."

"Alright. I have one more question for you. And I need you to give me an honest answer."

"Alright, what is it this time?"

"Who is Sam? And why are you so worried about his reaction to this?"

Nik clenched his fist and bit his lip. He wasn't supposed to tell her this. She wasn't supposed to find out until her wedding. He took a deep breath, knowing he was going to regret this.

"Sam is your fiancé. He's very protective of you. And hasn't wanted you living there since Kelley died. He's been telling your father to get you out of there, but we didn't listen. Henry's brother is Sam's first mate. They are close."

"How can someone who doesn't know me be protective of me?"

"Damnit Aquaria! Don't you understand who you are? Anyone who knows who you are would give their life to protect you."

"No one is like that with my siblings, so you can't say it's because of my father."

"Damnit I wish Sam was here. He could get this through your head."

"Then get his ass here and let me meet him."

"No! You know the law in this. You cannot meet until your wedding."

"This is bull sharks Nikoli! I should be allowed to know who I'm marrying! He knows who I am, so why can't I know who he is?"

"Because of Delanson. He is hunting both of you down."

"Why would he care about a pirate?"

"To stop your wedding. To keep from a permanent bridge between land and sea."

"Then send him to me to finish him off. I'm not afraid to end him."

"Not happening. We're getting you out of here first thing in the morning."

She glared at him, beyond irritated with the situation. "Fine. But understand this. No one kills Patrick. As much as I wanted to let him bleed out, I healed him and kept him alive so Lucy and Peggy wouldn't hate me. So if anyone kills him, I will finish them. Am I making myself clear?"

"Crystal. Now finish healing those wounds and get upstairs to get some sleep."

33

She rubbed her wrist, looking down at the floor. Her voice was stuck in her throat. Not a word would come out. She was terrified to go to bed, or even be alone right now.

"No... I'll wait here till everyone is gone. I won't be able to sleep anyways."

Her meek voice worried them all. None of them had ever heard her sound like that. There was always some form of dignified presence in everything she said.

"Alright, but at least clean yourself up a bit. I can't stand seeing you covered in that much of your blood."

She gave him a small nod before stepping out of the room. She sat outside the door shaking, afraid to be alone again. She could hear Gerard arguing with Nik. The only phrase she could understand through the door was Gerard shouting "If Kelley knew about this-" only to be stopped by Nik.

"But he doesn't!"

Her ears perked. What does he mean he doesn't? Shouldn't he have said well he's dead or something to that extent? She pressed her ear hard to the door but could only hear a slight murmur. They lowered their voices too much for her to hear. She heard the knob begin to jiggle and scooted away. Gerard left the office slamming the door behind him.

"What did he mean by but he doesn't?" Gerard froze and turned around. He hadn't noticed her sitting outside the door. "Explain what you know."

"I asked him that same thing, all he said was he misspoke."

"I don't believe that one bit. That's what he says when he's covering for a lie. What did he say to you?"

He leaned against the wall, scrubbing his hands down his face.

"He told me I need to stop hiding what's going on from him. That I need to tell him everything and that this could have been prevented if I had told him sooner." He looked at the ground as he let out a sigh. "That's when I yelled if Kelley knew about this. Then he shouted but he doesn't. I asked him what was that supposed to mean and he had this look on his face... it was like he knew he messed up. But I don't know if the mess up was because he knows that's a sore subject for all of us or because of something else. He apologized for yelling that at me, said he was still trying to cool down after seeing you like this. That's when they sent me out of the room to make sure you were alright." He noticed her beginning to rub her wrist again. "How about you go take a bath. I'll make you that hot chocolate that ma makes you when you have a bad day."

"A-Alright."

"Do you want me to sleep on the floor in your room tonight?"

"No... you need your sleep... Nik probably will be sleeping on the sofa anyways..."

"I can tell you don't feel safe. What do you think will help?"

She fell into his chest gripping his shirt as tears streamed down her cheeks. He wrapped his arms tightly around her, trying to give her a little comfort. Shannon finally came walking out of her bedroom.

"What's all the commotion been tonight? Usually these little outburst of emergency town leader meetings only last about-" she stopped when she saw Gemma crying in Gerard's arms. She saw the blood soaking through the shirt he had given her, as well as in her hair and covering most of her skin. "Gemma darling! What happened to you? Gerard, who did this?" She shrieked

"Da's taking care of it. Rackem and Morgan are already handling it, while Da is speaking with Nik and Henry."

"Gemma, let me take a look at you. Then we'll get you cleaned up and-"

"Ma... I've got this." He began leading her to the stairs so she could wash up.

"Have you lost your mind? What will Lucy say about you seeing her without clothes? She will be devastated."

"Lucy already knows, she's in one of the guest rooms with Peggy. This isn't the first time I've helped Gemma with something like this. Probably won't be the last either. Now let me help her, I know how."

"Gerard-"

"Shannon. Let him take care of her, he knows how to help her." William said from the doorway of his office. "Come in here, Nik has something's to explain to you about Gemma."

"Why is Nik here? It's not poker night."

"We'll explain everything in the office. Gemma doesn't want to talk about it right now."

Gerard walked her upstairs to the bathroom and started the bath. She watched the water fill the tub, becoming lost in a trance. She felt him nudge her arm, shaking her loose from the trance. She looked up at him. The concern on his face was worse than the last time. She sighed, taking the box of salt from his hand, pouring it into the tub.

"Just say it."

She took the shirt off and climbed into the tub. The salt giving her a burning relief in the remaining cuts as her legs transformed into her beautiful tail. Gods she missed her tail.

"Why? It's not like you'll listen."

"We're not telling him."

"He won't punish them for what Patrick did to you."

"Please don't say that name... I can't hear it right now."

"Let Nik tell him."

"No."

"Would you be fighting it this much if Kelley was here?"

"No, but-"

"Then let me tell him."

"What?"

"You want someone as a witness of the abuse you've endured while also being able to defend Lucy and Peggy. That's why you won't tell him. You're afraid that he won't believe you. But he will. There is no way he would ever think they had anything to do with this other than trying to protect you."

She sunk deeper into the water fully immersing herself. Washing the blood out of her hair and off her face. She pondered the idea under the water. She desperately wished she was at the lagoon. She could hide in that water for days if she wanted. She knew he was right though. She was just afraid of what her father would do, and how Lucy and Peggy would blame her for it.

"Fine." She grumbled from the water.

"I'm not a bloody fish. I can't understand you when you're underwater."

She sat back up. Flicked a little water at him with her tail. "I said fine. But I have one condition."

"Alright..."

"We tell your mother who and what I am."

"I have a feeling they're doing that right now."

The door opened and Shannon came walking in, yelling over her shoulder at William.

"You're insane. Mermaids aren't real. If you look for your-"

She froze when she saw Gemma. She was told her entire life that mermaids were just fairytales. William and Gerard had intended to keep it that way over the years.

"I'm sorry you had to find out this way Shannon. But I'm honestly surprised you didn't find out sooner."

"See Shannon. This is why Nik is here. And why it's such a delicate situation."

"Delicate?! This is all madness! How have we had a mermaid in our house and no one tell me?"

"Shannon, my father didn't want anyone to know I was here. He knows my brothers are hunting me down, so I'm here in hiding until my wedding to some pirate I've never met."

"Your father?"

"Poseidon. King of land and sea. Most powerful being in the world."

Shannon collapsed, William thankful caught her before she hit her head.

"Good job Gem. Now she's out cold. Think you could have waited on the whole royalty part until after the whole mermaids are real thing sank in?"

"It's best to just get it all out at once. Why wait until everyone is used to everything to fire another cannon ball at her. That just causes lack of trust. She'll be fine."

Nik walked in as William carried Shannon to the couch.

"Sharks! Aquaria! What'd you do?!"

"She told my mother she was Poseidon's daughter."

"You know you're supposed to keep that part of your identity a secret!"

"It's not like the rest of the family doesn't already know! Why keep that small portion a secret from her."

34

She sank back under the water, pulling her tail in with her as she curled up. Holding her tail tight to her chest. She just wanted to be alone, but at the same time, she was terrified to be alone at that moment. Nik heard the rain on the roof and knew she was hurting more than she let them think. He took Gerard out of the room to speak with him alone as she tried to cry it all out.

"You cannot tell her what I said in the other room."

"What are you talking about?"

"She knows my speech pattern... she will know something is off. I can't think straight right now. It's taking everything in me not to kill Patrick myself, but you and I both know I can't. So please don't tell her."

"I already did... I told her right when I left the room. She could hear us outside the door."

"That drive to the lagoon is goin to be an absolute nightmare." Nik groaned, running a hand through his hair, pushing his head back as he stared at the ceiling for a moment. "Listen, I have to deal with this with them. Stay with her all night. She will tell you not to, don't listen to her. She needs someone with her tonight, and I'm pretty sure she is too pissed at me right now to allow me to keep an eye on her."

"I was already planning on it. But when they get here with her stuff, bring Lux to her. She needs her."

"I'll make sure to put it in the room with her… if they find it. Those things are a nightmare to catch."

Gerard went back into the bathroom and leaned against the wall waiting for her to come back to the surface. When she finally did, Gerard was sitting on the cold tile floor, back against the door as he was carving something in a piece of wood.

"Finally decided to come back up?"

"I figured I should get to bed before I fall asleep in the tub. I don't think Shannon would survive seeing me asleep in the bloody water."

He gave her a little chuckle, imagining his mother's reaction to finding her like that. "As funny as that would be, she probably wouldn't." He paused for a moment trying to figure out how to word the question that had been haunting his mind all night. "How did he get into your room? I put a strong lock on that door, so how did he get in?"

"I got up to go to the bathroom, when I got back into my room… there was a sharp pain in my head and everything went dark. I woke up to his hand around my throat and he was already…"

"Why didn't you stop him with your magic?"

She sat in the water starring at her scales. She didn't think he would believe her that she tried but it wouldn't work. That no matter what she did, she was too scared to get anything to work. She pulled her tail tighter to her chest. Her eyes burned as tears filled them. She hated her life, she desperately wished she could just be wherever Kelley was. She had been trying to contact Hades for months, but he never showed. She just wanted proof that Kelley was gone. Everything in her heart told her he wasn't. She could feel his heart still beating. She knew deep down he was alive somewhere.

"I hate my life." She screamed through her tears. "Why? Why does everything go horribly wrong for me? Some days I wish I had died when my mother died. I wouldn't know this pain. I wouldn't have gone through all of this. I wouldn't have-"

"Met Kelley."

She turned towards him with a deathly glare. Her teeth tightly clenched. "That's not what I was going to say. I could never regret Kelley. I would trade my own life for his if I could."

"If you had died when your mother died, you never would have met him. Never come on land. Never met any of us."

"You know what I mean though."

"I know your life is horrible. You've probably gone through more physical and emotional torture and abuse in your life so far, than most people go through in their entire lifespan. You don't deserve it, but those are the cards you've been dealt. We don't get to choose the life we've been given, but we are challenged daily on if we are strong enough to survive it. You are more than strong enough to survive it. You don't give up. You brush yourself off and keep going. It's something I truly envy. I would've given up by now. Shit. I would've given up if Lucy died. But you haven't given up yet. And I know you won't. You're too stubborn to give up on yourself."

She watched her scales shimmer in the red water. She had no argument against what he had said. It was all completely true. She wiped a tear from her eye. She didn't know how to tell him everything.

"Do you believe he's dead?"

"We were both at the service."

"That's not what I asked."

"He's dead. We heard the story of how he-."

"We never saw the body. The five of us never laid eyes on the body. You can't tell me that deep down, you don't feel it too. You know something is off about his death. I saw your face at the service. You weren't crying or upset. You were pissed."

"You want my honest opinion?"

"Obviously."

"I don't for one god damn second think he's dead. I haven't believed them since they told us."

"Then why haven't you said anything about it?"

"Because I've been looking for proof. I've been trying to find proof that he died."

"Like what?"

"I go to the docks weekly to try to see if anyone has seen him. I keep getting told that I've lost my mind, that I need to face facts. But I can't. I keep waiting for his ship to come in so I can ask, but I always miss them by a day. I don't know what it is... but something just feels off about it. Something doesn't add up."

"No sharks it doesn't add up! None of it does! I just wish he was here! Or that if he was hiding and making everyone believe he was dead for some reason, that I could get a message to him about what has happened."

"All of it?"

"All of it."

"If I hear even a whisper that he's alive, I'll make sure he knows. I'll keep looking into it until I get some sort of proof that he is actually gone. And if I do find it... I'll tell you."

"Thanks."

"For what?"

"Not thinking I'm crazy for not believing he's dead. For wanting to keep searching for him. For keeping all my secrets for me."

"You still haven't told her?"

"No... she has no need to know."

"But I know."

"Things have always been different between us compared to me and Lucy. You've always been someone I can talk to and depend on without worrying that you want to be with me. I know when I tell you something, you have my best interest at heart, no alterer motive."

"Lucy doesn't have alterer motives either."

"No... but with her... there are things that are hard to talk with her about... even before he was gone. It's uncomfortable to tell her certain things."

"You know she'll always be here for you."

"I know... but with all the things going on with..."

"I know. We don't talk about it. She's afraid to say anything to anyone about it. She doesn't even know what to say about it."

"Well, she's not alone there."

"You need out of here."

"Permanently."

"Your father won't allow that."

She let out a sigh as she rested her back against the tub. "I know.

Otherwise I would have left with Kelley."

"You would have gotten yourself killed."

"No I wouldn't. ...I can't die. My father told me recently that I'm Immortal. So I would be fine. And Kelley... well he would still be alive because I would have healed any wound he sustained."

"Well you're not wrong." He went back to what he was carving as she closed her eyes.

"Will you stay with me?"

"I was already planning on it."

"Thanks. Please don't let anyone in here. I don't feel safe around anyone else right now."

"Not even Nik?"

"I feel safe around him. I just don't want to deal with that mess right now. I've never seen him so angry before."

"Well... you are his niece, so I can see why."

"Yeah. It all makes a lot of sense now." She watched the water drain from the tub as he handed her a towel. "Did I ever tell you what happened when my sister visited?"

"No. You two kept to yourselves."

She let out a sigh. This one was going to hurt again. "We we're speaking with our father when a note was slipped under the door. It was in Kelley's handwriting."

He froze. "What? Why am I just now hearing about this?"

"Cause I didn't know you didn't believe it either. I would've told you right away if I knew you thought the same thing."

"What did it say? What did you do?"

"It asked if I was alright... I searched the halls... but I couldn't find anyone. It was empty... unusually empty."

"What did your father say?"

"That it was from someone on my fiancé's ship."

"You know that's the same ship Kelley was on."

"What?!"

"Yeah. I figured it out tonight when I heard you say Sam."

"How would that-"

"Captain Samuel Jones. I heard his name mentioned at the docks several times when I was helping Kelley there or when I asked about the Crimson Cutlass. It's the same ship. Your fiancé... is Kelley's captain."

35

Her tail had dried and her legs came back. She stood up wrapping herself in a towel. She stormed out of the room, down the stairs and back into William's office.

"I want that black crystal from father's desk now!" Her low growl quaked the ground. All three stared at her. But her eyes didn't come off of Nik's.

"Why?"

"I need proof that he's dead."

"Why right now? Don't you think you've been through enough tonight?"

"Sam Jones."

Nik froze. His face emotionless. But his eyes told her she struck the right cord finally. Gerard came running in with a robe for her. She wrapped herself in the robe not taking her eyes off Nik's. If she could get her magic to work, she could just read him, but of all times. It was no use right now.

"How do you know that name?"

"You think I wouldn't put all the pieces together? I want the crystal now!"

"No."

"Excuse me?"

"No. I'm not swimming all the way back to Atlantis at four am, hunt down the ship, get permission from the owner of the memory, then come back to take us to your palace a few hours later. If you really want to see it, you can wait till we get there."

The floorboards quaked hard under their feet. Nails coming loose as the floor began to tear apart piece by piece. The rain outside hit the window hard. Cracking the glass.

"Knock it off Aquaria! Nothing you say or do will make me change my mind. I'll get it for you tomorrow. It will make no difference if you get it now or tomorrow. It's just a memory."

"Where is the ship now? I'll swim there right now to get permission."

"No you won't."

"Don't test me Nikoli! I want that memory! I need the proof!"

"You don't even-"

"I will hunt each man from that ship till I find the owner of that memory. I'll kill them all if I have to. If that crystal isn't in my hand by 9pm tomorrow. I will find them and get it myself."

"It's my brother's memory." Henry chimed in. He was holding tight to the wall. Not used to feeling the floor quake beneath him. "I'm giving my permission by proxy to allow her to see it tomorrow. However. You have to prepare yourself for what your going to see. You will be watching his death, unable to save him. All you can do is watch. So think long and hard about wanting to see it."

"Is permission by proxy allowed?" Her glare vanished as she turned to Henry.

"Yes. My brother has given me proxy to all decisions that don't involve his piracy. A memory isn't considered piracy unless you're stealing the memory. I'm granting permission. Just please make the quaking stop before I vomit!"

She blew out a deep breath, stopping the quaking. "Nikoli? Is he correct?"

Nik scrubbed his face. "He's correct. But he has to sign paperwork stating that he gave you permission."

"Sign it now or so help me, you'll all regret it."

"William, draw up the paperwork."

"Are you sure?"

Nik and Henry turned and glared at him. William pulled out a piece of paper quickly and began writing.

"You understand what you're doing?"

"I need to see it to believe that he's actually dead."

"You know-"

"He's still out there! I saw his handwriting on that note when I last saw father."

"It was just similar."

"It was his! He has a distinct way of writing certain letters!"

"You're not going to like what you see."

"I'm not alone in believing he's not dead."

"What? Who else?"

"Me." Gerard finally broke his silence. Leaned up against the doorframe. His emerald green eyes burrowed deep into Nik's skull. "I know everything Kelley knew. There is no way I'll ever believe he's dead until I see proof."

"He told you everything?"

He gave him a small nod.

"Fine. I'll retrieve the crystal tomorrow. William, is it ready?"

William slid the paper across the desk. Four names written at the bottom of the contract. Nik for proxy for Poseidon. Henry giving permission. Gemma's full name and title. But under her's was Gerard's full name. Nik and Henry quickly signed. They had no actual stake in this. They weren't the ones who were going to watch it. She snatched the pen out of Nik's hand. The pen hit the paper. But she pulled back.

"Why does Gerard have to sign?"

"What?!" Gerard rushed over and looked at the paper. "Why the bloody hell is my name on there?"

"You want proof. This is the only way you can be allowed to watch it." William said.

"Da' I never said-"

William stood up. "First." His voice boomed similar to her father.

"You said you don't believe he's dead. That you won't believe he's dead until you have proof. Second. She is going to need someone to help her through watching that. And finally. I'm doing this as a town leader not as your father. So understand that this is not something that as your father I would agree too. However. This is a legal matter. Which is why I had to write it all out for you two. Now sign the damn contract so you two can get your proof and we can all move past this!"

She watched as Gerard took the pen from his father's hand. A shaky signature placed above his full name, *Gerard Benjamin Collins – Digitate II.* He slid the paper over to her. Her signature took the longest. She looked up midway through, brows furrowed, letting out a sigh as she finished with her full title. The elegant loops and swirls of her lettering. Unlike any version of her handwriting that anyone there besides Nik had seen. *Tritonia Aquaria Oceana, Crowned Princess of Atlantis, Goddess of the earth and sea.* She set the pen down. Her hand hovered over the pen for a moment. She knew Nik was the only one in the room who knew why she stopped. She had to take a moment before she could finish. She hated her full title. The worst part was the goddess part was recently added after her father revealed to her that she was a goddess. She picked the pen back up. Took a breath. "Protector of land, sea & life." She slammed the pen onto the desk, turning to leave.

"I expect that crystal no later than tomorrow night." She stormed out of the room. Leaving to cry herself to sleep in the guest room that by this point was now considered her room.

Gerard chased after her, he promised he wouldn't leave her side, and now was definitely not a moment to break that promise. When he reached her room, she was curled up on the bed. Tears streaming down her face. He closed the door behind him before sitting on the bed next to her. Placing his hand on her back. He didn't know what else to say to her. He wasn't even sure which part of the nights events she was crying about. All he knew was that she needed him there. She didn't need protection. But she needed the comfort of feeling safe again. They heard the sound of the front door opening then closing. A soft patting against the door to the room. She sat up quick. She heard the humming.

"Lux?!"

Gerard opened the door. Lux ran in and curled up with her on the bed.

"I'm so sorry I left you there. You must've been terrified!"

"You need to just keep her with you at all times. Even at work. You need each other."

She began stroking Lux's fur. Listening to the soothing hum of a purr she was creating. "I think your right. She's the only thing making me feel even the tiniest bit better."

"Probably because she's part Kelley."

"Probably."

"You should get some rest. I'm going to grab my pillow. I'll be back in a moment."

He stepped out of the room, freezing at the stairs. He could hear them talking in his fathers office. He snuck down the stairs to listen outside the door. He knew they were hiding something Big from them.

"Thanks for getting Lux. I didn't even know she had one."

"I'm surprised Patrick didn't come after it as well."

"Well it can't die and it tends to go invisible. That's probably why he didn't notice."

"Add that to the list of things to fill Shannon in on."

"Is Shannon going to be alright with this?"

"It's a cat. She'll be fine with it."

"Not the cat... everything. Her royal highness... a mermaid, living here."

"She's going to have to be, at least for the time being. She loves the girl as if she were her own daughter, I don't see this changing that at all."

"Nik, when are you telling Gerard about Sam? He needs to know. He's the only one Sam will trust with that information." Henry's voice was lower than the rest. He was the only one being cautious of the possibility of someone listening.

"I don't know. Maybe this weekend when I take them away. I know I need to tell him. I know Poseidon will forbid it, but after what happened tonight... I know that he needs to know what's going on."

"I don't think it will be that difficult for him to handle. He already knows... even though he doesn't actually know."

"I've been wondering how long it would take both of them to piece it all together. I'm surprised it took this long."

"What about the crystal?"

"That's going to be rough for both of them. I've watched it... it's thankfully not gruesome, but still... I don't know if she'll recover from seeing it."

"Wait, I thought you were there."

"I was. I was in the water when he fell in. How else would he have gotten to Poseidon in time? That wound was so deep, I'm still surprised he survived that."

Gerard took a step back. Backing into the wall, knocking a frame to the ground. The door opened. Nik's eyes narrowed in on him.

"What did you hear?"

"He-he's ali-"

Nik's hand flew to Gerard's mouth. Holding it shut. Pulling him into the room & slamming the door.

"You're to say nothin' about what you just heard. Do you understand?"

"So he is-"

"Sam will explain everything to you. I'll make sure he contacts you next time he's here."

"But he's-"

"Sam is alive and trying to stay that way. The more people that know the more his life is in danger. Piracy isn't what's putting his life in danger, it's her brothers."

"Why? Why put her through this? Bloody hell! None of this would've happened if you'd never told Patrick he was dead!"

"Yeah. Well we didn't know this would happen."

"He needs to know. Maybe then he'll finally stop."

"No. He's goin to be sentenced by Poseidon as soon as Sam finds out."

"And who the bloody hell is telling him?"

"You are."

"What?! Why me?"

"Cause he trusts you most. I was planning to tell you all of this after we got to the palace, but you over heard us. So the fish is out of the net. Now get back up there and keep an eye on her. Lux can only help her so much after what happened."

He turned. Fist clenched. He knew better than to try to fight them about this. It was all four town leaders, one of which is his father, and Poseidon's most trusted adviser. Yeah… there was no argument he could win with them.

"Tomorrow night when she locks herself back in her room. You and I are going to have a nice long discussion in private." Nik said.

"Fine." Gerard growled back. "But you tell me everything!"

"Only if you agree to tell Sam everything. And I mean everything. Even what you keep from me. You tell him. Got it?"

"Yeah. Deal."

Gerard left the office. Slamming the door shut. This was nowhere near the end of that discussion. This was only the beginning.

36

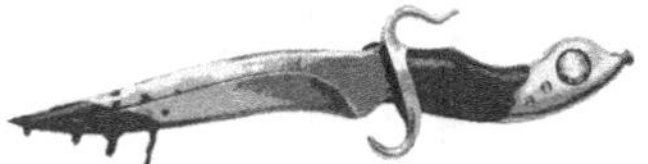

When they got to the Lagoon, Gemma told Nik he could stay in Kelley's room, she knew it was nicer than the room he usually stayed in. Nik turned the offer down, he liked his room because he had it just how he liked it. He also didn't want to make things harder on Gemma by staying in Kelley's room. He didn't know that Gemma never thought of that as Kelley's room, he only slept in there a couple of times. To her that room was just used as a way to sneak into her room. That night no one talked about what happened, they just talked about what they wanted to do to celebrate Gemma's birthday on Sunday. She noticed that Gerard and Nik were acting a little strange towards one another. She couldn't figure out what was going on with them, but she knew it was something. They never acted this way around one another before. Gemma and Peggy cleaned up dinner, while Nik and Gerard went to the study to speak privately, locking the door so no one could come in and hear what they were saying.

The next morning Nik took everyone to the nearby town of Carraroe, it was about 10 minutes away from her palace. Gemma and

Peggy and been there a couple times before, but no one else had. It was much smaller than what they were used to, but it was the perfect size for Gemma. They wandered around town for a bit, looking at what types of shops they had there. They went to the market and picked up some food for dinner, and ingredients to make Gemma a cake for her birthday. Nik told everyone they could head back without him, he had another way of getting back. They didn't understand how, but they knew to trust him.

As soon as they got back Gemma went right to the lagoon for a swim, she brought the trident with her to practice her magic a little bit, but spent most of her time just trying to relax again. She was now able to make shapes out of bubbles while in the water and when out of the water she could bend the water into whatever she wanted. She was able to make whirlpools and massive typhoons just by a small wave of her trident.

After a few hours Nik had showed up, he jumped into the water with Gemma, they sat underwater with the coral and fish to talk.

"Are you going to tell me what's going on yet?" She asked as she sat on a pile of sea sponge.

"I can tell you a little, but you know I can't tell you everything."

"I know, but I want to know the family stuff. Like the fact that you are my uncle and no one thought to tell me." She said in a snarky tone.

"Did you know on the day you were born I was the third one to hold you? The first one to meet you besides your parents. Your father hired me as a guard before he met Theia. I worked for him for a few years, then at one of the events, she came with me. Your father instantly fell in love with her, his hair turned pink, like yours when you're with Kelley."

Gemma blushed when he said that, she knew how much her parents loved each other.

"Your father kept the fact that I was her brother a secret. We became very close, he knew he could trust me with anything. Mostly because he knew I would always do whatever I could to keep Theia safe. I moved up fast in the ranks of the guards, became your mother's personal guard when they were married. Your brothers became suspicious of everything going on. It was unusual for someone to move up so fast. When no one else is around he treats me as family, and a friend. Just as Kelley and Gerard are together. When you were born, I was the only one besides them and the doctor that was there. They both entrusted your safety with me, knowing that no one else would care for you the way I do. I have no other family left besides you, and I promised your mother the day you were born, that I would protect and treat you as if you were my own child."

"Why keep all this a secret from me while I have been here? Why couldn't you have told me earlier?"

"I didn't see a point. I thought if I told you that you would be upset with me for keeping this from you for so long, and then would stop speaking to me, like you did with your father."

"It's different with him, you know that. We have always argued about everything. Why have you never tried to start your own family?"

"I care more about your safety, and don't want to risk someone finding out anything about you that can be sent to your brothers. You are my complete priority."

"But don't you want to find someone to love? Have a family of your own?"

"I would love to, but I have never met anyone who I have truly felt a connection with. If that day ever comes I will try, but until then I want to keep you safe."

"Well one day, I hope you find someone that makes you feel that way." She smiled at him.

"I almost forgot, your father and I talked and we got you a present."

"We?"

"It was my idea, and he helped me pay for it for you. He said it could be from both of us. It will help you, especially with everything that has been going on."

"What is it?" She said excitedly.

"It's in front of your house, you can go see it anytime you are ready."

"Well let's go." Gemma swam to the shore and got out of the water. As soon as she got out of the water, she got her legs back with her trident. "Come on! Let's go!"

"Aquaria do you mind giving me my legs back? I don't change as fast as you do."

"Oh right, sorry! Why did you call me Aquaria? You know I can't use that name on land." She used her trident to give him his legs and then they went up to the front of the house.

"Because that is your name. And no one else is around, I would prefer to call you by the name that your mother gave you." He said giving her a smile and a slight nudge.

Gerard and Lucy were already out front looking at her gift. Gemma saw it and was amazed.

"You got me a car? But why?"

"Well you need to be able to get back and forth from places. This can at least keep you safe from the rain whenever you are out. It will also get you here faster, you won't need to have that boy drive you home anymore. You can do it yourself."

"But I don't know how to drive."

"I DO!" Gerard said excitedly. "My Da' taught me how to drive ours. I'll teach you."

Lucy just laughed, "He wants a car for us one day."

"Can we go for a drive now?" Gerard asked

"How about after lunch, I'm pretty hungry." Gemma laughed

"Okay, after lunch." Gerard said, Lucy then dragged him inside to go make some lunch.

Gemma gave Nik a big hug, "Thank you so much! This is wonderful."

"Make sure you thank your father too, I couldn't have done this without his help."

"I will. I promise. Do you know when I could see him next to thank him?"

"You can see him anytime, let me know when you want to speak with him and I will set it up for you."

"Thank you!" She said smiling at him. She was excited but scared, she had never driven a car before. She rode in Finn's all the time now, but never even thought to ask him to teach her to drive.

37

After lunch Gerard and Gemma got into the car and went for a little test drive, and to teach Gemma how to drive a little. Nik stayed behind with Lucy and Peggy, he needed to speak with them. He took them to the study and closed the door. He first told them what crimes Patrick committed, and everything that he learned from Gerard and the town leaders.

"Can you two truthfully tell me what has been happening with Patrick and Gemma? Anything I might have not heard about the other night. From what I saw it seems this has been going on for a while."

Lucy sat quietly with a worried look on her face. Peggy excused herself for a moment to throw up. When she returned she sat back down without saying a word.

"Listen, I'm not going to try to extend his contract. Poseidon and I do not want to change any of that. We are just concerned for her, from what Gemma, Gerard and Callie have told me, it doesn't sound as if she is safe there anymore."

"Alright." Peggy said with a big sigh. "Patrick has been drunk for the past 6 months. He has been violent lately, mostly towards Gemma. Lucy and I have been hurt a few times trying to protect her. He stabbed me the other night, that's why we were also at the Collin's house. Luckily Gemma has her healing powers and has been able to heal not just us but herself. We have to call Callie a lot and have her keep Patrick there. Gerard's family has been helping us too. They know how rough it has been at home."

"Gerard has rescued us a lot, there are many nights that Gemma just doesn't come home anymore. Gerard and I have been looking all over to find a house in town, once we find one we were planning on Gemma staying there. We just haven't been very successful, in finding anything."

"Would you two be upset if we sent Patrick away for a while?"

"Take him. And don't bring him back. After what he did, I never want to see him again." Peggy snarled. Lucy had never seen her mother so angry before.

"I will talk with Poseidon and see if maybe we can help you and Gerard get a house faster." Nik said while trying to think of a solution. "I will talk to Callie, see if she can cut him off from the pub for a little while, until we can get the ship that will take him to Poseidon. Callie will talk to the owner of the market and have him do the same. Maybe if we cut him off from drinking all together, things can get better. Until then, Gemma will be staying here every other week. Then she will stay with Gerard's family, when she's in town."

"Should we let them know who she really is? Shannon has already gotten a glimpse of Gemma as a mermaid once. Luckily she changed back quickly and we just told her she was tired. But if she is going to be there that much, shouldn't they know?" Lucy said

"They already know."

"Will we be punished for what Patrick did?" Peggy nervously asked.

"No. I will ensure that you two receive no punishment. I'll also see if I can get Poseidon to give you two some compensation for the abuse you've received trying to protect her. But I'm not going to lie to you. He's in a lot of trouble. The only reason he's still alive is because Gemma has forbidden anyone from killing him. She says you two would never forgive her."

"Speaking for myself. Once he sobers up. I'm done with him. I'm only waiting till he sobers up so he will remember. But Gemma has no reason to worry, I would never hold his death against her after everything he has done to her the last six months." Peggy was furious. She had looked past so many of his flaws and indiscretions. But he crossed a line and she was now done. "Lucille, you will be staying with Gerard's family as well. I don't want you to come home for any reason, I will bring whatever you need to you. I don't trust him around either of you girls anymore. Stay away from him. Do you understand?"

She was still frozen in shock. Unable to respond. How could her father do such a thing. It took a while but it all clicked as to what happened. No one had told her that night and after everyone was silent.

She shook Lucy's shoulders. "Lucille! Did you hear anything we've said?"

"I-I… excuse me." She ran out the front door. Taking deep breath's. She looked up to the sound of a car coming to a halt. She ran to Gemma, holding her as tight as she could. Tears streaming down her cheeks soaking into Gemma's hair. Quietly repeating "I'm so sorry."

"Did you tell her?" Gemma asked.

"No, but I wouldn't be surprised if Nik did."

She rubbed Lucy's back until the crying slowed. Then passed her off to Gerard. "I need a moment." She went upstairs, locking herself in her room.

Nik said he need to step out for a little bit and that he would be back late. He told them not to wait up for him. Gemma watched him leave, he took the stairs in the lagoon to the tunnel. She knew he was going to talk to her father. She snuck out, and followed him, she needed to speak with him as well. She followed him down the tunnel for a long way, then he disappeared. She kept swimming down the tunnel when someone grabbed her from behind. She had a dagger with her and held it to the throat of whoever grabbed her. They let her go and turned her around.

"Aquaria what are you doing here?" Nik whispered

"Following you. I wanted to speak with my father, thank him for the gift."

Nik sighed, "You should have told me, I would have arranged for you to speak with him, I don't know who all is in the castle right now."

"Why can't I just see him for a moment?"

"If one of your brothers is here, you could be in danger. I will take you back to the stairs, and have him meet you there."

"Alright." Gemma sighed

She waited by the stairs for anyone to show up. She waited for a while, she was starting to get impatient. She could feel the stairs quaking, and the water around the tunnel becoming rough. That only meant one thing, Poseidon was furious about something. She knew she had to tread lightly when she saw him. Nik showed up and pulled her into the hallway. Then took her to the room that she went to for her 18th birthday. He closed the door behind them, and they waited for Poseidon. About 5 minutes later he came through a different door. Gemma swam right to him and gave him a big hug.

"Aquaria, what did you need to see me for? You know it is dangerous for you to be here."

"I just wanted to thank you for my gift. And talk to you for a minute."

"About what?"

"About me staying here at the lagoon, and not going back"

"Like Nik already told you. You can stay every other week. You will get too lonely being here by yourself for that long."

"I can't be in the same house as Patrick anymore. I just can't do it. Please!" She begged

"Nik and I were talking about that before he got you. We think we have come up with a solution for that. Until Gerard buys a house for himself and Lucy, you can stay with his family or Callie if Gerard's parents say you can not stay there. We have both agreed that it is best for you to not be in the same place as Patrick until his drinking stops. Have Lucy and Peggy gather all of your things from their house and bring them here. You can then just bring things to wherever you stay while in town. Bring Peggy with you to the lagoon occasionally, keep checking in with her at all times."

"Peggy is very worried about you, she just wants to be sure that you are safe. We all do, and right now, her home is not safe." Nik chimed in.

"How will that work with Callie? Won't she find out who I am?"

"Callie knows everything that has been going on, so we don't have to worry too much about her." Nik said

"Set up a meeting for them to meet me and we will figure this all out. Now if we can get Gerard his own place quickly, then we will not need to."

"What about Patrick? What is going to happen to him?" She asked

"We are going to have Callie help us to get the whole town to cut him off from all alcohol. I'm sure that the members of your club will help keep you safe. Once Patrick has sobered up and is acting like his normal self again, Nik and I will have a meeting with him, out at sea."

"Why did everything have to get so terrible? I just hate that all this has happened because of me." Her voice cracked as she held back the sobs. She wasn't allowed to cry in front of anyone especially her father.

"Aquaria, this is not because of you. It is because of past deals and contracts that had been made with me. Do not blame yourself, or let anyone blame you. None of this is your fault." Poseidon spoke softly to her, he knew he messed up, and nothing was going to make it better.

"I should get back, Peggy will start to worry about me." She said as she turned to swim away.

Poseidon pulled her into a hug. "I love you my pearl. Happy Birthday!"

"I love you too. And thank you. You are more than welcome to join us tomorrow!"

"I wish I could, but I can not, I need to take care of some things. But I will try to come by sometime this week."

She gave him a flat smile. She knew he would never show up. Then swam out the door and back towards the lagoon.

"So how are we going to help Gerard and Lucy get a house?" Nik asked

"Use the extra money that Patrick was getting to take care of her. Gerard and Lucy need it more, and are the ones actually taking care of her."

"What about Peggy?"

"We will send her a little something, but send it only to Aquaria, she can give it to her."

"This isn't how everything was supposed to go. We really need to have that meeting with Patrick, on the ship."

"I know, but we have to wait until the ship gets there. It is already on its way there, but you know it takes a few days from where they were."

"You could always send him to retrieve him."

"He would kill Patrick."

"That's not a bad thing."

"Aquaria forbids it. But accidents happen while at sea." Poseidon's voice lowered as a wicked grin showed the cruelty in his intent. He had no intention of letting Patrick die quickly.

38

It was the first week that Gemma was allowed to be alone at the Lagoon, everyone else went home after her birthday celebration. She thought that since this would be her future home and that she would be there a lot more, she should go into the nearby town by herself. She got into her car and left. She looked at everything around her, trying to be sure she could find her way back home. No one would be around to help her, so she needed to be sure that she could make it on her own. Luckily Gerard spent the whole weekend teaching her how to drive, she felt a little more confident, but her nerves were starting to get to her. She got into town and wondered around a bit, stopping in at a small café.

"What would you like to drink?" The waitress stood across from her, notebook in hand to scribble down her order. She had light brown hair, that looked almost blonde in the right light, and bright hazel eyes.

"Just water is fine."

As she left Gemma began looking over the menu. She had gotten used to human food, but the options on this menu were a little different from clew. She returned with a glass of water and stood across from her. She was looking her up and down, a curious look written upon her face.

"How long are you visiting for?"

"I didn't say I was visiting."

"Oh sorry. I just assumed cause I've never seen you here before. Or anywhere in town."

"Well I'm not visiting. I live here part-time."

"How do you live somewhere part-time?"

"I recently inherited a house a little ways out of town, I don't live there all the time yet. I plan to be here and my current residence for about a year. Then move here permanently."

"I'm just going to go with you being new in town." She smiled, "Now do you know what you would like?"

"Can I just get some soup?"

"Sure. I'll bring it right out." The girl said as she left. She returned a few moments later with a basket of bread and sat across from her. "I'm Anna-Maria. I'm about to go on my break, do you mind if I join you?"

"Umm… I guess not." Gemma grabbed a dagger from her boot, and held it close under the table.

Anna-Maria leaned in close to her, she gripped her dagger tighter. Trying to regulate her breathing. Then she whispered to Gemma, "You might want to keep those daggers closer than your boot. It's not safe for young girls to walk around this town alone. Trust me, I know." She pulled up the sleeve on her left arm revealing a wrist brace holding a dagger. She quickly covered it back up before anyone else could see it.

"How did you know about my daggers?" Gemma whispered back.

"You're new around here, you don't know what it is really like here. I can spot someone who is extra cautious. If you ever need a friend come find me, I can help."

"Why would you do this for me? You don't even know me."

"Because I've been where you are before. When I first moved here, I wasn't lucky enough to have someone watch my back. I don't want you to have to suffer the way that I did."

"Thank you. And my name is Gemma."

"I'll go get our food, and we will talk more."

Anna-Maria got up and walked away. She came back with some food and sat down with Gemma.

"You don't need to worry about me. I'm not trying to hurt you, I just thought it would be nice to make a new friend."

"What happened to you? Why do I need to be so careful? This doesn't seem like a bad town at all. Nothing compared to where I live now."

"Almost two years ago, I left home. I wanted to go see more of the world. I wasn't as prepared for the world as I thought I was. I didn't carry any weapons on me, or even know how to use them. I didn't make it here until December that year. I walked passed the pub and got pulled into an alley, held at knife point while a man stole every coin I had. Then after he took everything I had, he began to defile me. After he had finished with me, he stabbed me and left me for dead, in the snow. I was found later by a different man, he brought me into the back of this café. He didn't see what had happened to me, but he helped take care of me for a couple of days. He got Jerry to give me a job here, so I could earn some money back to try and get out of here one day. I've been here ever since."

"What happened to the man who found you?"

"I don't know, never saw him again. He worked on a pirate ship, he was very kind, didn't seem to belong there. His crew was at the nearby port for a little bit, and a few of them came to our town for a few days."

"I'm sorry that happened to you. I've had a similar experiences years ago and again more recently. Which is why I carry the daggers on me."

"Did they ever find the man who hurt you?"

"Yes, to 2 of them, but one got away. I unfortunately knew them both of the ones they caught. One is dead, the other isn't… yet. I'll get my revenge one day. I did it once, I can do it again."

"Weren't you afraid of him hurting you?"

"Of course I was! But after that first time I was attacked, I had more training in fighting. When I saw him again, I got him back the exact same way he got me. I wasn't going to let him know that he held any power over me."

"I couldn't imagine being up against my assailant. I would probably freeze up."

"Well I wasn't alone, I had my boyfriend and his best friend with me. My attacker was someone we all knew, his attack was for revenge."

"I'm so sorry. I know talking about something like this is hard."

"It's alright, you're the first person I have ever felt okay telling this to."

"It's because we have that in common." Anna-Maria got up from the table. "If you ever need anything, or just want a friend. I'm here for you. It's always good to have a friend around here."

"Thanks, I will definitely come visit you when I'm in town."

Anna-Maria gave her a soft smile, and walked back to the kitchen. Her smile seemed familiar. But she couldn't figure out why. She was certain she had never met her before. But something about her smile was familiar.

39

The next few days Gemma stayed at her house, practicing all of the magic she could. When she wasn't practicing her magic, she was reading one of the scrolls her father had sent her. They were boring and made her want to sleep, but occasionally they would teach her new magic. With her trident, she was nearly perfect. Most of her magic had become so strong that she could nearly rival her father. When she didn't use the trident, she wasn't nearly as strong. She wanted to get stronger without the trident, she knew that should be her focus while here. She searched the scrolls & books to try to find a way to make herself stronger, she could never find a straight answer on how to make herself stronger. All it ever said was that she needed to use all of her inner strength. No matter how hard she concentrated, she couldn't do it.

It was Friday morning, Lucy and Gerard would be coming back for the weekend and to see how she was doing. She thought she should go into town again, stop at the market to pick up a few things. When she got to town she went directly to the café to see if she could find

Anna-Maria. She walked in and saw her bringing some food to a few customers, she had a smile on her face. She was walking back to the kitchen when she saw Gemma.

"Gems! What are you doing here today?"

"I needed to stop by the market, a friend of mine is coming to visit me tomorrow. I thought I would come say hi, see if you wanted to come with me."

"Oh okay. Let me see if I can take my break a little early."

"Okay."

Anna-Maria went into the back and then came back out, she had taken her apron off and had a coat on. "Alright, I have an hour until I have to be back. We're slow right now so he's giving me a little bit longer of a break."

They walked to the market together and chatted the whole way. Gemma felt a close connection with her, it was nice to have someone somewhat understand what she has gone through.

"So where are you really from?" Gemma asked

"I grew up in a small town outside of Dublin, then when I turned 18 I decided I wanted to see more, so I left. I was supposed to be catching a ship in Clew Bay, but I never made it."

"Clew Bay? Where were you trying to go? The only ships that leave out of there go west."

"Exactly! I want to get far from Ireland, I want to go somewhere warm. I found a ship that was leaving out of there that was going to take me to the islands."

"Why do you want to go so far?"

"I have nothing here. There's nothing that keeps me here, I just want to feel free."

"What about your family, won't you miss your parents?"

"My mum left the same time I did, but she went back to Italy. She's hoping to find my father there, that's where she met him."

"So you don't know who he is?"

"I've met him a few times when I was very young. His name is Sebastiano, he had light brown hair, and brown eyes. Every time he was with my mother, his hair changed. It was strange, I still have never seen anything like it."

"What do you mean?"

"I was probably just imagining it, but it looked like little bits of pink would show up, but only when he would be with my mother."

Gemma remained silent for a moment, realizing who Anna-Maria was, and that she had no idea. She now understood why she felt such a close connection to her. Anna-Maria was her niece. Her favorite brother's daughter. But she must've been a secret because the only child she knew that Sebastiano had, was Nicoletta, and she was much younger than her.

"Why don't you just go to Italy where your mother is?"

"I don't know, I just don't want to deal with it. She's been wanting to find him for so long, I just can't figure out why. He left us, before I was born, only visiting a few times. He wouldn't even know what I look like now."

"Don't you just look like your mother?"

"No, she always said I looked like a perfect combination of her and my father. I just don't see it though. Anyways, going to the islands will keep me away from all of that. I dealt with it my whole life, and just don't want to do it anymore."

"You know its dangerous down in the islands, right?"

"I know, but I still have time. I don't have nearly enough money yet."

"If you want I can teach you to fight really well. Help keep you safe."

"I don't know, how well do you fight?"

"Well I won two competitions in Clew. I was fighting just the boys, so I'm pretty decent. But if you are trying to go to Port Royal or anywhere in the islands, you need to know how to protect yourself."

"Well, we can give it a try. I work every day, maybe after work?"

"I'm only here every other week, so we can start when I come back. I leave on Sunday for the week, and will be back Friday night. I work during the week when I'm not here."

"Where do you go?"

"I normally live in Clew, I work in the local pub there."

"You work in a pub? That's pretty dangerous. Especially in Clew. I've heard stories about the pirates that go there."

"They are pretty rough, but they're afraid of me. I can take care of myself." She said with a smile.

"You really could teach me a few things. I don't know if I could survive there on my own."

"The rest of Clew is fine, the pub is just rough. Callie and I take care of ourselves, they know not to mess with us."

"You're tougher than you appear."

Gemma laughed, "I get that a lot."

"What do you do for fun?"

"I like to fight, and I love to swim. I don't get to swim that much anymore, but I still love it."

"Why not just swim by the port?"

"The water is too cold, I grew up a lot further south than here, the water is a lot warmer there."

"Like southern Ireland?"

"No I am not originally from Ireland, I have been staying with some family friends while my father is away at sea."

"What's it like? Living somewhere other than here?"

"It's very different. I don't really know how to describe it."

"I would love to see the world. I just need to find someone to go with me, it would be safer." Anna-Maria sighed.

"If I ever think of anyone, I will let you know." Gemma already had someone in mind.

"Thanks! I probably won't save enough for at least another two years."

"Well then that will give me plenty of time to teach you to fight." Gemma laughed

"Maybe you could teach me to swim too."

"You don't know how to swim? And you were going to travel the world on a ship?"

"I guess I didn't think that all the way through. My mother never let me go swimming growing up. Or even take long baths, it was always wash quick and get out. I never understood why, but I didn't like to question her."

She knew why. If she was half mermaid her tail would appear after being in the water for a few minutes. Taking less time the more she changed. "Well I will try to teach you to swim, if we have time." She knew she couldn't. It would give away both of them.

"Thanks!"

They walked further into town, Gemma stopped when she saw a strange statue. Well to her it wasn't strange, it being there was what was strange.

"Why is this statue here?"

"Oh, it was given to the town by Poseidon. Supposedly he used to come into town once every couple of months, but no one has seen him in years."

"Why did he give the town a statue of himself?"

"Something about him helping the town. Supposedly he was building a castle near here, no one has ever seen it. I think it was all just a myth."

Gemma shrugged, acting as if she didn't know what Anna-Maria was saying. They finished their shopping then Gemma walked her back to the café.

"Where did you get your wrist brace? I have been thinking about it a lot and would love to get one."

"It was actually a gift, from the man who helped me."

"Really? Did he say where he got it?"

"No, he showed me how to wear it and said it would keep me safe. It's strange though, it had the letter 'A' on it. He didn't even know my name, no one in town did."

"Do you mind if I look at it?" Gemma asked nervously.

"Go ahead." Anna-Maria took it off and handed it to Gemma. Gemma looked very carefully at the brace, the leather, the stitching, even the A were the exact same as her fighting gear. There was no difference in it. Gemma took the holster off her hip and handed it to Anna-Maria.

"I know who rescued you."

"Really? How?"

"It was my boyfriend. He got me fighting gear that looks exactly like this, same leather, stitching, even the 'A'."

"But your name is Gemma, what does the A stand for?"

"My real name. Only three people outside my family know it. My best friend Lucy, her fiancé, and Kelley."

"Who is Kelley?"

"The man who gave this to you. He was the love of my life."

"Was?"

"He died, almost a year ago." Gemma said wiping a tear away.

"I'm so sorry. He was one of the nicest men I had ever met. You were very lucky to have him."

"Thank you." She handed Anna-Maria back her brace. She knew it was made for her, knew it wasn't meant to for Anna-Maria. But she didn't want to take away her only way to protect herself. "I should be going. I will be back in a week."

"Gems wait." She handed her the brace back. "You should have this. It was meant for you."

"You need it much more than I do. Thank you though. I will see you soon." Gemma went to her car and went home.

40

When she got home Lucy and Gerard had just arrived.

"Where have you been?" Lucy asked

"I went into town, I got a few things for while you are here. I made a friend while I was there too."

"Oh really? What's his name?" Gerard teased

"Her name is Anna-Maria. We met earlier this week, she's really nice."

"Well, be careful. You never know who you can trust." Gerard said.

"Don't worry I will be. It's just nice to have someone here when you're not."

"She better not replace me as your best friend." Lucy teased

"Oh you know no one could ever do that." Gemma laughed

"Well except maybe me." Gerard laughed, "You know we think a lot alike." He winked at Gemma. It was a little joke between them, and it drove Lucy crazy.

"I swear you two will be the end of me." Lucy grumbled.

"You sounded just like Peggy!" Gemma laughed

Gerard and Gemma were laughing so hard that they had tears. That was another comment that they knew drove Lucy crazy, yet they loved to say it.

"You know we love you! Besides someone has to pick up the slack of teasing you with Kelley gone." Gerard said as he kissed her head.

"Say what you want, but I'm the one that you both trust with all your secrets." She teased back.

"Come on, let's go inside and get dinner." Gemma laughed

Later that night, Lucy snuck into Gemma's room to find out more about Anna-Maria.

"So tell me about this new friend of yours."

Gemma told her everything that she knew about Anna-Maria. How she wasn't from here, and was attacked when she got here. How she is stuck here until she can save enough money to get on a ship to leave. The fact that she's almost positive that Anna-Maria is her niece.

"Your niece? Are you sure?"

"Only myself, my siblings and my father, have hair that changes color. How else would you explain it?"

"A small child with a strong imagination."

"Her father has the same name as my brother and she's from his region. I'm almost certain she's his daughter. If she is, I wouldn't be surprised that no one knows about her."

"Why?"

"Because her existence is illegal. She's half human half mermaid. You know the law, she shouldn't exist."

"I'm sure your father wouldn't do anything to her."

"To her, no. He adores all of his granddaughters. But my brother would be in a lot of trouble. And she would have a security detail on her. And trust me, she is the only merperson in this town. I didn't sense any one else."

"Do you plan to tell her?"

"Not until I get confirmation that she is his. I don't have any photos of him so it'll be hard to get. Even then, I don't know if it would be safe for her to know. She might be better off not knowing."

"Well I agree with you on that. I've seen how it's been for you, and she would probably have a target on her back if they knew of her."

"There is one more thing about her that I haven't told you yet."

"What's that?"

"She knew Kelley."

"How? How do you know for sure it was Kelley?"

"Kelley's the one who saved her. I know it was him because of something she had." Gemma pulled out her holster and handed it to Lucy. "She had a brace for her wrist that matched exactly with my fighting gear."

"It's just a wrist brace, that doesn't mean it was Kelley."

"It had my initial on it, exactly the same." She showed Lucy the A on the holster. "The only people who knew about it were us, and Kelley. No one else knew. She said she was surprised that it had her initial on it, seeing as how he didn't even know her name. When I showed her that it was the same as mine, she tried to give it to me."

"Well why didn't you keep it? It belongs to you."

"Because she needed it, I don't. I have more weapons than her, she has just the one dagger. She needs it. I've been where she is, I know the pain and fear that she's been living with. That dagger is what makes her feel safe. I can't take that away from her. Besides the only thing she even knows about Kelley is that he saved her. If this one little thing makes her feel even the slightest bit safer, then I want her to have it."

"Wow, I'm surprised."

"By what?"

"That you are willing to give up something from Kelley. I know that must have been hard for you."

"It wasn't as hard as I thought it would be. I guess because, he didn't give it to me personally. It didn't feel like it was truly from him."

"I'm sorry."

"Don't be, besides I still have one thing left from him that he gave me. I think It might be time that I actually open it."

"You still haven't opened that letter? It's been almost a year since you got it. I thought you opened it months ago."

"I just couldn't, it never felt right. But I think I might be ready."

"Do you want me to stay?"

"No, this is something I have to do on my own. Thank you though. Talking through all of this really made me feel a little better."

"If you need me, you know where I'll be. Just knock before you come in."

Gemma laughed, "I always knock. Goodnight."

Lucy left the room, closing the door behind her. Gemma got up and walked over to her desk, she opened the top drawer and there it sat. Kelley's last letter, and the photo of the two of them. She took them both back to her bed, she knew that she would be crying after reading this. Lux jumped onto the bed curling onto her lap. Humming softly to comfort her. She took a deep breath and opened the letter, tears already rolling down her cheeks.

My dearest Gem,

My love, I miss you more than you could ever know. I feel as if every moment without you, pulls me further away from myself. Every port we stop at, I think of you and only you. How much you would have loved everything I have seen, and how one day we will be together and explore. I've learned how to sail the waters, we could get a ship of our own and go wherever we wanted. Just be free together. Nothing else matters to me, only you. When I return, I plan on spending the rest of our lives together. I will do whatever it takes to make that happen. We will be together one day, I promise. Never forget how much I love you, how much you mean to me. No one in the whole world compares to you.

I might not be able to get a letter to you next week, we will be arriving at the fountain around the time Nik gets here. He gave me a memory crystal and showed me how to use it, I will send it with him next week instead of a letter. Never forget what I told you on the dock. Not even death.

I love you my beautiful Gem. Don't let your hair be blue all the time, let some golden happiness shine through. I miss you, please keep writing to me, these letters get me though every day. You are the only light I have in all this dark, please stay my light and guide me out of the darkness.

Love you forever and always

Kelley

Gemma curled up her bed and cried herself to sleep. It had been a while since she cried herself to sleep, but she needed to read that letter. It was the only way she would ever be able to move on. She dozed off to the sweet sounds of Lux humming, calming every nerve in her body, until she drifted off to sleep.

PART THREE

41

Once she stopped going to the O'Reilly's house, she started working every weekday at the pub. She got off a little early on Tuesday's and Thursdays so she could train Molly.

While she was working one afternoon, Callie had to leave for a few hours, leaving Gemma in charge. Luckily it was a quiet day, no ships were supposed to come into port today. Those were always Gemma's favorite days. She knew she could handle being there alone on these days. Gerard stopped by and brought her some lunch, he knew Callie would be gone. She took a small break and sat down with him to eat.

"Did you find a place yet?"

"We're looking at a house not far from here. It's not directly in town, but its walking distance."

"Near your parents or the other end of town?"

"Other end. Between port and here, it's not as close as Lucy wants. But she does like that living there, we will be between both of our parents, and closer for your drive to the Lagoon."

"Do you have enough for it?"

"Almost, we've been trying to get them to lower the price, just a little bit."

"Take me with you next time you talk to them."

"We're going today after I get off work. I can pick you up when we leave if you would like."

"That would be great."

"Alright! I'll see you then. I have to go get back to work."

Right as Gerard was walking out, Finn walked in. Gemma was already behind the bar again, cleaning some glasses. Finn walked right up to her and handed her a bouquet of flowers.

"What's this for?" She asked.

"Gemma, I know your answer will probably be no... again, but will you please accompany me for dinner tomorrow night. Just the two of us, not at either of our houses." Finn asked nervously, his eyes were closed tightly with his head down. He was preparing for the sting of rejection for the fifth time.

Gemma stood there speechless, she wasn't sure if she should say yes, but she knew she needed to move on. "That sounds like a lovely evening. What time will you be picking me up?"

"Is 5:30 too soon after you get off work?" He asked excitedly.

"5:30 is fine, I'll be at the Collins house."

"Alright, I'll see you then."

Gemma watched him leave. She had never seen him so happy before, she couldn't help but giggle when she saw how happy he was.

A few hours later when Gerard showed up, Gemma was throwing some drunk out of the pub. His hand was bleeding and his head had a big gash above his left eyebrow, dripping blood into his eye.

"One of these days they will learn not to upset you." Gerard said walking up to her.

"One of these days they will stop fighting, and acting like vile insolent cretins." She shouted at the man who she kicked out as he ran off.

"Having a rough afternoon?"

"I'm just fed up today, apparently a ship came in this morning and this group is just awful. I've thrown out so many of them today." She said while wiping the blood off her dagger.

"Well are you ready to go?"

"Let me just tell Callie I'm leaving, then we can go." Gemma went to find Callie to tell her she was leaving, when another fight broke out.

"We just can't catch a break today." Gemma said

"Help me with this fight then you can go."

"Alright, I got this." Gemma pulled a few daggers out of her boots and started to throw them. She hit one man in the hand, they just continued fighting. She hit another in the shoulder, and the fighting continued. The third dagger went right into another man's eye. The fighting stopped, the man was screaming in agony. He pulled the dagger out of his eye and threw it to the ground. Gemma stood on a table, being shorter than him, she needed to be able to be right in his face. She held another dagger at his throat and her sword at another man's throat.

"All of you get out, NOW! I swear on Poseidon's name that I will cut each of you, limb from limb if you come back in here drunk again. NOW LEAVE!" The ground beneath the pub was quaking as she spoke.

All the men scattered, she stayed on the table until they were all gone. Gerard walked over to her and helped her down from the table.

"Ready to go?"

"Beyond ready! Callie, I'll see you tomorrow." Gemma waved to Callie as she left.

When they arrived at the house they were looking at, Lucy was already there.

"I don't know, it's wonderful, I just don't know if we can afford it." Lucy said softly.

"We'll figure it out. It's the perfect location, perfect size. We will figure it out." He said

"What if it's already gone by then?"

"Then we will find something else."

Gemma walked over to the owner of the house, she asked him what his absolute bottom of the barrel price was. She knew that they were a little short, but also knew that the amount he said, they wouldn't be able to get in time. But she had more than enough to cover that amount. Her father had been sending her extra money to put towards a house for Gerard and Lucy.

"If I give you what they don't have right now, can you just tell them that you will lower the price. I don't want them to know that I'm taking care of it for them. I don't want them to feel in debt to me."

"Alright, but I'm sure you don't have enough to cover it."

"I do, let me get it out of my car. And don't say a word to them."

Gemma ran to her car and grabbed some money she had stashed in there. She counted it out and put it in a small sack, then went back inside. She had the man follow her into the kitchen to give him the money.

"I even added a little more, so say nothing to them about this."

He counted the money, then put the sack in his pocket. "You have a deal." He shook her hand, then went and told them he would be willing to lower the price.

"Really?" Lucy said excitedly.

"We will sign the papers tomorrow morning at the bank." He said

"Thank you so much!" Gerard said shaking his hand. "We will see you tomorrow morning."

They headed for the door, the owner looked over at Gemma and gave her a nod. She gave him a thank you nod and left.

When they got back to Gerard's parents' house, Gemma needed to talk to Lucy.

"Finn came in again today. This time he brought me flowers."

"Did you finally say yes to him? He's determined to keep trying until you say yes."

Gemma laughed, "I did, I caved in. I'm just a little nervous."

"Why? It's not like you haven't been with someone before."

"It was different with Kelley. We never went out in public alone. So I don't really know what to do."

"You'll be fine, trust me. You can handle yourself better than anyone."

"I don't know how to act, what am I supposed to do."

"Just be yourself, but you know, don't try to kill him." Lucy laughed

"I wouldn't try to kill him... well unless he tries something, then it's his fault." Gemma laughed

"So where is he taking you on your date?"

"He didn't say, he just wanted to go to dinner just the two of us."

"Well if he brought you flowers just to ask you to dinner, it will probably be somewhere nice. So you should dress nice, and not in black. I know the perfect dress!" Lucy ran to Gemma's wardrobe and pulled out a short pink dress. Gemma had bought it months ago, but only wore it once. "Here, this is perfect!"

"I don't know, what else do I have? Pink reminds me too much of Kelley."

"Everything reminds you of Kelley." Lucy sighed, "I'll try to find something else." She rummaged through the wardrobe more and found a dark green dress. It wasn't very fancy, no elaborate stitching, no gems or jewels, just simple. She had never even seen Gemma wear it before. "How about this."

"That should work just fine."

"When did you get this one? I've never seen it before."

"I got in the town by the lagoon. I was bored one day and went shopping with Anna-Maria."

"I'm surprised you picked this out, it's not really your style of dress."

"What do you mean?"

"Well most of your dresses have some sort of elaborate stitching or something that sparkles. This doesn't have any of that."

"I liked it when I had it on, so I figured that it would be worth having."

"Well I'm sure you will still look incredible in it. Finn will love anything you wear."

Gemma just gave her a small smile. Lucy knew that Gemma was just doing this to get over Kelley, that she just didn't know what to do anymore.

She had a late start to her day, spending her morning on a ship where Patrick would receive his punishment. She had made a deal with Nik that she would get to speak to him right before the ship left port. She knew he wasn't coming back, everyone except Lucy knew he wasn't coming back. She wanted to be the one to tell him his fate if she couldn't do it herself. She rushed to the pub when she was finished on the ship. Her fear of seeing him around town had completely vanished.

The day was going fine at the pub until a new ship came in. The locales were a buzz about the new ship. Unsure how they would act compared to the other pirates that frequented there. Unfortunately they turned out to be one of the more rowdy group of pirates. A chair went flying across the room. She threw a dagger into a pirates shoulder. She started breaking up the fight when a drunk grabbed the shoulder of her dress. Ripping it and exposing her tattoos. She pushed him down, grabbed her dagger and went back behind the bar. A tall, large built, scruffy man with wild strawberry blonde hair approached her at the bar.

"Rough crowd tonight."

"Ha! This is nothing."

"Interesting that someone like you would consider this an easy night. I figured you of all mermaids would be locked up until your wedding. Your highness."

Her eyes widened with every word he spoke. Her highlights went white before flickering to a deep crimson. She slammed her hands on the bar in front of him. Radiating a red burst locking everyone in their place. She glared into his eyes.

"Who in the underworld are you?" Her growl was deep. Silencing the room and muting their conversation from everyone else.

"Well your tattoo gave you away for one thing, you look identical to your mother when she married grandfather, oh and I'm your nephew. Any other questions darling?"

"What do you want from me?"

"Well I'm in a pub, so obviously I would like a drink. Just ale. I don't drink the hard stuff in port."

"Why are you here?"

"To get a drink? What part of me being in a pub are you not understanding?"

She slammed a pint in front of him. "Who sent you to find me?"

"Who sent me? No one. This is just a port we stopped at. Who in the oceans do you think would send me?"

"I don't know. You haven't told me which one of my siblings you belong to."

"Technically I don't belong to anyone. I'm captain of a ship you see."

"Your dodging my question. Which sibling."

"Listen. I don't do the whole royal family thing. I took off the day I got my powers. You're the first one in the family I've seen and spoken to since then."

"Who damn it!"

"Fjord."

"Erik..." her voice caught. She knew he had been missing for years, her father refused to help fjord find him because he wanted to protect Erik from something. "If you even breathe my name to him. I will pull every ounce of salt water from your veins and watch you writhe in pain until you're dead."

"Honey. I'm the last one you have to worry about telling the family where you are. I left that life. Actually I was banished by my father."

"For what? What could you have possibly done to make Fjord of all mermen banish his only male heir?"

"He doesn't approve of who I want to be with."

"Let me guess, a human?"

"I mean, sure. A human works for me, but so do mermen. I'm not that hard to please."

"If you're interested in men, then why are you acting like you're trying to flirt with me and those other women you were talking to earlier."

"Because I'm a siren darling. I flirt with whoever I need to, to get the info I need. How do you think I became captain of a pirate ship?"

"I swear if I find out that you've told someone who I really am-"

"If I did, that means exposing myself. I quite enjoy my life. Don't plan on changing it anytime soon. Now be a dear sweet auntie and fetch me another pint. I see some fresh meat that seems to be oozing with information for me."

She handed him another pint. "You call me your highness or by my real name one more time in this pub and I'll personally slit your throat. And in this pub no one would even blink. Do I make myself clear?"

"Quite clear, auntie. Best to cover up that tattoo. You're giving yourself away."

She released everyone and went in back to change her dress. She knew he was right. Her tattoo exposed who she was. She kept a close eye on him as he drank and flirted with everyone who walked into the pub. It was like watching a bee go from flower to flower. After a few hours he returned to the bar to grab another drink. He waved her down.

"What do you want Erik?"

"Woah careful with the Erik thing. I don't want anyone knowing where I come from."

"Then what do I call you." She rolled her eyes.

"Damion Drake is what I go by now, auntie."

"Keep calling me auntie and I'll start calling you nephew, loud enough for everyone to hear."

He raised his hands in surrender. "Alright, I concede. Would you prefer I use your real name? Or have you changed your name as well."

"I go by Gemma here. But you so much as breathe a syllable of who I am here or anywhere else. I will cut out your tongue, eyes and hands before pulling the salt. Understand?"

"Listen you can stop with the threats. We want the same thing. For no one to know who we are. I've kept myself hidden from my father and the rest of the family since you were one. I don't intend to ever return to the family. I enjoy my life. So no need to threaten me."

"The threats are needed. Your father and Delanson are hunting me down. How do I know you don't have one of your father's spies on your ship?"

"Because I'm not stupid. I would never allow anyone who works for the family near my ship. The last thing I want is for them to find me. I've lived in peace for nearly twenty years. I plan to keep it that way."

"Then why expose yourself to me?"

"I wouldn't have if your sleeve hadn't ripped and nearly exposed your identity. You get exposed and my father and uncle will be here before I can get out of port. The last merman I ever want to see again is him."

"So you we're doing it to cover your own tail." She said flatly. She rolled her eyes and continued working. "Just do me a favor anytime you stop at this port. Don't call me auntie."

"But you are my auntie."

"Keep throwing that around and the humans will get suspicious. You want to keep your identity a secret? Don't call me auntie. I'm half your age."

"How about this, I won't call you auntie unless you become queen. You are the only legitimate heir to the throne. While grandfather is immortal, and very unlikely for you to be crowned."

"Fine. But if that day comes, I want your unconditional loyalty."

"Only if you promise to kill my father and Delanson." He extended his hand for her to shake.

She gave him a nod before accepting his terms. She handed him another pint and walked further down the bar to help other customers. Making that deal with him would help them both. If she did ever become queen, she would at least have one member of the royal family on her side. Although she didn't really want to deal with him to have that loyalty, it was a start. Especially since he could help with the pirates as well.

With all the things Nik & Hades had been hinting at with an underwater war. It was clear that something's might be changing. Maybe not anytime soon, but eventually. She noticed the time and knew Erik needed to get out of there before Nik showed up for poker night.

"You might want to leave."

"Why? I'm having a great time chatting with you, my dear."

"Well if you don't mind being caught by Nikoli, then I guess you can stay."

His eyes widened. He reached into his pocket, handing her a very large sum of money. Way more that what he owed.

"Thanks for the warning. I'll see you next time."

He left quickly, going the opposite direction of the docks. She shrugged as she went back to work. Only to see Nik there a minute later.

43

Gemma was upstairs getting ready, when Finn came to the door.

"Finley, please come in. Don't you look charming tonight." Shannon said, "Gemma should be down shortly."

Finn handed Shannon a small bouquet of flowers, then sat patiently downstairs while waiting for Gemma.

"Oh thank you Finley! That was very thoughtful of you."

Gerard knocked on Gemma's door and went in.

"Gemma, Finn is waiting for you."

Gemma sighed, "I know, I'm just really nervous. Am I ready for this?"

"I don't know, I'm not you. However, you will never know until you try. If it doesn't feel right, then you don't have to do it again. But it is worth a try, right?"

"I guess you're right. How do I look?"

"You look great. Now get down there before he gets more nervous than he already is."

"Alright." She sighed

She walked downstairs and into the living room. As soon as she walked into the room Finn stood up and walked over to her. He handed her a large bouquet of roses, Gemma didn't know what to do.

"Thank you, they are beautiful." She smiled at him.

"Not as beautiful as you." He said.

Gemma blushed, she started to feel a bit awkward, Shannon was watching them with a big smile on her face. Gerard was at the top of the stairs, watching them like an over protective big brother.

"Ready to go?" He asked, feeling uncomfortable as well.

"Yeah, let's get going. Shannon do you mind putting these in some water for me?"

"Of course. I will put them in your room."

"Thank you." They were just about to walk out the door when Gerard ran down the stairs and stopped them.

"I will come get you if it starts to rain. Okay?" He whispered, Gemma just nodded.

When they arrived she froze when she saw where he took them. It was Donovan's, the nicest restaurant in town. It had a strict dress code. She had never been there before, but had heard Lucy talk about how much she wanted to go there. She looked down at the dress she chose and knew she was underdressed. She wrapped her shawl around her tighter. She had never been underdressed before, her father would never accept that. She looked around at the other women going into the restaurant in their elegantly dresses. Her plain deep green dress that she thought would be perfect for a first date of going to the cafe, was nowhere near appropriate for there. The collar of the dress feeling increasingly tighter by the second. A suffocating feeling she had never felt about clothes before. The fear of her father's repercussions for her not following the rules was causing her hand to slightly tremble.

Finn looked back at her, his smile dropping. The fear in her eyes was not something he expected. He thought she would be ecstatic to be going to Donovan's, everyone else in town always were. He screwed up. He made her uncomfortable. After months of asking her to dinner. Rejection after rejection. She finally says yes, and he blew it. He needed to think of a way to salvage this. He was head over heels for her and refused to let his one chance be ruined.

"Do you want to go somewhere else?" He said softly.

"No, its fine. I just feel underdressed for this place. I didn't know we were going to such a nice place, I would've worn something more appropriate."

"You look wonderful. But if you don't feel comfortable here, we can go somewhere else. I just want us to have a good time. I won't be upset if you want to go somewhere else."

"No, really its fine, we can stay." She was looking down at her dress, unable to look him in the eye as she lied. She desperately wanted to leave.

"Wait here." He walked off further into the restaurant.

Gemma sat waiting for a little while, no one had come to take her to her seat or anything. She was starting to feel discouraged, wanting to leave, but then Finn came back. He was carrying a few boxes with him, with a big smile on his face. One of the waiters was following him carrying more things.

"Come on Gemma, I have a better idea."

Gemma followed them back out to the car, Finn and the waiter put everything in the car. Finn opened the door for Gemma and told her he would be right back, he just needed to get one more thing. Finn walked back in with the waiter, while Gemma sat and waited again. She couldn't help but think that this wasn't going so well. Maybe she had made a mistake. Finn came back with a bottle of wine and another rose. He got back in the car, and they left.

He handed her the rose and said, "I'm sorry that took so long, and that I took you there. I should have taken you somewhere less formal for a first date. I just really wanted to impress you, and thought that you would like it there."

"It was fine, we didn't have to leave."

"You were uncomfortable, and I didn't want you to be uncomfortable. I want you to enjoy yourself tonight. I really like you, and wanted to do something special for you."

"Thank you. I would've been fine, but I felt so underdressed. I'm pretty sure I would be grounded for eternity if my father caught me that underdressed."

"I promise I will take you back again, but I will tell you that we are going there so you can dress how appropriately you feel necessary."

"Thank you, that would be helpful." She said giving him a little smile.

"Sounds like your father is really strict."

"He is, but his reason for appearances makes sense. So where are we going now?"

"Some place I think you would feel better at."

They drove for a little bit longer, finally they stopped when they reached a grassy area by a cliff. He had Gemma stay in the car a little bit longer while he set up, but told her to not turn around and see what he was doing. After about ten minutes of waiting he opened her door and held out his hand. She gently placed her hand in his, a bit nervous. He told her to close her eyes, so she did. He walked her behind the car and had her open her eyes. He had set up a picnic for them. There was a blanket laid out on the ground. A dozen small lanterns giving them some light. On the blanket he had a basket, plates and glasses, as well as a bottle of wine. When he walked her over to the blanket she saw the view, it was of the ocean.

"Finn, this is incredible! How did you come up with this?"

"Well you always talk about the sea, and you looked so upset, that I thought this would make you feel the best."

"It's absolutely wonderful! I love it. Thank you."

They sat, ate and chatted for hours. Gemma was actually feeling a little bit happy, something she hadn't felt in a long time. She began shivering in the cool evening air. Finn took his jacket off and wrapped it around her shoulders. After they finished eating he ran back to the car and came back with a small white box.

"Another surprise?" She said

Finn just laughed. "It's just dessert don't worry." He opened the box and there sat two chocolate cupcakes.

"They look delicious."

"Well I hope they are. Otherwise I will have to have a talk with Francis." He laughed

"Who is Francis?"

"He is the pastry chef at the restaurant. He helped me get everything I needed."

"How do you know him?"

"I work at the restaurant, he's a good friend of mine now."

"Really? But I thought you worked at one of the shops in town."

"I've only worked there a few weeks, Francis got me the job. He knows I really want to learn how to cook and hopefully be a chef there one day."

"I never knew that. Why didn't you tell me?"

"I haven't told many people. My father wants me to do what he did, but I am not interested in what he did."

"What did he do?"

"He worked on a merchant ship for years, then retired from there to run his shop in town. Its where I used to work, but I hated every minute I would be there. I really hope to one day be able to cook as good as some of the chefs in the restaurant."

"I'm sure you will, it will just take time and practice. One day we have to get you out of this town though. Then you could learn to cook from different places."

"I never really thought about that, I've always heard that France, Italy and Spain are great places for food. My father talks about it all the time, and how much he misses it."

"I'm sure if you learned to cook some recipes from places that he likes a lot, he would be very happy that you were a chef. Who knows maybe one day you could open your own restaurant."

"That would actually be a dream come true for me." He said with a smile

"Well one day when you are confident in what you cook, I would love to try something."

"Really?" He said excitedly

"Of course. Why wouldn't I?"

"I don't know. I just didn't think anyone would want to try anything I made."

"I promise, one day I will try something you make me." She smiled and grabbed his hand. "This has really been lovely. Thank you."

"Thank you for finally saying yes." He laughed. "I honestly didn't think it would ever happen."

"Sorry it took so long, I have been trying to get over some things."

"Oh. I'm sorry. I really didn't want to bring up anything to remind you. I hope that didn't just ruin everything."

"No, no. Its fine. I really am having a great time. However, I think we should get going soon. It is really late, I'm sure Gerard is sitting up waiting for me to get home."

"He treats you like a little sister doesn't he?" He laughed

"Yeah. It's okay though, I treat him like a big brother." She laughed, "We are the closest thing to siblings that either one of us have."

"I thought you had a bunch of siblings."

"I do, but they are much older than me. I didn't grow up with them around or anything. I only ever saw them once every couple of years. They don't like me, and always fight with our father. They never really felt like siblings, just estranged relatives. I do have an adopted sister who I'm close with, Gerard and Lucy met her while I was away for a few months. But she lives across the ocean from here so seeing her is rare."

"Why aren't you staying with one of them?"

"I'm not safe around them. I'm safe with my sister, but my brothers know I would be staying with her so it's not safe there either."

"Oh."

"Sorry, my whole family life is complicated. That's why I really don't like to talk about it. It's too confusing to explain to everyone. Lucy and Gerard don't even know much about my family. They just know to never bring it up."

"Well thank you for telling me. I like when you talk to me, and not try to hide yourself."

"It's just easier to hide everything."

"I understand that. Why do you think I haven't told my father where I work now."

"Because it's easier to just not tell him." She giggled.

"Exactly." He smiled at her, and interlocked his fingers with hers.

They stared at the stars for a little longer. Then he helped her up and they put everything back in the car and left. When they got back to the Collins house he walked her to the door. She thanked him for such a wonderful evening, and she gave him a small peck on the cheek, then went inside. When she got inside, Gerard was sitting up waiting for her.

"You didn't have to wait up for me." She said to him.

"What if it had rained?"

"I would have either called, or he would have figured it out. Still you didn't have to wait up for me."

"I was just being cautious. So where did he take you?"

"Well first he took me to Donovan's."

"Really? Wow! Please don't tell Lucy that. I haven't even taken her there."

"Why not? It seemed really nice, and the food was incredible."

"I can't afford that place, especially now. Maybe for our anniversary I can save up enough to take her there and not worry about the cost."

"I didn't realize it was that expensive. I knew it had to be, I felt so underdressed that we ended up leaving."

"What? Really? Why? And where did you go after that?"

"Well he noticed that I felt uncomfortable there, because of how underdressed I felt. So he had the chefs and waiter put everything in boxes, including dishes, a blanket, lanterns and even a bottle of wine. Then they put it in the car and he drove us to this field by the cliff that overlooks the bay. He made me wait in the car while he set it all up. When I got out of the car there were lanterns everywhere and the picnic was laid out so perfectly. It was really wonderful."

"Wow! He went all out on the first date. I'm surprised he could afford that place."

"Well he works there now, so I guess they gave him a lower price or something."

"When did he start working there? I thought he worked for his father."

"He said he has been there for a few weeks, he hated the shop that his father owns. He says that he wants to be a chef one day, and that one of the chef's at Donovan's got him the job there."

"Well you will have to tell Lucy all of this tomorrow. You know she is really wanting to know how it went."

"Don't worry I plan on it." Gemma then went upstairs and went to bed.

She sat there thinking about how great of a night it was. Still unsure of her feelings towards Finn, but glad she at least gave him a chance. She knew she could never be with Kelley again, he could never come back. She realized that she had to accept that, accept that all their hopes were gone. That he wasn't going to show up after her wedding and save her, that she would never see him again. It was time for her to accept her fate, the future she dreaded more than anything. Time for dreams of running away to be happy were gone. She was stuck, her acceptance was mandatory now. She had to go along with the marriage, no matter how horrible it will be. Game, set, match, her father's plan continues as he wants.

44

Gemma helped Gerard and Lucy start settling into their new house. They were so happy to have their own place. It was not normal for a couple to live together before they were married, however given the circumstances of everything that had happened, it was understood. They were all excited, Lucy was already figuring out how she wanted every room. She let Gemma design her own room though, she would be living with them until her own wedding. Lucy had Gemma spending every free moment she had, helping her plan the wedding. It was good for Gemma, she kept herself so busy, that it took her mind off of everything. She was so busy that when she would go to the Lagoon, all she wanted to do was relax. Even there she was busy though, Gemma spent most days teaching Anna-Maria how to fight. When they weren't training, they were just spending time together, becoming closer friends.

"Gemma, what do you think of this color?" Lucy asked,

"For what?"

"For the wedding, what else?"

"I know that, but what at the wedding? Table cloths? The dress? Other décor?"

"For your dress!"

"It's nice, but you have to see what it would look like as a dress and if it looks good."

"Good point. Let's just go to the dress shop and see what they have."

"Okay, and if you don't find anything here, we can look at the dress shop near the lagoon."

"I never thought about that! That will be very helpful!"

"So I talked to Henry about using the ball room for the reception, he says that's fine. The only thing is they don't have any openings until January."

"Well, I guess we can push it back a month. As long as we can get the banquet hall, we really want the reception to be held there."

"I will let him know that January is fine. He said he can have the tent set up for the same day as well."

"Perfect!" Lucy was excited that things were already starting to come together. "How are things going with Finn? You seem to be spending a decent amount of time with him."

"Things are fine. He wants to spend more time with me, but I'm so busy I don't get as much time for him as he wants."

"Well make time."

Gemma laughed, "I can't! I work everyday, then after work I'm helping you with wedding stuff, and training Molly. On weekends and every other week I am at the lagoon. And he works afternoons and evenings, so my free time he is at work. It's just hard to figure it out."

"Well you don't have to go to the lagoon every weekend! You can stay here sometimes and spend some time with him. And I can come with you to the lagoon sometimes and we can work on wedding planning there, so you have a little free time while here."

"I guess we could give that a try. Maybe I can see if he can get a day off this weekend, or some other night this week."

"You really should, you need to have a little fun."

"Would you mind coming with me to the lagoon this week? I would love for you to meet Anna-Maria, and then we can work on wedding planning there. You can see the dress shop, see some different options."

"I guess I can. I have to check with Ma, and Gerard."

"Do you think Peggy would want to come with us to the lagoon this week? It might be good for her to get away, she hasn't been back since my birthday."

"I'm sure she would love it. I'll ask her when I go home for dinner."

"You know that this is your home now right?" Gemma laughed

"I know, but It's still home, it's where I lived my whole life. Just like your home is still the castle in Atlantis."

"Atlantis hasn't been my *home* for a long time."

"Just because you moved here doesn't mean it's not your home."

"No, that's not why. It stopped feeling like home before I moved here. Before I even knew I was moving here. The ocean will always be my home, but the castle isn't. That's my father's home, all of my siblings feel the same. My home is the lagoon, even without Kelley, that is my home."

"Well the lagoon will always feel a second home to all of us. There is no other place in the world like it, it's magical."

Gemma smiled, she knew how magical it truly was there. It was the big reason why she loved it so much there. She just hoped that whoever she marries, doesn't ruin all of the magic and memories she already had there. She knew those memories were going to be the only thing to get her through all of this.

"Can Gerard come too?"

"Sure, you know he's always welcome."

"Well I wasn't sure if you just wanted a girl's weekend or something."

"We will have that weekend right before your wedding." Gemma laughed.

45

The next day while Gemma was working Finn decided to stop in and see her, hoping that he could possibly get to spend lunch with her. He walked right up to the bar, it was extremely busy, so he knew that it would probably be the only spot he could actually talk to her.

"You seem unusually busy today, are you going to get a lunch break at all?" He asked

"Hi Finn! I'm not sure, it's kind of crazy in here right now. I don't have any plans after work today though, I'm not sure if you are working or anything."

"Unfortunately I am working tonight. I was just hoping to catch lunch with you before going to work. That doesn't look possible though."

"I'm sorry, it's horrible in here today. When is your next day off?"

"Tomorrow night, but you are training Molly then."

"We can ask Molly if she would mind taking a night off. I'm sure she would understand if I cancelled on her one night."

"Alright, I will talk to her, I will come pick you up at six. Is that alright?"

"That's fine." Gemma said smiling at him. Then she heard the sound of glass shattering, and a fight starting. She sighed. "I have to get back to work. I will see you tomorrow."

"Gemma, we are going to Donovan's, so wear whatever you will feel comfortable in there." He teased

"Alright, I will find something. Thank you." She smiled at him, then heard a table being knocked over. Finn saw her grab her sword from behind the bar, and watched her storm over to the fight. He lightly chuckled to himself as he walked out of the pub.

It was easy to tell who had been in there before, and knew who she was. When they would see her walking their way, they would instantly stop. If this was someone's first time meeting her, they didn't stop, and always regretted it.

She marched right up to the men fighting. One of them saw her, he knew who she was and instantly backed away. The other didn't know any better and kept trying to fight. He had his fist in the air, about to throw a punch at the other man. Gemma threw a dagger at his fist, it landed directly between his middle and pointer knuckles.
"WHAT THE HELL!" The man groaned in pain. He looked around, trying to find out where it came from. Then he saw her holding a sword, still walking towards him. The look on her face struck fear into all of the other men there. He just stood there and began to laugh.

"You can't tell me you are all afraid of some little girl. Go on girl, go back to the dress shop." He laughed.

"Ugh! Why does everyone think I belong in a dress shop." She mumbled under her breath.

His laughter was stopped instantly when she threw him against the wall holding her sword to his throat. "You think this is some kind of joke? You think I'm afraid to cause you an immense amount of pain?" She shouted. The other men backed further away, they all knew better.

"Go home child! This is a matter that is to be dealt with by men." He said

Everyone in the room stopped what they were doing, and stared at them. Gemma looked over at Callie, she gave her a nod, which always meant *do as you wish*. Callie hated it whenever anyone told either of them that something was for men. Callie then began walking towards them as well. More of the men scattered.

"Oh really, this is a matter for men?" Callie said, "Gemma, you can finish him, however you please. Quick, slow, ruthless. I don't care, just finish this vial piece of scum."

"I think slow and painful, sounds more appropriate." Gemma said, glaring at the man.

"Wait, What?" He said, "Yer gonna have this little girl kill me for starting a fight?"

"No, for saying *this is a matter for men.* Ask anyone here what happens if someone tries to belittled the two of us for being women." Callie now had a sword to his throat as well.

"That is no reason to kill a man!"

"In this pub it is!" Gemma said through her teeth. "The town knows how things work in here. Now enough talking!" She drove her sword deep between his ribs, puncturing his lung. She pulled her sword out. "Your lung should be filling up with blood, becoming harder to breathe."
The man began coughing up blood, spitting it on the floor at her feet. Holding his chest and wound.

"Shall I continue Callie? Or should we just let this be a warning for him?"

"Let's just have this be a warning. But if he ever comes back in here and disrespects either of us, again, then finish him."

Gemma pulled the dagger from his hand. "I better never see you in here again, or you will be in more pain than you can imagine." She growled.

He was in pain, but angry. Gemma began to walk away, Callie stayed where she was. She moved the sword from his throat and let go of him, about to walk away as well. He grabbed his own dagger from his belt and threw it at Gemma. It hit her right shoulder, piercing her trident tattoo. She screamed in pain as the floor quaked. A golden electrical current coursed through her body, radiating from her tattoo. Callie threw the man back against the wall, dagger to his throat, seconds away from finishing him. Gemma whipped around, she pulled the dagger from her shoulder. She started storming towards him again. One of the other men grabbed a chair and put it in front of the man, giving Gemma more height. She took his dagger and drove it through his right eye.

"YOU DARE TEST ME?" She shouted, as a clap of thunder followed her words. A massive storm was now stirring outside. "YOU HAVE NO IDEA WHO YOU ARE DEALING WITH!" There was another loud clap of thunder as lightning struck the ground right outside of the pub.

"Gemma would you like me to finish this piece of scum?"

"NO! This one is MINE!" She boomed through the room, making the room start shaking. She sounded as terrifying as her father. Callie was becoming worried about her identity staying a secret. Only Poseidon and Gemma could cause a room to shake like this.

"Then make it quick. Who was fighting this man?"

"Him" Gemma pointed to a man who had a bloody nose.

"You will dispose of his body after we finish him. If you ever want to come back in here again, you will do as we say. UNDERSTAND?" Callie said to the other man,

"Yes ma'am" He said in a terrified voice.

"Alright, let's get this over with!" Callie said to Gemma.

Gemma took her dagger, slicing his throat fast and deep. He dropped to the ground gripping tight to his throat. Gemma stood over him as his blood soaked the floor. "Never underestimate a woman." She said while glaring at him. The pirate that got her the chair, extended his hand to help her down. She looked at who it was, it was Jamison, the one who saved her before. She gave him a slight smile then gently placed her hand in his, held her head high and stepped down from the chair. "Someone clean this up." She shouted while storming off to the back room, slamming the door behind her.

Callie just smiled when she watched Gemma walked away. Two men grabbed his body and dragged it out of the pub. Another grabbed a mop and began to clean up the blood, while some of the others picked up the chairs and tables.

Gemma unbuttoned the top of her dress and pulled the shoulder down. She inspected her wound, there was too much blood to see where it really was. She grabbed a wet rag trying to clean up as much blood as possible. Once it was cleaned up she pressed her hand on the wound and healed herself. Callie walked into the room. Gemma quickly held some gauze in place, to be sure Callie didn't see that she had healed herself. Callie grabbed some clean clothes off of one of the shelves and handed them to Gemma.

"You handled yourself well in there. I didn't think you had it in you to finish the job." Callie said proudly

"Not the first time I've killed someone, and it probably won't be the last. I try my best to hold back, but I couldn't this time." Gemma grumbled, her blood was still boiling.

"Well I'm proud of you. You have no need to continue training anymore. I have taught you everything that I could."

"Wait, you don't want to train me anymore?" Gemma said, a bit confused.

"There is no need, you can take care of yourself perfectly. We can still practice some mornings, but I have nothing left that I could possibly teach you."

"Really?"

"Really. You can handle anything. Unless you want to start learning how to use a pistol, then we will have some more work cut out of us."

"Well I would like to be familiar with one, just to know how to use one in case I ever need it."

"Alright, we will work on that now with your training. Go home for the day, your shift ends in an hour, take off a little early today. You earned it."

"Thanks Callie, I will."

Once Callie left the room, Gemma finished healing herself then changed. When she left the back room, all of the men were very quiet. All filled with fear from this petite young girl. The storm had stopped, so she left. When she got back to Lucy and Gerard's house, Lucy saw Gemma's bloody clothes in her arms.

"What happened this time?" Lucy sighed.

"Just another piece of sea scum that I had to deal with."

"This is a lot more blood than usual. What happened?" She said as she inspected Gemma's clothes.

"I didn't hold back this time, I did as my father would have. I showed no mercy."

Lucy just shook her head. "Why? What did he do to cause you to end his life?"

"He insulted the fact that I was a woman. I was just going to leave him injured but he threw a dagger at me and it stuck into my shoulder. That was the final straw. I was not going to hold back on someone who hurt me." She said confidently.

"Well Gerard is going to love this story when he gets home." Lucy sighed. "Come on, let's go get this cleaned up."

The next day at the pub, there wasn't a single fight. Everyone behaved themselves, not wanting to irritate Gemma and Callie again. Then Nik and a tall man she had seen a few times before came in. A man she knew was her fiancé's first mate. Callie took them in back, Gemma wanted to talk to them both, but knew it was best not to. When Nik came out, he had Gemma come sit with him at a table to talk.

"Did you really kill a man yesterday?"

"Yes." She said confidently. "Do you have a problem with that?"

"No, but your fiancé does. That man was a member of his crew, he isn't happy with what you did."

"Well maybe you should inform him that his men need to learn to have some respect, and not test me! It's always his crew that I have the most trouble with. Maybe that's saying something about him." She said sarcastically while glaring at him. "Please inform him that if another one of his men show's me that kind of disrespect and hurt me again. I will be much more ruthless than I was yesterday."

"He hurt you? Are you alright? What happened?"

"Callie didn't tell you what happened?"

"No, she thought you would enjoy telling me what happened."

"He started a fight and wouldn't stop. I threw a dagger at his hand, and he began to insult me for being a woman. He said this was a matter for men."

"Well that right there was his death wish in this pub." Nik laughed,

"I then drove my sword through his ribs, puncturing his lung. Callie said I could finish him, but we decided to give him a chance to learn some respect. As I walked away he threw a dagger at my shoulder. So I stabbed him in the eye, yelled at him for being stupid enough to test me. Then slit his throat."

"This is going to be a story your father will be very proud of you for." Nik said with a smile.

Gemma smiled when he said that. She knew that he would be proud of her for that.

"However, you need to be more careful. The only reason I knew that something happened was the storm you created yesterday."

"I'm sorry about the storm, but not about what I did yesterday."

"Well, just try to control your temper, I know it's hard. I have to deal with your father having the same problem. However, you can still learn how to control yourself. Please just work on that for me."

"I will try. But I think the only reason the storm happened is because the dagger pierced my trident tattoo. I wasn't angry enough to cause a storm, and I felt an electrical current going through my body."

"It landed in your trident." Nik's face drained of all color, his eyes widening as he looked her over. "Were you able to heal it?"

"Of course. It looks like nothing had happened. The storm stopped once I finished healing it. That's how I figured out that's what caused the storm."

"Thankfully you were able to heal it. I was worried that I would have to get your father to use his trident to heal it. Whenever one of your siblings got an injury there, they became comatose until your father healed it. Ty and Cane couldn't control their own powers until the other was healed. It's why the family armor is so strong at the shoulder. An injury there won't kill you but it can cause serious problems with your powers and if not healed quick enough, can cause a coma. Bash was in a coma for a while because of his injury there."

"Good to know. I guess that's where I should target Delanson and Fjord. It would at least slow them down." She stood up knowing she needed to get back to work. "I should get back to work, I get off in a couple of hours. I have plans after work and I can't be late."

"More wedding planning with Lucy?"

"No... I have a date."

"A date?" He said in a concerned tone. "With who? How long has this been going on?"

"Don't worry this won't affect father's plans. It's just a boy in town. It's nothing serious, I've only been seeing him for a month. It's nothing to be concerned about. He's nice, and keeps me distracted from the reality of my life."

"Tell him nothing, no matter what he says. He can know nothing about who you really are."

"I know, and I wasn't planning on ever telling him. The only thing I might tell him one day, is the fact that I am in an arranged marriage."

"Fine, but nothing else. I don't care how much he begs, tell him nothing."

"I know Nik. I know not to tell anyone. You don't have to remind me."

"Well with how reckless you have been lately, I had to be sure you remembered."

"I've told you to stop saying that I am being reckless. I have control of myself!"

"I'm sorry, I mean with your emotions, not your actions. You just need to learn to control your temper better."

Gemma sighed. "I know. I will work on that. Now I really have to get going. I don't want to be late tonight."

"Gemma." He said grabbing her hand. "Please be careful."

"I will. I promise." She said as she went back to work.

46

When Finn showed up that night, Gemma was dressed in a teal knee length dress. Completely covered in silver and teal beading, it seemed to be low cut, but had sheer covering her chest. The back was almost completely bare, showing every bit of her tattoos.

Finn handed her flowers he brought for her, and said "You look stunning." Then kissed her cheek.

"Thank you." She smiled at him.

Gerard and Lucy were sitting in the room watching them. Gerard was watching like a protective big brother, but also as Kelley's best friend. Making sure that he was good enough for her, even if it was only temporary. Lucy was watching as her best friend, just happy to see her trying to move on.

"Ready to go?" Finn said smiling at her.

"Yeah, let's go." She looked over at Gerard and Lucy, "No need to wait up for me."

"You know we will anyways." Lucy said smiling. "Have fun!"

"Bye…" Gemma laughed while walking out the door.

When they got to the restaurant they were taken to a small table, close to the kitchen. Gemma could tell that Finn wasn't like his normal self, he seemed nervous. He kept getting up from the table and leaving, constantly going into the kitchen. She spent a lot of time at the table alone, then he stopped leaving right before dinner arrived.

"Is everything alright?" She asked

"Umm, yeah. Why?" He replied nervously.

"You're not acting like yourself. Usually you're excited every chance we get to spend together, but you seem nervous about something." She said.

"It's nothing." He answered.

"Do you want to leave?" She asked

"What?"

"Do you want to leave? You're not happy here right now, so do you want to leave?"

"No, it's nothing like that. I'm just a little nervous right now."

Gemma reached across the table and grabbed his hand. "What are you nervous about? It's not like we haven't been out to dinner before."

Finn looked into her eyes, he could see she was genuinely concerned for him. He held her hand a little tighter, and took a deep breath. "Remember on our first date, how I told you wanted to be a chef?"

"Of course! I think it's wonderful." She said with a smile.

"Well, you told me if I ever made something you would try it."

"What does that have to do with how you are acting tonight?" She asked.

"Well, I have been running off to the kitchen the whole time because I made our dinner tonight. I still had Francis make our dessert, he wanted to make sure that if our dinner is awful that at least our dessert would be good." He explained

Gemma giggled a little bit, "You don't need to be nervous, I'm sure that it is wonderful. Should we try it, just to be sure?"

"I don't know, you will be the first person besides Francis to try anything I have made."

"What does Francis say?"

"He says it's good, I change the recipes a little bit, so it always throws him off."

Gemma took her fork and took a piece of the steak, getting ready to take a bite when someone came out of the kitchen.

"Be careful! You never know what he might have put in there."

Francis said

"Francis stop! You know how nervous I am about this." Finn said.

"Oh you're fine! Don't worry my dear, I tried some before I let them bring it out here. Trust me it's safe." Francis winked at her.

"Francis this is Gemma." Finn said as he rolled his eyes.

"It's nice to finally meet you miss Gemma. I've heard a lot about you, he is *always* talking about you. I'm not sure if he has anything else to talk about." Francis teased.

"Francis..." Finn said through his teeth in the most irritated and embarrassed tone possible.

Gemma giggled a little. Finn's face was bright red, she had never seen him embarrassed like this.

"Alright I'll leave, but I'm coming back when it's time for dessert."

Gemma and Finn ate their dinner, Gemma loved it. It was one of the best meals she had, had in a long time. Finn thought she was just trying to be nice, but she really loved it. She could tell that he was still uneasy about his cooking. Francis came out with their dessert, it was something that Gemma had never seen before. It looked strange to her, she couldn't figure out what it was. Francis and Finn just laughed at her facial expressions to the dessert.

"It's called a soufflé." Finn laughed, "Francis only makes this for special guests, so be honored that we get them."

"But what is it?" She asked as she inspected it.

"It's a dessert from France, I spent a decent amount of time there learning how to cook." Francis said with a smile.

"That is why he is the best pastry chef around, and why so many people want to eat here. It's all because of Francis." Finn bragged.

"Until you start cooking here, then people will be coming here for both of us. But first you need to get out of this town and learn about food from other places." Francis said nudging Finn.

"I've been saying the same thing! He needs to go see the world." Gemma said

"You two are never going to stop are you?" Finn groaned putting his face in his hands.

"Probably not." Francis said, winking at Gemma again. She couldn't help but smile. "Gemma, it looks like we are going to have to work harder on getting him to leave this place."

"It will take a lot, he doesn't seem to even want to leave the town." She giggled.

"Why do I need to leave? I have everything I could possibly need right here." Finn said.

"Finn, there is so much more to the world out there. You really need to get out of here. Explore, learn about more than what is directly around you. You might be surprised at how much you enjoy it." She said with a smile.

"I already told you Finn, if you go explore, when you get back we can open our own restaurant together. It would be incredible! I'm sure Gemma would come try our food." Francis said.

"Of course I would." She said smiling.

"Maybe one day I will go, but not alone." He looked at Gemma, smiling at her.

Gemma blushed, she was flattered, but knew it could never happen. "We will have to see." She said cautiously.

They quietly finished their dessert, then got ready to leave. Thanking Francis for their dessert before they left. They walked back to the car, still silent. They got back to the car, but before he opened the door for her, he pulled her close and kissed her. It was a nice kiss, but she didn't feel any spark between them. No fish swimming in her stomach, no color change, no tingling feelings. Just a simple kiss, no feelings associated with it. She knew instantly that she didn't have the same feeling for him, as he did for her. After he kissed her, he opened the car door and she got in. She sat there quietly as they drove back to Lucy and Gerard's. When they arrived the lights were still on, which meant that they were still up waiting for her.

Gemma sighed. "I should go inside, they're waiting up for me."

"Gemma wait." He said as he grabbed her hand. "What's going on? You've been quiet the whole way home"

"It's nothing, I just really should be going inside."

"Gemma there's something that I have been wanting to tell you. I have been wanting to say this for a long time, I just couldn't figure out when or how to say it."

"Finn, I have to go. I can't do this tonight."

"Gemma please, wait." He pulled her in for another kiss, she still felt nothing from it. "I love you."

Gemma pulled back slowly, "I have to go." She said opening the car door and getting out of the car. She had tears running down her cheeks as she ran to the front door.

"Gemma wait!" Finn shouted back to her, he tried chasing after her. She got inside the house right after the rain started. "Gemma please, can we talk." He said through the door.

She was sitting on the floor, her back against the door. Tears still streaming down her face. Lucy and Gerard heard Gemma crying and came running to her. Her tail had appeared from the rain. Gerard picked her up and carried her to her room. She was crying the whole way there. Lucy opened the door after Gemma was out of sight, and spoke with Finn alone.

"He didn't see did he?" Gerard asked

"No, I was inside with the door closed when I changed." She said through the tears.

"Okay, good. So do you want to talk about what's going on?" He asked.

"I do, but right now I just need to talk to Lucy."

"I'll go get her."

"Thank you."

"Lucy, can I please talk to her." Finn asked

"Tell me what happened and I will think about it." Lucy answered.

"I told her I love her, then she ran out of the car crying." He said

"You can talk to her tomorrow, right now she needs to talk to me." Lucy said sounding concerned.

Gerard came to the door, and told Lucy that Gemma needed her. Lucy ran up the stairs.

"Finn, go home. You can talk to her tomorrow." Gerard said.

"Please, I just need to talk to her. I don't know what I did wrong. I just told her that I love her." Finn said.

Gerard sighed "Finn, tonight... there is nothing you can do to make things better. Tomorrow will be better."

"Why is she crying because I said I love you?" Finn asked

"Because the last man that said that to her was Kelley, and now he is dead. She isn't ready for that type of relationship again. It's been a rough year for her, and anytime something reminds her of not just him, but those type of feelings, she becomes depressed again. Her life is much more complicated than you know. One day she will be able to explain but for now you have to trust me when I say that she isn't ready for that. Just think of how long it took her to finally say yes to going out to dinner with you. Even after she said yes, she was asking me if she was doing the right thing, if she was ready. She doesn't know what her emotional limits are right now, which causes her to break. Come back tomorrow to talk to her, just don't say that to her." Gerard explained.

Finn left, and Gerard joined the girl's upstairs. Gemma was still crying, Lucy was holding Gemma in her arms.

"I can't do this. I just can't! I can't put him through what I'm going through. He deserves better than this." She cried.

"Gemma what happened?" Lucy asked.

"He told me he loves me." She cried

"And you're upset because you feel the same and can't change your fate?" Lucy asked

"No, I don't love him. I like him, I just don't want him to feel this pain that I feel. I care about him a lot, just not in that way." She said through her tears. Lux came bounding into the room, jumping onto the bed and snuggling close to her.

"I don't understand." Lucy said confused.

"I do." Gerard said walking in, "She truly cares about him, just not in a romantic way. He loves her the way that she loves Kelley. She is in pain because she can't be with Kelley. She knows that if Finn feels that strongly for her, he will be completely crushed when she has to get married. She doesn't want him to feel that kind of pain. It's hard to watch someone you care about go through that kind of pain."

"Exactly." Gemma said through her tears. Gerard came over to her and held her like Lucy was just doing.

"How did you understand all of that?" Lucy asked

"This whole time we have been helping Gemma get through that same thing. You know how hard all of this has been for her. She just doesn't want to put him through the same thing. Come on Lucy, she needs to cry this one out, she needs to be alone for a little bit."

Lucy gave Gemma a hug, then they left her to be alone for a little bit. Gemma's legs were back so she quickly changed into something more comfortable. She searched her room for her memory crystal of Kelley and put it in a cup of water. She curled up in her bed with Lux humming and fell asleep to their memories.

The next night Finn showed up before work to talk to her. He needed to find out what happened. She tried to explain it to him, he said he understood and wouldn't say that again. But she could feel it in how he spoke to her, he didn't understand at all. He just said he did.

47

A month later he arrived early to pick her up for their date night. She loved going on dates with him, he really knew how to make her feel special. She felt as if he treated her as royalty, even though he had no idea who she really was. She was always excited for her date nights with him, it was one of the only things she looked forward to. When he walked into the house she was dressed as warm as she could, and even had some extra blankets, just to be prepared.

"Gemma, you really don't need to bring the blankets, we will be fine." He laughed while walking to the car.

"You told me to dress warm, it's freezing out, I'm just being prepared. I don't know what you have planned. You never tell me what our plans are."

"Well I like to surprise you." Finn laughed, "You can bring them if you want, but I don't think you will need it."

"I don't like to be cold!" She laughed, "I'm going to bring the blankets."

"How do you live here and not like the cold?" He laughed.

"You know I'm not from here. It's much warmer where I am from." She laughed.

"And where is that? You still won't tell me." He said placing his hand on her leg.

"I will tell you one day." She said taking his hand off her leg.

He looked down and saw the sparkling of her ring from Kelley. It killed him that she never took it off. Even when they were together, she always wore it. He knew that he could never tell her how he felt about it. If it had been from anyone other than from Kelley, or on any other finger, he wouldn't care so much. But it was a constant reminder that her whole heart still belonged to Kelley. Making him want to go to great lengths to get her over him. Help her realize that Kelley was never going to come back, that he was right here and madly in love with her.

When they pulled up to Donovan's, Gemma was confused. "I don't understand. Why did you tell me to dress warm if we were coming here? I would have dressed nicer."

"You will see. Trust me, you will love it. Now don't get upset with me, but I am going to blindfold you. It's just to make the surprise even better." He said as he kissed her as passionately as he could. She wrapped her arms around him, desperately trying to feel the same as he did. They stopped kissing and she smiled at him, not wanting him to know that she didn't feel the same as him.

"Why would you need to blindfold me?" Gemma giggled as he covered her eyes with a dark silk scarf.

"Just trust me, it's going to be great." He said as he finished putting the blindfold on her.

"Alright. Just don't let me get hurt okay?"

"I would never let you get hurt." He said as he kissed her again.

He walked her inside and upstairs, where you have to rent out the whole floor to be able to even go up there. Then he took her up another flight of stairs and opened another door. He took her outside somewhere, she now knew why he told her to dress warm, it was quite cold, but not as cold as it was down by the car. There was no wind or anything, it was just chilly.

"Finn, where are we? Can I take this thing off yet?" She lightly laughed.

"Not just yet. Give me another minute beautiful."

"Okay, but I might not be able to wait much longer." She was anxious, she loved surprises, but hated them at the same time.

"Alright, you can take it off now."

She slowly took off the scarf and looked around. She wasn't outside like she thought, she was in a room made completely out of glass. The walls, celling everything was glass. There were lights hanging from strings all over the room. Roses of every color were all over. In the center of the room was a small table for two, and an ice bucket holding a bottle of champagne. Finn came up to her and grabbed her hand and brought her to the table.

"Finn this is incredible! It's too much!" She said, completely in shock.

"Nothing is too much for you." He said pulling out her chair, then giving her a kiss.

"What's the special occasion?" She asked.

"Just enjoy this, please?" He said as he got their food for them.

"I am. I just can't believe that you did all this!" She said smiling.

Finn laughed, "Well this room is always here, only the staff know about it."

"Well it's beautiful! Thank you."

They enjoyed their dinner talking the whole time, everything they ate was amazing. Gemma couldn't believe that this was food he cooked for her. When they finished dinner Francis showed up with dessert.

"Thank you Francis. This looks delicious." Gemma said with a big smile.

"Well I hope you love it. Have you been enjoying yourself tonight?" Francis asked.

"I have! This room is incredible. I can't believe that no one knows about it."

"Well we try to keep it as a secret for special occasions for the staff." Francis said.

Right after Francis spoke, he saw Finn glaring at him. Francis then quickly left. "What's the special occasion?" Gemma asked with a smile on her face.

Finn took a deep breath, looking extremely nervous. "Gemma, you know that I love you. I have been thinking lately, about what you and Francis have been constantly telling me."

"You mean about you needing to get out of this town?" She teased.

"Yeah. Well I decided that I want to go, but I don't want to go alone." He stood up and walked over to her and held her hands. "I don't want to go with just anyone, I want to go with someone who means more to me than anything."

"Finn… where are you going with this?" Her smile vanished, she became nervous and worried.

"Just let me finish." Gemma became more nervous, her hands began trembling.
"Gemma, I want to share this experience with only one person."

"No no no no no… Finn please stop…. We can't…" She frantically cried.

"Gemma will you travel the world with me?" He asked.

Gemma quickly let go of his hand. "Finn, I can't." She got up quickly and started to head for the door.

Finn was in shock, he didn't understand what just happened. He quickly chased after her. "Gemma, wait! What just happened? What do you mean you can't?"

She turned around to face him, with tears starting to roll down her cheeks. "Finn, I can't. I can't go away with you." She said as they heard the rain hitting the glass roof.

"If you're just not ready, we can wait. I know we haven't been together long. I just know you are the one I want to be with." He said as he tried to wipe the tears from her eyes.

She pushed his hand away, "No Finn… I CAN'T go away with you, ever."

"What do you mean you can't ever? You're always saying I need to see the world. Why can't you come with me?"

Gemma took a deep breath, trying to calm herself a little more so he could understand her better. "I'm getting married, my wedding is in four months."

"You're getting married? To who? Why are you just telling me this now? How long have you been engaged?"

"I don't know who it is. It's an arranged marriage, this has been in place since before I came here."

"Why are you just telling me this now?"

"I've been wanting to tell you for a long time, I just didn't know how. I didn't know you were even thinking about taking things further."

"I just don't understand. I…"

"Finn… I'm so sorry. I never wanted to hurt you. This is the reason I said no to you for so long. I knew one day I would have to tell you, and that it would hurt you." She began to walk away, wiping a tear from her eye.

He grabbed her hand and tried to stop her. "Gemma, let's just run away together. We can be together, you can get out of this! Please!" He begged.

"I understand if you never want to speak with me again. I just can't, I'm so sorry."

She turned, ran out the door, and down the stairs crying. She hid in one of the bathrooms and cried. She knew he couldn't go in there and try to talk to her. She couldn't run home because of the rain, she had to wait until she stopped crying. She was in there for a while, then she heard a knock on the door.

"Gemma, are you in there?" Finn asked.

"Go away Finn. Please."

"Gemma, can we please talk about this?"

"There is nothing to talk about. Nothing I can do."

Gerard showed up and tapped Finn on the shoulder "Let me try."

"How did you know we were here?" Finn asked.

"She called me to come get her." She didn't, but he knew when he saw the rain.

"Gemma, can you please open the door. Come on, I'll take you home. Lucy is at the house waiting for us."

"I can't. You know I can't." She cried.

"Stop crying and you can. Now come on, you have to get out of there." Gerard said firmly.

Gemma slowly unlocked the door, she wasn't crying anymore, but she still had tears in her eyes. She walked out, Gerard put his coat around her shoulders and began walking her to the door. Finn was confused about everything.

"Gemma wait, please don't go. Can we please talk about this?" Finn said grabbing her hand.

She pulled her hand away. "Finn, I can't."

Gerard opened the car door for her and she got in. It was still raining so she only had a few seconds before she changed. She took Gerard's coat and covered her legs with it.

Gerard went over to talk to Finn. "What happened?"

"I told her I wanted her to go travel the world with me."

Gerard sighed, "I'm sorry, I wish there was a way for that to be possible for you two. Unfortunately, it's not something she can do. Did she tell you?"

"She just told me she's getting married, but why didn't she tell me until now?"

"She didn't know how. It's not something she's happy about, but she has no choice. All of us are unhappy about this, but she really has no choice. She HAS to marry this man, and none of us even know who it is."

"Why? I don't understand!" Finn shouted. "Why can't she just say no, or run away?"

"She tried that once, with Kelley. They were stopped. So they came up with a plan for Kelley to kill whoever it was right after her wedding. Her father found out and had Kelley killed. It's why Patrick hates her so much, and why she can't get over him. Their love is what got him killed." Gerard sighed. "She doesn't want the same to happen to you. She cares about you, but she can't get out of this."

"What if I try to do what she planned with Kelley?"

"Do you really want her to feel guilty for your death as well? She's trying to protect you. You have to just let her protect you. She would never forgive herself if she was the reason for your death as well."

"Why won't she explain this to me? Or anything else in her life? What is the big secret?" Finn shouted again.

"Maybe one day she will be allowed to tell you, but for now she can't, and I'm sorry about that." Gerard said "Give her a couple of days, and come over to the house to try to talk to her. She will be going out of town again soon, so you will want to be here before Friday." Gerard then got into the car and left. Gemma sat in the car silently wiping the tears from her eyes, ready to just be back at the house. Finn stood outside the restaurant, confused and hurt.

48

Gemma couldn't wait until the weekend to go to the lagoon, she needed to get there sooner. She couldn't face Finn yet, she felt horrible. She talked to Callie the next day, and told her that she needed to leave. She couldn't explain why, but she needed to go away earlier than planned. Callie told her it was okay, but that she needed to explain when she came back. She got in her car and left, Lux watching the world go by in the window. She told Lucy where she was going but no one else. She needed to be alone, and Lucy would be showing up there this weekend.

When she arrived, she went straight to the lagoon for a swim, it helped her feel a little better just to be herself. She didn't have time to grab any food, she was in such a rush to get out of there. She had to go into town to get food. She just hoped that Anna-Maria was working. When she got to the café, Anna-Maria was just getting off work.

"Gems? I thought you weren't getting here till Friday. What a wonderful surprise!" Anna-Maria said walking over to her.

"Do you have time to grab some dinner? I could really use a friend to talk to right now."

"Of course. I'll get us a table and send in our orders." She looked at Gemma's face and noticed that something was very wrong. When they sat down she brought them each a cup of warm tea.

"Alright, what's bothering you? I've known you long enough to know when you're upset, so spill."

Gemma sighed. "You know that boy that I told you about, Finn."

"Of course! He sounds wonderful and extremely romantic."

"Oh he is… but… last night we went out on a date. The most romantic date I have ever been on, it was incredible, until…"

"Oh no, what happened?"

"During dessert he told me that he was wanting to go away, travel the world. He asked me to go with him."

"That sounds fantastic! Can I come too? I have almost enough!" Anna-Maria said excitedly.

"I told him no." Gemma said.

"What? Why? It would be so much fun!" Anna-Maria said sounding a bit confused.

"I can't go. I had to tell him one of my secrets that I have been keeping from him. I haven't been able to tell him because I didn't want to break his heart. But I had no choice, I had to." Gemma said, close to tears.

"Gemma, what did you tell him? What happened?" Anna-Maria said becoming worried about her.

"I'm in an arranged marriage, and I can't go with him because I am getting married in four months." She said with her head hanging low.

"Oh." Anna-Maria said, shocked and a little confused.

"It's not something easy to talk about, or even something I'm happy about."

"Then why go through with it? Don't you care about him?"

"I care about him but…. I don't love him. I have tried this whole time. I have tried everything possible to feel the same, and I mean everything. It doesn't matter how much I kiss him, or even when we slept together, those feelings are just not there. I wish they were, but at the same time I would be even more heart broken when I get married. He is absolutely wonderful, and I care about him a lot. That spark, that feeling you get in your stomach that makes you feel sick and happy at the same time. None of those feelings have ever been there with him."

"Did you ever tell him you don't love him?" Anna-Maria asked.

"I've tried, he tells me he loves me all the time, but I never once said it back. I told him several times that he shouldn't love me, but he never listened. I just had to run away, I can't face him right now, not yet."

"You need to talk to him."

"I will when I go back, but… I just couldn't today. I have to end this with him, and I know he won't think of last night as me ending it."

"Really? Isn't that normally what anyone else think is ending it?"

"Normally yes. With Finn, he won't give up that easily. He asked me to dinner every week for three months before I finally said yes."

"Well hopefully being away will help, and not make things worse."

"I hope so too." They finished eating, then made plans for tomorrow.

Gemma spent the next few days trying to take her mind off of things, she swam a lot, worked on her magic and spent time with Anna-Maria in town. Lucy, Gerard and Peggy arrived on Friday night. They spent all their time at the house and lagoon. It was cold out so only Gemma ever wanted to go for a swim, and even then, she didn't swim long. On Sunday afternoon Gerard and Peggy left, Lucy was staying the week at the Lagoon with Gemma. Gemma and Lucy worked on wedding planning, and were going into town to look at the dresses in the dress shop.

"I hope you don't mind, I invited my friend Anna-Maria to join us." Gemma said.

"I don't mind, but don't you think she will be bored?" Lucy asked.

"No, she loves going into the dress shop. She knows the owner really well, so she said she has access to the stuff that he doesn't normally show on display."

"Alright, I guess it is about time I actually met her."

"I would really like you two to know who one another is." Gemma smiled at her.

They arrived at the shop and Anna-Maria was standing outside waiting for them.

"Anna-Maria! Why are you waiting outside for us? Its freezing!" Gemma said

"I haven't been out here long. I saw your car pull into town, so I decided to wait out here for you."

"I still would have waited inside. It's too cold." Gemma laughed

"Gemma, you should be used to this weather by now. You've been here for almost four years." Lucy said.

"I still prefer warmer weather." Gemma laughed.

"Lucy this is Anna-Maria."

"It's great to finally meet you! Gems has told me so much about you. I can't believe that it has taken so long for us to finally meet." Anna-Maria said excitedly.

"Nice to finally meet you as well." Lucy replied.

"Come on, let's go inside. I will go find Neil." Anna-Maria said

They walked into the store and began to look around. Anna-Maria instantly went into the back of the store, looking for the owner. The style of dresses were very different, not one was the same. They looked as if they were from different parts of the world, and were all beautiful in their own way. Lucy noticed Gemma looking at a certain dress for a long time. It was off white, covered in crystals and pearls, it looked tight at the top then flared out at the knees.

"Are you alright?" Lucy asked

"Huh? Oh… yeah… I'm fine." Gemma said

"You don't seem fine, something is bothering you."

"It's nothing, I'm fine… really"

Then Anna-Maria came back out. "He will be right out." She said smiling, then she noticed Gemma. "What's wrong Gems?"

"Nothing. Why do you both keep asking what's wrong?" Gemma said a bit irritated.

"I don't know, maybe because you look more upset than usual." Anna-Maria said sarcastically

"I'm fine." She snapped.

Anna-Maria walked over to Lucy and whispered to her, "You're seeing this too, right? Something is wrong."

"Oh I see it, I'll try to talk to her a little later about it. It's best if we don't upset her though." Lucy whispered back.

"Alright, but please let me know what's wrong, I worry about her." Anna-Maria whispered.

"I will. Let's look at the dresses, maybe I will finally find something."

They were taken into the back to look at some of the other dresses, Lucy wasn't impressed by what he was showing her. She was just about ready to leave when she spotted something on the table. It was a white gown with a lace top. She asked him if she could take a look, he was hesitant, it wasn't nearly finished yet. He held it up for her to inspect, and asked him what was needed to finish it. He told her the top wasn't close to being finished yet, he still had to add the quarter sleeves, it was supposed to be an off the shoulder completely lace top. The bottom needed an extra few layers to make it poof out more, and add a few lace accents to it. She asked him if it was already sold, he told her no, but that it was very expensive. Gemma told him she would take care of it, just size it for her and have it ready in two weeks. Lucy was excited, it was exactly what she was looking for. She then found another dress, perfect for Gemma's dress at the wedding. She had her try it on and decided that it was perfect. They purchased the dresses and then left to get some lunch. Anna-Maria had to start work, but told them she would make time to sit and chat with them some more while they ate.

"Gemma, what was wrong in there? And don't tell me that its nothing, we both knew something was up with you." Lucy asked.

Gemma sighed, "That dress was just perfect. It made me think about if Kelley and I were ever to get married, that was what I would have wanted to wear. It then reminded me that he was gone, and how that dream would never come true. It's really not a big deal."

"Oh, I'm sorry. I shouldn't have made you come with me." Lucy said.

"No, I wanted to come with you. I wanted to help you with this. I just feel bad that I always feel upset, and then you get upset." Gemma said as a tear rolled down her cheek.

"Well maybe you can wear something like that at your wedding." Lucy said, trying to cheer her up.

"I don't get to choose my dress. I have to wear this awful dress that is used for all the land and sea weddings. Even your dress for my wedding is already picked out. I don't really get to do anything for my wedding, everything is already decided." Gemma whispered.

"That's terrible! You can't choose anything?"

"Nothing, everything is already decided."

"Why can't you choose your dress?" Lucy asked.

"This is the exact same dress that is used in every land and sea wedding. It's supposed to symbolize joining of the two worlds, my dress is to represent the sea, looking as if it is made of seaweed. It's absolutely awful. I hate that dress, I have seen it before and its atrocious. But as usual I have no choice."

"Well, soon this will all be over. Only four more months."

"Only four months till I have nothing left." Gemma hung her head low. She hated all of this, she didn't love Finn, or even have the same type of feelings for him. But she wanted to run away with him, just to get away. She knew she couldn't, but it was becoming tempting.

Gemma and Lucy returned to Clew a few days later. Lucy was so happy to be back and tell Gerard everything. Gemma was dreading being back and having to talk to Finn. Finn showed up the next morning, before Gemma left for work.

"Gemma, can we please talk?" He asked

Gemma sighed, "We can talk on my way to work. Callie won't be happy if I'm late."

"Why didn't you tell me sooner? Why did you wait so long?" He asked

"I didn't know how to tell you. How do you bring something like that up? What am I supposed to say something like; *just so you know I'm in an arranged marriage. I hope you're okay with that, even though I'm not.* It's not easy to tell anyone. It's even harder because they are not common here so then I get a lot of questions." She said. "I'm sorry."

"I guess you are right. Are there a lot of arranged marriages where you are from?" He asked sounding upset.

"Somewhat, it depends on the family. In my family, it is almost mandatory. Very few members of my family don't have an arranged marriage." She explained.

"Why can't you get out of it?" He asked.

"It's complicated, I can't tell anyone anything about it." She said.

"Why not?"

"It has to do with my safety, if people find out who I really am, my life will be in danger."

"What you mean who you really are?"

"Gemma isn't my real name, no one here knows my real name, not even Peggy. Lucy somewhat knows where I'm from, but not really. Anyone who knows anything about who I really am, is in danger." She explained.

"Danger? What kind of danger? And why?" He asked fear written on his face.

"If you know who I really am, it could cost you your life. That is why the O'Reilly's don't know my name."

"But why?" He asked even more confused.

"Because of who I am, who my father is. I honestly can't tell you anymore, I have already told you a lot more than I should have."

"Okay." Finn hung his head low.

"I'm sorry, I really do understand if you never want to see me again. There isn't much of a point. It will just be dragging out the inevitable."

"No, I want to be with you. I love you, I'm just upset that you have to do this. Maybe we can find a way for you to get out of it."

"Trust me, I can't. There is a lot of things dependent on this marriage. If I don't go through with it, bad things will happen."

"Can I at least continue seeing you until then? I love spending time with you." He said hopefully

"We can if you really want to, but there is no way out of this."

"Alright. Well can I take you to dinner sometime this week?"

"I don't see why not."

"Great! I will pick you up tomorrow night." He kissed her then left. He needed to come up with a plan to save her.

49

Lucy was getting frustrated, she didn't like any of the flowers at the flower shop in town. They didn't seem to have what she wanted, which were certain wildflowers. The flowers that Gerard would bring home for her when she was upset. She wanted to be sure that those flowers were part of their wedding. Everyone thought Lucy just wanted the wedding to be perfect, but her idea of perfect, was showing their love for one another through all the little details that only they knew. The location of the ceremony was where they first danced, the location of the reception is where they went to the ball together. She wanted it to be perfect for them, make things easier on Gerard. He hated the idea of a big wedding; he doesn't like being the center of attention unlike Lucy. So Lucy wanted to make sure that there were subtle hints for him that this was for them. That evening Lucy curled up on the couch with Gerard, he knew something was wrong, she was not her normal bubbly self.

"What's the secret?" He asked.

"What are you talking about?"

"You're only like this when you are hiding something, so what is it?"

"Oh, I don't have any secrets that you don't already know. I just am stressed about the wedding. Things just aren't coming together like I want."

"Everything will be fine, you have been planning this for almost two years. Trust me everything will be okay." He said as he kissed her head.

"I'm just worried about you."

"Me? Why?"

"I know how much you hate when everyone is looking at you. You are only okay with it when you are in the ring, other than that, you like to keep to yourself."

"I'll be fine, I just have to remember to keep my eyes on you the whole time. I know that will help. Just try not to worry about everything. Just be happy that it's almost time."

"I am, but I still worry about you. I also worry about Da' he still isn't back yet."

"Be prepared he might not make it back at all."

"Why did they have to cut it so close to the wedding?"

"Gemma has pleaded with Nik and her father to make sure he comes back alive. But Nik doesn't seem hopeful about it, her father is furious and his crime against the crown is punishable by death. So I wouldn't get your hopes up that he'll make it back."

"I didn't know that. I can't believe that she would fight so hard to get him back here."

"She did it for you. You are like a sister to her, all she wants is for you to be happy. She knows that you would feel as if our wedding would be ruined if he wasn't there."

"I know, but I still can't believe it. After what he did to her..."

"She stopped all of us from killing him that night, including me. She even healed the wound on his neck enough so he wouldn't die. She did all this for you, and you alone. If he doesn't make it back, that's not because of her."

"I understand."

"Everything will be fine. Stop worrying so much."

"I just hope his time away actually helped him. I can't have things go back to the way they used to be. He may only see it as Gemma only here for a few more months, but what he doesn't realize is that she will be in our lives forever." She said.

"Well that's because he doesn't know our plans for the future." He pulled her closer to him.

"He would if he was coherent enough to actually have a conversation with." She said starting to get angry.

"Don't worry, everything will be just fine." He kissed her head, "Come on, let's get to bed, it's getting late, and I have to get up early."

"I'll be there in a few minutes."

Lucy had become anxious over the recent days. She was going home more frequently to see if there was any news. Gemma and Peggy only hoped for one outcome, while Lucy was torn. As horrified as she was by what he did, she had a hard time breaking away from all the good memories she had with him. It was a week before her wedding, and she needed to know if he would be back for it or if she would need to make other arrangements.

She saw Gemma's car outside the house and ran in. Hoping for good news. But they weren't in the living room or kitchen. She could hear them talking though. Following the sounds of their voices to Patrick's office.

"I'm not telling her. I told everyone not to tell my father of any harm he caused me yet someone told him. I'm not taking the blame for this." Gemma snapped.

"Taking the blame? Do you honestly believe that she'll blame you for this?" Peggy questioned.

"I don't know. When it comes to him, she's all over the place. I know exactly where you stand. You've been in the same boat as me. But I don't know with her."

"I'm sure she won't blame you. Your father and uncle didn't blame me for what happened to Zeus."

"That's because you saved them from having to do it." She muttered.

"Nevertheless, I doubt she will blame you for it."

"I hope you're right. And thanks for having my back through all of this. I know it can't be easy, this being your husband and all."

"He stopped being my husband the day he locked Kelley's room. He became dead to me on your birthday when Nik told us what he did to you." She placed her hand on Gemma's shoulder. "Even if she gets mad at first, she'll forgive you. You did nothing wrong in all of this."

Gemma wiped a tear away. "I still can't bring myself to go upstairs."

"You will one day, once I get that bloody door open. That key has to be in here somewhere."

"I still think we should just call the blacksmith. They might have something to break it open. Or I can just take an axe to the door. I'm sure Gerard will replace it for you if we let him get a couple of swings in. He's been looking for a way to get his aggression out."

Peggy laughed. "I'll think about it. What do you need in there before you leave anyway?"

"It's a book. One that we took turns reading and leaving notes for one another. Nothing special to anyone but me. It's actually my book from the lagoon so I'm sure Marsali would be thrilled to have that no longer missing."

"I'm sure she's losing her mind over a single book." Peggy rolled her eyes.

"Trust me she is. She keeps asking when I will have it back so she can mark it returned in the ledger. Hmm. I wonder if Gerard has figured out how to pick a lock yet. He's been trying to learn for months to be able to open that door. I'll send him over when I get to work." She looked at the time and sighed. "As much as I love our time together, I should get going. Callie is expecting me. Let me know when you find it and don't forget, your telling her, not-"

Lucy stepped into the room, arms crossed hard against her chest. "Telling me what?" She snarled.

She handed Lucy a letter from Nik. "I'm sorry." She patted Lucy on the shoulder and began walking out the door.

"What was she saying about Zeus?"

"You should read the letter my dear. Then we will have a long chat over some tea, alright?"

Her hands trembled reading the letter. "He's gone?" Tears fell from her eyes landing on the letter. She noticed that not a tear was shed by even her own mother over this, hers alone were on the paper.

50

Lucy went into town the next morning and went straight to the pub, hoping to find Gemma, but she wasn't there.

"Callie, where is Gemma?"

"I told her not to come in until later this afternoon."

"Oh, ummm… alright. I'll see if she's at home. Thanks."

Lucy said as she ran out of the pub.

She walked to her house and went inside. Gemma was sitting in the living room talking with Finn. Finn had his arm around her, Gemma was stiff as a board. Trying to not get too close to him. Finn was smiling from ear to ear. While Gemma's face was unreadable. He would occasionally kiss her cheek and neck. Gemma would flinch and tell him to stop. The closer he got the further away she tried to be.

"Oh, hi Lucy, I didn't know you were coming home so early." Gemma said, as soon as she saw Lucy.

"I came looking for you. I need your help with something."

"Oh, alright. Do you need me right now? Or a little later?"

"Right now. I will explain on the way."

"I can help too if you need me." Finn was obviously trying to spend more time with Gemma.

"This is something only Gemma can help me with. She's all yours later tonight, but I just really need her right now."

"Alright." Finn said. He gave Gemma a kiss. "I will pick you up later, after you are off work."

"See you then." Gemma said as Finn left. "Lucy what's going on? You're not acting like yourself."

"Gerard got the door to Kelley's room open."

Gemma's eyes widened "Are you sure?"

"Positive, I saw him open it this morning. He then had to leave immediately after to get to work. Can you please come look with me?"

Gemma sighed, she wanted to go, she wanted to be in his room again. But at the same time, she knew that it would just make things harder on her. She hadn't been able to even make it up those stairs since that night. "Fine, let's go."

They got in Gemma's car and went to Peggy's house. They walked inside and Peggy gave both girls big hugs.

"Gemma! Two days in a row, this must be my lucky week!" Peggy said with a big smile.

Gemma laughed, "Well Lucy insisted that I come over for something."

"Oh really? And what is that?" Peggy said in a curious tone.

"Gerard opened Kelley's room."

"Alright, so why did you insist Gemma come over?"

"I just want her to see something."

"Okay... well, try not to spend all day in there. That much dust won't be good for either of you."

Lucy and Gemma went upstairs, Gemma stopped at Kelley's door, nervous to open it. She could hear her heart pounding, her hand began to shake as she reached for the door knob.

"Gemma, are you alright?"

"I... I don't know if I can do this."

"What do you mean? You've been in here a million times."

Gemma took a deep breath, "It has taken a lot to get over him. I know going in there that all of those feelings will instantly come rushing back. Including the heart shattering feeling of when he died. I don't know if I can go through that again."

"Gemma, can you please try for me? I really need help finding something of his for the wedding."

"Lucy, I'm sure Peggy would be more helpful with this."

"Please Gemma, just look." Lucy begged.

"Fine, but you owe me."

Gemma took a deep breath. Her shaking hand on the door knob. she slowly turned it and pushed it open. Her heart pounding louder and louder as the door slowly opened. She slowly stepped into his room, looking around. It looked exactly the same as when she was last in there, only covered in a thick layer of dust. She looked over at his desk and instantly knew what was missing. Her heart sank, she had wanted that very thing. She wiped away the tears that started to roll down her cheeks.

"Everything is exactly where it was before, except one book."

"What was it?"

"You don't need to worry about it. It was mine that he probably took with him when he left. I never checked for it before the room was locked up."

"Oh. Well we are in here now, do you want to look at anything? Or was there something that really meant a lot to you?"

"I already have most of the things that meant a lot to me. That was the last thing, but it doesn't matter anyways. It will just make things harder." Gemma wiped another tear from her eye, "I really need to go." She turned around, about to leave when she saw something above his door, it was sparkling. She reached up trying to grab it but couldn't reach.

"What is it?"

"I don't know, but I have never seen it before. Bring me the chair, I want to see if I can reach it."

Lucy brought her the chair and Gemma climbed up to grab it. She brushed the pile of dust off of it. It had more dust than the rest of the room, as if it had been there the whole time and she just didn't notice it.

"Gemma what is it?"

"It's a pendant of my family crest." She felt something carved into the back, normally the back of these pendants were smooth. She flipped it over to see what it was. It was a heart with 'K+A' inside it. She couldn't help but wonder how that got there. It felt familiar, but she couldn't figure out how. As she ran her fingers across the carving, the carving lit up a little. She felt as if half of her was missing, but the way she did when Kelley left, not since he died. It was as if a small glimmer of hope sparked through her, that he wasn't truly gone.

"Why would that be there?"

"I don't know. He said he was taking it with him... I... I don't know. It's the first time I've seen it but both Gerard and Kelley had mentioned it to me before. I need to talk to Gerard about this."

"Well there must be a reason for it to be here. Maybe he just forgot it."

"Maybe." She took a deep breath. She put the pendant in her pocket and the chair back. "I have to go to work."

"Can you help me put a few things in your car to take to the house?"

"I thought we got it all last time."

"No, there are just a few things left."

They went to Lucy's old room, there were 2 trunks and a suitcase. Much more than she thought there would be.

"Alright, let's get these to my car then I have to get to work."

They each grabbed a chest and brought it downstairs. Gemma went right back upstairs to grab the suitcase, while Lucy put the chests in Gemma's car for her. Peggy came out and gave them both a hug. She invited Gemma to dinner but she already had dinner plans and told her some other time soon. She hated telling her no to dinner, she loved Peggy's cooking but even with him gone, she didn't feel safe in that house.

51

"Gemma, your later than I thought you would be."

Callie said as Gemma ran into the pub. She was tying an apron around her waist.

"I know, I'm sorry. Lucy wanted me to help her with a few things."

"Well you didn't miss that much. We are just now starting to get a little busy. Our least favorite crew is back."

Gemma groaned, "Great, so it is going to be a rough afternoon."

"Sorry, but it seems like they will be here for a few days."

"Can you get a message to my fiancé. Let him know that his crew is unruly, and I will not hold back anymore. I don't care that it's his crew! If he wants me to be merciful towards them then they need to learn how to act more like civilized men, and less like the degenerate Cretans they continue to act like. I'm done with them! I refuse to let them act this way any longer in here! The only two from that crew that don't act like that is the one who is always talking with you in the back room and Jamison who doesn't say anything ever." Gemma spoke in her royal voice to Callie. Callie knew instantly that this was a royal order, not just a request. Gemma was no longer going to sit around and let them act this way towards her.

"I will send a message to him right away, but I can't promise that there will be much of a change, especially today."

"Then there will be a lot of bloodshed today." Gemma spoke with no remorse, she was done with their behavior.

"Ever since that night, Jamison has never been the same in here." Callie said

"What do you mean?"

"I mean that he used to be like he is at every other port. David tells me all the stories of their crew, and Jamison has quite the reputation at the other ports. He was like that here too, until that night." Callie explained, "Something about you had him acting different, and we are all fine with that." Callie laughed.

Gemma thought about it for a few minutes. She had taken him out of the trance so what else could it be? Maybe it's because she pays for his drinks whenever he is there. She couldn't think of any other way to show him how grateful she was towards him. As usual he was quiet the whole time he was there. Callie told her after that incident, that Jamison liked whiskey. So whenever he would walk in she would give him a glass. Sometimes a hug if there were not many people in there. Anytime his glass was empty she would bring him a new one, without him saying a word. She knew she owed him. While she knew she was immortal, she also knew that her surviving that would have gotten word back to Delanson. The last person she ever wanted to find her.

There were several fights that afternoon, Gemma was through with them. She made sure they knew that she would not put up with this anymore. Every fight that started, she stopped before Callie got a chance to say anything. She didn't care about Callie being okay with how she stopped the fights. She just did as she wanted today. She was angry about so many things, she honestly just wanted to fight today. At the end of her shift, Callie went to speak with her in back.

"Alright, let's hear it." Callie said.

"Hear what?" Gemma grumbled.

"What is going on with you today? I haven't seen you in a mood like this in a long time. Now what is going on?"

"Nothing, I'm fine." She snapped.

"Gemma! Don't lie to me! I know you very well now, and I know when you are having a bad day. What happened today?"

Gemma sighed, "Its nothing! I'm just in a bad mood."

"There's more to it than that! I've seen you in *'just a bad mood'* this is not that."

"Fine!" Gemma shouted, "Lucy had me go with her into Kelley's room today. It just brought back a lot of feelings and rage towards a certain someone."

"Do you think you will be back to yourself tomorrow? Or do you need some extra fight time?"

"I would love some extra fight time. It will help me feel better."

"Alright, show up early and we will spar for a few hours, or until you feel better."

"Thanks Callie." Gemma had a slight smile on her face. "I need to get going, I have to clean up before Finn picks me up."

"Good luck with that. Are you ending it yet?"

"No, I can't end it a couple of days before Lucy's wedding. It would just make him being there extremely uncomfortable."

"Well don't string him along for too much longer. You leave in a few months."

"I know. I will see you in the morning."

She already knew when she would end it, right after the wedding. No point in staying any longer. She wanted to end it now but it was so close to Lucy's wedding that she needed to wait a few more days.

When Gemma got back to Gerard's house, Finn was already there.

"I'm so sorry I'm late Finn. Just give me a few minutes to change."

"Its fine, but you are covered in blood. Are you alright?" Finn said with concern

"I'm fine, it was just a long rough day."

"Well, I'm glad you are okay. I hate to see you like this."

"I will be back down in a few minutes."

"No rush. Take your time."

Gemma ran upstairs and started to clean herself up. She looked at herself in the mirror, she was a mess. Her hair was a complete disaster, her arms had blood splatter on them. Her face looked tired, and angry. There was no joy left in her today. She washed the blood off her and washed her face. Changed into something clean and fixed her hair to the best of her ability. She took the pendent from her pocket and put it on her bedside table. Then went back downstairs, Gerard pulled her aside before she left.

"Are you okay? Lucy told me about today. Do you need me to do anything for you?"

"I will be fine, I just need to get through this myself. Nothing anyone can do to help me right now."

"Are you sure? You seem to have more blood on you than usual today."

"My fiancé is at port and his crew is just unruly. I honestly just wanted to finish them all off tonight. I can't handle them in there anymore, they don't listen to anything. No matter how many of them I have hurt in the past, they just continue to act like vile degenerate pieces of sea scum. It's just bull sharks that I have to deal with them all the time. I just want to yell at him for not stopping them from acting this way towards me! He doesn't even have the decency to get off his ship to apologize for how they act."

"You know he can't, he isn't allowed to meet you until the wedding."

"I know, but it doesn't change how I feel."

"I know. I think I know who his first mate is. I can send a message back with him when he comes in to pick up their supplies in the morning."

"That would be wonderful actually. I keep sending them with Callie but they don't seem to make a difference. I will write a note and give it to you when we leave in the morning."

"Alright, but you know I am not working much tomorrow."

"I know. Neither am I. I'm getting off when you get off. Just stop by on your way out and we will go to the rehearsal together."

"Alright I will. Try not to be too late tonight. I will try to wait up for you."

"Thank you. Now you should probably be heading over to Peggy's house, you know how much she hates when you are late."

"I know. I will see you tonight. If you need anything, just create a storm and I will be right there."

"I know." She laughed, then walked out to the car with Finn.

Gemma was enjoying their quiet evening together. He didn't try to question her about anything. He didn't even try to get her to run away with him. He knew when she had bad days at the pub that she just needed a nice quiet evening.

"Gemma, do you want me to help you with any of the stuff for Lucy's wedding? I know it has gotten you stressed out a bit."

"I will let you know, I don't know what else she is going to need my help with."

"Well what did she have you do today?"

"She had me bring some of her stuff home, but also something else. I don't really feel like talking about it."

"Oh, alright. Well if you need any help, please let me know. You seem like you need some help or to just take some time off from it."

"I just need some time off from everything. The day after the wedding, I'm going out of town for a week again. I just need that time to myself right now."

"I hope it helps make you feel better. If you want I can come with you."

"No, I just need to be alone after all of this. It has all been just a little too much for me."

"Okay. If you change your mind, let me know."

"I won't change my mind, but thank you for the offer." Gemma looked at the time, "We should get going, it's getting late and I have an early day tomorrow."

Finn took Gemma back to Gerard's and gave her a small kiss goodnight. She was tired and just wanted to go to sleep, but Gerard was up waiting for her.

"How did everything go? You alright?"

"I'm fine, I just want to go to bed and forget about today."

"Then I will see you in the morning."

"Good night." Gemma said while walking up to her room. Just wanting to be alone. She changed her clothes and curled up in bed looking at the pendant. Trying to figure out what it meant, why it was in Kelley's room. She ran her fingers along the carving on the back, watching it glow. Something felt familiar about it, but she couldn't remember. She felt as if she had seen the carving before, as if it was something that she was meant to know. She only wished she could remember.

"Kelley what is this supposed to mean?" She whispered to herself. Lux curled up next to her and began to hum. "Why are there all these things that keep me from getting over you. Why can't I just move on? Why do I have to love you so much?"

She now had a few tears roll down her cheeks. She kissed the gems on her ring and watched them glow. Something inside her was telling her to touch the gems to the carving. She didn't know what, or why, but her gut was saying that she had to. She nervously touched them together and a small pink burst shot through the room. Nowhere else, just her room. She instantly felt better than she had in years. She felt like her old self again, like she could take on anything. Then she had the strangest feeling rush through her. She felt as if she not only had to go through with this marriage, but that she now wanted to. Something inside her was telling her to not give up. That everything would be alright. She got out of her bed and wrote a note for Gerard to give to her fiancé's first mate in the morning. She went to bed feeling better than she had in years, knowing that she was strong enough to do this. She just needed that reminder, that push that the burst gave her.

52

It was the day of the rehearsal for Gerard and Lucy's wedding, and Gemma's fiancé's crew was still at port. Callie and Gemma had their hands full with this group. There were constant fights that they had to break up. Gemma began to feel as if someone was watching her. It wasn't a feeling that made her worry about her safety, it was more of a feeling of comfort, as if someone was watching over her.

"Gemma, can you take care of that one over there?" Callie shouted from across the room.

"No problem" She shouted back.

She went back behind the bar, there was a tall man wearing a big hat, that hung low over his face. All you could see was a shadow covering his mouth. She noticed his drink was empty so she went over to him.

"Would you like another?" She asked

"Yes" He said in a deep raspy voice.

She poured him another drink, tried to talk to him but he never said anything other than an occasional word or grunt.

She reached into her boot, pulled out a dagger, and threw it across the room. It stuck straight in the middle of a man's hand, and held his hand to the wall. She calmly walked over to the man. Her royal presence radiating from her. It had instantly stopped the fight. She got right in his face. Holding another dagger to his throat and spoke through gritted teeth.

"Cruze! I've told you how many times you start a fight I will finish it! Now pay your tab and get out before I cut off your favorite appendage!"

He reached into his pocket and quickly paid her. She pulled the dagger from his hand, still not moving the other from his throat. She counted the money then lowered her dagger. Cruze ran out of there fast, wrapping his hand in his shirt to stop the bleeding. She went back behind the bar, and put the money away. The man she had spoken to before was still sitting there. She went to check on him to see if he needed anything else.

"He start fights often?" He asked

"At least once a week. The part of his hand I hit has a permanent hole from how many times that dagger has gone through his hand. I never miss my target. I always hit exactly that spot on his hand." She said.

"Why?"

"The hole is already there, so this way it will hold his hand to the wall easier."

"Interesting tactic."

"Well I do what I have to, and with him that is what works the best." She tried to get a better look at him, but it was hard with how much his hat was covering his face. "I haven't seen you here before, is this your first time to our port?"

"No, just first time I've been to the pub in years."

"Well if you remain this peaceful and quite you are more than welcome to come back anytime." She said with a smile. "I'm Gemma, what's your name?"

"Sam." He paused for a moment, "What does your fiancé say about you working here?" He said pointing at her finger with Kelley's ring on it

"Oh... I don't know, he probably would have hated it. He died two years ago."

"I'm sorry, that must have been painful for you."

"It is, I just take it one day at a time. I know I will never fully recover."

He just nodded and took a drink, she noticed a few rings on his hand. He had a gold one with a crest on it. Right as she began looking at it he twisted the ring and put the crest in the palm of his hand. She couldn't make out what the crest was, he moved it too fast, but she knew it looked familiar. Then there was another gold one on his left ring finger. It had some intricate carvings in it. It also looked familiar to her, but she couldn't figure out how. Then she noticed a tattoo on his left forearm that said the word light, but how it was written, it looked like something was different about it.

"You're married?" She asked.

"What?" He coughed, his drink going down the wrong tube.

"Your ring, on your left finger."

"Umm, no. Engaged."

"I've never seen a man have an engagement ring before."

"My soon to be father-in-law insisted, as a reminder."

"A reminder of what?"

"Why I'm doing all of this."

"Well it was lovely to meet you Sam." She said, as she started to get back to work.

She began to walk away when he grabbed her hand and held it for a second. She was startled at first but his hand felt comforting to her, the black in her hair started to slightly fade away. She tried to pull away, then she saw him pull out a handful of coins and placed them in her hand. Her hair instantly went back to black when he let go.

"This is more than your tab." She said

"Keep the rest." He said as he got up to leave, bumping into Gerard as he was walking out the door.

"Oh sorry mate. I didn't see you." Gerard said as he nearly knocked Sam's hat off.

Sam quickly fixed his hat and ran. Gerard watched him run, and shrugged, then saw Gemma.

"Ready to go? Lucy is getting very anxious about tomorrow."

"I know. I will be right there. Let me just finish putting the money away, and clean up this area."

"Don't take too long."

Gemma watched Sam through the window as he walked away.

She put the money away, Callie told her to keep her tip. They usually split the tips, but Sam gave her a very generous tip, so Callie thought she should keep the whole thing. Gemma went to grab Sam's glass and wipe down his area when she noticed something. There was a small crystal sitting next to the glass. She picked it up and examined it. She quickly ran over to Callie.

"Callie what ship is in port right now?"

"There are a few, most of the Crimson Cutlass crew is in here now. Why?"

"That's the ship Kelley was on. I just found this next to that man's glass." Gemma said excitedly.

"So it's just a crystal. It doesn't look like it would even fetch very much. He probably just dropped it when handing you the money." Callie said.

"You're probably right." She sighed, hope evaporating from her thoughts. "Think I should try to return it to him?"

"I will have it sent back with someone from the crew. Did he tell you his name?"

"He said his name is Sam." Gemma sighed, "Alright, well I have to get going."

"I know, Lucy's wedding rehearsal. Good luck with that."

"Thanks. I will be going away after the wedding for the week. So I will see you when I return."

"I will see you tomorrow at the wedding."

Gemma smiled then left with Gerard. After she left she had that feeling again, that someone was watching her.

"Everything alright?" Gerard asked

"Yeah, I'm fine. I just have this strange feeling like someone is watching me. And that man that ran into you when you came in. Something was familiar about him, it was as if I knew him."

"I thought the same thing, I thought maybe I was going crazy or something. Who knows, maybe it's someone we have fought in the ring years ago."

"Maybe. It was just strange."

They got into her car and left for Gerard's parents' house, Lucy was already there waiting for them.

When they got inside Lucy ran right to Gemma, and pulled her into a different room.

"Gemma! There is still so much to do. I don't know if I will get it all done in time. I have to get the flowers for tomorrow, and I don't know how either of us are going to wear our hair. We have the rehearsal in about 20 minutes, and I don't know what to wear." Lucy was pacing as her speech got faster by the second.

Gemma grabbed Lucy by the shoulders holding her still. "Lucy, calm down. Breathe. It will all work out. Tomorrow morning, I will go out and get the flowers. We will figure our hair out tonight, and I will help you pick out what to wear to the rehearsal. Just take a deep breath. Everything will work out fine." Gemma spoke calmly.

"I wish he was here. He was supposed to be standing next to Gerard, slightly teasing me like he always did. I just wish he was going to be here." Lucy said.

Gemma hugged Lucy, with tears running down both their faces. "I wish he was here too, we all do. It's hard on all of us. You know he would be giving you a hard time right now."

"What? Why would he be giving me a hard time?"

"How worried you are about the wedding. You know what he would tell you?"

"That it's out of my control, and to just go with it."

"Exactly! Now let's get going. We have to get to the rehearsal."

"I just want everything to be perfect."

"There is no such thing as perfect. It's just a high standard set to make you feel like nothing you do is good enough. The only thing that should matter is at the end of day, you and Gerard will be married. When you look back on this one day, you won't be thinking about if the decorations were perfect, or if your hair was perfect. You will only be thinking about you two."

"When did you get so smart and insightful?" Lucy laughed

"I've always been this way. You would know that if you listened when I talk." Gemma laughed, "Here wear this dress tonight. You will look amazing, but not quite as stunning as you will tomorrow."

"Thanks Gemma, you always know how to make me feel better."

They finished getting ready and went to the rehearsal, when they arrived Lucy lost it. Nothing was the way she wanted, the alter was missing, only half the chairs were there. Gerard tried to calm her down, but she was so worried that nothing would be ready in time, that nothing he said could calm her down. Gemma looked around, she knew it was nowhere near perfect like Lucy wanted, and a lot of things were not ready for tomorrow. There was something that was missing, something that no matter how much they tried, would never be there. Gemma whispered into Gerard's ear, and the two of them left. Lucy didn't even notice the two of them leave. They returned 10 minutes later, Gerard's arms were full, everyone stopped and watched the two of them. Gemma grabbed one of the chairs from the back and placed it up front, right next to where Gerard was going to stand. She took a black table cloth out and draped it over the chair. Gerard then put a portrait of Kelley in the chair, and Gemma placed a white rose in front of the portrait. Lucy began to cry, Gerard held her close. Lucy and Peggy both ran to hug Gemma.

"Thank you Gemma! This is exactly what I needed. What we all needed." Lucy said

"Gemma dear, this is the best idea you have had in a long time. Thank you!" Peggy cried.

"It wouldn't be right for him to not be here somehow. This was the only way I could think of."

"It's perfect! I couldn't think of a better way to have him represented." Lucy said as she wiped the tears from her eyes. "Really, thank you! Alright, just get the rest of the chairs and the alter, fix the holes in the tent and everything will be great."

Lucy grabbed Gerard's hand, and thanked him, then told him she was ready to actually rehearse. They had to perform the rehearsal a few times, Gerard got a little nervous and kept messing up the words. He was never good with crowds and hated the idea of all those people looking at him tomorrow. He finally relaxed when Lucy kissed him and reminded him that the only thing that mattered was the two of them.

That night Lucy, Gemma and Peggy, stayed at Gerard and Lucy's house, while Gerard stayed with his parents. They could have gone to Peggy's house, but Gemma hadn't been back there for a full night in almost a year. She felt safe and happy when at Gerard and Lucy's house.

53

The morning came fast. Gemma and Peggy brought Lucy breakfast in bed. Then Gemma took off to get the flowers. Lucy didn't want an elaborate bouquet from a flower shop. She told Gemma that she really wanted to just have wild flowers, picked from a specific field. It was winter so getting flowers from the field that she wanted was out of the question. Gemma spoke with the florist and told them exactly what Lucy wanted, she gave them a list of flowers and told them to keep it simple. She told them she needed: Forget-me-nots, violets, White field roses, pink sea peas and trailing bellflowers. She went back to the house and showed Lucy the flowers, she loved them. They were exactly what she wanted. Gemma made two bouquets, two boutonnières and a special flower setting for Kelley's chair. She teared up a little while making the flowers for Kelley, just wishing he was there with all of them.

She went to Lucy's room to help her get ready. Peggy was much better at hair, so Gemma told her what to do for both of their hair. Lucy had her hair pulled to the side, gently draped over her shoulder in big elegant curls. They placed some small white flowers in her hair, then Gemma took out her gold hair comb and used that to hold Lucy's hair in place.

"Gemma, why did you put your mom's hair comb in my hair? Don't you want to wear it?" Lucy asked

"I want you to wear it. It's your special day! Anyways, you need something borrowed, right? What are the four things you said you need? Something old, new, borrowed and blue?" Gemma said smiling at her.

Lucy laughed at Gemma, she knew Gemma had no idea about how their traditions worked or why this was even a tradition.

"Yes, those are the four. Thank you, it's beautiful."

Gemma finished Lucy's makeup then helped her get into her dress. She wore a long white, off the shoulder gown. The whole top was lace, including the sleeves that went down to her elbows. The rest of the dress was silk and chiffon, right at the waist the dress lightly flared out, giving the dress a light poof. Lucy did a small twirl, her dress spun out beautifully, exactly what she wanted.

"What do you think?"

"I think it's perfectly you. Nothing else would be more perfect for you."

Lucy beamed with happiness. Gemma got dressed, she wore a long sage green, off the shoulder flowing gown, it had sleeves that went down to her wrist. She had a cream colored shawl to keep her warm. Gemma looked around for somewhere to keep her dagger on her. She knew better than to go anywhere without one.

"Gemma, are you really brining your dagger to my wedding?"

"Of course! You know I never leave without one anymore. It's the only way I feel safe going anywhere. You know this." Gemma said while still searching for a place to keep it.

"I know, I just don't understand why you would need it at my wedding."

"Well we didn't think I would need it at the festival dance."

Lucy sighed, "Good point. You do seem to be a target for attacks at formal events. Just please don't have it visible. I don't want everyone thinking that we are all armed. Gerard already insists on having his sword and dagger on him as well."

"For the same reason I assume."

"Yes for the same reason. You two think way too much alike." Lucy sighed as she rolled her eyes.

"You love us for it." Gemma laughed, while still searching.

"You're both lucky I love you two so much, otherwise I wouldn't allow it. If Kelley was here he would insist that you have multiple ones on you." Lucy laughed.

"He would probably insist you carry one as well." Gemma laughed, "I got it!" she took her bouquet removed the ribbon, placed her dagger in the center of the bouquet. She placed it blade up, the butt of the dagger barely sticking out for her to grab if she needed it. She neatly re-wrapped the stems in the ribbon. It looked just as it did before she put it in there. Lucy just shook her head.

"I really hope no one sees that."

"We will test it on Peggy. She notices everything." Gemma laughed.

"So, is Finn coming today?" Lucy asked

"Yes."

"You don't seem too happy about that."

"You know why."

"Then why are you still with him? You only have three months until your wedding with the captain."

"I just know that when I do end it, I will have to stop training Molly. It'll crush her, and I really enjoy training her.

"Maybe you should talk to Molly about it."

"I have, she wants me to stay with him. He has asked me several times to run away with him. I just can't, and I really don't want to. I just don't feel the same way about him, as he does about me."

"Then end it already. Tell him you just don't feel the same. Why keep him around if you don't want him around."

"I like him as a friend, but there is just no spark between us. I don't know, maybe I just wasn't ready to be with anyone yet."

"Then why did you start seeing him?"

"I don't know. I guess I felt like I should give him a chance. He asked me so many times, and has always been so sweet to me, I just thought I should try."

"But you didn't really want to?"

"No. I didn't feel anything like that towards him. Why do you think I never took him to the ball? I knew he couldn't ask me, because he's not a member, but I didn't want him to go at all. So I went alone. I only invited him today because I felt like I had no other choice."

"Well tomorrow, end it. Gerard and I will be leaving first thing in the morning, for a whole week. End it tomorrow before you go to the lagoon."

"I don't know."

"Just do it. If you don't you will spend the next three months trying to figure out how to end it. And he will keep trying to get you to run away with him."

"I guess you're right. Alright. Let's just not talk about this today. We have your wedding to focus on, and it's almost time to leave. Are you ready?"

"I'm ready! We just have to wait for William to get here. Where are you staying tonight?"

"Probably above the pub with Callie unless William and Shannon say I can stay with them."

Lucy just laughed, "I swear you basically live at that pub with Callie!"

"I oddly enough feel safe there, even though it is the most dangerous place in town." Gemma laughed, as Peggy walked in.

"What are you two laughing about this time?" She asked as she walked in.

"I was just teasing Gemma about how she basically lives at the pub."

"Well she does, I hardly see you anymore." Peggy said softly.

"You see me just about every day that I'm in town, and come by almost every weekend at my palace." Gemma laughed.

"I know, it's just not the same."

"I know, I'm sorry."

"You have no need to be sorry dear. It was something we all decided."

Gemma smiled as Peggy spoke to her. Gemma loved how Peggy treated her as if she was her own daughter.

"Lucy my dear, you look beautiful! He won't be able to take his eyes off you for a second." Peggy gave Lucy a proud smile.

"Of course he will, when she is pulling his shirt off him tonight." Gemma laughed

"Gemma!" Peggy snapped

"What? You know it's true!" Gemma laughed.

Lucy blushed, then they all started to laugh. Peggy grabbed the veil and Gemma got the flowers and a rope of 13 colors that Gemma spent a week making, and the three of them went into the living room. William was standing there waiting for them. He was in a nice suit and had combed his hair neatly, he had a smile on his face. Lucy ran to him and gave him a big hug.

"You look so beautiful! I'm so happy that you're about to become my daughter. Are you ready? Everyone is waiting on us."

"Thank you! And yes, we are ready." Lucy said happily

"Gemma and I will take her car separately so you two can make your grand entrance." Peggy said.

When Gemma and Peggy arrived, Peggy looked in to see if everyone was there. Gemma quickly fixed Kelley's memorial chair. She took the table cloth and folded it to look like a sash, she hung it as if someone was wearing a sash and pinned it in place. Placed his portrait and the flowers, as well as a small dagger. She wiped a tear from her eye, then quickly left the tent, lightly bumping into someone, dropping her flowers.

"Oh, I'm so sorry." She said.

He picked up the flowers and handed them to her, he lightly touched her hand. She had never seen him before, but something about him was familiar. She looked into his eyes, getting lost in them, feeling as if she could look into them forever. If she didn't know any better she would have sworn that it was Kelley. The black in her hair began to fade.

"Thank you." She said taking the flowers from him. He walked away to his seat as she left.

"There are just a few more stragglers, come help me put the veil on Lucy. She can't be seen by anyone yet." Gemma and Peggy went to Lucy and put the veil on her head, keeping it in place with some hair pins. It had elegant lace around the edges, and pearls that she asked Gemma to sew into it. After they finished, Gemma and Peggy stood outside the tent. Gerard walked Peggy and Shannon to their seats, then waited at the front. Gemma took a deep breath and walked into the tent. She held her head up high, and had a slight smile on her face for Gerard and Lucy. Gerard noticed something shinny in Gemma's flowers, and whispered to her when she got to the front.

"I'm surprised Lucy let you bring that."

"I told her she could choose between in the flowers or the dress." She whispered back smiling at him. "She said we think too much alike."

"Isn't that what she loves about us."

"I said the same thing." She lightly giggled. "Oh here she comes!"

Lucy and William walked into the tent, all eyes were on her. She glided gracefully down the aisle, her head up high, biggest smile in the world on her face. Her rose gold hair shining brightly against the white dress. Tears fell from Gerard's eyes when he saw her, he was amazed at how beautiful she looked. His smile was so big and happy, nothing could upset him right now. Lucy gave William a kiss on the cheek as he handed her off to Gerard. Lucy and Gerard were smiles the whole time, nothing could take away the happiness they were feeling. Gemma looked over at the chair with Kelley's photo and a tear rolled down her cheek. She knew how much he wanted to be there for Lucy, it was something that they had all talked about ever since they got engaged. She wiped the tear from her face, but kept a slight smile. She occasionally looked out in the crowd of people, she didn't like big crowds, she never felt safe in them. She saw Finn in the crowd he was smiling at her, she gave him a quick glance, avoiding eye contact. She looked further in the crowd, at the very back of the tent she spotted Callie. Then next to Callie was a man she had seen before, he was the first mate of her future husband. She knew she needed to talk to him, he had no reason to be here, so why was he there? She was about to look back at Gerard and Lucy when something caught her eye. The man she bumped into that handed her, her bouquet back, he was sitting next to the first mate. The first mate whispered something to him. This was not a coincidence, she needed to know more. She turned back to Lucy and Gerard just as they were exchanging rings.

"I Gerard Benjamin Collins pledge my love and everything I own to Lucille Adeline. I promise the first sip from my cup, to you and only you. I promise to only ever cry your name in the middle of the night, and be the only face I look upon when I wake. I promise to remain loyal and true, in this life and our next. I promise to defend your honor and protect you from all harm. I promise to be by your side, in all of the moments in our lives, the easy and the hard ones. I promise our love will remain never-ending, and we shall be equals in all aspects of our marriage, forever and always. This is the vow I pledge to you on our wedding day." Gerard said as he slowly slid the ring on her finger.

"I Lucille Adeline O'Rilley, pledge my love and everything my heart possess to Gerard Benjamin Collins. I promise the first sip from my cup, to you and only you. I promise to only ever cry your name in the middle of the night, and be the only face I look upon when I wake. I promise to remain loyal and true to you, in this life and the next. I promise to stand up for you, when you feel you cannot. I promise to be your voice when you no longer have one. I promise to stay by your side, no matter what comes our way. I promise our love will remain never-ending, and we shall be equals in all aspects of our marriage, forever and always. This is the vow I pledge to you on our wedding day." Lucy said excitedly, she quickly slid the ring on his finger, with the biggest smile on her face.

Finally, they began the handfasting ritual. She handed the minister the rope, and the colors were explained, Gemma listened closely, she wanted to understand this tradition. Lucy handed her bouquet to Gemma, then grasped Gerard's hands, gazing into his eyes.

"Every color of this rope represents many different aspects of a marriage." The minister went on to explain each of the thirteen colors: red, orange, yellow, green, blue, purple, black, white, grey, pink, brown, silver and gold. Then continued to slowly wrap the rope around their hands, making an eternity symbol out of the rope, then tying it into a knot. "Gerard and Lucille, this along with your rings, signify the unity of your marriage, and the vows that you have made to one another. This knot forever binds your hearts and souls as one, and to be used as a reminder of what you have pledged to one another. With this bond you two become one, one love, one family."

Gerard kissed Lucy and everyone started to applaud, Gemma couldn't because she was holding two bouquets, but she had a big smile on her face. They walked back down the aisle and left the tent, Gemma followed behind them, alone. She stopped at the end of the aisle to speak with her aunt and uncle who were hiding in the back.

"What are you two doing here?" She asked as she hugged Persephone.

"You know we wouldn't miss our goddaughter's wedding. But we're only here for the ceremony." Persephone held her at arms length. "You look gorgeous today my dear, but why do you look so upset to see us?"

"Why have neither of you responded to any of my messages or requests?"

"Because we didn't know what else to say."

"But you could've answered with that at least. Or checked on me. I've felt so alone."

"I told you when I gave you Lux what would happen if anything happened to Kelley. We would never even know that he died. We didn't know anything until you sent us that message and we've been trying to search for answers since then." Hades explained. "If we find anything we will let you know, you know I don't like lying, so take me at my word that we are still searching for answers."

"Okay, but can you two please come visit me at my palace sometime. I miss you both and could use some company while I'm there."

"We will try to make a trip there this week." Persephone said with a smile. "Now go join the wedding party."

She gave them both a hug then went outside to walk to the reception, Finn ran right to Gemma and grabbed her hand. She quietly held his hand, didn't say a word. When they got inside she spoke to Lucy immediately, telling her that she saw Nik outside and needed to speak with him for a few minutes. Lucy told her not to worry, but to not be gone too long. Gemma told Finn she would return in a few minutes, and that she didn't want him to come with her. She left the reception hall and looked all around for either of the two men, then she saw them in the distance. She ran after them, the one who she bumped into didn't stop when she yelled to them, but the other did.

"Wait! I need to talk to you." She shouted, "I know you, I've seen you before. You are my Fiancé's first mate. What are you doing here?" She said slightly breathless when she reached him.

"I was invited by Callie, she wanted someone to come with her." The man said

"Then why are you not going to reception with her?"

"My mate over there, isn't up for a party, so I was helping him get back to the ship."

"Alright," She said, not believing a word he said. She pulled a dagger from her flowers and held it at his throat. "Now, what is the real reason you are here?" She spoke with no fear towards him.

"That is the truth, Callie just wanted to have someone to come with her, and my best mate wanted to leave."

"If there wasn't more than that, you would have told him to walk back by himself. Now who are you both?" she shouted.

"My name is David, I'm your fiancé's first mate. That is my friend, he thought he wanted to join Callie and I, then decided he wanted to go back."

"Who is he?" She said pressing the dagger harder to his throat.

"He is just a friend of mine. He has been on the ship with me for years. That's all! You met him yesterday at the pub, when he saw you walk off with that boy he decided he wanted to leave."

"Sam" She whispered to herself "You know exactly who I am, and what I'm capable of. Now tell me, who is Sam really?" She shouted.

"I already told you! He is just one of my friends." He said.

She looked into his eyes and knew he was hiding something. He looked worried with a hint of fear in his eyes. She pulled the dagger from his throat, then ran in the direction where Sam went. She tried to catch him, but was unsuccessful. She made it to the docks, there were four ships there, she knew she would never find him. Then she felt a hand on her shoulder, she turned quickly dagger in hand.

"Nik? What are you doing here?" She said.

"I saw you run off from the wedding. What are you doing out here? You should be with everyone at the reception."

"I... I saw someone, I... needed to know who he was. There was something about him, something so familiar. I... I just had to know." She said stumbling on her words, still looking all around her.

"Well did you find him?"

"No, I didn't."

"Alright, let's go back, Lucy is probably worried about you."

Gemma sighed, hung her head low, "Alright." Gemma was quiet as they walked back.

"Come on, don't be like that. It was probably no one." Nik said.

"But what if it wasn't."

"Who did you think it was?"

"I don't know, but I met him in the pub yesterday. I didn't see his face then, but he touched my hand and I began to feel whole again. Then today I bumped into him dropping my bouquet and as he handed it to me, our hands touched. I started to feel whole again, and his eyes, I started to get lost in them. If I didn't know any better, I would swear it was Kelley. Those are his eyes, I know his eyes anywhere."

"Gemma, you know it's not him."

"I know, but it felt like he was there today, and then that man's eyes, and how I felt when he touched me. I... I just had to be sure it wasn't him." She continued.

"I'm sorry." Nik said

"Why?"

"That you couldn't find out, but I'm sure it wasn't him."

She sighed, "I know." She wrapped her shawl around herself, it was quite cold out. She didn't notice before how cold it was, the adrenaline and running made her feel warm. Nik took his jacket off and put it around her shoulders.

"It's too cold for you to be out here like this. Your mother would kill me if she knew I let you run off into the snow, without a coat." He laughed

"She would not!" She said giving him a slight push.

"Oh trust me she would. Think of your mother and I, like Lucy and Kelley. You know Lucy would kill Kelley if he had her daughter out in the snow."

Gemma just laughed at him. "Yeah she would."

54

When they got back to the reception, dinner was being served. She asked Nik to come sit with her and Finn, she didn't want to be stuck alone with Finn. She knew Finn didn't like or trust Nik, and that he rarely ever said anything when he was around. It was the perfect way to keep Finn from asking her to run away with him again. They all danced and had a wonderful time. Gemma was happy to have Nik there, she was happier to dance with him than Finn. Every time Finn was alone with her he would bring up the same thing. Eventually Finn pulled Gemma outside to talk.

"Gemma, I can't let you go through with this. Please just run away with me. We can leave all of this behind us, start a life somewhere else. You always tell me I need to travel to other places, we can do that together." He begged.

"Finn, you know I can't! This has been set my entire life. I can't run away from this." She said firmly.

"Yes you can! We can get in your car and leave right now."

"We are not running away. There are things you don't understand."

"Because you won't tell me!" He shouted.

"I can't and you know that!" She shouted back.

"Why can't you? Lucy and Gerard know. I'm sure Kelley knew. Even that Nik guy knows! So why can't I know?" He began to shout louder.

"Because my life isn't what you think! I can't tell you any of this. I have no choice. One day you will know and understand, but until then, I can't tell you or anyone."

"Then why do they know?"

"Because they have been entrusted with my life. You think I want to live like this? You think I like having to keep everything from everyone? I hate it! I just want to go home and I can't! I can't tell anyone where I'm from or who I really am! My life has to be a complete secret!" She shouted, filling with rage.

"Why? Why do you have to live like this?"

"Because my life is constantly threatened! Even if I did tell you everything, you wouldn't believe me!"

"Yes I would! Just tell me!"

"I told you I can't tell you! If I do you could be in danger too. Trust me when I say it's better you don't know!"

He could see the hurt in her eyes, and began to speak softly towards her. "I will be fine. It just kills me that you keep something like this from me. You know how I feel about you." He grabbed Gemma's hands, interlocking their fingers.

"Finley stop, that won't work! It won't get me to tell you. I have to go." She started to pull away, trying to go back to the reception. He pulled her close and kissed her. She pushed herself away from him.

"No! That's not going to work this time!" She shouted again, "We can't keep doing this. I can't keep doing this. It's not fair to you."

"Just tell me and everything will be fine."

"No Finn. I can't do this anymore! I can't keep leading you on. I'm done." She shouted

"Done with what? This conversation? Fine, but we have to finish this one day." He shouted back.

She let out a deep sigh, "No. Finn, I'm done with us. Our relationship. I'm done."

"What?" He said in shock, "But why? You know how much I love you."

"But I don't love you. I like you as a friend, but I don't have those same feelings you have. I've spent months trying to feel the same, I just don't. I was going to end this tomorrow morning before I left, but I can't do this again tomorrow."

Gemma began to walk off, he chased after her.

"Wait! What can I do to fix this? Please Gemma, I don't want to lose you!" He begged.

"There is nothing you can do. I have led you on for far too long. I should have ended everything the moment you said I love you, but I didn't. I wanted to try to have those feelings for you, but I just don't. And now... now there is no point in trying anymore. I will be married in three months, and I am not going to run away and risk chaos happening if I do."

"What is that supposed to mean? So some guy you are going to marry is out of this arrangement too. That doesn't sound like a bad thing!"

"It's something that you don't understand. I will explain everything one day, but I can't now, not yet. It's too big of a secret for you to have to keep, and it won't change anything once I tell you."

"I can handle whatever secret you have, just please. Don't leave me, I don't know what I will do without you."

"Finn, you will be fine without me, you were fine for years without me. There is a girl out there who is perfect for you. I'm just not that girl. It would never work between us. If you knew, you would understand."

"Then tell me so I can understand. If we can't be together I want to at least understand why. I won't tell anyone. I promise."

"I will tell you when it is safe, but for now, you have to move on."

"How long will it be until it's safe?"

"After my wedding. That is when everything will be over and I will be safe."

"How will you tell me?"

"I will send you a letter, telling you to meet me somewhere. I know the perfect place, but you would have to travel there, it will not be here. Now I have to go back inside, I'm sorry."

Gemma went back inside, Finn stood there in the cold not sure what to do. He loved Gemma, but knew that once she made up her mind, there was no changing it. It killed him that she didn't want to be with him, and that he couldn't understand why. Why she wouldn't tell him anything at all. He didn't want to go back in there, not now after what just happened.

Shortly after she returned, Lucy and Gerard were getting ready to leave. Gemma gave them both big hugs and told them to let her know when they were back. She gathered her things, and the memorial left for Kelley. Then left for Shannon's and went to bed, ready to leave first thing in the morning.

55

It had been three months since Gerard and Lucy got married. And now Gemma's wedding was in a week and a half. Gemma got up and started packing her bags. She was going to the Lagoon to take more of her things there. She wanted to make sure she had everything there before she moved there. She didn't know if her future husband would allow her to go see Gerard and Lucy. She even brought Lux to leave at the castle for when she returned from her wedding. She finished packing her car and knew there was one last thing to deal with, Finn. She gave Lucy and Gerard hugs, and told them she would see them this weekend. She drove over to Finn's house and knocked on the door, Molly answered.

"Gemma? What are you doing here? I've missed you so much!" Molly said excited and confused.

"Hi Molly. I've missed you too. Is Finn home? I need to talk to him about something."

"Yeah, he's outback. You are more than welcome to just go back and get him."

"Thanks Molly."

"He's still hurting though, so he might not be too thrilled." Molly said as Gemma was turning to go find Finn.

"I know, but it's something that I need to talk to him about." She sighed

"Why did you have to end it? Why couldn't you two just stay together?" Molly asked

"You know why. I'm getting married in a week and a half." Gemma said.

"I know, I just don't understand why you couldn't just run away with him." Molly said.

"Give it a few weeks, I will tell Finn everything after the wedding. You will understand then." Gemma said as she walked away.

Gemma went around back and found Finn in the barn. She knocked on the side of the doorway.

"Finn?"

Finn turned around quick, "Gemma? What are you doing here?"

"I need to talk to you about something."

"Alright, what is it?" He said in an annoyed tone.

"Can we sit down?"

Finn nodded and gestured to a couple of crates sitting near him.

"You know how I always told you that you need to go see the world?"

"Yeah, I was actually considering doing it, but only with you." He said, still sounding annoyed.

"Would you still want to travel a bit? See other places?"

Finn's ears perked, he was hoping that she was asking him to run away with her "Maybe."

"If you are willing to think about it, I have an idea, but I would need you to come with me for just a couple of days. I have to take the rest of my things to my house. It would at least get you out of this town for once."

"When are you leaving?"

"Now. It's just for three days."

Finn sat there and thought about it for a few minutes. He knew she was up to something, but couldn't figure out what. "Alright, let me go pack a bag, and I would need to stop by my work and let them know." He said hesitantly.

"I will be waiting in my car." She said with a smile

"Alright."

Gemma walked back around the house and sat in her car waiting for Finn. He got in the car, they stopped by Donovan's and then they left. Finn saw the whole back seat was filled with trunks. He noticed that all of the trunks had elaborate carvings all over them. Embedded with jewels and sea life. He was starting to wonder who she really was, and where these trunks came from. It was a long silent drive. Gemma was afraid to tell him anything just yet. She didn't want him to try to back out of it before he met her. She pulled into town and parked her car.

"Where are we?" He asked

"This is the town near my house. This is where I go every other week, and where I will be from now on." She said.

"I don't understand, why are we here?" He asked

"I want you to meet a friend of mine." She said with a smile.

"Alright…" He said hesitantly.

They went right to the Café, she knew that Anna-Maria would be getting off soon, so she would be able to join them. As soon as they walked in Anna-Maria saw Gemma and ran to her giving her a big hug. His heart skipped a beat the moment his eyes landed on her.

"Gems! I thought you weren't going to be here until tomorrow. I took the whole day off to spend with you." She said extremely excited. "Oh, who's this?" She said when she saw Finn, then whispered to Gemma, "He's gorgeous! Where have you been hiding him?"

Gemma laughed. "I missed you too! This is Finn, I've told you about him before. Can you get a table for the three of us?"

"Of course! Away from the window as usual?" Anna-Maria asked

"You know me so well." Gemma laughed.

She took them to a table in the corner, set for four. "I get off in about five minutes, do you mind waiting for me?"

"Of course not, that's why I said for three." Gemma said with a smile. Anna-Maria smiled and walked off to get them some drinks.

"Gemma who is that?" Finn asked.

"That is my close friend Anna-Maria. She is the one I spend all my time with while I'm here. She's pretty incredible. We have been through some of the same things, so we understand one another pretty well."

"Oh, so is she set in an arranged marriage as well?" He asked sounding glum.

"No. She had been attacked a couple of years ago, we help one another feel safe."

"Really?" Finn said, not taking his eyes off of her. Anna-Maria returned with drinks for the three of them and sat down

"I ordered your favorite for you, but I didn't know what to order for Finn. So I just got him what I got."

"What did you order?" Finn asked

"Half a Cornish hen. Gems ALWAYS gets seafood, I swear she doesn't eat anything else."

Finn laughed, "Yeah I know, I tried for a while to get her to eat other things, but she always went right back to seafood."

"It's like she lives in the sea." Anna-Maria laughed.

"You know how much I love the sea. Salt water is in my blood." Gemma laughed

"Oh Gems, I have missed you this last week! We had some of the worst men come in recently. Thankfully I remembered everything you taught me. It was very helpful."

"What did she teach you?" Finn asked.

"How to defend myself. I was attacked a couple of years ago, my first day in this town. I was robbed of all the money that I had, and was left for dead. I was rescued and then given this job to try to save up my money and get out of here. I have enough, I just don't want to go alone, and Gems refuses to go with me." Anna-Maria explained.

"It's not that I don't want to, you know I can't." Gemma said.

"I know I just really like to give you a hard time." Anna-Maria teased.

"Where are you trying to go?" Finn asked, becoming more intrigued by the second.

"Well first I'm going to Clew Bay to catch a ship. Then I plan on just exploring for a little while, and hopefully one day make it down to the islands."

"Why such a long trip?" Finn asked.

"Haven't you ever wanted to just see the world? See what is out there besides Ireland?" She asked

"I've thought about it, but I never wanted to go without Gemma. She is the one who gave me the idea of seeing other places." Finn said.

"Really? You never wanted to leave before that?" Anna-Maria said sounding confused.

"No. This is actually the first time I have left Clew Bay." He said, sounding a bit embarrassed.

"What? How have you never left your town before? Gems! Why didn't you bring him here sooner?" Anna-Maria asked

Gemma laughed at the two of them. "I don't know. Maybe because he kept trying to get me to run away with him."

"Well you should have, I know I would! ...I mean, he seems pretty great." Anna-Maria blushed with her last comment.

"There is no changing her mind once it's made up." Finn said smiling at Anna-Maria.

Anna-Maria's cheeks began to burn. "Have you seen her house yet? I have been begging her to take me there, but she never does. Something to do with the big secret of who she really is."

"Everything has to do with that big secret. She still won't tell me anything."

"You both know I can't." Gemma sighed.

"That doesn't mean we can't tease you about it." Anna-Maria teased.

They all sat and chatted for a couple of hours. So far everything was going the way Gemma wanted it. Finn and Anna-Maria couldn't take their eyes off each other. Finn was fascinated by her. She reminded him of Gemma, but not full of secrets. She was an open book, not afraid of anyone finding out anything about her.

"I will be back in a few minutes, I have to check Finn into his room at the inn." Gemma said.

"Wait I'm not staying with you?" Finn asked, a bit confused.

"No, you can't stay at my house."

"We know, the big secret. One day you will have to tell us." Anna-Maria said. "Don't worry the inn is really nice, that's where I live." She whispered to him. He just smiled back at her.

When Gemma came back, the two of them were still talking. She looked at the table and saw that his hand was on top of hers. *Perfect*, she thought to herself. They were hitting it off just like she knew they would. She sat back down with them and they chatted a bit longer. Gemma paid for all their meals, then told them she needed to go. They all got up and left.

"I can walk you to the Inn if you would like." Finn said, even though he didn't know where it was.

"That would be lovely!" Anna-Maria said smiling and blushing at the same time.

"I just need to get my things from Gemma's car." They went to Gemma's car and Finn grabbed his bag. Gemma gave them both hugs and told them she would see them in the morning. She watched as they walked off holding hands. She got home just before it had started to rain a little.

56

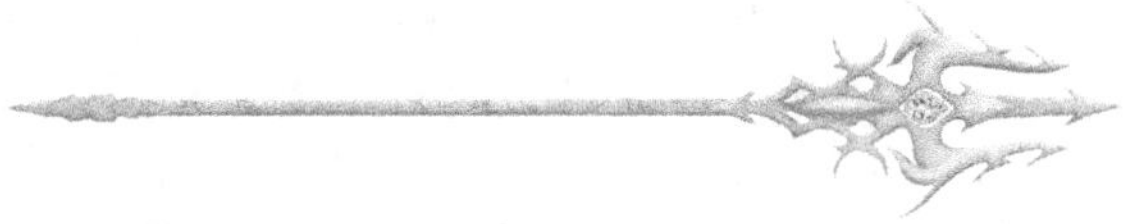

When she got to town in the morning, Finn and Anna-Maria had already had breakfast together.

"Well it looks like you two have hit it off." Gemma teased.

"Gems, he's amazing! Why are you not still with him? Actually that doesn't matter, because now I can have a chance with him." Anna-Maria whispered to her.

"I thought you would like him."

"Like him? Gems I am falling for him, I'm thinking about asking him if he would want to go with me."

"You should."

"What are you two whispering about?" Finn asked

"You of course!" Anna-Maria said smiling at him. She then turned back to Gemma. "We stayed up all night just talking. I have never met someone like him. He is gorgeous, kind, smart, funny. I honestly can't believe that he isn't already married. I would keep him forever if I could." She gushed about him. Gemma had never seen her act like this, and couldn't help but giggle.

Finn held Anna-Maria's hand as they walked around the town. "I need to stop at the market, do you two want to come with or just meet up with me again in a few?"

"Ummm… well I don't actually need anything from there today. I need to stop by the dress shop though." Anna-Maria said.

"Well I can go to the market, and get whatever Gemma needs while you two go to the dress shop." Finn said.

"That sounds perfect!" Anna-Maria said

Gemma handed him two pieces of silver and a list of what she needed. It wasn't much, but it was food essentials for her and Marsali. The girls went to the dress shop and picked up a couple of things that Anna-Maria needed. They talked the whole time, she told Gemma everything that Finn and her talked about that night. She had never felt so comfortable with any man before. She told her that she was afraid though, afraid that he wouldn't want to go with her. She wasn't going to give up the trip she had saved for so long for. She was willing to not move to Port Royal though, she had realized that she didn't know what it was really like there. She needed to know what it was like somewhere before she decided to settle down anywhere. When they left the dress shop Finn was standing by Gemma's car waiting for them. Gemma noticed that he had some flowers behind his back, and smiled, she knew they were for Anna-Maria. He handed her the flowers and she squealed with excitement. No one had ever given her flowers before. They spent the rest of the day wandering around town. Gemma tried to give them time alone, but Anna-Maria still wanted to spend time with Gemma. They all had dinner together again, after they had been there for a couple of hours, Gemma told them that she needed to get going. She went back to her car, and looked at them through the window. They were laughing and talking with smiles on their faces the whole time.

When Gemma came back in the morning, Anna-Maria was already at work. That meant she had to entertain Finn the whole time. The two of them talked a little bit, but it was not like how they used to talk. He seemed afraid to say anything to her.

"So what did you two do after I left?"

"We just went back to the inn, and talked some more."

"You two have really hit it off."

"Yeah, I guess." He said blushing

"You know it's okay if you like her, or want to be with her."

"You're okay with that?"

"Of course I am. Why wouldn't I be?"

"Well because of us, and you brought me here. Which I still don't know why."

Gemma laughed, "You really don't get it do you?"

"Get what?"

"I brought you here to meet her."

"What? Why?" He asked, confused by why she would want him to meet Anna-Maria.

"Because you two seemed perfect for each other. I wanted to make sure you at least met her before she leaves."

"She is pretty perfect. Not that you aren't... but I mean, she is different than you."

"Finn it's okay!" She laughed. "Honestly I wanted you two to meet before we got together. But you kept asking me, so I thought I should give us a try. I knew as soon as I met her, that you would love her."

"I really like her, a lot. She isn't afraid of her feelings, and tells me everything. I... just don't know. Am I rushing into this? Should I just wait for her to come back?" He asked.

"She might not come back though. She might find somewhere that she truly loves. She doesn't have any family here, nothing keeping her anywhere." She said

"Oh, I guess I was just hoping that she would want to come back here with me."

"She might, that is something you should talk to her about."

"I'm scared to, what if she says no?" He said nervously.

"You won't ever know until you talk to her. Why don't we ask her to come back with us tomorrow? I have to come back here again this weekend anyways. This way she can spend a few more days with you, it would give you both more of a chance to decide."

"That sounds like a great idea. Let's go ask her!" He said now excited

"We have to wait a little bit, she is at work right now. She should be done in a couple of hours."

"Oh, right. Are you sure you are alright with all of this?"

"Of course I am. I care about you both a lot. You might not think I care about you because I ended things with us. But I did that because I care about you. I just didn't have the same type of feelings that you did, and it wasn't right for me to keep stringing you along."

"I'm sorry." Finn said hanging his head low.

"For what?" She asked.

"Making you feel as if you had to be with me, that I wouldn't just let us be friends like you wanted."

"You don't need to be sorry. Honestly I needed to learn to move on, it's a lot harder than I thought it would be. You helped me, I still haven't fully recovered. But you did help me a little. I just hope I will have those feelings for someone else one day."

"Well hopefully it will be your husband."

"I really hope so. The wedding is in a week, and I'm not ready or looking forward to it. The only thing that will make it a little better is that I will get to see my father."

"When was the last time you saw him?"

"My birthday last year."

"I thought he was out to sea for a few years."

"He made a special trip to see me, because it was my birthday."

"Oh, well I'm glad you were able to see him, especially with everything that was going on around your birthday."

"Thanks, it wasn't the best birthday. Seeing him did make it a little better, then he gave me my car as a gift."

"So that's where you got it from. I never asked because I figured you would never tell me." Finn said smiling.

She laughed. "I don't blame you. Sorry I keep so much from you, I really can't tell people anything about me. The only people who know are the O'Reilly's because they are supposed to be watching me. Gerard only knows because he found out, then we had to explain everything to him. He knows if he tells anyone it could put himself and his family in danger."

"I wish you could just tell me, so does Anna-Maria."

"I know, and I will tell you both sometime after the wedding, but until then, it's just not safe. I truly don't want any harm to come to either of you."

"I understand." He said. "Can I ask you something? It's not about any of that stuff."

"I guess."

"Were you pushing me to travel because of Anna-Maria?"

She sighed. "That was a big part of it. I knew she would leave one day. She would never give up this trip for anyone. But I thought that if you two hit it off, it would be great for both of you. Even if you don't end up dating seriously, having someone with you is safer. I wanted her to have someone to go with her… and I wanted you to see other parts of the world. You can learn so much from other cultures. More than just cooking. It gives you a sense of what is most important to you. You learn to adapt to your surroundings. For a chef, that's a really good talent to have." She reached into her bag and pulled out a book. "If you decide to go, this will help you survive. It's common phrases in languages around the world. If you don't go, then give it to Lucy and Gerard. They can get it back to me."

"Shouldn't you be giving this to Anna?"

"She already memorized the countries she plans to visit." She laughed. "I let her borrow it last year."

"Why do you even have something like this?"

"Salt water's in my blood. I've traveled all around the world. Learning other languages was something my father insisted on. To the point where I can fluently speak most languages."

"And your mother?"

"Not as much as him, but she saw the value. She preferred I learn more about helping those less fortunate, or who need the help."

"Thanks… I have a lot to think about."

When they picked Anna-Maria up from work Finn asked her if she would be willing to take a few days off from work and come back with them. He told her he was really considering going on her trip with her, but he wanted to spend a few more days with her before he was sure. She asked Jerry, and he gave her the time off. Anna-Maria was excited, it had been three years since she first arrived there, and still hadn't left even once. They told her they would be leaving in the morning, so to make sure she packed that night. Gemma said good night to them, she looked back at them as she walked away and smiled. She was glad they were happy, she just hoped that Finn would actually go with her.

57

They arrived back at Clew, Gemma was happy to be back, she went straight to Gerard and Lucy's house. Finn took Anna-Maria around town, it was very different than where she spent the past three years. Her port was much smaller, and didn't get as many ships into port. Usually the ships that did come in were already from there, maybe once a month they would get a different ship in. Gemma asked Lucy if it was okay for Anna-Maria to stay there for the next few nights. Lucy was hesitant at first, but then said it was alright. She knew how close Gemma and Anna-Maria had become, and that they both had been through a lot of the same things. Gemma told Finn and Anna-Maria to do whatever they wanted, just make sure that Anna-Maria was ready to go back on Friday.

Gemma hardly saw either of them the entire time that they were there. Gemma was running around town all week with Lucy, getting everything ready for the wedding. Gemma didn't care too much about all of the wedding stuff, but Lucy wanted to try to make the ceremony as perfect as possible. Gemma didn't understand why, they had no say in anything for the wedding. She wasn't even excited about the wedding. She couldn't choose anything that had to do with the wedding. She was never a fan of the requirements of Land and Sea weddings, everything had to be a particular way for it to be legal. She went to a land and sea wedding once, when she was very little. She watched from the water with her mother, and remembered how much she hated the outfits that they all had to wear. The only thing that was making any of this worthwhile, was that Lucy would be the one standing next to her. Lucy helped Gemma pick out flowers, and other decorations, but there wasn't too much they could really do to make it special. Everything was supposedly taken care of by Poseidon, which didn't make Gemma any happier. Gemma's mood just got darker each day they got closer to the wedding.

She walked into Callie's pub to say her goodbyes. She wasn't sure how she felt about leaving the pub. She was happy to be done with dealing with the degenerates that would come off the ships, but she enjoyed her time with Callie and a few of the regulars. She spotted Callie in her usual spot behind the bar.

"Gemma! What are you doing here? I thought you already left."

"I leave tomorrow morning. Just a few last minute things I need to take care of. Do you mind if we talk privately in back?"

"Of course. Fredrick, can you handle being left alone?"

"Y-yes ma'am" Fredrick's words shook as the pirates laughed.

"He's not going to last long." She whispered to Gemma.

Callie took them into the back room. She locked the door and opened up a panel in the wall placing a golden key in it. The sound of steam escaping the walls as the room began to move. She gave Callie a suspicious look. When the room stopped moving Callie opened the door to another room.

Deep cherrywood throughout the room. The shelves on the walls filled with scrolls and trinkets. A large desk that looked to be the twin of the desk she had at her palace sat in the center of the room, behind it was a portrait of Callie, as a pirate. She smirked. She knew she was right this whole time. Callie worked for her father. And the crest sitting on her desk said it all.

"So you have the other one." She laughed picking up the pendant. "Safe to say you know exactly who I am."

"I do, your highness." She pulled out a box wrapped in white paper with a silver ribbon. "A wedding gift from me. Your father doesn't know about this." She gave her a small wink.

"Well this just makes my request so much easier."

Callie took a seat and gestured for Gemma to do the same.

"I have a friend who is going to be traveling around the world soon. I don't feel she is safe with the papers she has. I feel some will try to take advantage of her. I know you can make travel documents, I've seen you do it before. Could you make her some, but change her last name and put a specific seal on it?"

"That shouldn't be a problem. Which seal do you need me to put on there?"

"The royal seal for the Mediterranean."

She narrowed her eyes. "Why?"

"Because she is my niece and doesn't know it. She doesn't know she's a royal and I would prefer she be treated better than she has been in the past. But I want her last name changed to her boyfriend's last name so her father can't find her."

"So you found his half human daughter. I was wondering when someone would find out about her."

"How do you know about her?"

"Your father sent me to bring him home. When I found him, he was with his daughter."

"Hmm." She looked around the room, admiring the woodworking. "I'm surprised you didn't tell my father."

"Your brother made it worth my while."

"Add an HRH to her name, she deserves to have her title. Just don't tell her what it means."

Callie was writing down notes for the papers. "And the name?"

"Ana-Maria Isabelle Gallagher"

"Gallagher huh. So she's the one seeing Finley now. A little strange, isn't it?"

"No, I wanted them to date the whole time but Finn wouldn't take no for an answer. He fell head over fins for her the second he saw her though."

"I can have them ready in a few days. Have her stop by to pick them up. Does Finley know you're putting his name on her papers?"

"It was his idea, seeing as how he's the one going with her. He said it would probably be safer for people to think they're married."

"Well he's not wrong. Do me a quick favor. Sign this note with your real name and title. I'll seal it and have her give it to the captain.

It'll give them extra protection on their ship out of here. After that, they're on their own."

"Add one thing to the note. To notify Nikoli what port they arrived in. This way I can try to help them the best I can. Those two are not great at fighting and need all the help they can get to survive."

That night Anna-Maria brought Finn over for dinner, they needed to talk to Gemma about something before they all had to leave in the morning. After dinner they all sat in the living room and chatted.

"So we have spent this whole week getting to know each other better." Finn started,

Then Anna-Maria interjected. "Finn is going to come with me!" She was so happy, "Sorry I couldn't contain myself any longer."

"I already know. Finn told me this morning. I'm thrilled for you both!"

"We have to wait a couple of weeks before we go, but she is going to be staying at my parent's house while we wait to leave. You won't have to drive her back tomorrow. We will be going back together to get all of her things."

"What do your parents think of all this?" Gemma asked, "I mean, I know they can't really say much because you're 22."

"My mum is not happy about this at all, she thinks I'm throwing my life away. She is pretty upset with you right now."

"When is she not upset with me? I'm pretty sure that she has been upset with me since the moment I met you." Gemma laughed

"My Da' on the other hand thinks it's the best decision I have ever made. He completely supports me in this, and thinks it will be good for me to see the world."

"How's Molly taking this?"

"She's unsure. She's going to miss me a lot, but also really likes Anna-Maria, and wishes she could just come with us. She's a little jealous that we are going off and exploring the world and that she is stuck here."

"Well I'm very excited for you two. Do you know where you are going first?"

"We are planning on going to France and staying there for a couple of weeks or so, but it will take a few days to get there. Then we want to go to Spain for few weeks. Finn wants to go to Madrid and then Italy after that, but I still want to go down to the islands. So we are just going to play it by ear once we get to Spain."

"You know I want to go down there too, I just think going to Italy would be great. Maybe spend a few days in Rome, it's not like we'll be too far away from it when in Spain. Besides I can learn different recipes from all the different places we go, and my father and Francis, both said I need to see Italy."

"We will just have to see how everything is going by that point. Who knows where we will want to go by the time we get to Spain."

"We just thought you should know. We are so grateful that you introduced us to each other. We couldn't be happier or more excited." Finn said as he smiled at Anna-Maria. "Well, we should get going, I know you have to get up early to leave."

"Thanks for letting me know. I'm really happy for you both! I hope that your trip is enlightening."

Anna-Maria gave Gemma a big hug and whispered to her. "Thank you so much! Finn is the greatest thing to ever happen to me. I will send you letters all the time. I will have them sent to Jerry, so you can get them anytime you are in town."

"Thank you. I will miss you."

"I will miss you too! Don't forget me. Oh I almost forgot, I want you to have this. I should have been yours in the first place. I had Neil make me my own, and a holster for my thigh as well." She handed Gemma her wrist brace. Gemma had a tear roll down her cheek, she was happy to have it, but also sad that the only friend she had near her house was leaving. Gemma hugged her again and thanked her. Then she gave Finn a hug goodbye.

"Thank you Gemma, I'm glad that you had me come with you this week. None of this would be happening without you. Good luck at your wedding, I hope that he is a good man."

"Thanks Finn, me too. Be safe when traveling, please bring a few swords and daggers. They will keep you both safe." Gemma said.

"Don't worry, we were already planning on it." Finn laughed. Gemma walked them out, then waved to them as they left.

58

Gemma stared out the window the entire three day trek to the ship. It should've only taken them half a day, but her father made them stop at two other ships and pretend that was where they were going. She was already drained from traveling there. But a deep sinking feeling filled her heart. No turning back now. This was the destiny that was made for her. Despite the fact that she wanted nothing to do with it. And as much as she hated to admit it, her gut was telling her this was not only what she needed to do, but what was right for her. What's the point in trying to find love or anything now? Kelley was gone. No one else mattered to her. She knew deep down he was the one that was meant for her. Everyone else was going to just be subpar compared to him. She rubbed the pink stones of her ring, as a tear rolled down her cheek.

Dark grey overcast as far as the eye could see, no sign of sun or blue skies. Terrible weather for a wedding at sea, not that she was looking forward to it anyways. It was the final day of their journey, the day she has been dreading for four years, and now it was finally here. She had a trunk with the remainder of her things that were at Gerard and Lucy's house. Which was just a few outfits and knives. Everything else was already at her palace at the lagoon. Even Lux was at the lagoon with Marsali. Gerard and Lucy were going to be staying there to keep an eye on her after the wedding when she was on the dreaded honeymoon. Gerard and Lucy had decided to drive her. They knew it was the best decision to not have her drive herself. She wouldn't follow her father's rules and stop where he told her to.

The ship was huge, larger than any ship she had ever seen. The front of the ship had a golden mermaid, the rest of the ship had a beautiful caramel stain, with white and teal accents. Adorned with sheer white fabric draped everywhere, pink, blue and white flowers were placed all along the ship. Diamond encrusted golden star fish were hung from all of the flowers, giving everything an elegant sparkle. It was absolutely beautiful. Much more elegant than the other land and sea wedding she went to. It was how she had always imagined her wedding to be if she had been allowed to marry Kelley. It made it even harder to be there, it was just how she wanted everything, but not with who she wanted it with. She stepped on the ship knowing that she would never be called Gemma again, she had to go back to being called Aquaria. Her days of hiding were done, time to be a princess again. Throw on the crown and be miserable under her father's laws and rules of royalty.

She entered the captain's quarters, this was to be where she would spend the night and get ready in the morning. She walked around the room, it looked similar to the study at her home at the lagoon. There was one big difference, the whole back wall was windows, covered in sheer curtains, it let in so much light that you would have thought you were outside. She went and sat on the bed, where Lucy joined her. There was a mannequin in a corner of the room, it had her wedding dress on it, something Aquaria didn't even want to look at. She cringed at the thought of having to wear that dress, and what it signified. She hated all of this, that she had no choice in anything. She just wanted it to be all over, not be forced into this life.

"Gemma, I asked Gerard if he would stay guard for us tonight."

"You can't call me that anymore. That name and part of my life is over now." She said in a solemn tone. "I have to go by my real name now."

"You will always be Gemma to us. It's going to be alright, you can come stay with Gerard and I anytime you want. You will always be my sister, and any time you need to or just want to run away, you can."

"Lucy, you know I can't, and I have no reason to." She said with tears welling up in her eyes.

"After tomorrow you can run away. It won't matter what happens after the wedding, you can run if you want."

"The only reason I ever had to run, died remember?"

"Of course I remember. He's my brother. How could I forget my own brother's death?" Lucy snapped.

"I don't know, you don't seem to be as upset about it as I am."

"I can't live my life being depressed about my brother's death. I loved my brother and miss him, but I have to keep living my life. Gerard and I can't live our lives like this, not if we are…. Never mind, now is not the time."

"Not the time for what?"

"Nothing, it can wait until after the wedding. Speaking of… it looks like your father has made it absolutely perfect for you."

"Stop trying to change the subject. Are you saying what I think your saying? Are you two having a baby?"

Lucy's cheeks burned, she had a huge smile on her face.

"How long have you known?"

"We found out the day before we left. We wanted to wait to tell you until after all of this."

She gave Lucy a big hug. "I'm so happy for you" The black in her hair started to fade. Then Gerard came walking in with Lucy's trunk and set it by her bed. He saw the smile on her face.

"So can I assume that you told her?" He said smiling, Gemma got up and ran over to him to give him a big hug.

"I didn't tell her everything yet."

"There is more? What more could there possibly be?"

"Gerard you tell her!"

"Well since I have no siblings, our child will not have any aunts or uncles. We wanted to ask you if you would be our child's aunt. You have been our family for the past four years, it only seems fitting that you stay that way."

"Really?" She cried, "I… I don't know what to say, other than of course." Her hair faded even more,

"You will always be our family." Lucy said hugging her.

Peggy came in the room, bringing in dinner for everyone. Everyone sat and ate quietly, After dinner, Peggy left, she was sleeping at the inn off the ship. Gerard was only staying with the girls to keep them safe, and to stay with his wife. Everyone went to bed early, the next day was going to be long, and Gemma was dreading it more than anything.

59

Gemma was woken up by the sound of a loud knock on the door. Gerard got up, wearing only sleeping shorts and opened the door, he was quickly knocked out of the way by a group of young girls pushing their way into the room. He closed the door behind them, yawned and scratched the back of his head. He went back over to Lucy, he kissed her and told her he loved her, then he went into the dressing room to change. Gemma sat up in her bed, and saw all the girls line up in front of her. Not one of them said a word, Lucy came and sat next to her.

"Who are these girls? Why are they just standing there not speaking?" Lucy whispered.

"I'm assuming this is the rest of my bridal party." She sighed, "Did he have a message for you to give to me?"

One of the girls handed her a letter, she opened it, and read it quietly to Lucy.

My Dearest Aquaria,

You might not recognize your maids, they are actually your nieces, it has been many years since you have seen them. Shelby is the oldest and will do your hair,

Marina will do you're make up, Alexia, Amara and Nicolette will be assisting with everything else. Lucy shall be by your side the entire time, never separate from her for the entire day. No Men are allowed in the room while you are getting dressed. Two of my guards will be at your door at all times. Nikoli will be arriving before I do, he will be bringing your tiara. I will arrive at 4, the wedding is at sunset. I will see you this evening.

Love your father

Gemma sighed, she looked at the girls, and just shook her head. Her hair had already turned to black, the girls whispered when they saw her hair change. None of them had ever seen color streaks turn black before, each of the girls have a parent with color streaks, but none ever turned black before.

"Out with it. What are you all whispering about?"
Shelby stepped forward. She was a tall lanky girl who looked just like her father Delanson. She always hated Aquaria, jealous that her fiancé, Macsen always wanted her more. Her snarling tone made her voice sound scratchy and deep. Sounding even more like Delanson. She wasn't even sure if Shelby had any traits that look after her mother. "Why did your hair turn black? We have never seen that happen before."

"Have your parents ever lost someone that they love?"

"Not that I know of."

"Well that is why you have never seen it turn black. Do you not remember 4 years ago when my mother died? Your grandfather's hair did the same thing."

"Then who died?" Nicolette asked. She was the youngest there. She couldn't be more than 15. She always adored Nicolette. She was small and dainty. Dark chestnut hair that reached halfway down her back. But her eyes were the exact same as her sister, Anna-Maria. Gemma looked at her with tears welling up in her eyes.

"My brother." Lucy said, "They were in love, he was killed two years ago." The girls started whispering again, all except Nicolette, whose eyes were welling up with tears.
"You girls start getting ready, she needs a moment."

Gerard came out of the dressing room and the girls all pushed him out of the way and went in to change. Gerard was confused as to what had just happened.

"What's with them?" He asked, then he saw Gemma's face, and

knew something was wrong. "Gemma is everything alright? What happened?"

"We can't call her that anymore remember?" Lucy gently reminded him

"I'm sorry, I forgot. It's going to take some getting used to. So what happened?"

"Those are her nieces, they are the rest of the bridal party. They were being a bit nosey, asking about, why her hair is black."

Gerard walked over to Gemma and held her hand. "If you need anything, just ask. I will escort them out of the room if they are upsetting you."

"Thank you Gerard, I might need that."

"Anytime." He kissed Lucy on her head. "I'm going to grab some breakfast for the three of us, I will be back in just a few moments."

"Thank you love." Lucy said as he left.

The girls came out of the dressing room, all in matching off white tops and skirts. They looked almost exactly the same as Gemma's the only difference was that hers had jewels all over it. Lucy grabbed both of their dresses and went into the changing room, Lucy changed first, so she could help Gemma get dressed. Gemma took a white box out of her trunk, she pulled out a special garter that Callie had made for her, it was made to securely and discretely hide a dagger.

"Do you think you will need that today?"

"I can never be too careful."

"It's your wedding, what could happen?"

"You never know. I would rather be safe than sorry."

Gemma started getting ready, she stripped down to nothing but her underwear. Everything was a pearl color, having an iridescent glow to it. She pulled her skirt on, it came halfway down her thigh, barely covering her dagger. It had sheer overlaying it, the sheer was down to the floor and cut into small strips, looking like pearl seaweed. Her top had a white half corset that cut off halfway down her sternum, there was a sheer overlay that also had the strips like the skirt. The straps were tight and off the shoulder, holding her arms tight to her sides. It was so tight she was barely even able to move her arms away from her sides, let alone freely. The whole corset portion was covered in diamonds, and pearls, into patterns of seashells and flowers. She was given a small golden chain belt, it had many other chains hanging down from it, with pearls and diamonds all over them. She had Lucy put her necklace on her. It was the necklace that she got from her father in the trunk for her eighteenth birthday. She was already wearing Kelley's ring on her finger, and her championship rings on her other fingers. Lucy saw the ring and knew she had to say something.

"You shouldn't wear, that today."

"What?"

"Kelley's ring, today isn't the day to wear that. You can put it on tomorrow, but it will only make today harder."

A tear rolled down her cheek as she stared at her finger. She slowly twisted it off her finger, more tears began to flow. She stared at the engraving on the inside, her heart breaking even more. She hadn't taken it off since Kelley put it on that finger. She slowly handed Lucy the ring, having a hard time letting go.

"I will have Gerard hold it for today. You know he will keep it safe." Lucy said.

"I know. I just can't lose more of him. It's all I have left." She wept.

"I will be right back, let me go give this to him."

Lucy left the room and luckily Gerard had just walked in with their breakfast. She kissed him, then handed him the ring and whispered in his ear. He nodded and placed the ring in his pocket, then tried to find a ring box to put it in. Lucy went to get Gemma, and found her sitting on the floor crying, Lucy brought her, her breakfast. They sat on the floor together, both crying. This day was hard on Lucy as well, only three months prior was her wedding. All either of them wanted was for Kelley to be there. When they finally stopped crying, Lucy forced her to eat something. When they left the dressing room, Gemma went and sat in a chair while Shelby and Marina took care of her hair and make-up. Lucy did her own hair and make-up, she kept her hair in a simple fishtail braid, placing gold starfish pins in the braid. The girls took a long time to do Gemma's hair and make-up, Lucy helped the younger girls with their hair and make-up, giving them the same style that she had. Gemma's hair and make-up was finally done, she had two braids in her hair, across the top of her head like a crown, then big curls were pinned up in the back. Gemma looked over at Lucy, not happy with her hair. Lucy took over for

Shelby and fixed her hair, she knew how she liked her hair. She liked her hair simple, Lucy had a braid start on her left side, brought it all around to her right side then pinned it in a low side bun. She pinned some pearls and starfish in her hair as well. Her eyes were dusted with gold, it made her eyes shine brighter than usual.

"You look beautiful" Lucy said

"Thank you." She said quietly.

All of a sudden, they heard the sound of fighting, several thuds and grunts.

"Lucy, get in the changing room, we have to keep you and the baby safe." Gemma said

"What about you?"

"We will be fine, no matter what happens, keep that baby safe!" Gemma said.

Lucy ran into the dressing room and hid, behind all the clothes and the big mirror. Gemma grabbed her sword that she had kept next to her bed. She tried to hold it up, but the straps of the dress made it nearly impossible. Her arms were completely pinned to her sides. The other girls clung to one another, terrified of what was coming their way. She heard the guards at her door it wasn't good. She held her sword out, not afraid of whatever was at the door. The door was kicked in and a large, older pirate came walking in, followed by many others. He had long dark, greying hair, a long deep scar across his right eye. His right eye was a light grey, looking as if it was damaged.

"Well look what we have here, these girls will fetch a pretty penny don't you think." He sneered "This is a feisty one, she might fetch even more than the others. Take them all."

Gemma tried to fight them off, but there were too many of them. The dress restrained her so much that she wasn't able to fight how she normally did. They quickly overpowered her, but not before she stabbed a couple of them. They dragged the other girls out, hitting her in the back of the head with the butt of his cutlass, everything going black.

* * *

The girls were dragged off the ship and taken to another ship nearby, they pushed off from the dock right as Gerard woke back up after being knocked out from behind. He could see the girls on the other ship, he instantly ran to their room to find Lucy. He looked around and saw blood on the floor and his heart started to race, terrified that, that was Lucy's blood. Then he looked in the changing room and still couldn't see anyone.

"Lucy?" He whispered, there was no response, "Lucy please say you are here." He said louder

"Gerard?" She said peeking out from behind a mirror. When she saw him, she ran into his arms.

"Lucy I was so worried! I saw the blood and I just…"

"I'm fine, Gemma told me to hide, she wanted to keep us safe, especially the baby."

"I'm just so happy you are okay. I don't know what I would have done if something happened to you."

"What happened out there?"

"I don't know, I was on the deck trying to get things ready, then someone hit me over the head from behind. When I woke up all the guards were either knocked out as well or dead. I saw another ship taking off and saw some of the girls on there. So I came running in here and saw the blood on the floor…"

"What are we going to do?" She said franticly, "Nik, Poseidon, the groom…. Everyone will be here soon. We need to tell Nik now! How do we get ahold of him?"

"Get ahold of who? And what in the hell happened here? Where are the other girls?" Nik walked into the room holding two wooden cases.

"Someone took them!" Lucy cried, "Gemma had me hide, she tried to fight them off but there were too many of them!"

"Why did she make you hide but not hide herself or the others?"

"She wanted to keep our baby safe." Gerard said.

"Ahhh… I see a congratulations is in order, but we will celebrate that later." Nik said, now noticing that Gerard had his hand on Lucy's stomach the whole time.

Gerard explained everything that he saw, he described the ship to him as best he could. Nik handed Lucy and Gerard the cases. "I need to alert Poseidon. I know someone who can help! When he gets here, keep him calm. This is not how today was supposed to go at all!" he said running out of the room.

"Keep who calm? Poseidon?" Lucy shouted to him.

"Not Poseidon, I'm dealing with him! The groom. Keep the groom calm!" Nik shouted back, then dove in the water and took off.

They stood there baffled by what had just happened. After four years of keeping her safe, she is taken on the day of her wedding. They checked on all the guards, only the two at the door were killed, the rest were knocked out or injured. Lucy helped stitch up the injured ones, and Gerard moved the two who were killed onto the dock. They cleaned up all of the blood off the deck and tried to make everything look nice again. They saw another ship come into to port, two pirates came off the ship and walked toward theirs. A pirate that looked to be about Patrick's age began running up the gangway when he saw the bodies on the dock, then a younger one slowly followed.

"WHAT THE HELL HAPPENED HERE?" The older one shouted, before the younger pirate even made it on the ship.

"We were attacked sir. You must be Captain Jones. Poseidon has been alerted and is working on getting them back." Gerard said

"I'm not Captain Jones. He is!" He said pointing to the younger man who was still walking up the gangway. "Now where the bloody hell is she? I'm going to need an answer before he gets up here."

"She was taken by some pirates about 20 minutes ago." Lucy said

Captain Jones finally stepped onto the ship, Lucy was speechless when she saw him.

"What happened? Where is she?" Captain Jones said in a firm tone

"I'm sorry captain, but she has been kidnapped, just 20 minutes ago." Herriott said

"So that ship we passed, she is on there?" He asked.

"Most likely captain."

He gave a small nod, then turned around and headed back to his ship. "HERRIOTT!" He shouted while leaving.

Herriott followed, quickly. "We will return with her."

Lucy and Gerard were still silent. She looked at him with wide eyes, trying to process what she just saw.

60

She awoke to a throbbing in her head. The smell of urine and molding wood assaulted her nostrils. Whispers and quiet sobs fought against the sound of the waves lapping against the ship. Slowly opening her eyes her blurred vision slowly coming back. The girls were huddled in a corner together. A couple were crying as the others tried to comfort them. Marina appearing to be the one doing most of the comforting, she knew she was the one who could help her.

"Marina, I need your help." Marina walked over to her and crouched beside her. "On my garter there's a dagger, grab it and hand it to me, I'll cut your ropes."

Marina did as she asked, it was a struggle with her hands tied together, but at least they were in front of her unlike Gemma's who were tied behind her back. Once she was cut free she helped Gemma out of her ropes and they both quickly and quietly helped the other girls. She kept checking to see if any guards were near. Thankfully they were a little further away so they could get their hands free.

"Alright I don't know how much time we have before they come back. No one can know who your parents are or your grandfather. Do you understand me?" She whispered.

"Aquaria. What do they want with us?" Shelby asked

"They want to sell us, and If they find out what we really are, it will only make things harder on us. Especially if they find out what family we come from."

The creaking of a door startled the guards back to the cell. The girls all froze. Their eyes wide as the footsteps got closer. Gemma put the dagger back in her garter, and placing her hands behind her back. The cell door flew open, a large man filling the opening. The stench of whisky dripping from his pores and mouth. She was quite sure he drank more than a bottle for the stench to be so strong. His eyes trailing over each girl. Assessing every detail he could see. His eyes lingered on Gemma's chest as he licked his lips. She shuddered at the thought. She gripped her wrist, holding it tight to keep them from knowing she's free from the ropes.

"The one who is in the more elaborate dress must be the bride, she should fetch even more than the others." He said in a rough voice. "I just might try her out before the buyer arrives." He began to laugh. Gemma knew exactly what that meant.

"Are you sure that one? She isn't the normal size and shape you prefer. Her tits alone are enough of a reason that you would normally walk away from a woman." Another one said.

"Well if that elaborate wedding is for her, there must be some reason she is worth all of this fuss." He laughed

"You don't have much time, the buyer should be here soon. If you're going to take that one for a ride, now is your only chance."

He grabbed her arm. His nails digging into her skin. His rough grip leaving a searing pain in her arm. He pulled her out of the cell and threw her against the wall. Her vision doubled from the impact. *Sharks.* She knew how her siren abilities wouldn't be working right away. She had hoped to put them all in a trance and escape. He held her against the wall by her throat. Constricting her airway, she was close to losing consciousness again.

"Lock them up and leave. I. Want to play with this one. She seems like she'll be worth more." His slimy voice made her skin crawl.

She began reaching for her dagger. Grabbing it off her garter and stabbing him in the ribs.

"Ahh. You stupid bitch!" He punched the right side of her face. She fell to the ground coughing and trying to catch her breath. Her eyes narrowed on him as he approached her. She stared into his eyes, as she clenched her fist tightly. He began grasping at his throat. Her fist tightening he fell to his knees trying to get the tightness around his throat to stop.

"You must've had no idea who you just kidnapped." She gave a curt laugh. "I'll be sure to tell my uncle what you tried to do to me. He'll have fun torturing you for all eternity."

She kicked him onto his side. Grabbing her dagger from his ribs. She wiped the blood off the knife on the dress. She hated that dress and wanted to ruin it. She kept her fist tight as she cut the strap of the left arm. Freeing her arm from constraint. Releasing her fist and taking the dagger in that hand to remove the other strap. Seconds after she made the cut she was hit with a heavy blow. Knocking her to the ground. She rubbed her jaw as she looked up at him. Fire in her eyes as she got herself to her feet. He threw her against the wall. Driving a dagger through her right hand, pinning it to the wall. And snapping her left wrist. She screamed from the pain, sending a shockwave through the ship. He took her dagger lightly pressing it on her collarbone, cutting her skin ever so slightly. Just enough to have a couple drops of blood. He then took the dagger and did the same to her other shoulder, leaving two cuts below her collar bone. His rough dirty hands began roaming her body. She kicked him hard between his legs. He doubled over, but didn't release her wrist. Instead he plunged the dagger deep in her thigh. She cried out as the pain was radiating from her thigh. A tall woman came up behind him, Gemma couldn't make out her face in the dark. She only knew it was a woman by the silhouette. She grabbed him and threw him against the wall holding a dagger to his throat.

"What have I told you about playing with the merchandise before I buy it? You think I was going to be lenient on my terms? I told you I would slit your throat and send you to the locker next time you broke our terms." She spoke through her teeth, in a stern angry tone. A voice that sounded a little too familiar to Gemma, but she was too distraught and busy trying to get the dagger out of her hand to figure out who it was.

"I didn't think you would be here for a while longer, I wanted to make sure the merchandise was worth it." His voice trembled fearing for his life.

"They lose value after they have been defiled, you idiot." She shouted.

"I'm sorry, I won't do it again."

"No you won't!" She slit his throat, blood splattering across her blouse and face. She watched his body drop to the floor and bleed out. She stepped over the body and walked over to Gemma. She had a large brim on her hat, making it even harder to see who she was. She wore black leather pants and boots, with a white shirt and a red leather vest.

"Your highness, are you alright? Did he hurt you?" The woman said.

Then Gemma recognized the voice. "Callie? What are you doing here?"

"I'm here to save you. Nik found me and told me what happened. My whole crew is up on deck, we are acting as if we are buying you. You think you can play along?" Callie asked while getting the dagger out of Gemma's hand.

"Yes of course, but what crew? I thought you weren't leaving for another week." Gemma asked. She placed her bleeding hand on her wrists, once that was healed she moved on to heal her hand, head and leg. She had more wounds but those were the most crucial. She would deal with the others later.

"I left early to surprise you at your wedding. You were supposed to find out everything at the ceremony." She said "You're covered in blood! What did he do to you?"

"He cut me a few times and tried to do other things. I'll be fine." She said as she began rubbing her wrist. "Just get me out of here."

"Your fiancé is going to kill us when he finds out what happened to you. His fury rivals yours and your fathers." She handed Gemma her dagger that had been thrown on the ground.

"How well do you really know him?"

"I've known him for many years. Now we have to go, I'll explain some more when we get back to my ship. My crew will bring no harm to any of you. We have to get you back to your wedding as fast as possible." She unlocked the cell door and Gemma had the girls follow them. Instructing them to keep their mouths shut and just do as they told them. They all kept their heads down and followed her off the ship, acting as if they all still had their hands bound. Once on Callie's ship the girls were taken somewhere safe. Gemma and Callie went to Callie's quarters to speak privately.

"Who all knew who you really are?" Gemma asked.

"All the pirates know who I am, they just don't know I work for your father. I'm very well-known and feared on the seas, Kelley knew as well. He hated keeping that secret from you, but he knew that it would upset you to have another one of your father's workers watching you."

"I can't believe he knew. What else did he know?"

"He found out everything right before he left, and he only knew that I worked for your father. He didn't know my backstory or even my name, although he did always suspect that I was a pirate. Enough talking for now, we need to get you into something that you can keep yourself safe in, and about those cuts..."

"I can take care of them. I just need to wash the blood off." She handed Gemma a rag and some water, then a set of leather fighting clothes, they looked just like the ones she had worn back in the ring. "So you're the one that Kelley got these from?" Gemma said as she started to heal herself and wash the blood off.

"Yes, he knew I would be able to make you some that would keep you safe. Now get dressed, you will be more like yourself again." Callie said with a smile.

Gemma quickly changed, Callie was right, she did feel more like herself once she changed. She borrowed one of Callie's swords and kept it close to her. Suddenly they heard one of Callie's men yelling.

"We're being boarded!" Callie jumped up from behind her desk and headed to the deck, Gemma followed her.

"Gemma stay here. We still have to keep you safe, and I don't know who is coming on board."

Everyone on deck drew their swords as several pirates swung onto their ship by rope, then tied the ships together. Callie made Gemma stay near the door, she had to keep her safe somehow. None of Callie's men were fighting. They were talking with the other pirates. Confusion written on all their faces. Then a large plank was placed between the two ships, Callie walked over to it and waited at the end.

Her sword was drawn and ready to attack whoever came on her ship. Two tall men walked onto the ship, and Callie put her sword away. She shook hands and began to speak with the first one to come on board. Then the other one stepped on the ship, he was tall with short dark hair, he looked much younger than the other one. Gemma couldn't see his face from where she was standing. She was still at the doorway of the captain's quarters. She kept trying to see who it was, but something was always blocking his face. Callie pointed to where she was and they all came over to her. She recognized the older one, it was David Herriott, she had met him a few times. Which meant one thing... the other one was her fiancé. She gripped tight to her dagger, ready to drive it right into his heart. She wanted nothing to do with him. When they got to her, her fiancé pushed the other two aside, quickly grabbed Gemma and kissed her. Her dagger gripped tightly in her hand, pointed at the left side of his neck. She was ready to drive it deep into his neck. Sever an artery. But he moved so fast she didn't even get a chance to see his face. The second his lips touched hers, she felt a spark, she knew that kiss anywhere. There was no denying who it was. Her hair turned pink the second his lips touched hers. She dropped her dagger and wrapped her arms around him, knowing exactly who it was. He let go of her and took a step back.

"Kelley? You're alive!" She said, her eyes welling up with tears.

"We have a lot to talk about my love." He wiped the tears from her eyes, and kissed her again. "I told you I would come back for you."

She smiled at him with a huge smile, tears in her eyes, and her hair lightly glowing.

More from J.A. Johnson

Gem of the Sea

Aquaria Oceana Book 1

What if the daughter of a god fell for the one person she could never have?

Aquaria has spent her entire life hiding. As the youngest daughter of Poseidon and heir to the Throne of the Sea, she should be wielding elemental magic and ruling the ocean depths. Instead, she's disguised as "Gemma" living among humans, betrothed to a pirate captain she's never met, and forbidden from revealing who she truly is. Four years. That's how long she has to survive on land before the marriage that will seal a fragile peace between worlds. But Aquaria didn't plan on Kelley, the pirate's son who teaches her to sword fight in secret, who looks at her like she's more than a pawn in her father's game, who makes her want a life she was never meant to have. With her eighteenth birthday approaching, Aquaria faces the deadly trials that will unlock her true power. The same prophecy that has haunted her family for generations. Now she must choose: Accept the fate Poseidon has chosen for her, or fight for the love and life she wants, even if it means igniting a war between land and sea.

Coming soon

Gem of the Captain

Aquaria Oceana book 3

Kelley has been lost to the world for over a year, declared dead, his past buried beneath the waves. But in truth, he sails on, living a dangerous lie as Captain Jones, the ruthless master of the infamous pirate ship *The Crimson Cutlass*. To survive, he must become someone else entirely, commanding fear, masking his heart, and never letting his true identity slip.

Surrounded by bloodthirsty pirates, relentless assassins, and admirers who threaten to see through his disguise, Kelley walks a razor's edge every day. Yet his mission is clear: he must endure long enough to return to the one person who matters most, Aquaria.

But Aquaria is no ordinary bride. As a daughter of the sea, her destiny is bound to an ancient power. Together, she and Kelley are fated to rise as the new rulers of the ocean, taking the place of Poseidon himself. If they can survive long enough to say "I do."

Because the sea is watching.

And Aquaria's brothers are hunting.

As Kelley struggles to master not only the life of a pirate captain but also the secrets of the merpeople, the line between who he is and who he pretends to be begins to blur. With enemies closing in and destiny pulling him deeper into the tides, one question remains:

Will love be enough to save him… or will the sea claim him first?

Popstars in the Backyard

A second chance celebrity romance

Six years. One accident. A chance to rewrite their ending. Andi Cooper spent six years trying to forget Ryker Thomas, her former best friend who walked away and never looked back. Now he's one of the biggest popstars in the world, and she's just trying to survive the summer before her senior year. Then fate intervenes. When an accident throws them back together, Andi wakes up with no memory of what tore them apart, and hallucinations that won't stop. The only thing that makes them disappear? Him. Ryker's returning home one last time before moving to LA, but saving Andi's life changes everything. She doesn't remember the fight. She doesn't remember why he left. And hiding her condition from the media hounding his every move is nearly impossible. Now they're trapped in forced proximity, with the past erased and the spotlight closing in. Can she trust the boy who abandoned her? Can he protect her from the truth that broke them the first time?